Resuscitated

Peter Budetti

This is a work of fiction. All incidents and dialogue, and all characters in the novel, are products of the author's imagination and are not to be construed as real. No one should take offense or be pleased at thinking they are characters in this book because any resemblance to persons living or deceased is entirely coincidental. Nothing in this book is intended to depict actual events or to alter the entirely fictional character of the work.

Cover photo by Ilya Haykinson

DEDICATION

To all the good physicians and nurses who care for the tiniest babies, and to the parents of the little ones

Resuscitated

Chapter 1: The Call

Senior Pediatric Resident Sarah Belden shuffled into the on-call room, her eyes hazy, half-open, her shoulders drooping. Glancing at her wristwatch, she groaned: *three-fifteen!* Twenty-one hours into her shift at Memorial General Hospital she still had three hours to go before she could sign out. Alone in the tiny windowless room, she was surrounded by drab grey walls barren except for metal hooks and an old mirror speckled with dark streaks and bare spots. A pair of steel bunk beds tantalized her with a promise of blissful sleep, but a black wall phone hanging between the stacked beds loomed like a bugler threatening to blare reveille at any moment.

Eager to shed clothes grungy from her long day caring for sick children, Sarah removed her white coat, hung it on one of the hooks, then peeled off her crumpled green scrubs and tossed them onto an overflowing laundry hamper. When she glanced at her reflection in the mirror she chuckled at seeing her trim young body in the matronly underwear she wore for sheer comfort during the long hours on duty. Baggy white cotton panties hung like bloomers around her shapely hips, while a soft, oversized brassiere cushioned her ample breasts. She had the urge to collapse onto the bed in her underwear but couldn't risk the embarrassment should one of the male residents show up and see her old-lady undergarments. So she pulled on a starched pair of clean scrubs just before she dropped onto one of the lower bunks, not bothering to get under the covers. She closed her eyes, hoping against hope that her exhausted body would let her fall asleep instantly, that she was not so wired she would lie frozen in semi-consciousness while the intense scenes from her tedious day swirled in her head. In an earlier life Sarah had been a deep sleeper but now the anxiety of being on call kept her on edge, knowing that any second she might be summoned. Mercifully, exhaustion gave way to light sleep.

But not for long. Barely fifteen minutes had passed before the shrill ringing of the telephone startled her wide awake. She bolted upright from her pillow, nearly smacking her forehead on the bottom of the upper bunk. She pulled the handset from its cradle, coughed to clear her throat, and said, "Dr. Belden."

A shrill voice pierced her ear, the words urgent, hurried, more pleading than commanding.

"This is the charge nurse in Obstetrics and Delivery. We have an emergency, you'd better come *stat* to the delivery room. Preemie, extremely small, any second."

"On my way."

Sarah jumped out of bed, tossed the phone onto its cradle, pushed her feet into her slip-on shoes and charged out of the on-call room. She flew down the hall to the nearest stairwell, contorting her body to pull on her white coat as she ran.

An adrenaline rush surged through her, triggering equal measures of exhilaration and alarm. This was *her* moment, this was what she had gone through medical school, internship, two years of junior residency for. This was it, now *she* was the senior pediatrician in the hospital, it was all on her to deal with a life-and-death situation. The life of someone's baby would depend on her.

But would she be up to whatever challenge awaited her in that delivery room?

Her heart pounded in her chest as she raced up three flights of stairs two steps at a time, gasping for air. She pushed through a heavy metal door with a faded sign that read "*Obstetrics*," ran down a hallway jammed with empty hospital beds, gurneys, random pieces of medical equipment, and burst through a pair of swinging doors into the small washing-up area just outside the delivery room. She ripped off her white coat, pulled a pair of paper shoe covers over the slip-ons, tucked her hair into an operating room cap, tied a surgical mask over her face, and started scrubbing her hands under the high faucet in the oversized stainless-steel sink. Yellowish-brown antiseptic foam bubbled over her fingers and nails as she brushed them with iodine soap and warm water. Still panting heavily, Sarah glanced over her shoulder through the large windows in the delivery room doors.

What she saw twisted her stomach into spasms, filling her throat with the foul taste of bile. She belched hard and swallowed back the surging vomit.

"NO!" she screamed into her face mask, drowning out the muffled sounds of her paper-shrouded foot smashing repeatedly on the floor. *"NO!"*

The woman on the delivery table was Martina Johnson. Again.

Chapter 2: Twenty-One Hours Earlier

Memorial General Hospital served indigents, undocumented immigrants, inner-city gunshot victims—anyone who could find nowhere else to go for medical care. A county hospital long dependent on the vagaries of public financing, Memorial General was a hodgepodge of interconnected buildings constructed at various times between the early 1900s and the 1950s, the newest now nearly forty years old. One building housed the pediatric wards, delivery rooms, and nurseries, another the surgical wards and operating rooms, others the medical, orthopedic, and psychiatry wards, the radiology department, and the infectious disease ward where long-term tuberculosis patients were quarantined. From the outside the buildings were strikingly attractive—the architects had stayed true to the original neo-Spanish design over the years. Stuccoed adobe brick walls topped by red clay tile roofs, brick-and-stone archways aside long arcades, and a terraced inner courtyard with a massive brick fountain, all created the appearance of an elegant Spanish Colonial compound, a grand medical campus of stately haciendas spread across two city blocks.

But the stylized Spanish elegance was a façade, as make-believe as the replica of the Alamo built for the movie *Viva Max!* some twenty years earlier. Inside the hospital the exterior charm dissolved into an endless vista of pale yellow ceramic tiles covering the floors and walls below a patchwork of crumbling drop-ceilings with empty squares where some of the pock-marked fiberboard panels had gone missing. Bundles of jerry-rigged wiring hung randomly from exposed pipes of various sizes running along the top of the walls. Bare light bulbs and flickering fluorescent fixtures provided the only lighting. The wards for patients resembled wartime military barracks, cavernous rooms crammed with row after row of slender beds.

At ten minutes to six the morning of Saturday, November 9, 1988, Sarah Belden arrived at the hospital to relieve the other senior pediatric resident, Jane Zimmerman, who was due to go off duty. She walked down a long, dreary corridor into the women's locker room, cramped quarters that had been converted from a storage area back when women were first accepted as interns and residents at Memorial General in the 1950s. Thumbing through the stack of clean, freshly ironed unisex scrubs, she pulled out a pair of Mediums, just big enough to be comfortable, not so loose she would have to contend with gaping décolletage displays while bending over little kids. She slipped into the shapeless green outfit, then pulled on a hip-length white cotton coat, making fists with both hands to poke her arms down the heavily starched sleeves.

Sarah pushed hard on the pin of her nametag to drive it through the stiff cotton lapel of the white coat. Letters etched through the top layer of the white-on-black plastic sandwich displayed her name and title: "Dr. Sarah Belden. Senior Pediatric Resident." The nametag was indispensable for a woman physician. Together with the white coat, the badge broadcast an essential message: *"I'm a Doctor, don't call me Nurse."* The male physicians could get by without their nametags or even their white coats and no one would think they were nurses, but the women had to keep them on at all times to avoid those persistent, aggravating moments explaining to patients, lab techs, social workers, police, that they were doctors, not nurses. Sarah had a very high regard for nurses, but to get her job done she needed people to acknowledge her authority as a physician.

Next, Sarah methodically stuffed her coat pockets with her mobile doctor's office—more pens than a sophomore engineering student and a combination flashlight/otoscope in the single breast pocket, stethoscope in the left waist pocket, her precious little black notebook with notes to herself on all her patients and abridged versions of everything she'd ever learned in medical school and residency in the right waist pocket. Finally, she packed in the latest *Harriet Lane Handbook*, the small, shorthand medical Bible of *"what to do and how to do it"* that pediatric residents everywhere relied on. In the outside world Sarah's long brown hair hung free, setting off her sharp features, but now she wound the hair and pinned it into a bun to keep it under control until her next shower and shampoo, which as yet were off in some unforeseeable future.

Outfitted now to take on the upcoming day, her uniform and tools in place, her game face set, Dr. Sarah Belden, Senior Pediatric Resident, studied her reflection in the mirror on the wall between the rows of women's lockers. She felt a rush of pride at seeing her transformation from a carefree young woman into a high-ranking medical house officer. A little girl still lived somewhere inside her but that was no longer the person she was. Now she was a physician with real responsibilities for life and death decisions. It felt good, that was why she had worked so hard, studied so much. She deserved to be there, she had earned it.

She walked briskly to the pediatric ward to find Jane Zimmerman and send her on her way. At exactly six o'clock the two budding pediatricians started their weekend making rounds on the pediatric inpatients. Sarah would check in later with the Interns assigned to the different wards—for now this was time for the two most senior residents to speak candidly and move quickly, Sarah brimming with energy to take on a challenging but rewarding day, Jane eager to go home.

Wishing to intrude as little as possible on her colleague's incipient time off, and also keen to assume control in her own right, Sarah greeted her counterpart with a friendly smile but wasted no time with pleasantries.

"Hi, Jane. I know most of these kids pretty well, so this shouldn't take long. Just tell me what big-time pitfalls I might need to be aware of."

Jane, an affable but serious woman much taller than Sarah, peered down at her colleague over her small wire-rimmed eyeglasses that always seemed about to slip off of her elongated Ichabod Crane nose and smiled back at Sarah.

"Not a problem, Sarah, I'm just going home to crash in bed as soon as I walk in the door anyway."

Sarah and Jane, like all the physicians in training at Memorial General, had no time for real life outside the hospital. They worked every weekday and every other night, enduring an endless cycle of 36-hour shifts for at least three years with the help of gallons of coffee. Both young doctors had worked all day Thursday, then Sarah stayed on duty Thursday night while Jane went home overnight. Then they worked all day Friday until 6PM, when Sarah went home and Jane took over. Now it was Saturday morning and the treasured weekend schedule would provide a short respite for Jane. She could leave the hospital after turning things over to Sarah and would be free until Sunday morning, a precious 24-hour break until she returned to relieve Sarah.

Sarah's weekday assignment that month was to oversee the newborn nurseries. But when the senior pediatric residents were on duty at night or on weekends they had responsibilities all over the hospital. They cared for patients and supervised the pediatric interns and junior residents in the emergency room, inpatient pediatric wards, delivery rooms and nurseries, even the infectious disease ward where some children were in quarantine. Sarah had to allot her time among the different parts of the hospital as best she could, so it was critical for her to know what problems awaited her, who the sickest patients were, which interns and junior residents she had to watch carefully and which ones she could trust to call her on their own if they needed help.

As they began their quick walk, Jane said, "You're in for a big day, I'm afraid, Sarah. The ER has been overflowing. I had to see lots of patients myself to try to help with the logjam, and it's still packed. And I hate to remind you, but the intern on duty in the ER today is Sandy Kischer. You know how insecure and cautious Sandy is. He'll never be able to handle the crowd of patients on his own so you'll be busy there for sure. A couple of kids on the wards are in real danger, but at least Jimmy Yoder is the intern there, he's so reliable and smart you shouldn't have to worry about him. And who knows what might happen in the delivery room."

When they finished their rounds, Sarah envisioned Jane heading home, soon to be sound asleep in her own bed, and felt the irrepressible wave of jealousy that appeared at every change of shift. Suppressing her own fantasy of heading back to bed for ten or twelve hours and awakening to do something other than return to the hospital, Sarah managed to say, quite cheerfully, "Thanks, Jane, as usual you're on top of everything. Time for the fresh troops to go into battle."

"You bet, Sarah. I'll see you in the morning. Hope it's not too bad."

As Jane disappeared down the corridor Sarah headed straight for the ER to make sure the situation was under control. She checked in with the nurses to find out how the pediatric patients had been

7

triaged, which children in the queue needed prompt attention, which ones might pose special problems. Then she settled in to consult with the marginally-competent Sandy Kischer and do her part to keep the flow of patients moving at a reasonable pace.

For the next five hours Sarah Belden slogged through a nonstop flood of children with fevers, rashes, scrapes and bruises, coughs, belly pains, earaches, headaches. Kids with profuse diarrhea and kids whose bowel movements weren't regular enough for their worried parents. It was all seemingly a matter of life and death to each family, but routine to her by now. Constantly smiling, upbeat, reassuring, she worked without a single break, seeing patients at a rate of about three for every one Dr. Sandy Kischer managed to stumble through, and also checking in on every one of his. Finally, Sarah was dealt a merciful lull—time enough, she figured, to head to the cafeteria for a quick lunch.

But all thoughts of lunch vanished as Sarah passed a bay reserved for treating orthopedic patients. A small boy, probably not quite two years old, was sitting on the examining table as an orthopedic resident bandaged the toddler's feet and ankles. Ducking into the orthopedics bay she walked up to the resident, a tall, handsome man so impeccably preppy in his designer scrubs and wavy blond hair he might have been a Yale freshman masquerading as a doctor at a frat house costume party. Sarah glanced at his nametag and asked, "What's going on, Dr. Robinson?"

Some six inches taller than Sarah Belden, Dr. Farley Robinson glared down at her, making no effort to conceal his surgeon's resentment that a mere pediatric trainee, and a woman at that, had the temerity to question him.

"Oh, nothing of importance," he replied in a patronizing, faux-patrician voice. "Just some burns on his feet and lower calves from stepping into a tub full of scalding water. Not too bright this child, I suppose."

Sarah knew immediately that Farley Robinson had been blind to a clear case of child abuse.

She gritted her teeth, struggling to control her anger. This was all too familiar. For three years she had dealt with countless surgery residents like Farley Robinson, bright but dense fellows who thought they were God's gift to medicine, so cocky they would often fail to see what was in front of them unless they thought it was something they could use a scalpel to cut on.

8

"Where are his parents?"

"Mother and aunt—they stepped outside for a smoke," he muttered.

That's enough, she thought. She moved closer, her body seeming to extend upward to meet him eye-to-eye. Despite the height difference, Sarah didn't feel short. She knew she had the upper hand. Suppressing an unprofessional urge to rip his nametag off and send him packing, she asked, "Tell me, Dr. Robinson, why would a two year old child put both feet into a tub full of scalding water at the same time? Actually, how could he even do it? Did he hop into the tub like a gymnast?"

Farley Robinson had a surgeon's tunnel vision but was no dummy—he had brains enough to discern the implication of Sarah's question. He quickly filled with anger at himself, not for missing the diagnosis of an obvious case of child abuse, but for having condescended to take care of the child in the first place. He had been bored—no trauma victims with multiple fractures or other interesting cases worthy of his advanced skills as an orthopedic surgeon had come into the ER for a few hours. So, when a charge nurse asked him to help out since the pediatric section was so busy, he had agreed to treat the child with burns on his little feet. Now, his lapse in judgment exposed, he kept quiet and stared down at Sarah, who continued her interrogation.

"Why would this child be taking a bath on his own, anyway? Do you think that maybe there might be something else to consider here?"

Just then two enormous women burst into the stall, sputtering with laughter and reeking of stale cigarette smoke and fetid smells of unwashed bodies and squalid clothes. An impressively obese pair, their bulk overwhelmed the small space around the examining table. Their massive hind quarters indented the curtains with four large round bulges that protruded well into the neighboring stall.

"You done yet with those bandages?" the taller and slightly broader one asked, snarling at Farley Robinson while ignoring Sarah. "We need to get going. He's tough, he'll be OK."

The big woman wore a faded grey overcoat held partially closed by a mismatched belt that strained to encircle her waist. Tattered work-shoes with knotted shoelaces looked to be barely up to the task of supporting her. Her hair was wrapped in a bright pink-and-white flowered scarf that was as threadbare as an old dust cloth.

Glaring at Sarah Belden, the stubbier one blurted through a mouthful of twisted and tar-stained teeth, "What's the nurse doin' here?" She sported a frayed leather biker-jacket, the surviving paper-thin leather worn through to the underlying mesh framework at the elbows. The jacket was wide open, revealing a near-empty pack of Camels crushed into the narrow space between her ponderous left breast and the front flap of her shirt pocket.

Seeing his mother, the little boy started shaking and crying, "Momma, Momma."

"Shut up, you!" the one in the overcoat replied. She advanced toward the boy, raising her arm to strike a blow to his head.

Infuriated by the threat of physical aggression toward a small child, Sarah stepped between the enormous woman and her son. She announced calmly, "I'm Dr. Belden. I'm in charge of taking care of children in this hospital, and he's not ready to go anywhere just yet. We need to run a few more tests."

"Tests? What d'you mean, tests? He just burned hisself, and we got to go," yelled the boy's mother.

She started to push past Dr. Belden to reach the boy, but Sarah had been through similar encounters and didn't flinch. These women dwarfed her, making her feel like Alice after eating the cookies that made you shrink, yet Sarah stood her ground, her voice composed, her words defying the woman to advance.

"Stay where you are or I'll call security and have you restrained. He needs to have some blood tests and X-rays, and I have to examine him myself. We need to know if he has any other injuries or medical problems."

Sarah was rolling the dice, guessing that the women knew that security at Memorial General was the real thing—on duty, regular City police, tough cops in uniforms with badges, nightsticks, handcuffs, loaded guns in leather holsters. This ER was a harsh place, the destination for all the city's gunshot victims who survived long enough to be transported somewhere other than the morgue, the dumping ground for all the drug addicts when their sources dried up and they went into withdrawal or their supply suddenly improved in quality so that their customary dose nearly killed them.

Sarah's gamble paid off.

"He don't have no medical problems," the woman muttered, but she retreated a few feet.

Farley Robinson taped the gauze in place, said "He's all yours, *Doctor*," and slipped through the curtains, leaving the mess to Sarah Belden.

Sarah did a brief physical, speaking softly to calm the boy down. As soon as she uncovered his chest her worst fears were confirmed: old scars nearly covered the front and back of his thin torso. Small round bulls-eyes, pale in the center with a halo of dark pigment, dotted his skin—the unmistakable hallmarks of healed burns from cigarettes pressed into the little boy's flesh. Bigger crescent-shaped blemishes, traumatic tattoos imprinted by beatings with a belt buckle so vicious the whelps had turned into scars. Stifling a rising fury at what had been done to the child, Sarah said only, "I'm taking him to the lab and to X-ray. You're welcome to come along."

Sarah then endured a tense hour-long interview with the toddler's mother and aunt who repeated the same implausible story that the child had jumped into a scalding bath on his own. When the radiologist reported that the X-rays showed old rib fractures, the classic sign that the boy had been beaten repeatedly with enough force to shatter the bones, Sarah called in the social worker and the police. She then spent the next two hours ducking in and out of a series of interviews while continuing to examine countless patients and oversee the slowpoke Intern in the ER. Orthopedic Resident Farley Robinson was ordered to recount his experience with the injured child and left nursing a serious blow to his smugness. Finally, the child was taken into protective custody and the mother and aunt were hauled off to the police station.

By now Dr. Sarah Belden was well behind schedule. On her way to the pediatric wards she stopped at a bank of vending machines and bought two *Snickers* bars to substitute for the lunch that had never been. Her green scrubs were now soiled and her formerly brilliant white coat was a wrinkled mass of off-white cotton, its pockets yawning open from the weight of their contents. But there was no time to change clothes, barely enough for a long-overdue pit stop in the bathroom.

Her first stop was the nursery for normal newborns. Army-surplus canvas cots for parents to sleep next to their babies were wedged in among countless cribs. After the nurse in charge reported no problems, Sarah walked to the ward for older children. The long, narrow room was jammed with more than thirty low beds with rails and so much medical equipment that the staff and parents had to navigate down narrow pathways. Brightly-colored comic book figures, clown faces, and playfully smiling animals had been painted on the walls by well-intentioned volunteers to calm the young patients, but Sarah knew nothing could distract the sick children from the noisy medical paraphernalia or the stream of strangers in green outfits who constantly touched them and jabbed them with needles.

Sarah scanned the room through a sea of pale blue curtains surrounding the beds and spotted Jimmy Yoder. She maneuvered through the maze, walked up to the young physician, and said, "Hi Jimmy," as cheerfully as she could muster. "How're things tonight? Sorry I'm a bit later than I had intended. Things were pretty difficult in the ER—bad battered-child case."

"Yes, I heard. So awful about that child in the ER, Dr. Belden. I'll never understand how people can hurt little children like that."

"Yes, it turns my stomach to see."

"At least the child's safe now."

"For a while, anyway. So, looks like you've got your hands full up here."

"We're really busy tonight."

Jimmy Yoder was pleased that Sarah Belden was on duty. He would feel forever grateful to her for having recently extricated him from an encounter that might have been humorous for someone else, but for Jimmy had nearly developed into a painfully embarrassing experience.

Some twelve members of a Gypsy family, complete with an ancient grandfather, had tumbled en masse into the ER with a feverish little boy late one night when Jimmy was on call. "Your son has an infection," Jimmy explained to the child's mother after a thorough examination. Seeking to impress her with the potential gravity of the situation, he cautioned her in his most serious life-or-death tone of voice, "He can go home, but you should bring him back right away if his fever remains high or he sleeps too much or won't eat or drink."

"Home? Bring him back?" his mother said softly, with an accent Jimmy had never heard before. "We are Gypsies, *Roma*, we are always on the road. We could be in LA or Seattle tomorrow, how could we bring him back here?"

Jimmy had just started to say, "Wherever you go, there are hospitals you could take him to…," but lost his voice as the woman's beautiful dark face moved closer and closer until the tip of her nose nearly touched his. Her blue-green eyes twinkled as a smile formed on her lips. Then her sister moved in as well, pressing her breasts against Jimmy's arm, her long black hair tickling his neck. He felt the mother's breath as she whispered in his ear, "So he needs a doctor, huh? You're cute. Why don't you just come with us? Then the boy will be fine…and so will we."

Jimmy Yoder felt his knees going limp, then feared he might even wet himself. He was utterly helpless.

Just then Sarah Belden had saved the day, pushing aside the curtain and stepping between the alluring sisters and the struggling intern. "Hello," she said, sizing up the situation quickly, "I'm Dr. Belden. Can I help?"

The spell was broken. Jimmy finished giving the family written instructions on what to look for, and Sarah had become Jimmy's heroine forever.

That memorable incident in the ER with the Gypsy family had been some six weeks earlier, and now Jimmy was assigned to the pediatric ward for a two-month rotation.

"The ward is unusually crowded for this time of year, Dr. Belden. Lots of the kids are from the latest round of flu spreading through the day care centers, but we also have some chronically ill ones who are back in the hospital for the ten thousandth time, or so it seems. My main concern is for one of the Frons, Julie Fron."

Jimmy was talking about a child whose cystic fibrosis—CF, they all called the genetic disease—had once again relapsed. Sarah knew Julie Fron very well—the Frons had five kids, three of whom had the dreaded disease. Statistics mean nothing to people who actually get specific illnesses, Sarah thought—each new Fron baby had only a one-in-four chance of getting the defective gene from both parents and developing CF, but this family had hit the unfortunate jackpot three out of five times. Hardly a month went by without at least one Fron being admitted to the pediatric ward, and Sarah had attended to all of them many times over.

Charlie Fron, Julie's father, was at his daughter's bedside. He understood the drill for dealing with exacerbations of this deadly disease well—better than most interns did, certainly better than Sarah had when she showed up for her first month as a doctor fresh out of medical school.

"Hi Mr. Fron. How's Julie doing?"

Charlie Fron struggled to work up a friendly smile on a face whose eyes were sunken and surrounded with dark circles. He looked far older than his 35 years. He had four more kids at home, two of whom were probably coughing away but not quite bad enough to come into the hospital yet, just enough to keep him and his wife up for several nights in a row.

"It's been rough, Dr. Belden. She started getting worse two days ago, and we had to bring her in to the hospital tonight. But now she looks a little better, thanks. We're always grateful for everything you doctors do for her."

Addressing Sarah directly, the perpetually optimistic and compassionate Dr. Jimmy said without hesitation, "She's doing well, Dr. Belden. Julie is really coming along, she's a trooper."

Sarah wondered if Jimmy ever got depressed, let alone despondent, dealing with all these sick children. She hoped his optimism wouldn't sour over the years.

"I'm sure she is, she's in good hands," Sarah replied. She turned to the little blond girl and said, "Hi Julie."

Still drained from the emotional encounter over the burned and battered child in the ER, Sarah forced herself to sound cheerful. She was determined to leave that sorry situation behind for now.

Julie turned her eyes toward Sarah and nodded slightly. Her lips mouthed, "Hi," but no sound came out.

Sarah could see the papery skin between Julie's ribs and above her collarbone suck in with every strained breath. She was exhausted from her struggle to breathe and from her workout at the hands of the respiratory technicians who had clapped her on her chest for hours, moving her body around head-down to drain her lungs.

Jimmy Yoder interjected, "The respiratory treatments have really helped, Dr. Belden. Her chart shows that the oxygen level in her blood is stable."

What he didn't say, Sarah knew, was the real message: he hoped he wouldn't need to put Julie on a respirator. Dr. Jimmy and the nurses on the ward would keep a careful watch on her and do everything possible to help her survive this episode. When the kids with CF had to be intubated that was all too often a death knell.

After doing a quick exam on Julie Fron, Sarah said, "Looking good, Julie. Dr. Jimmy will have you out of here soon. Get some rest," she added, to both Julie and her father.

Sarah moved on. She wanted to make sure the blood sugar levels were stable on a new patient whose juvenile diabetes she had diagnosed earlier that week, and spent the rest of the time making rounds on the seventeen other kids who were straining her and Dr. Jimmy and the nurses to their limits. Still no time for a break—the nurses in the ER called her repeatedly over the next few hours as Dr. Sandy Kischer fell further and further behind, she was paged twice to the delivery room for what turned out to be uncomplicated deliveries, then she went back to the ward to check on Julie and the other patients. One more short stint in the ER, and finally, Sarah was off to the on-call room for that overdue change of clothes and some precious sleep before Jane Zimmerman would arrive for the change of shift.

Chapter 3: Martina and Derek Johnson

If General Howard Q. Olsen Senior High School had ever had good days, by the mid-1980s they were long since past. A sprawling collection of two-story buildings with outdoor loggias and flat roofs constructed toward the end of World War II, Olsen High looked like a cheap motel on the outskirts of a rust-belt city. As if announcing the sad state of the school to the public, the battered sign over the main entrance read *Ol_en High _chool*. The cafeteria and gymnasium had been condemned and boarded up, and were languishing in disrepair as the school district's budget priorities perennially ignored Olsen. Classrooms and administrative offices provided the only indoor spaces—even the lunch area was outside, under a makeshift canopied shelter, and the only basketball courts were on the paved parking area. School assemblies were held in the ramshackle bleachers at the football field in good weather and moved to the auditorium of the nearby junior college in foul.

The buildings and grounds may have been decrepit, but the students were alive. Very much alive.

In homeroom section 10-7 for Olsen High sophomores, Derek Johnson was passing a suggestive note to Betsy Williams, the precociously buxom girl whose figure had embarrassed countless boys when called on to stand up in class with an uncomfortable bulge in their blue jeans from ogling her. Derek was concentrating on projecting a threatening look to discourage any of his classmates from opening his note to Betsy as they passed it along, so he didn't notice Martina Solyanskaya when the new student entered the dilapidated classroom. But once Betsy got his tightly folded piece of notebook paper, he shifted quickly in his seat to avoid having her catch him staring at her. That was when he saw Martina and forgot all about Betsy or any other girl. Forever, as it turned out.

Martina Solyanskaya stood in the doorway, waiting for Jeptha Hillock, the aging homeroom teacher calling the daily roll call in his slow southern drawl, to acknowledge her presence and invite her in. Martina wore a thin, off-white shawl draped over her shoulders and wrapped around her chest. It was nothing like any piece of clothing Derek had ever seen, and the young woman wearing it was like no one he had ever seen. Shimmering blond hair flowed over the shawl and hung halfway down her back. Under the shawl she wore a simple white blouse with colorful decorations he could not make out from the distance, tiny embroidered flowers he would come to be quite familiar with. An old leather book bag dangled from her right shoulder on a thin strap. In her left hand she held a manila file folder with her school papers. When she at last caught Jeptha Hillock's attention she smiled, a smile that transfixed Derek. Her face seemed to radiate, from the corners of her eyes to her glistening lips, her smile conveying just a hint of self-deprecating humor but also a sense of confidence, of knowing who she was and where she was.

"Come in, come in, young lady," Mr. Hillock said in an enthusiastic welcome to the newcomer, getting up from his desk and accepting the file folder she handed to him. He squinted his puffy eyes as he read from the folder and struggled to pronounce her name: "Martina Sol...Sol-yank, no, sorry, Sol-yan-sky-yaw?"

The smile broadened on her soft white face, but not in mockery; it was gracious, respectful.

"Close enough, thank you, Sir."

"I am Mr. Hillock, your home room teacher, Marty. Should we call you 'Marty,' Marty?"

He laughed at his own joke, revealing an array of random gaps where teeth had gone missing, a mouthful of decay that would never be brought to a dentist on his teacher's salary.

"Pleased to meet you, Mr. Hillock." Then she added courteously but assertively, "It's Martina, thank you."

Derek was stunned. Her beauty, her presence, her self-confidence, were all things he had never seen in his female schoolmates. Or, perhaps the long familiarity from having known the girls in his class for most of their lives may have blinded him to the minuscule increments of their steady transition into maturity. Except for Betsy, whose breasts and hips had exploded like a time-lapse video. But the way Derek looked at the young woman who had just entered the classroom wasn't anything like the way he would undress

Betsy with his eyes. No, this reaction was an altogether different feeling, a fascination, a previously unknown sense of connection he had never felt before. The young man was undergoing a moment of instantaneous maturation, he was being propelled from the quagmire of adolescence to the periphery of adulthood in the wink of an eye. The sudden transition was something he had neither anticipated nor was prepared for, a rapid change that brought its own energy and direction and carried him irreversibly into a new phase of life. Later he was to realize that this moment was the first awakening of love.

Mr. Hillock pointed and said, "OK, Martina, Martina it is," and chuckled again at his revised little joke. "Take that empty desk one row over and two seats down from the front, please."

The desk afforded Derek a perfect view of this entrancing new creature. As she turned her body to slide gracefully into the desk she looked back and made eye contact with him, captivating him with her smile. He was frozen, unable to return the smile, not managing even a faint nod of recognition.

When Martina turned forward to face Mr. Hillock, Derek immediately regretted having missed the opportunity to return her glance. A word he had seen in print but never used before popped into his head: *gorgeous*. To that exact moment he had always thought of attractive girls as *hot* or *nasty* or some cruder sexually-tinged term from the endless adolescent male vernacular. Never *gorgeous*. He knew then that he would have to get to know her, understand who she was. She seemed so...so different. She had told the teacher not to call her Marty, wasn't that what she had said? Martina, that's her name, Martina. Martina—what kind of name was Martina? Who cared?

Derek's musings were interrupted by the school bell signaling the onset of the 5-minute break between home room and their first class. He saw Martina thumb through the papers in her file folder and pull out her class schedule, then stand and look around somewhat perplexed, clearly unsure of where she should go. Derek sensed a second opportunity and found the strength to approach her and say, "You lost? Want some help?"

He was rewarded with another soft, entrancing smile—not alluring, not a come-on or in any way projecting sexual overtones. Just captivating. Her smile connected the two of them in an unfamiliar bond, drawing him in to her presence without triggering his pubescent erotic fantasies.

"Hi," she said, not answering his question. "I'm Martina," she added, extending her hand.

Derek's shoulders dropped. He had no idea how to respond. *Shake hands with a girl?* The unexpected, entirely novel invitation to shake her hand caught him off guard. He had held hands before with girls, had experimented with holding various other parts of their bodies, but had never just shaken hands with anyone his own age, boy or girl. He had hardly ever done so with an adult. But she was standing in front of him, reaching toward him, waiting for him to take her hand; he had to respond. As he stuck out his right hand the gesture seemed as foreign to him as throwing a football with his left arm. But everything changed when they made contact, as the touch of her soft, thin hand sent a warm tingle up his arm and across his neck to his hairline, radiating out to his ears. By the time the handshake ended it seemed far too brief. He found himself wishing the moment would have lasted much longer.

"Derek. Derek Johnson," was all he could muster, his heart pounding furiously from the contact with her hand. He managed to add, "OK, show me your schedule."

She handed him the paper and he glanced it over, excited to see that he could, indeed, be helpful. "We're in the same class first period, American History. We can walk there together."

He felt a tiny sense of triumph: he had gotten the right words out. He told himself to calm down, maybe she had a boyfriend. Maybe she knew she was too classy for him. He forced himself to take a deep breath, not realizing he was clenching his teeth so tight the muscles in his jaw were pulsating visibly through the skin.

"That would be great," she said. "Thanks. It'll probably take me a day or two to find my way around."

As they headed off to the classroom Derek passed two of his buddies standing in front of their lockers, staring at him with the new girl. He had to appear cool, to keep the boys from seeing through his nonchalant façade into the jumble of emotion swirling inside. Those guys were punks, he thought, they'd be real assholes about seeing him with the new girl. No way he would risk introducing her. Derek pursed his lips slightly, stiffened his back and turned his shoulders away from his friends and continued down the hall without looking at them.

***

Over the next two months Derek and Martina exchanged small talk in hallway chats between classes, occasionally at first, then regularly. Soon they started meeting for lunch, sitting together on the low brick wall surrounding the school's outdoor eating area. They spoke about their classes or families or other mundane matters, never about whether they might be developing feelings for each other. By teenage standards, their simple act of eating lunch together was more than enough to mark them as a couple as surely as if they had been caught making out behind the school buildings, but they never got together outside of school hours. Derek wasn't sure why he was so hesitant, he just felt an unaccustomed, overwhelming sense that he should not push things. And, strangest of all, he found that he enjoyed cultivating a real friendship with this girl. Over time they began to open up with each other and he discovered she was someone he could actually explore thoughts, feelings, personal histories, all the expanding richness of life with. They even discussed books they were reading in sophomore English, most recently sharing their reactions to *The Catcher in the Rye*. He felt comfortable entering into this new bond with a young woman, a chaste, pristine camaraderie.

So it came as a shock when she was the one to cross the line and propel them into uncharted territory. It was the last week in October, barely two months after they had met.

"Derek," she said, "I'd like to ask you something."

"Sure, whatever."

He was calm in his innocence, having no clue that she was about to spring something quite unexpected on him.

"I'd like you to take me to the Sadie Hawkins Dance in a couple of weeks. The girls tell me it's the one time every year that we get to do the inviting, so I'm inviting you to take me. Would you like to do that?"

Derek was stunned. She was looking at him in a new way, her smile deliciously mischievous, conveying a different type of interest than ever before. Her question carried a suggestive air he was not prepared to deal with. As conscious as he was of her beauty and charm, he had not foreseen anything like this. She might as well have hit him between the eyes with her lunch pail.

"Mmm..me," he blubbered, "Me?"

She laughed, not harshly but with good-natured amusement.

"Is there anyone else named Derek here? Of course, you." She curled down her perfect lower lip and lowered her upper eyelids in a coy expression of mock disappointment. "Don't you want to go with me?"

He stumbled to find his footing.

"Uh, sure, sure, I'd really like to go, that's great. It's just…just that I thought you were going to talk about something else, you know, one of our books or something."

The bell calling them to their separate after-lunch classes rang just then, mercifully cutting off the conversation before Derek had to grope for anything else to say. As it developed, that was fortunate since he was about to go utterly speechless when she rattled him completely with yet another surprise.

"Call me tonight," she said softly as she stood to walk away, ratifying their new adventure with another smile, only this time the smile was followed with a slight pursing motion of her lips.

Oh my god, he thought, shaken to the quick. *Was that a kiss?* Had she blown him a kiss? Derek remained seated on the brick wall for several moments watching her disappear into the crowd of students hurrying in every possible direction out of the courtyard. He sat until he realized he was the only one left, then picked up his schoolbag and ran, ran hard, barely getting to his next class before the door was closed. He might as well have skipped class that afternoon—there was no room in his mind for anything but thoughts about Martina. He was in a daze, trying to sort out his feelings, his adolescent emotions straining to cope with this new situation, his nether parts tingling with the realization that she might be thinking about him *in that way.* The thought careened around inside his head like a steel ball in a wild pinball game, pinging, screeching, exploding across his brain. Was this really happening? Was she really interested in him, in…*whatever?*

The Sadie Hawkins dance was to seal their new relationship. But before that could happen Derek had to make that phone call, had to take the torturous step that would launch their after-hours contact. Phoning girls was not part of his 10th grade boy's world yet, but she had said, "Call me tonight." He had no choice, any more than he had with that first handshake. He asked himself what was the big deal about a phone call. After all, didn't he talk to her all the time at school? Then it came to him. How would he get any privacy to use the telephone without his parents or brother listening? Even worse, he became terrified about who would answer the phone once he did make the call. What if her mother answered? How would he ask for her? What if he sounded stupid to her mother on the phone?

In the end, it was easy. Derek's older brother Albert had a basketball game that night and their parents went to see him play. Derek had the house to himself. He paced around the living room for nearly fifteen minutes, then finally sat down on the couch in the living room, picked up the phone and dialed Martina's number.

"Hello," said a deep, almost gruff, heavily accented female voice that startled Derek. It was his worst fear: Martina's mother. He nearly hung up the receiver, but froze when he heard the voice then say, in a commanding tone not to be ignored, "Who is this calling?"

Derek's brain was a mass of putty, but his mouth somehow replied as if it were on auto-pilot. "Derek, Derek Johnson."

"What you want, Derek Johnson?"

Again, the voice seemed severe, but Derek also detected a note of something lighter, an inquisitiveness that was not aimed at just any caller, but was focused on him. The other person was testing him. After all, she had not even asked him to explain who he was after he said his name, she only asked what he wanted.

Derek heard his voice saying very politely, "Is this Mrs. Solyanskaya? Mrs. Solyanskaya, I would like to speak with your daughter, Martina, please. I'm a friend of hers from school."

The voice that had seemed so stern at first softened in response. Derek heard a slight chuckle, then, "Good, that's good, you know how to pronounce our name just right. You got good manners, too. Good boy, you must be good boy. OK, you can speak with Martina."

Derek had passed the test. He realized that Martina's mother had anticipated the call, she had not answered the phone by accident. She had to hear his voice, make her own decision about what this boy was like. Martina must have told her all about him.

"Hi, Derek."

Martina's disembodied greeting came directly into his ear through the handset, a thrilling new sensation. Then she sealed their privacy saying, "Hang on a second. I'm taking the phone into my bedroom."

This was exciting, so intimate, Martina in her bedroom, he in his empty house, just the two of them speaking mouth-to-ear

22

through the phone line. They spoke for nearly two hours, until he saw the lights of his family's car in the driveway.

"I gotta go now."

"OK. You hang up first."

"No, you hang up first."

"You're the one who said you have to go. You hang up."

"I'll count three, then we'll both hang up at the same time. One. Two. Three." He did nothing, waiting for the dial tone. It didn't come. Then a laugh.

"You didn't hang up, you're still on the line."

"So are you!" He heard the key in the front door. This was it. "This time for real. See you tomorrow. Gotta go. Bye." He repeated as fast as he could, "One-two-three," and hung up the phone.

It was a silly game that was to be repeated many times in the next two-and-a-half years, all through high school, every night that they weren't actually together.

There were three Solyanskaya women and Derek charmed two of them. Charmed the pants off of one them, as it turned out. Martina became his constant companion, his best friend, his lover. They floated together in a world of deep emotion, neither of them with any thought of anyone else, both consumed by the passions that surged through their rapidly maturing bodies.

Mrs. Solyanskaya was also taken with Derek, impressed with his polite demeanor toward her, his genuine interest in speaking directly with her and learning about the forlorn existence that she had endured in the Soviet Union. He seemed fascinated and sympathetic as she described the unimaginable years of never feeling that she actually owned her own life. She was equally delighted to see her daughter so happy being wooed by this well-mannered boy, satisfied that the sacrifices she had endured in her painstaking struggles to gain freedom in the West had indeed given her daughters a more worthwhile life than they would have known in her native land. Derek also filled a void in the family, there being no man in the Solyanskaya household. Derek was never to learn the full story, knowing only that Martina's father had been much loved but had disappeared into a part of their past that was not to be discussed.

The third Solyanskaya woman, Martina's sister Ivana, was never to come into Derek's sphere of admirers—nor she into his. The void between them was difficult for Derek to understand. Ivana looked so much like her younger sister, they were clearly made by the same tailor, but unmistakably cut from different bolts of cloth. It was as though their creator had used the roughest lots of the same fabrics to craft Ivana but reserved the finest bolts for Martina. They had similar features, from striking blond hair to curvaceous bodies to identically painted toenails. They might have passed for twins at first glance, yet they were like night and day. Martina had a softness in her manner and displayed an appealing sensitivity to her surroundings, while Ivana was hard and distant. Derek was struck that they did share one thing: a degree of self-confidence he had never seen in other girls. But while Martina emanated a confident sense of herself that invited him to relate to her as his equal, the same trait in Ivana played out as cockiness, arrogance, harshness.

No trace of jealousy festered in Ivana over Derek's presence in the lives of her sister and mother—she had her eyes set on a different kind of boy, a go-getter, someone who would do well in business or otherwise elevate her into the comfortable American lifestyle that she craved. She would find a man who would give her children, a big house, oodles of spare money. As far as Ivana was concerned Derek was fine for her sister, but she had her own life to pursue.

Ivana went off to college the next year. Derek and Martina drew ever closer, developing a comfortable bond that seemed capable of movement in only one direction. Then, shortly before graduation from high school, their lives changed forever.

"No, Derek," she whispered, pushing his hand off of her breast one night as they sat in his car looking out over the city. "I can't. We can't. Not tonight."

Martina's refusal to have sex left him more surprised than angry—it was the first time she had ever interrupted an affectionate moment, the first time he had experienced rejection from her. Their lovemaking had always been spontaneous, entirely mutual, shared with an ease, an enthusiasm that never called for submission on either one's part. They had progressed seamlessly from the first kiss that night of the Sadie Hawkins dance through the exploration and finally the consummation of sex. All the while their relationship had seemed perfectly symbiotic. Now, what was happening? Why was she shutting him out? He felt stunned, intruded upon by an unwelcome visitation. He sensed some permanent change unfolding, a seismic jolt to their idyllic state. Until that moment they had been one organic unit but now her side was asserting its independence, drawing

24

a line between them. He might have been a Siamese twin who had not seen a razor-sharp cleaver descending from nowhere, irreversibly severing their lifeline of flesh and blood in one instant. He felt as though he had fallen to the ground at the separation and now needed to recover his footing.

He struggled for words.

"OK, sure. OK, no problem. Whatever you say."

Derek tried to collect his bearings, to find not just the right words but the right message, the right thoughts to bridge the chasm that had suddenly opened between them. One thing he was grateful for was that Martina had stopped him before he was fully aroused, or he would have been in serious distress, too distracted by his erection to deal with whatever was intruding so unexpectedly on their relationship. But he had to find his way in this alien terrain. Something important was coming between them.

"What's up, Martina?"

She didn't hesitate.

"I'm pregnant."

"Are you sure? How do you know?"

"I know. I'm sure. My breasts are swelling up, I haven't had a period in two months, I'm throwing up every morning. It's real."

He went silent.

She mistook his shocked silence for disappointment, or anger, or any of a million signs of rejection. Her deep-seated strength failed her.

"Derek!" she shrieked, her scream shaking the car.

It was an anguished cry, not a howl of anger. Now the other separated Siamese twin felt the partition, the shattered bond. She sobbed violently, gasping for breath between loud, explosive moans.

"Martina, Martina, it's OK, please, it's OK. I love you. Please, it's OK, I was just…just stunned. But it's OK, it's really OK."

She took a deep breath, exhaled, then spoke in a soft, loving tone as she wrapped her arms around him, burying her face on his chest.

"Derek. Derek. Yes, OK, I love you too."

They were two children about to have a child. Their own childhood had come to an abrupt end, and now they had to become older than they were. They faced a transition that they had anticipated, even longed for, but that they had expected to glide slowly into. Building a family together was supposed to be some years in the future, not now, not overnight. A baby meant Martina would have to give up her scholarship to the State University. Derek would still take the construction job he had lined up but he'd have to abandon his plan to begin a technical program at night at the local J.C. They had anticipated playing together on weekends, spending every summer together, but now they would have little time for anything but work and caring for a baby. Their plans were gone, all gone. Something—someone—else was now demanding their attention, directing their lives down a different path.

The wedding was a simple civil ceremony at the County Courthouse early in June, right after graduation. Wearing his first suit and a bright red tie that Martina had bought him as a wedding present, Derek felt like a little boy in a costume. Martina wore an unadorned white dress, her only jewelry a gold cross on a thin chain that Derek had given her.

"I love you," they repeated to each other as they exchanged simple wedding bands.

Mrs. Solyanskaya was not pleased that Martina would forego college, but the woman had suffered through so much cruelty and hardship that she knew life was more likely to lead down unforeseen pathways than to reward human efforts at planning the future. Her instincts told her that Martina could have done far worse than marrying this well-meaning boy, albeit prematurely. She looked at Derek and gave him a hug, saying only, "You are a good boy, you are doing the right thing by my daughter. You will be a good man, a loving husband and father, I know you will be." Before she released Derek from her arms she kissed him softly on his right cheek, then his left, then again on the right, sealing her approval.

While the mother was resigned to the situation, relieved that her daughter had not simply been abandoned to raise a child on her own, the sister was smugly triumphant. Ivana was openly self-righteous over what she saw as Martina's folly. She berated her sister for having let this working-class boy drag her down, truncate her future, deprive her of the comfortable life that might have opened before her. Having just returned home from her freshman year at the State University, Ivana was all the more convinced that she was on track for a far better life than her sister would ever know. She had spent much of the year learning how to pursue the appropriate candidates for a future husband—which sorority she should join, which fraternity she should accept dates from, which major course of study she should follow. She was not kind to Martina, mocking her mercilessly. "You are a damn fool. You will pay the consequences." Ivana was exultant in her victory.

Derek's family simply adapted to what was happening. His brother Albert had graduated from high school and gone to work, the family had no real expectations about whether the boys would go to college or not. And, getting married to a girl that one of them had knocked up was the honorable thing to do. As it turned out, unbeknownst to Derek or Albert that was precisely how their own parents had conceived Albert and gotten married. The family had never discussed the chronology of marital and birth events with their sons, and somehow neither Albert nor Derek ever thought to broach the subject or to do the math. But once Martina's pregnancy was revealed to the family Derek's father had confessed casually to him, "Here we go again, son. There will be more people in your wedding photos than anyone can see, just like at ours. You're keeping up a family tradition." Derek stared at the wry smile on his father's face and needed no explanation.

Mrs. Solyanskaya was right—up to a point. Derek was indeed the loving husband to her daughter that she had hoped for. His job as an apprentice to a carpenter paid decent wages and the couple rented a small house that Derek was fixing up in his off hours. Martina was beautiful in her pregnancy once the ravages of morning sickness and heartburn had abated in her second trimester. Life seemed to be progressing in a tolerable, even promising, way.

Just as the young couple seemed to be finding their way, the first of the disasters they would endure exploded on them, imposing penance far out of proportion to their sin of passion.

Chapter 4: Number One

The first time Sarah Belden had been called to the delivery room for an emergency she was but a fledgling doctor left to fly on her own. During medical school she had helped deliver babies, had examined many newborns, but barely six weeks after graduating from medical school she was the rawest of raw pediatric interns when she heard the page: *Dr. Belden, Stat! Dr. Belden, delivery room, STAT!* The sound of her name blaring urgently over the hospital's loudspeakers made her tingle with excitement, confident she had done everything possible to prepare for this moment, yet anxious that she might forget something critical. She ran a string of memory-stimulating mnemonics through her head to reassure herself she could deal with any catastrophe: *ABC—airway, breathing, circulation; PPV—positive pressure ventilation; APGAR—appearance, pulse, grimace, activity, respiration.* Her heart raced with her new sense of responsibility—if the baby had serious problems, if it weren't breathing or went limp or turned blue, it would be up to *her* to take action, no one would be around to take over if she couldn't remember the right drug to give or the proper dose for a newborn, or bungled her attempt to insert a breathing tube or start an IV. There would be no Dr. Virginia Apgar in the delivery room with Dr. Sarah Belden.

As she entered the delivery room, Sarah had been thinking only of the baby, and herself. But when she saw the woman lying on the table, her legs up in stirrups, her face contorted in pain as she pushed hard through a contraction, Sarah shuddered: the woman in labor was a child herself, a teenager too young to be having a baby. Sarah glanced at the clip board hanging from an IV pole next to the mother-to-be. It read, "Martina Johnson."

Sarah's excitement and fear of failure, her astonishment at the woman's youth, her recitation of life-saving procedures, everything tumbling through her mind vanished in the next instant as the woman pushed hard one last time and the obstetrics resident, Dr. Alan Martindale, caught a baby. But there would be no infant for Sarah to attend to, no life to save. The Johnson baby was stillborn. Seriously malformed, its contorted face no more than a mask in front of a truncated skull that ended just behind the ears, the lifeless infant looked as though someone had scooped away the back of the head, *horrible,* Sarah gasped, *the baby has no brain.* The scientific name popped into her head: *Total anencephaly with multiple anomalies,* not viable with or without medical attention.

Shocked by being so close to a disfigured creature she had previously seen only in garish textbook photos, Sarah struggled to come to grips with what was happening. Her heart pounded, the arteries on both sides of her head throbbed as a new wave of anxiety consumed her: how could she break the bad news to this poor woman? What could she possibly say to comfort her? Even as the thought made her cringe, she was mercifully reprieved: Alan Martindale was taking on that grim responsibility. Sarah breathed out a sigh of relief and watched in silence, deeply grateful, as the obstetrics resident walked around the delivery table to speak with the young Mrs. Johnson.

"I'm very sorry but it's not good news, Mrs. Johnson, not at all," Martindale said in a soft but straightforward and professional manner that made a deep impression on Sarah. "The baby is not alive. He had such serious problems that he never had a chance."

"Can I hold him, please?" murmured Martina through little sobs, the plea of a helpless child.

"Sure, of course. But, Mrs. Johnson, I need to tell you, he doesn't look like a healthy baby. His little body is not like anything you have ever seen. He has a number of severe malformations."

Martindale was doing his best to prepare the woman for a sight she could not possibly imagine, but he might as well have been trying to cushion a blow from a sledgehammer. This woman-child had come to the hospital anticipating the wonders of motherhood, and now all she had to show for weeks of morning sickness, for nine months of carrying a baby inside her, for the hours of labor pains, was the unthinkable tragedy of losing her first child, dead before it was even born, its body grotesquely distorted.

"It's OK," she said, still sobbing, "he's my baby."

Martindale wrapped the baby in a soft cloth but he couldn't hide the featureless face with the sunken nose and bulging eyes. He handed the lifeless baby to Martina Johnson and stood silently next to her for what seemed to Sarah a very long time. Then he turned to the delivery room nurse and said, "Please stay with Mrs. Johnson for a few minutes." The nurse nodded and moved close to the mother and baby as Martindale stepped outside and approached Martina's husband, Derek Johnson. Sarah followed closely behind.

This time Martindale didn't have to speak first. Derek took one look at the two doctors and went pale. He dropped his head and seemed to be staring at his right foot as it tapped rapidly on the floor, his whole body shaking to the beat of his foot. Without looking up he murmured, "It's not good, is it?"

"No, it's very bad, the baby wasn't born alive," responded Dr. Martindale, with the same compassionate but professional tone he had used with Martina. "He wasn't fully formed and had no chance to live. His heart wasn't beating, his brain just wasn't what it needed to be. I'm so sorry for you and your wife."

"OK," said Derek, still not lifting his head. His foot had now grown still. Like Martina he was being propelled through an unfathomable heartbreak with no time for emotional growth, a child dragged into another burden of adult life. "OK," he repeated. "How's Martina? Can I see her?"

"She's fine, and she's holding the baby. Come with me," Martindale gestured to Derek to follow him through the door to the delivery room to his wife's side. Martindale pulled over a stainless steel stool for Derek to sit on, then signaled the nurse to give the couple a few minutes together before wheeling Martina out to the recovery room.

Sarah had learned a lot from Alan Martindale that night about how to deal with being a family's first link with the gravest disappointment of all. But she was to discover that she had not learned everything she would need to deal with the tragic moments her patients were to experience. The obstetrician had shown compassion and empathy, the interpersonal skills of a seasoned diplomat, qualities Sarah had not been born with or learned in college or in four years as a student doctor in medical school. Watching Martindale deal with the Johnson couple taught her that she must gather her wits to face terrified family members and deliver bad news, the worst they could be hearing. However ghastly the result for the baby and parents—death, horrific deformity, a thousand other tragedies—it would be up to her to burst their bubble of joyous expectation, let them down, console them as they searched for an explanation. Perhaps even bear the brunt of their anger, as messengers of bad news throughout the ages had done. Each terrible time she would have to perform impromptu with no chance to rehearse, each first take would be the only take.

Martindale had maintained seemingly perfect self-control without going cold, without appearing to distance himself entirely from the human concerns of the people he was speaking to about the pall had been cast over their lives. But Martindale taught by example. He never said anything to Sarah about how to ward off the effect these piercing encounters might have on her. He never told her how to compartmentalize her involvement, how to seal off the excruciating encounter from the rest of her life. He had left a void in her learning, a void that would later come back to haunt her: how to disengage her inner self from the tragedies of others, how to develop a proper distance while demonstrating genuine compassion to those who were suffering. How to be a good, caring doctor while protecting her own core in a shell of clinical detachment.

Emotionally defenseless, with no shield, no filter, no reserve of experience to buffer her reaction to the tragedy that had befallen the Johnsons, the vulnerable young doctor let her heart go out to Martina Johnson. Sarah visited her often in the maternity ward during the next few days. She would hold Martina's hand, repeating words of encouragement over and over. "Martina, this was horrible for you and Derek but you are both young, there will be other babies, and they will do just fine."

Dr. Sarah Belden's reassurances were well-intentioned but she had no power to make good on them. Yes, there were to be other Johnson babies, but they would not do just fine.

Chapter 5: Lenny

Barely one year after the tragedy of her deformed first-born, Martina Johnson delivered twins. Sarah Belden, now a more seasoned second-year pediatric resident, was not on duty the night the twins were born, but she was working in the newborn unit that month so the two little boys with their two happy, loving parents were waiting for her when she arrived for work the next morning. Sarah examined them carefully: they were perfect. She was buoyant seeing the Johnsons cuddling the newborns, taking turns holding each of the twins, laughing at every tiny burp, treasuring even the slightest change of expression on either face. She smiled when Martina told her that Derek had come up with their cute twin names, Lenny and Denny.

Sarah resolved that she would make sure the boys went home healthy. They had to, for her as well as for the Johnsons. The memory of the malformed stillborn hung like a black veil between her and Martina, never mentioned but always present. She would *not* let anything happen to Lenny and Denny. She assured the Johnsons the boys would do just fine in the normal newborn nursery, then go home with them very soon.

But once again Sarah had no power to make good on her well-intentioned reassurances.

On the third day Lenny began refusing to feed, always a grim sign in a newborn. Sarah saw that he had a rapid pulse and was having difficulty breathing. She listened to his chest with her stethoscope. A heart murmur and signs of congestive heart failure— the boy had most likely been born with a congenital heart defect. Sarah transferred him to the neonatal intensive care unit, letting Denny remain in the normal nursery. She would have to explain to the Johnsons why she had separated the twins and tell the young couple that something might be seriously wrong. Sarah steeled herself, took a deep breath, walked down the hall toward their room, then stopped when she felt her stomach churning and a foul bilious taste bubbling up in her mouth. She ran to the ladies room and retched into the sink, not able to make it to the toilet bowl. She rinsed her mouth and gargled with handfuls of water, then splashed cold water on her face until she got her bearings. This was her job, just as Martindale had said, this was her job, no matter how grave the situation.

Sarah headed back to the Johnson's room. Derek was sitting in the only chair, holding Denny. She looked from him to Martina, then, sounding more apologetic than she had intended, said, "I am so, so sorry to tell you but I'm afraid Lenny has a problem. I think he has some kind of hole in his heart, and it may be serious. I called in the heart specialist, the pediatric cardiologist, Dr. Lesley Kahn. She's the best there is."

Sarah expected the young parents to start peppering her with questions, or break down crying, accusing her of something, but they just stared at her.

Surprised at their lack of reaction, Sarah wondered whether the parents had any idea what she had told them.

Martina was the first to speak. "When will she be here?"

"Soon," Sarah said. "She'll be here soon."

Less than ten minutes later a short, trim, woman with long, flowing brown hair that hung nearly to her waist, entered and commandeered the room with an immediate air of authority.

"Mr. and Mrs. Johnson?" she said. "I'm Dr. Lesley Kahn. Dr. Belden tells me your baby has a heart problem. I'll examine him and then I will come back to talk with you." Turning to Sarah she said, "Come with me, Dr. Belden," leading her out of the room before the parents could say anything.

With eyes that always seemed to be critical, judgmental, Dr. Lesley Kahn was straightforward to the point of being blunt. Sarah never knew whether Kahn was in fact as insensitive as she seemed or whether her tactless treatment of families like the Johnsons was her way of insulating herself from her own feelings. But she was a truly gifted cardiologist whose initial diagnosis was almost always correct. And she took great pleasure in making sure all the pediatric residents knew just how good she was. As soon as she had examined Lenny Johnson, studied the paper strip from an electrocardiogram, and looked at an X-ray of his chest, she announced her preliminary diagnosis: "This boy has a fatal heart defect, Dr. Belden. I believe he has only one ventricle in his heart to pump blood instead of two. I need to perform a cardiac catheterization immediately to confirm the diagnosis. Go speak with the parents and get them to sign the consent forms while I get things ready in the cath lab."

Sarah walked back to the Johnson's room feeling the weight of her growing responsibility. The Martindale moment was continuing, she would have to endure another heartrending encounter with the Johnson. She stopped at the nursing station to collect the paperwork, then gritted her teeth and entered their room. Sarah wished she could take her time with the young couple, explain everything in detail, give them time to adjust, but she knew that she needed to get them to move quickly or the impatient Dr. Kahn would burst in and take over.

"Martina, Derek," she said, shifting her glance slowly from mother to father and back, her eyes sad, her lower lip curled up slightly. "Dr. Kahn thinks that the baby...sorry, Lenny, needs to have a test so she can be sure what the problem is with his heart. The test is called a cardiac catheterization, a type of X-ray. It involves putting some medicine, some dye actually, into Lenny's bloodstream so that his heart will show up clearly on the X-ray. Dr. Kahn has done many cardiac catheterizations on babies. As I said, she's the very best there is."

"What do you think we should do, Dr. Belden?" asked Martina.

"Dr. Kahn is the expert. If she says Lenny needs the cardiac catheterization then I agree with her. She's always right." She handed a clipboard with a pen attached on a beaded chain to Derek and said, "I don't want to rush you, but Dr. Kahn thinks she needs to do the test right away. Please sign these consent forms, at the bottom of each page."

Derek looked at Martina, who nodded slowly. He scribbled his signature and handed her the clipboard. She signed and handed the papers back to Sarah.

"Please, Dr. Belden, please make him be O.K."

Sarah's voice stuck in her throat. No more promises she couldn't deliver on. She coughed once, then said, "He's in very good hands with Dr. Kahn, and I'll be with him the whole time. I'll be back as soon as the test is finished."

Sarah wheeled the cart holding the baby in his bassinet away from Martina's bedside, through the door and down a short hallway into the cardiac cath lab. Already cloaked in a sterile gown, gloves and cap, Leslie Kahn was pacing quickly back and forth, bursting at the seams to get started. "About time," she said without greeting Sarah. She lifted Lenny out of the bassinet with a clean blanket and lowered him face-up on the X-ray table. With precision and skill that amazed Sarah, Kahn started an I.V. in a vein in the baby's arm and opened a slow drip from the bottle of saline hanging nearby. She injected a tiny dose of sedative into the line, waited for a brief moment while he relaxed, then scrubbed his groin with iodine soap, dabbed the area with gauze dipped in sterile water, and dried it with a sterile towel. She injected a small amount of local anesthetic into one side of the baby's groin then inserted a tiny catheter through the skin and into a blood vessel and threaded it up to his heart. Kahn injected dye into Lenny's bloodstream and Sarah watched, mesmerized, as the minute organ about the size of a walnut lit up, appearing much larger than life-sized on the video monitor. The image on the screen showed a severely undersized left ventricle and underdeveloped heart valves and aorta, just as Kahn had predicted. The self-absorbed cardiologist startled Sarah with a triumphal outburst: "*Yes! Yes! Nailed it! Hypoplastic Left Heart Syndrome! Yes!*" The highly-skilled but tactless physician was cheering her success as if she had scored a game-winning buzzer-beater in a basketball game rather than having confirmed the inevitable death of a baby.

Striding quickly out of the cardiac catheterization lab several paces ahead of Sarah, Dr. Kahn walked directly up to the Johnsons and launched into her monologue with no prelude, saying, "There's no hope for this baby. The heart has only one ventricle and it can't pump his blood around his body adequately. I'll talk to the cardiac surgeons and see if they want to try something. They're surgeons, they usually want to operate," she said with an obvious sneer, "but in my opinion there's no real hope. Any questions?" Pausing for but a few seconds to give the stunned couple little chance to respond, Kahn spoke before they said anything. "OK, I'll let the surgeons know and they'll talk with you," she said, then disappeared down the hall.

Sarah moved close to the Johnsons. As well as she knew Lesley Kahn's brusque style, Sarah was caught off guard by such a curt delivery of bad news. She wondered whether Kahn had even seen the bewildered look on the Johnsons' faces. She had to do something, help them somehow understand what was going on. "Please, come with me," she said. With Derek's arm around his wife, the two trembling parents walked with Sarah down the hallway, tracing Lesley Kahn's footsteps to the cardiology suite.

"Take a seat, please," Sarah said, gesturing to the old aluminum chairs with faded red plastic bucket seats that comprised the only furniture in the stark waiting room. Pointing to an inner door that led to the viewing room she added, "Dr. Morton Scheld, the chief pediatric cardiac surgeon, and Dr. Kahn are just inside, reviewing the videotape of Lenny's cardiac catheterization. They'll be out in a few minutes."

Posters depicting drawings of human hearts covered the wall. Sarah was never sure if the sketches meant anything to people who hadn't studied anatomy, but they gave her a visual aid to help her explain Lenny's problem. Sarah pointed to one drawing labeled *"Normal Newborn Heart"* and asked "Do you know how a heart is supposed to work?" The Johnsons looked at each other briefly before nodding slowly, unconvincingly, to Sarah. "A normal heart has four chambers," Sarah continued, "two that receive and hold blood between heartbeats and two bigger ones that contract to push out the blood during each heartbeat. The bigger ones are called ventricles. The right ventricle pumps blue blood to the lungs where it collects oxygen, and the left one pumps the fresh red blood around the body." The Johnsons nodded again.

Unsure whether any of this was making sense to the young couple, Sarah moved a few feet to another wall chart and pointed at a second drawing, titled *"Hypoplastic Left Heart Syndrome."* "This is what Lenny's heart looks like. See—the ventricle that pumps blood around the body, the left one, is hardly formed. The only hope for Lenny is if the surgeons can re-route the blood so that the right ventricle does all the work for both sides of his heart. Sometimes the operation works pretty well, at least for a few years. But sometimes the one pumping chamber just can't do the job for two. The surgeons will go over Lenny's condition in more detail and let you know what they think."

Inside the viewing room, cardiac surgeon Dr. Morton Scheld asked his cardiologist counterpart, "What have we got here, Dr. Kahn?" Despite working with her for many years, Scheld still addressed his colleague formally, as he did all the other physicians he encountered. Scheld was aloof, but had none of Kahn's rough edges.

Quite the opposite, he exuded patrician dignity. He was often referred to as *The Distinguished Dr. Scheld*, and he savored the praise, accepting it—expecting it, really—without a pretense of humility. He looked distinguished, he was distinguished, and that was that.

"Hypoplastic left heart syndrome, absolutely clear," replied Kahn, using her pointer to outline the defects being projected on the video monitor. "He hasn't got a chance."

Morton Scheld did not endorse her pessimistic conclusion. A consummately self-confident surgeon, he believed that a baby in his hands always had a chance to recover, however hopeless the situation might seem to others. "Thank you Dr. Kahn. Excellent catheterization, our work is clearly defined."

"You're wasting your time, Morton. This kid has no prospect for survival, none at all. But I knew you'd want to give it a try anyway."

Scheld walked out of the viewing room directly up to the Johnsons. Sarah stood immediately but the parents remained sitting. When Sarah realized that Scheld was not about to introduce himself, she quickly said, "Mr. and Mrs. Johnson, this is Dr. Scheld, the chief pediatric cardiac surgeon. The heart surgeon." Scheld ignored Sarah, speaking directly to the Johnsons. He remained standing as he addressed them.

"As Dr. Kahn has explained, your baby has a serious heart problem, but I believe I may be able to help him." Scheld had no idea that Lesley Kahn had said little more than that the baby was sure to die.

"What…what can you do, Doctor Scheld?" asked Derek. Martina looked down at her hands, clenched tightly together in her lap.

"I will connect the two sides of his heart so that the right ventricle will pump all the blood around his body."

"Will it work?"

"I have done this procedure many times, with excellent success."

How could he say that? thought Sarah, startled by the surgeon's self-assured response. Scheld was one of the best pediatric cardiac surgeons anywhere, but she knew that he was vastly exaggerating his experience performing that procedure. She had attended his own recent presentation at Grand Rounds where he had reported his results on all the babies with this specific heart defect that he had operated on in his entire career—and the list added up to less than a dozen babies, only two of whom had survived out of infancy. She grew anxious that the Johnsons were being misled but she dared not correct Scheld. Maybe later, maybe later she'd be able to say something.

"What are his chances, Doctor?" asked Derek.

"His heart is already giving out. With surgery, he may survive; without it, he cannot live more than a few weeks, perhaps months, but he will quickly outgrow his heart's capacity. We will not know what will happen for sure until the operation is finished."

"I guess…I guess we have no choice." He turned to his wife and said, "Martina?"

She nodded slowly in acquiescence, not raising her head to look at her husband or any of the physicians.

"OK, whatever it takes," he said to Scheld. "Thank you, Doctor."

"Fine," said Scheld. "We will transfer him to the University Hospital. We have the necessary resources to perform open-heart surgery on infants there. If we had the equipment here, of course, I could operate at Memorial General, but this hospital does not have what we need. The University will be much better for him."

Done, Sarah thought, she would never get a chance to say anything to them. But at least Lenny would be at the University. She knew that they had the right staff there, the cardiology fellows, the nurse specialists, the technicians who ran the heart-lung bypass equipment.

In less than an hour Lenny was transferred by ambulance across town to the University. As soon as her shift at Memorial General ended, Sarah hurried there to be with the Johnsons, arriving just before the surgery ended.

Some twenty minutes after Sarah sat down with the young couple, Morton Scheld came into the waiting room still wearing surgical scrubs, a white cotton mask over his nose and mouth, a paper hood over his hair. He walked directly up to the parents, untied the top strap of the mask so it dangled around his neck, and said, "I'm sorry to tell you, the baby didn't make it. He died on the operating table. We were able to connect the two sides of his heart, however his Right Ventricle wasn't strong enough to handle the load."

Sarah was aghast. Dr. Morton Scheld had not greeted the couple or called Lenny by his name. She clenched her teeth, suppressing her outrage, watching as Derek and Martina struggled to respond, all the while thinking, *I should have warned them, said something, I should have.*

"But you said he had a good chance to live, that's why we went ahead with the surgery," pleaded Derek at last. "What went wrong?"

"Nothing went wrong, nothing at all," Scheld said, with what sounded to Sarah like a note of indignance in his voice. "The surgery went perfectly well, just as we expected. His heart, the single ventricle, just couldn't take the pressure. Sometimes it just happens that way."

Scheld was already looking over their heads at the clock on the wall of the surgery waiting room. "Again, I regret that he couldn't make it. We did everything that could be done surgically," he said. With no further words he turned and headed back into the doctor's lounge in the operating suite to change into new scrubs and prepare for his next operation.

The distraught couple held each other without speaking, their silence broken only by an occasional soft whimper. Sarah could not say or do anything to cushion the fact that Martina and Derek had lost a second child. She sat with them for ten minutes, then left to return to Memorial General and check on the other twin. Nothing bad would happen to Denny, nothing. She wouldn't let it.

Chapter 6: Denny

In the normal newborn nursery with all the other healthy babies, Denny was thriving. Like Lenny, he was a little over four pounds at birth but he was feeding vigorously and gaining about one ounce each day. Sarah felt deeply gratified when she would see Martina suckling him at her breast or cuddling him while she and Derek giggled and made faces at the cooing infant. Martina was flourishing in her new role. The color was returning to her face, her cheeks were filling out, she was taking pains to shampoo and brush her long blond hair that once again shimmered in the light.

She's turning into a mother, thought Sarah as Martina held the baby, staring at him with a faint smile as she rocked him to sleep.

One morning Martina greeted Sarah with a cheerful question: "When will Denny go home, Dr. Belden? We have the nursery all set up, we can't wait." But then the words caught in her throat as she remembered that there were two cribs waiting in their little house, two wind-up musical mobiles with little circus animals hanging over them, two sets of fleece sleepers.

Sarah saw Martina's expression lose its joyful anticipation and grow distant, and guessed that Martina had realized she would be bringing one baby home, not two.

Hoping to break through Martina's sudden melancholy, Sarah smiled and answered, "Denny will go home when he gets close to five pounds. It won't be long now, the way he's feeding." She told herself that Martina would put all of the heartbreak behind her once she was in her own home, once she was living a mother's normal life with her baby son and husband.

But two days later the bottom dropped out of the Johnson's world. And Sarah's.

After a long night in the Neonatal Intensive Care Unit dealing with a newborn who was having breathing problems, Sarah went to the normal nursery to check on Denny. The nurse on duty greeted Sarah with ominous news: "Dr. Belden, you should take a look at Denny Johnson. He hasn't taken much the last two feedings, and he seems to be sleeping more than he had been."

"How are his vital signs?" asked Sarah.

"His pulse and breathing were up a little at 1AM and 3AM, and his temperature is just below ninety-eight degrees. We weren't sure if we should call you earlier since we knew you were so busy and would be coming by as soon as you were free."

Sarah wanted to scream at the woman—Denny could already be deathly ill. She cursed under her breath with frustration. How many times had she told the nurses to call her at the first sign of any problem! The nurse should have known that newborns might not develop fevers or show other obvious signs of infection like older kids or adults, yet be seriously ill and go downhill suddenly.

"I'll check him right away," Sarah said, struggling to keep her voice calm. She added in mild reproach, "Please, never hesitate to call me if you think something might be wrong. That's what I'm in the hospital for."

She had long been annoyed with the nurses in the normal nursery. They were good, well-meaning, but they simply didn't like looking for bad news and were often in denial until the signs of danger were unavoidable. Unlike the highly skilled nurses in the NICU who were far more experienced than even the interns and residents in caring for desperately ill and tiny newborns, the ones in the normal nursery were motherly figures who loved nurturing nearly two thousand normal babies every year, not taking care of the sick ones. Many were also gun-shy, having been embarrassed early in their careers by calling the pediatrician to examine a baby who looked worrisome to them but was just fine by the time the young physician arrived. So now they turned a blind eye to early signs of distress to avoid crying wolf and having another physician berate them and question their judgment.. But this time they had waited too long.

What Sarah found made her stomach churn: Denny was listless and hardly moved as she examined him. Her heart started racing as she thought through what she needed to do to search for an infection hiding somewhere in the little baby. A spinal tap to check for meningitis. Blood and urine specimens. Get the tests ordered

41

quickly, then start antibiotics while waiting for the results. She called out, "Get me LP, blood culture, and bladder collection setups, and let's bring him back to the NICU."

After cleansing the skin over the baby's pubic bone, Sarah deftly inserted a needle into Denny's tiny bladder and collected about two teaspoonfuls of urine for testing. Next she faced the challenge of drawing blood samples from a miniature vein on the back of his little hand. She put a rubber tourniquet around his tiny arm, wiped the skin with an alcohol pad, then guided an ultra-thin needle into the minuscule vessel, sighing under her breath with relief when drops of blood started flowing on the first attempt. After collecting a few micro-samples for testing, she taped the needle in place and connected it to a tube hanging from an IV bottle.

Then she put on sterile gloves and opened the sealed tray with the supplies she needed to perform a spinal tap. She scrubbed Denny's lower back, then, holding her breath, she slipped another thin needle through the skin between two vertebrae near the bottom of his spine and advanced the point a fraction of a millimeter at a time, trying desperately to avoid scratch any tissue and contaminate the spinal fluid with blood. Hoping to see crystal clear, healthy spinal fluid dripping from the needle, she saw instead cloudy liquid bubbling into the collection tube. She muttered, *"Aw, shit!"* under her breath, then bit her lip, turned to the nurse, and said, "We'll send most of the fluid off to the laboratory for examination and culture, but I'll keep a couple of drops to look at myself." She dripped the spinal fluid on a glass slide and slipped it under the lens of a microscope. As soon as the image came into focus she saw very bad news: white blood cells that didn't belong in spinal fluid, a sure sign that the baby's body was trying to mount its defenses against a life-threatening infection. She again muttered, *"Aw, shit!"* then pounded the table with her fist and said out loud, *"Dammit, dammit, dammit."* Sarah went back to Denny's incubator and started the antibiotics dripping through the IV as the nurses connected instruments to monitor his heart and breathing.

But Dr. Sarah Belden could not save the second twin. Denny was dead by early that evening. Sarah sobbed uncontrollably as she watched the Johnsons leave the hospital for a home with a nursery and two empty cribs.

Chapter 7: Resuscitated

A little over one year after Lenny and Denny died, and a short two years since the malformed stillbirth, Dr. Sarah Belden staggered at seeing Martina Johnson on the delivery room table. Exhausted from twenty-one hours of nonstop work, still reeling from the heartrending encounter in the emergency room with the battered little boy with cigarette-burn and belt-buckle scars, and now breathless from her sprint to the delivery suite, she could not believe it was happening all over again. But it was: Sarah was about to be responsible for the life of yet another Johnson baby. She had to steel herself for the task at hand, face the reality of where she was and what she had to do.

Sarah took several deep breaths, then pushed backward through the swinging double doors of the delivery room to avoid contaminating the hands she had just scrubbed. Bile swirled up in her throat when she glanced at Martina Johnson. She swallowed the foul liquid, took another deep breath, then coughed out a question to the maternity nurse through her surgical mask, "Did you alert the neonatal intensive care nursery and page the on-call neonatologist to come in *stat*?"

"Yes, Dr. Belden, the NICU is ready. And we put in a call right away for the neonatologist. It's Dr. Silvestre, she's coming as soon as she can, but she's over at St. Anne Moray Hospital so it'll be a few minutes."

Sarah felt a wave of relief mixed with frustration. Giuliana Silvestre was her favorite among the neonatologists, but at this moment she was miles away, she wouldn't arrive soon enough to help Sarah in the delivery room with what was sure to be a difficult baby. She, Dr. Sarah Belden, was the senior pediatrician in the hospital at the moment, it was up to her to deal with this situation.

Focus, she had to focus, this was on her. No time to grouse about where Dr. Silvestre was. No time to whine about her bad luck at being on call for another Johnson baby's birth. No time to think about anything or anybody other than the infant whose life was about to be in her hands. Her heart thumped hard in her chest. She felt sweat starting to ooze on her forehead and hoped it would not seep out from under the surgical cap and drip into her eyes.

She pushed her arms into the surgical gown the nurse held open for her, slipped her hands into a pair of sterile latex gloves, and looked around the room to locate the equipment and supplies she would need when the baby came out. Then her eyes came to rest on Martina Johnson. Sarah's heart went out to the still-young woman in labor. Her third pregnancy and nothing to show for it except three lost babies. The Johnsons had suffered repeated heartbreaks, more agony than anyone should have to endure in a lifetime, and yet it had all come upon them in a few short years. Sarah asked herself what more could happen to them, then cringed as she remembered that this pregnancy was ending prematurely, this Johnson baby would be fighting for life from the moment it was born.

A deep, friendly male voice distracted her from further painful thoughts on what the future might bring.

"Howdy, Sarah," said Fred Trilling, the OB resident perched on a stool at the end of the delivery table, "we're going to have a baby for you in a couple of minutes."

"Hi Fred. How far along do you estimate?"

Lowering his voice to a stage whisper, he said, "Not far enough, at most 24 weeks by dates. Just couldn't wait any longer, apparently."

"Do you know what happened?" said Sarah, moving close enough to speak privately into Trilling's right ear. "Did you try to stop her labor?"

"No time to stop labor, too far along. Seems she was having strong contractions all afternoon but didn't tell anyone. Finally told her husband when she was about to pop and he called an ambulance. I thumbed through her medical record. This poor kid has had a rough go with her pregnancies the last few years. My guess is she just didn't want to admit to herself that she was going into labor already so she didn't seek help until it was too late."

"Yes, I know her story," Sarah said flatly through closed teeth, loath to recount her own excruciating history with Martina

Johnson and the three dead babies. Trilling did not know, or thoughtfully did not mention, Sarah's role in Martina's earlier pregnancies, and raising all of that with him now wouldn't serve any purpose, would only distract her. She had to focus on this baby, the others were gone, she couldn't help them now.

"Here he comes," said Trilling, reaching forward with both arms extended. In an instant he was holding something in his hands: a baby so small Sarah couldn't recognize any features even though he was less than five feet away from her. Trilling put two clips onto the umbilical cord, cut between them with a scalpel, and handed the tiny baby to a nurse, who laid it onto the warming tray in front of Sarah.

As she began examining the smallest newborn she had ever seen, Sarah had to fight off her immediate reaction: the inert mass of pallid tissue lying in front of her did not look like a human child. The oversized head and bulging eyes were still covered with a thin membrane, the body was cloaked with eerily translucent reddish skin and soft, fine *lanugo* hair. She was looking at something so different than a beautiful full-term baby that the sight did not trigger the urge to jump in and take life-saving action that she always felt when disaster struck a newborn who looked like a baby is supposed to look. Then she would react instinctively with an immediate surge of energy to do everything to save the baby, or die a little herself trying. But *this*...this one was so small and undeveloped she could barely tell that he was another baby boy. She had seen pictures of newborns as tiny and undeveloped as this, but no photos could prepare her for seeing one in person.

Sarah fought to put those thoughts aside. Those were improper thoughts that did not belong in her brain, the brain of a physician, a healer. She needed to remember that she was looking at a fellow human being, however immature. The tiny creature in front of her was a baby. A baby who was not breathing, a baby who was not moving, a baby lying completely limp on his back. His glistening skin was rapidly darkening to a deep blue-purple color as his little body used up the oxygen he had been getting from his mother through the umbilical cord. A subconscious countdown clock started ticking in Sarah's head toward the moment when brain damage to the baby would be unavoidable, if there was any brain activity there to salvage. She was approaching the point beyond which it would be impossible for her to save the baby.

She listened to his chest with her stethoscope. No heartbeat. *Dammit*, she thought, reflexively stomping her paper-encased right shoe on the tile floor again. She put her index finger ever so lightly into the space at the top of his leg where it met his groin to feel for a pulse; nothing. Then she tried on his neck. Still she felt no pulse, nothing at all except the tiniest of bones. She lifted his miniature arms then let them loose but the baby showed no reaction, the flaccid limbs just fell aimlessly without a twitch.

"One minute," the maternity nurse called out. "Apgar, Dr. Belden?"

It didn't take long for Sarah to calculate the Apgar score: "Zero," she replied. "No pulse, no respirations, color blue-purple everywhere, floppy with no muscle tone, no response to stimulation. No sign of life whatsoever."

Sarah felt pressure building in her chest. This was it—she had but one chance to make a truly life-or-death decision. She had to react as much as think, to act quickly one way or the other. Since there were no signs of life, should she declare this a stillbirth and leave things alone? Or should she start to resuscitate him? If she hesitated too long she would be making the decision by default, but the result would still be her doing, her responsibility. She had no time to rouse Martina and have a coherent discussion, no time to run out of the delivery room and look for Derek. The decision was hers, hers alone, and she had to make it now.

The answer became starkly clear as images of the three lost Johnson babies flashed into Sarah's mind: she must try to resuscitate this one. This was her duty as a doctor, but it was also her chance to make amends, to shed the guilt she had carried with her, guilt she bore even though deep down she knew it was not her fault that the other babies had died. None of that mattered. Martina and Derek wanted a baby. She had promised them healthy babies, and she had failed. They would want her to try. She must make the effort to resuscitate this one, give him a chance at life. If he didn't respond, so be it, she would have done her best.

The decision made, her years of training took over. She went into action, following the steps that were so ingrained at this point. First, get some air into his lungs to inflate them for the first time. Every part of this baby was so undersized it was like working on a miniature model, a small-scale mock-up of a baby, less than a foot long. Sarah selected the tiniest endotracheal tube, only 2.5 millimeters across, not even as wide as a cocktail straw but big enough to provide a minute passageway for air. Standing behind the baby's head, she placed a flat, undersized laryngoscope blade the size of a coffee stir-stick gently into the baby's mouth and lifted his tongue up and out of the way, revealing a tiny pair of vocal cords. She slipped the narrow breathing tube past the cords directly into his trachea. Grateful that she had succeeded on the first try, she directed a silent prayer of thanks to whatever deity had come to her aid. She connected the stub end of the endotracheal tube to a soft rubbery airbag, squeezing it ever so delicately to give the minuscule infant his first few breaths. Just then Jimmy Yoder ran into the room and stood at her side. She handed him the bag and said, "Gently, very, *very* gently, Jimmy. Tiny, quick puffs, little taps on the bag."

The baby's veins were far too small to consider starting an I.V. in them to deliver fluids and medications, so she would have to use one of the severed vessels in the stump of his umbilical cord. The two arteries and the single vein staring at her from the cross section of the severed umbilical cord were the only blood vessels big enough to provide a pathway for a tube. She would have to thread a slender plastic catheter through one of those tiny blood vessels, a maneuver that required a lot of skill and even more luck. The catheter wasn't much thicker than a ballpoint pen refill but it would be the baby's only lifeline for drugs, fluids, nutrition, blood transfusions—if she could insert it into him in time. This was really a task for three hands: one hand to hold the slippery few centimeters of cord stump and stretch it out slightly to straighten the blood vessels, another to tease the severed end of the artery open with a small pair of curved tweezers, and a third to hold the catheter and slip it into the artery. Having only the usual two hands, Sarah held the limp cord stump as stable as possible with her left hand and used the prongs of the tweezers in her right hand to probe one of the arteries until the fleshy tube opened ever so slightly. Then she grasped the cord stump with the tweezers and pulled just enough to hold it in place while she picked up the catheter. In one smooth motion she deftly slid the lifeline into the baby. She advanced it just a few centimeters, measuring the correct distance by counting the fine lines imprinted on the catheter, then taped a length of the tubing to his belly to keep it from slipping back out.

Once again she was moved to silent prayer. *Thank you, Lord, thank you*, she thought. But her sense of relief disappeared quickly as she saw the deep blue-black color of the blood trickling from the baby back into the umbilical catheter.

"His heart isn't beating. I need some adrenaline to get his heart started," she said to Jimmy Yoder, to the nurse, to everyone, to no one in particular. Sarah picked up a syringe with a pre-measured minuscule amount of the drug and injected it through the umbilical artery catheter, then flushed the tube with a few milliliters of fluid and began gentle cardiac massage. She tapped lightly but rapidly with two fingers on his chest to pump blood through his body. When his color started to change from deep purple to faint pink and rapid pulsations of his heart appeared through his nearly-transparent chest wall, she felt like she might burst into tears.

"His heart's beating," she exclaimed, filling the room with her joyful cry. "He's *alive*."

Sarah watched the baby's chest long enough to be sure the heartbeats were continuing on their own, then pushed the cart with the tiny baby out of the delivery room and toward the neonatal intensive care unit. Jimmy Yoder ran beside her still squeezing puffs of air out of the *ambubag*. A bottle of IV fluid hanging from a short metal pole swung back and forth as they ran. In the NICU Sarah lifted the infant onto a scale for a quick weigh-in, then set him down in an incubator. The incubator was supported by an aluminum stand on wheels, with a storage cabinet below and a shelf above. With its own controlled air supply and heating system and numerous portholes for the nurses and doctors to reach in and touch the baby, the incubator would be the baby's home for the foreseeable future.

A few moments later Sarah looked up and saw a slender woman in fresh scrubs entering the NICU. Sarah sighed with relief as the experienced neonatologist walked to the other side of the incubator.

"Ah, me, such a small one this time," said Dr. Giuliana Silvestre in her perfect English with just a hint of an elegant Italian accent. "Did you weigh him yet? Looks about 23-24 weeks, eh?"

"By dates, he's no more than 24." said Sarah. "I think he might be even younger, or else he could be small for his dates. He's just over 600 grams, about 1 pound and 4 or 5 ounces. I haven't done a full exam yet. His eyelids are open, but his posture, his skin, those folded ears—he's pretty early."

"Probably closer to 24 weeks, yes. Have we ever had one this small here at Memorial General?" asked Dr. Silvestre. "I have had a few of this size who survived at the University Hospital, but have we had any here?"

"I don't think so," said Sarah, "but I wouldn't know all the babies who were born here."

Patty Jennings, an experienced NICU nurse, interposed. "None, not this small. We had a couple of extreme preemies who were well into the 800-gram range that made it out of here alive, but they were pushing two pounds and were much more developed."

"Ah, yes, an extra half-pound and a few weeks make a big difference," Silvestre said. "Let's do everything we can for this little one here, and we will consider transferring him to the NICU at the University later."

Sarah called to Patti Jennings, "Cover his eyes and hook up the monitor."

"I'm trimming the black patches now," she replied, as she cut tiny oval pieces of dark cloth to cover the miniature eyes to protect them from the bright lights in the NICU. She put the eye patches on the baby and placed two electrodes on his chest. When she snapped wires onto the electrodes the heart monitor on the shelf above the incubator came to life, beeping rapidly and displaying a pulsating series of EKG waves on its green screen.

Silvestre then said, "At this age he will need help with his breathing. Hook him up to the respirator at the lowest setting. His lungs are so immature they need some pressure to keep them inflated."

"OK," said Sarah, who knew that extremely premature babies lacked surfactant, the natural oily substance that keeps normal lungs from collapsing between breaths. Unable to stay open on their own, the underdeveloped lungs needed air pressure to force them to remain inflated, but it was an exquisitely delicate balance—too little pressure from the respirator and the premature infant's lungs would collapse, too much and they would pop like overblown balloons. She took the manual *ambubag* from Jimmy Yoder, disconnected it from the endotracheal tube, then quickly connected the tube to a mechanical respirator that delivered very small, frequent breaths. Once the respirator was attached, its soft *"ca-thump, ca-thump"* drummed with a new rhythm out of sync with the much more rapid *"beep, beep, beep"* from the cardiac monitor.

"Start with 100% oxygen?" Sarah asked.

She knew this was another delicate balance—too little oxygen and the baby would die or suffer brain damage, too much oxygen and it might cause scar tissue to grow in his eyes and blind him for life. Too much could also cause more lung damage.

Silvestre quickly replied, "Yes, his color is not good. He is already having trouble breathing and will only get worse over the next few hours. Give him pure oxygen to start, and we will run blood gases within 15 minutes and adjust the amount of oxygen as often as we need to. And you know we will need to give him some blood," Silvestre added, "so send a sample to determine his blood type and get the transfusions ready at the blood bank."

Testing his blood over and over again was crucial for keeping the oxygen level just right, but repeated testing held particular significance for a tiny premature infant whose body contained barely a dozen teaspoonfuls of blood. He would undergo so many blood tests over the coming weeks he would need a series of transfusions just to replace the countless blood samples. Sarah withdrew a small amount of blood from the umbilical artery catheter and distributed the samples into miniature test tubes with different colored corks sealing their tops. Pointing to each one in turn, she said to Patti Jennings, "Keep this one on ice for the blood gas analysis, that one goes to the lab for electrolytes, and that one to the blood bank."

Like a seasoned noncommissioned officer accustomed to being ordered around by brash new First Lieutenants, Patti Jennings nodded in silent compliance, even though she was well aware what each of the different blood sample tubes was used for. She would carry out orders from physicians who were learning the ropes themselves until they reached the point at which she would feel compelled to correct their mistakes. Fortunately it would not be necessary for her to intervene this time since Sarah Belden was good at what she was doing and Giuliana Silvestre was there just in case Sarah slipped up.

"Hook up the infusion pump, Sarah," said Silvestre.

Sarah threaded one section of the tubing running to the umbilical artery catheter through the rubber-covered wheels of a small pump that would squeeze the supple tube rhythmically in one direction to push fluids into the infant. She checked to make sure the device was set to pump at a very slow flow rate, since his body could only process about one teaspoonful of fluid an hour.

"That's good," said Silvestre, watching the deliberate drip-drip of lifesaving liquid moving from the hanging bottle, through the pump and tubing, into the baby.

Sarah labored over the baby for the next three hours, adjusting the respirator and oxygen and the flow through the IV as the results of the blood tests came in from the laboratory. Every spare moment she would walk down the hall to the room where Martina dozed on and off, with Derek always by her side. But mostly she stood staring at the baby in the incubator, feeling…feeling what? Conflicting emotions ping-ponged through her. Intense satisfaction that she had resuscitated the baby with such precision. Profound anxiety about the baby's chances to live. Apprehension over whether he would be normal if he did live. Near-exhilaration that Martina and Derek would at last have a son. Grave concern that the couple would have yet another tragedy blanketing their young lives.

6 AM Sunday morning came before Sarah knew it, time to sign over her patients to Jane Zimmerman. Starting their rounds in the NICU, she led Jane to the incubator where Patti Jennings had attached a small card to the IV pole that read "Baby J" in neat block letters. Sarah went over the medical details first, then the sad history of the other three lost Johnson babies. The tall and slender woman, her tiny eyeglasses as usual slipping down her nose, bent awkwardly over the infant, like a stork making one last check to be sure it had flown in with the right baby. Sarah liked her colleague, respected her knowledge of pediatrics, but Jane didn't have the emotional connection to the Johnsons and their newborn that Sarah Belden had. For better or for worse?, Sarah suddenly asked herself, unsure of the answer.

Unable to drag herself away from the Johnson baby or from the Johnson couple, Sarah stayed long after her shift had ended. Two hours later, Jane Zimmerman returned to the NICU from the Emergency Room and saw Sarah looking like a zombie in scrubs. Jane walked up to her, put a soft hand on her shoulder, and said, "You should go home now, Sarah. If you don't get some sleep you won't be worth anything tomorrow. Nothing's going to happen here that I can't handle."

Sarah nodded. Fatigue emanated from her body. Even the slight up-and-down nod of her head made her feel lightheaded, her arms and legs devoid of sensation. Her body had reached its limits, it needed rest. She said softly, "I'll be back in the morning."

Chapter 8: Revenue Center

While Sarah Belden was at home struggling to rest and recuperate, Giuliana Silvestre worked with Jane Zimmerman to keep Donny alive. By that evening she had made a decision and ordered that it be carried out immediately, but early Monday morning she discovered she had been rebuffed and her order had not been carried out. Furious, she set out a mission.

The administration building at Memorial General Hospital was at a distance from the clinical buildings, secluded behind trees on a low rise at the far end of the sprawling campus. Few of the hospital's employees ever went there, regarding the building and its occupants as uninviting as the Bates Motel. Giuliana Silvestre was one of the few exceptions. She had no fear of the hospital's center of power and could easily find her way there by maneuvering along the hodgepodge of open-air breezeways connecting Memorial General's ancient structures. But today there was a misty rain and, dressed as she was for combat in a stylish Milanese businesswoman's suit, she would not risk getting wet by taking the outdoor route. She chose instead to wend her way through the labyrinth of tunnels under the expansive complex.

Some ten or twelve minutes of negotiating the underground passageway led her to the door of an enormous elevator that only went up and down between the tunnel and the main floor. She boarded the old lift, pressed the M button, rose the one flight, and exited into a cavernous space the size and ambience of a warehouse. She walked the length of the room and paused in front of a locked door secured with an alarm and a bold EMERGENCY EXIT ONLY sign. She punched a code into a keypad on the wall, then passed through the doorway into a different world. She had entered the modern, well-lit lobby of an elite sanctuary frequented by only a few dozen high-level executives and their assistants. To her left, another secure door provided private access between the building and a small, gated parking lot where a huge white Cadillac occupied the CEO's space. Expensive sedans and sports cars sat in the other numbered spaces. She walked to her right, where a modern elevator, secured with another keypad, awaited her. She punched in the code, entered, and rose to the third floor.

The elevator door opened onto a space so unlike the rest of the rundown public hospital it was as if she had been beamed across town and rematerialized in a lavish office suite in the financial district. An oversized reception area with cathedral ceilings, modern light fixtures, and not a wire or pipe showing anywhere. An imposing mahogany counter intended to block whatever few unwanted visitors might make it this far into the hospital's inner sanctum. Thick carpeting below dark wood-paneled walls. Picture windows with spectacular views of the lush rolling hillside behind the hospital. Floor-to-ceiling windows overlooking the private parking lot.

She strode past the receptionist behind the counter, saying "Dr. Silvestre" with such poise and assurance the hapless sentry froze, not daring to stop her. She passed through a set of unmarked, heavy wooden doors into the Executive Suite and continued past a matronly executive secretary who stiffened her back and raised her shoulders as if she were about to stand up to intercept the interloper, then thought better of it and simply shook her head and remained seated at her desk. Finally she pulled open the door beyond the secretary's desk and let herself into the office of Everett Kappel, the President and CEO of Memorial General.

"Dr. Silvestre," said an unfazed Kappel, greeting her with a pleased look as if he had been expecting her all along. "So good to see you. Have a seat and tell me what I can do for you."

Giuliana Silvestre remained standing. "I understand that you have contravened my decision to transfer baby Johnson to the University," she said. She stared down at the short, slender man sitting at an oversized desk so out of proportion to him that he resembled a little boy who had climbed up into his father's chair. Kappel could have shaved by his reflection in the extravagant, highly polished desktop, a slab of Philippine mahogany that was barren save for the morning newspaper.

"The transfer is absolutely necessary," she continued. "He can not be treated properly here. We do not have the proper equipment or staff here for so small a baby. We have good nurses in the NICU, but not enough of them. We have competent pediatric residents, but at the University we have neonatology fellows on call every night, and we have all the pediatric subspecialists immediately available. And we have several research projects underway there that might help save his life. This baby must be moved to the University."

"I appreciate your concern, Dr. Silvestre, but it is imperative that the baby remains in this hospital," the little man said, his tone ostensibly courteous but unmistakably resolute, the general at his command post giving the orders. "You are an outstanding neonatologist. You have excellent nurses and pediatric house officers. Do what you can for him, but do it here."

"No, we cannot do what he needs in this hospital no matter how hard we work. We must make sure he gets all the best care. Why would you deny him the proper medical care?"

Kappel looked smugly at Silvestre, thinking that this demanding woman had no idea what it took to run an inner-city hospital and keep it on its feet financially while it cared for indigent patients that other hospitals avoided. In truth, he was correct—she didn't understand such things. Memorial Hospital's financial and political imperatives were, literally, foreign to her. Giuliana Silvestre was the product of an Italian health care system designed to care for patients in whichever hospital offered the appropriate level of technology and specialists for their illness. When Silvestre had requested that a patient be transferred, she was accustomed to seeing her directive carried out quickly, without question. Small village hospitals sent very sick patients to the bigger hospitals in major cities or regional centers, and they in turn referred the most advanced cases to the university hospitals. By and large it was a well-oiled, coordinated process that belied the chaotic stereotype of Italian disorganization.

Kappel was terse, though he did not sound overtly hostile as he replied, "It's best for everyone, including the baby."

Silvestre was taken aback. He had given her no answer, no explanation. She was a doctor wanting the best for her tiny patient, but now something she didn't comprehend stood in her way. She had to know what she was dealing with. Her voice was polite, but firm.

"Excuse me, Mr. Kappel, but what you say does not explain why we should not transfer this baby."

"Please, sit, Dr. Silvestre. I will try to clarify for you just how important this is." He spoke softly, graciously. When she did not move he repeated his request, "Please, have a seat and we can talk."

Gracefully, though reluctantly, Silvestre slipped onto the deep burgundy leather chair facing Kappel's desk. She sat forward, perfectly upright, and stared directly at him. It took a measure of her self-control to force herself to lock her gaze on his deep brown eyes and avoid staring at his fuzzy black mustache, which, with her doctor's eye, she correctly deduced he had grown on his upper lip to conceal the scar from the surgically repaired harelip he had been born with. Perhaps the hairy camouflage worked for many people, but it could not hide his disfiguring birthmark from the experienced pediatrician.

Kappel lifted the day's newspaper off his desk and turned it toward her.

"News about the Johnson baby being cared for here at Memorial General has already received a great deal of attention. It was the featured story on the front page of the *Metro* section of the newspaper this morning. '*Smallest Baby Ever Clings to Life,*' he said, pointing to a huge, above-the-fold headline, with the subheading, '*Baby J Defies the Odds at Memorial General.*' There will be stories on all three local television stations tonight—they want to interview you, the baby's internationally-famous doctor. This is very good publicity for the hospital, favorable publicity we do not get very often. Usually the public only hears about Memorial General when a police officer dies in our emergency room or someone gets shot in one of our clinics or we petition the County Commission for more money."

Kappel's rationalization passed through the air to Silvestre without sticking, like a cigarette smoke ring that caught her attention briefly but dispersed quickly, leaving nothing behind except an unpleasant aroma. She sensed something else was going on, something unstated, something he was holding back.

She persisted.

"Why should we risk his life for publicity? And, the publicity will not be good for the hospital if the baby dies."

"I have every confidence in you. He will not die. Not soon, in any case. If he lives even a few weeks, we will get credit for working a miracle."

Silvestre grew indignant. The man was toying with a human life, she must not give in.

"What difference does it make what the newspapers and television reporters say? This hospital is open to everyone, no matter how poor they are. We do not need to attract patients, we get all the patients we can handle already. The nursery and the clinics are full, we could not take any more cases even if people wanted to come here. And, respectfully, Sir, our duty is to the baby. We must give him all the medical care he needs."

"And so you shall. Right here in Memorial General."

She remained calm, determined to assert her authority. She was the baby's doctor, she must have the final say. She looked him directly in the eyes, clenching her teeth slightly as she said, "I am the physician in charge of this case. I am ordering that he be transferred to the University, and if you persist in preventing this from occurring, I will let the newspapers and the television stations know the full story."

Kappel did not flinch or show any expression on his face, but his eyes opened slightly, just enough so that his dark green pupils seemed to glow like a wolf's eyes in moonlight. His tone went cold.

"That would not be in anyone's interest. Not yours. Not the hospital's."

"I care about no one except the baby. My patient."

Everett Kappel was confident he would win this struggle. The 'Hospital Administrator' in the U.S. had long been a functionary, a backroom layperson subservient to the doctors on the medical staff of the hospital. But as medicine became more and more a commercial enterprise in the 1970s and 1980s, power shifted to the 'Chief Executive Officer,' whose job was focused on the bottom line, not on patient care. Kappel rode that wave. His success at Memorial General made him a powerful figure in local politics and the press. He was the one in charge, not doctors like this nuisance Silvestre. She posed no threat to him.

The old Memorial General had been a traditional public hospital that depended entirely on money appropriated by the County government. Kappel turned that around, cutting budgets mercilessly and finding ways to increase patient care revenues. He restructured the hospital from a government-owned facility to a public-private corporation under the control of his hand-picked Board of Trustees. Most of its revenue now came from Medicaid and Medicare, and a few privately insured patients. The hospital still needed local tax dollars to stay afloat, but the amounts stabilized, even going down in some years, so the Commission and his Board loved him.

Kappel was devious and clever at keeping off the hospital's books the true cost of the extravagant salaries and benefits he provided to himself and his senior executives. He formed a separate "MG Hospital Foundation" that received tax-deductible philanthropic gifts. The sleight of hand operated much the way universities channeled money from donors to pay their football coaches multi-million dollar salaries that would be scandalous if the funds were to come directly from public appropriations or tuition collections.

The little man demanded absolute loyalty from the hospital's employees and exerted constant pressure on physicians to practice in ways that would benefit the hospital—just as he was now doing with Giuliana Silvestre.

"Dr. Silvestre," he said with ostensible emotion that surprised Silvestre, "I would *never* presume to practice medicine, that is up to you and the other doctors in this hospital. But I must tell you that if you were to give the citizens of this city and county the impression that Memorial General Hospital cannot provide adequate medical care to this baby, that would be highly detrimental to our reputation. Perhaps, even, to the hospital's very survival."

He rose from his chair and began pacing around the room irregularly, with no apparent destination.

Silvestre found it disconcerting to track the little man as he walked behind her chair, then over to his window, now looking in her eyes, now turning his back to her, but never pausing in his speech. It was like trying to follow the random buzzing of a fly that would not alight for longer than a split second at a time. When Kappel stood still long enough for her eyes to focus, she stared at him and realized that he was in many ways a caricature of himself. If he had not walked and spoken with such commanding authority he would have made a comic figure in his finely tailored three-piece pinstripe suit, the little boy rising from his father's desk wearing the old man's clothes.

His monologue continued, the tone still filled with what seemed to Silvestre to be genuine passion.

"We all know that Memorial General needs better equipment, more modern technology, even some entirely new buildings. And I believe we are on the road to getting all of that accomplished. But we are also dangerously close to going in the opposite direction instead, even disappearing entirely. There is a very strong faction in this community that has wanted to close this hospital for years. If the quality of our medical care were to become suspect, it would not take much for our adversaries to succeed. You see, this hospital used to rely entirely on tax revenues from the County. But the cost of medical care grew so fast that the County could no longer pay for everything. So we started billing Medicare, Medicaid, private insurance, and we took some of the strain off of the County. But the public share is still very large, and many of the County Commissioners would love to cut us off and divert our funding to the private hospitals, or to schools, or roads, or jails. Do you know what the consequences would be? As you said, our clinics and wards are full. But they are filled with indigent patients with no health insurance who cannot pay for their medical care. Even the ones with Medicaid are costly, since we're lucky if the state Medicaid program pays us as much as one-third of the cost of taking care of them. Where will those patients go if Memorial General closes? Do you really believe that the private hospitals will care for them?"

"As you say, I can imagine it would be a terrible thing if the hospital were to be closed," she replied. "But, I am sorry, I do not see how any of this relates to this baby. He needs the kind of medical care that is not fully available here, so he must be moved."

Silvestre was unyielding, her thoughts focused on her tiny patient, on getting him into safer territory at the University.

"My dear doctor, there is clearly something you are not taking into consideration. This baby could be the linchpin for this hospital to go in one direction or in the opposite direction. He could be the straw that would break this camel's back, or the cornerstone for a momentous future for this hospital."

Despite Silvestre's fluency in English, Kappel's mixed metaphors and colloquialisms left her hanging.

"Please, sir, you must explain."

"The neonatal intensive care unit is one of the only parts of this hospital that generates any positive financial return—it's one of our few revenue centers in a sea of cost centers. The Johnson family came to this hospital the first two times because they had no money and had no choice other than right here, the county hospital. We welcomed them and gave them all the medical care they needed. We provided them with expensive care without hesitation even though they couldn't pay their bills."

Kappel was deviously selective in recounting history. He did not mention that the Johnsons had paid every penny they had for the medical care provided to Martina and the three ill-fated babies, and then billed them for the remainder and pursued them relentlessly, dunning them, threatening lawsuits. Before Kappel's time, Memorial General had the open-door approach of the traditional charity hospitals—everyone who came there could get whatever care the hospital could provide, all for free. No debts were booked, no bills were sent, collection agencies were unknown. But Kappel had realized there were millions of dollars to be collected from Medicaid and Medicare, from the few privately insured patients they saw, and, like the Johnsons, even from the many poor patients who simply felt obligated to pay as much as they could, regardless of the financial consequences for their families. So Memorial General started billing everyone, insured or not, hiring bill collectors who were paid a share of everything they could drain out of their patients. And that was what the hospital had done to Derek and Martina Johnson, devastating the young couple with enormous debt for what was widely ballyhooed as "free" medical care.

Kappel continued, his voice rising with ever more emotion.

"Mr. Johnson now has a job with good insurance coverage—one of the few health plans that actually pays what we charge."

Again, he was revealing barely half the truth—the Johnson's insurance did, indeed, pay the hospital very well, but it did not cover all of the bills. The Johnsons would be held responsible for thousands and thousands of dollars the insurance did not pay.

Kappel stopped circling suddenly, pausing directly in front of Giuliana Silvestre.

"With their private insurance, the Johnsons could have gone to any hospital for this pregnancy, but they came to Memorial General this time by choice. Patients with private insurance like the Johnsons help our bottom line. We need that money to stay in business. Threaten the reputation of our NICU and you threaten the viability of this hospital. That is why I say the NICU is the cornerstone, it is central to our finances, to our very survival."

"Surely the neonatal intensive care unit cannot be so important," she responded. "This is a big hospital, with so many different services. How can our little nursery keep the hospital financially sound on its own?"

Kappel sensed that her voice had become slightly less assertive. She was weakening, she was beginning to swallow his argument. He moved in for the kill.

"Ah, that is my very point. We need the money. The NICU is our most positive revenue center, it generates a surplus that helps support the Emergency Room and all the clinics that see patients who cannot pay. On the other hand, with all the publicity this case has attracted, negative stories saying that our NICU was not able to care for this baby would undermine our reputation. If you were to destroy our public standing in this case, you would be responsible for turning the city against us. The County Commission might withdraw its support and then Memorial General would have to close down. You would put over two thousand employees out of work. You would take away the only hospital that cares for tens of thousands of poor people in this city. Would you like to be known as the doctor who shut down Memorial General Hospital? Is that a legacy that you would wish for yourself? I can assure you that if this hospital slams its doors in the face of the poor of this city, Dr. Silvestre's role in the closing of Memorial General Hospital would be widely known."

The highest-paid hospital executive in the state, the cut-throat businessman eking profits from a hospital for indigent patients with an iron fist, slipped easily into his pretentious role of moral crusader. He delivered his righteous warning with a vengeance, the lies flowing smoothly, convincingly over his restored lips.

The cunning little man's act paid off. Giuliana Silvestre was disconcerted. Not intimidated, not really, she was too secure to be intimidated by the likes of Kappel, but she was deeply distressed to hear that her good intentions might have disastrous consequences that she could never have foreseen. How could this be? She had known that the private hospitals, the University even, all chased after profits from their patients. And the University coveted the millions of dollars in research grants she brought in. But the public hospitals in Italy were not businesses, they were public institutions, and the government gave them their entire budget. She had never considered that it might be different here, not for hospitals that served everyone.

She sat back on the leather chair and drew a deep breath. Exhaling with a sigh she said, "I am not concerned about myself, what people think about me is of no importance. I only want to do what is right for my patient. But I could not have known that so much might be at stake, that so many people might lose their ability to get medical care. You are correct, Mr. Kappel, what you have described is something I do not want to happen. We will do our best for Baby Johnson here in Memorial General."

Despite her assurances to Kappel, she was unfazed in her determination to see that Baby Johnson would receive whatever medical care he might need. She told herself that she would move the baby out of Memorial General to the University in one second if it proved to be necessary. But she held back for now. She had had enough of Everett Kappel for one day. And another defiant retort from her would surely trigger further lecturing, more arguments from the little man that she was not about to bring on herself.

Kappel looked directly at her, suppressing the smile that would cross his face as soon as the door closed behind her.

"You're an excellent doctor. I know the baby will be fine and we will all be proud of what Memorial General has done for him."

Silvestre stood up, nodded without speaking, and walked out through the wooden doors, into the elevator, and back into the world of pale yellow ceramic tile, bare pipes, hanging electrical wires. Everett Kappel at last let the smile form on his face, savoring his conquest. Giuliana Silvestre had become yet another dedicated doctor who had been taken in by his doomsday scenario.

Chapter 9: Home Away From Home

Still reeling from her encounter with Everett Kappel, Giuliana Silvestre met Sarah Belden as they had agreed, and they went together to see Martina Johnson. They found Martina in one of the few small semi-private rooms. Her husband Derek sat nearby in the worn, faux-leather recliner where he had spent the night. No one occupied the second bed, which had been pushed up against the window so Derek could move the recliner closer to Martina.

Sarah was immediately struck with how much the young couple had aged in the year since Lenny and Denny had died.

Still in his early twenties and dressed in the all-denim outfit of a young man, Derek no longer appeared youthful. Dark lines and furrows crossed his face, puffy bags drooped under his reddened eyes, patches of stubble littered his chin and neck. The anxious expression that crossed his weary face at seeing the two physicians told Sarah that he expected to hear them say yet again that he and Martina would not be taking a baby home.

Wrapped in a faded pink hospital gown held modestly closed by drawstrings, Martina no longer exuded the beauty and self-reliant strength that had always reminded Sarah of a Norse goddess. The young mother looked drained, distant, having no real connection with her surroundings. Her fair skin was pallid, too pale to look healthy. Her once-magnificent blond hair hung in clumps of twisted strands.

"Good morning," began Giuliana Silvestre, "I am Dr. Silvestre, the neonatologist. I know you are already acquainted with Dr. Belden, our fine Senior Pediatric Resident. How are you feeling?" she said, looking at Martina.

Martina glanced at Derek, who said, "Thanks, Doctor, we're hanging in there."

Silvestre was not familiar with this particular American idiom, but she quickly understood it to mean that the deeply stressed young couple was searching for the strength to endure their burdens.

Martina said softly, "I'm so, so sorry. I just…I just didn't think I was going to have the baby then, it was too soon. I thought I was having gas pains or those contractions that happen sometimes but don't mean anything. I didn't know what to do. I had just seen my doctor two days before, and everything was fine, we were so happy this time. It…"

Sarah cringed at hearing Martina's voice quaver with apology as if she had done something very wrong and now was confessing her misdeed.

Derek was holding his wife's hand, and now began stroking her gently on the arm. The many stresses that had been compressed into so few years had taken their toll on his body but had not lessened his love for Martina.

"It's OK, Sweetheart, it's OK. You had no way of knowing. It's not your fault."

"That is correct," intoned Silvestre. She pulled a chair up to the bedside and sat so that her eyes were level with Martina's. "It can be very difficult to know what is happening when the baby comes so soon."

"How is Donny?" asked Derek. "That's his name, Donny. Will he live? Can we see him?"

"You may look at him through the window of the newborn intensive care unit later today but it will not be easy to see him well. Donny is very young and very small, and he needs a lot of medical care, so he is surrounded with equipment and people. And he needs to stay in his incubator, so you cannot hold him just yet. Babies so very small must be kept warm and given oxygen, so he cannot come out of the incubator. Also, much of his face is covered; he is having some trouble breathing because his lungs are so immature, so he is hooked up to a respirator, a breathing machine."

"But…what's the hope?" asked Derek, quietly but with deep anticipation. Martina moved her eyes from him to Silvestre and raised her eyebrows as if to repeat the question with her glance.

"He is very tiny, very fragile, but he is alive and has a good chance to do well," answered Silvestre.

Sarah remained silent, wishing she could assure the Johnsons that what Silvestre was saying was sure to happen, but knowing that there was too much room for horrors lurking in Silvestre's words, "*a good chance*" to risk any assurances. She was also reluctant to say anything hopeful since her optimistic words to the Johnsons had so often led only to heartbreak.

Silvestre continued, "He will need a great deal of medical care for many weeks. The main problem is that his body did not have enough time to develop properly. So he is not fully formed, not yet. Even if everything goes perfectly well, as we hope it will, he needs to be cared for long enough for his body to grow as if it were still in his mother's womb."

Sarah noticed that Silvestre pronounced the "b" at the end of '*womb*,' a rare reminder of her Italian origins.

"Besides needing the warmth of the incubator and the oxygen, he is not ready to eat, so he must get nourishment and fluids directly into his bloodstream. In one sense you can think of him as not yet having been born, as if he were still in the womb. We are providing an artificial womb so he can grow and become like a full-term baby in another few months. We estimate that he was born about sixteen weeks early, so he has nearly four months of catching up to do."

"And if things don't go well?"

"Yes, there can be difficulties. I cannot tell you that there will not be difficulties. Perhaps the most important is that his lungs have a disorder we call RDS, respiratory distress syndrome." She said the three long words slowly, pronouncing each syllable precisely, as though enunciating the words carefully would make their meaning more easily understood. "It can be a serious problem, very serious, but we are getting better at treating it all the time, and if he does well it will go away when his lungs grow a little."

"Anything else?"

"I must be honest. When a baby is so premature, there are many things that can go wrong. Problems with his heart, with infections, with his body's chemistry. We will watch him very carefully and take care of anything that develops."

"What else can go wrong? What else? What about...what about his...his *brain*? Will Donny be normal if he lives?"

Sarah shuddered at the question of what might happen—or may have already happened—to Donny Johnson's brain. An uncontrollable spasm of her cheeks and eyebrows suddenly squeezed her eyes nearly closed and tightened her mouth into a pained grimace.

As her face relaxed she turned toward Derek and Martina and sighed with relief when she saw that they were both looking at Silvestre so they had not seen the tortured expression cross her face.

Silvestre paused, then said, "This we cannot predict for sure. It has only been the past few years that such small babies had any chance at all of living, so we do not have a lot of experience with how well they do later on. The very few babies this size who survived in the past were almost certainly not so premature. They were further along, more fully developed, just much lighter weight than they should have been for their age. Those babies by and large have grown up entirely normal."

"What if he isn't normal? What can happen?"

"It is too early to tell you. We will do everything we can, and we will hope for the best. If something goes wrong, we will let you know right away."

"Will…will we have any choice?"

Sarah grimaced again, grinding her teeth so hard her jaw hurt. The most important moment of choice had been hers, not theirs. She felt the weight of having usurped what might well turn out to be the only real life-or-death decision for Donny. It was her split-second decision in the delivery room to resuscitate a baby so premature he barely resembled a human child. Born with no heartbeat and not breathing, he was legally dead. No one would have criticized her if she had simply pronounced him stillborn, and the Johnsons would be home now coping with a known tragedy, instead of here, suffering through the unknown.

Silvestre harbored none of Sarah's self-recriminations. "There could be many choices for you to make, yes," she replied. "For example, we may need to do some procedures on his heart, and you would have to give your consent. We would not do anything such as surgery without your consent."

Derek and Martina nodded.

Silvestre's answer, however well-intentioned her reassurance that the parents would decide important aspects of Donny's medical care, sounded hollow to Sarah. She knew all too well that most of what was likely to transpire would emerge little by little, one small change at a time, never quite crystallizing into another true life-or-death choice for the parents unless the situation became desperate. Sarah had seen it all before: the moments when parents were asked to make decisions were stacked against them, postponed until they had no real choice. Necessity dictated that the doctors make countless day-to-day decisions that really determined whether the baby would live or die or be seriously impaired. They wouldn't ask the parents if they should increase the oxygen by 5% or add some supplemental sodium chloride to the IV or even treat infections or seizures. Even if the baby's heart stopped they would react without consulting the parents. No, it was only when the situation truly became hopeless that the medical staff would turn to the parents and ask whether they wanted to keep going, whether they should they pull the plug, turn off the respirator, disconnect the IV fluids, forswear further attempts at resuscitation. But Sarah could only bear the burden of such thoughts in silence, this was not the time or place to express them. Not now, not in front of the Johnsons.

In any case, it was up to Giuliana Silvestre to handle this situation. Sarah greatly admired the way she never lost her professional demeanor. She remained calm in the face of emergencies, warm and never condescending talking with parents who had endured unanticipated terrors. She always had a steady composure dealing with doctors who were bullies like some of the surgeons. Sarah couldn't help thinking that on top of everything else, Giuliana Silvestre always *looked* the part. She didn't have to play at it, she really was such an accomplished professional woman, all professional, all woman, inside as well as outside. She was never distracted, never rude, never seemed to be thinking about anything other than this baby and these people. Sarah told herself she would be satisfied if she could be only half the doctor Silvestre was.

The Johnsons nodded to Silvestre, not really in agreement but more in simple acquiescence to the hand they had been dealt. Little did they know what was coming.

Donny Johnson needed care 24 hours a day, measured not by the hour but by every second of every minute of hour. Unprepared to handle the demands of staying alive outside the womb, his body needed doctors, nurses, machines, and drugs to substitute for his immature organs. His lungs developed a fulminating case of RDS. Sarah, Giuliana Silvestre, Jane Zimmerman, Patty Jennings, and many other doctors, nurses, and technicians spent countless hours measuring the oxygen level in his blood, adjusting the amount he was breathing and the pressure setting on his respirator, reading fuzzy X-rays taken in the nursery with portable machines since it was too risky to transport the baby to the Radiology department. Then, just when his breathing was improving, Donny started having seizures. The tremors were small at first, just his arms and legs making jerky motions, but soon his tiny body exploded in full-blown convulsions. More blood tests and X-rays, then minute doses of Phenobarbital and other drugs to manage the seizures. When the seizures seemed to be controlled, they would slowly wean him off the drugs, only to have him start convulsing all over again.

The weeks went by in a continuous maelstrom of noise, drugs, medical procedures, discussions, all of which Martina and Derek could only watch from behind a glass wall. When one umbilical artery catheter clotted Sarah inserted a new one into the other umbilical artery. After those had run their course the surgeons were called to insert a catheter into blood vessels in his groin and later in his neck, until the veins in his scalp had grown big enough for the slenderest IV needles. The breathing tube in his mouth was replaced by one inserted through his nose, clearing the way to thread a feeding tube through his mouth, down his esophagus, and into his stomach.

When Sarah's assignment in the newborn nurseries came to an end she moved on to a stint in the endocrinology unit. There she took care of a number of children with juvenile diabetes, a few true dwarfs whose pituitary glands didn't produce enough growth hormone, and other young patients with a variety of rare, often deadly disorders. Among the most unfortunate were the misshapen, squat children whose bodies lacked the mechanisms for making certain essential enzymes or produced toxic chemicals that destroyed normal tissues. Caring for these children was a two-edged sword for Sarah: intellectually stimulating but at the same time emotionally draining. Intellectually stimulating because she enjoyed the challenge of discovering ways to stabilize or perhaps even treat the complications of the genetic mistakes ravaging their young bodies. Emotionally draining not only because of the plight these children faced, but also because the constant exposure to their problems aggravated Sarah's anguish over whether Donny would also be severely afflicted.

Over the ensuing months Sarah returned to the nursery to check in on Donny as often as the demands of her continuously-changing assignments permitted. Now that she was no longer watching him every day for hours on end she was able to appreciate that Donny was making stepwise progress. After one month he began to look like a baby to her. Then he started to breathe on his own, at first with help from the respirator, then, miraculously it seemed, his lungs actually took over. At last, one evening Sarah came in and saw Martina Johnson sitting next to Donny's incubator. She choked up when she realized that Martina was holding Donny in her arms.

"He's out!" said Sarah, with more emotion than she meant to demonstrate. "Terrific."

"Look, Dr. Belden, I'm feeding him. Look."

There it was: Madonna and the infant, a mother cradling her baby, feeding him, just as the Johnsons had always pictured things would be. Martina was holding a miniature baby bottle and gently putting the tiny nipple into Donny's mouth.

"He's sucking on it. Look. It's my breast milk, I've been pumping milk and storing it for him."

"What a joy," Sarah said. "You must feel wonderful. Derek must be so happy. Before long they'll be tossing baseballs around."

Donny Johnson was moved out of the intensive care nursery when he was about three months old, 'promoted' to the lower-level special care unit where he was still the smallest baby. He continued gaining weight and growing to his parents' delight. His eyes, now uncovered, would often be open wide and active, making contact with faces and exploring his strange hospital world. His mother hovered nearby, caring for her baby boy from early morning until his last nighttime feeding. Derek would drop Martina off at the hospital in the early morning and stay for a quarter-hour before going to work, then come back every evening to spend time with his son and bring his wife home.

Sarah's visits were irregular, depending on her other duties, but she never went more than a few days without checking on Donny. The thought grew on her that saving him had been a turning point for her as a pediatrician—his very life had been in her hands, and now he was thriving. Her decision to bring his limp body to life had been the right choice, she had done her job well. Donny Johnson was her reward for all that studying, all those hours of work, all that stress. She had helped to give the Johnsons the child they had so dearly longed for. At last her self-doubts began to wane.

Chapter 10: Transitions

"Careful, Honey, careful. Watch yourself."

"He won't break, Derek, he's a baby, not a china doll. He weighs over five pounds, remember?"

Martina cuddled Donny in her arms as they walked toward Derek's van, the baby's tiny head covered with a bright blue wool cap that one of the nurses in the NICU had knitted for him. Walking with his new family, Derek was beaming. He carried bags with presents that the nursery staff had brought to a surprise going-away party for Donny. The hospital staff had chipped in to buy basic baby supplies—four blue sleepers, giant boxes of diapers from Costco, soft baby blankets, nothing overly frivolous. And several cases of formula samples in individual disposable glass bottles. Martina had cried when she saw the chocolate cake decorated with *"Bye Bye Donny, We Love You."*

Derek and Martina could not believe that the President and CEO of Memorial General, Everett Kappel himself, had come to the party and given a brief speech. The little man glowed with satisfaction as he spoke.

"Donny Johnson is the pride and joy of his parents and of Memorial General Hospital. He is the smallest baby ever to survive in this town, weighing just over one-and-a-quarter pounds at birth. Everyone in this room, and many others, deserve our thanks for what they have accomplished. Donny Johnson's survival is a testimony to the wonders of modern medicine, to the dedication, perseverance, and skill of the physicians, nurses and all the staff here at Memorial General. His parents, Derek and Martina Johnson, have been exemplary in their loving devotion to their son. Many of you know that the Johnsons had suffered the loss of three sons before Donny. Their enduring commitment to Donny is inspirational. This is a great day for him, for his parents, and for Memorial General Hospital. Congratulations."

The hospital's official photographer took dozens of photos, and Kappel had arranged for a newspaper reporter and two local television crews to record the event. Later that night, Kappel was chagrined at his own limited visibility on the piece that appeared on the evening news—it pictured him speaking briefly, but did not identify who he was or broadcast his words, instead highlighting the NICU staff singing,

For he's a jolly good baby,
For he's a jolly good baby,
For he's a jolly good bay-ay-bee,
And now we say Bye Bye.
Bye Bye Donny,
Bye Bye Donny,
Bye Bye Donny,
We love you, little guy.

Kappel had one brief moment of gratification at the end of the short news report: both TV stations had shown the Johnsons leaving by the main door, walking with Donny under the archway with the antiquated sign that read, unmistakably, *"Memorial General Hospital."*

The little Napoleon smugly praised himself for keeping Donny Johnson at Memorial General. This was all his doing, he deserved all the credit. That bitch Silvestre would have taken him to the University and none of this would have happened. Everything had turned out just as he knew it would and his hospital had received all the recognition. He reveled in his triumph.

***

Driving his family home for the first time, Derek could not control the smile on his face as he anticipated Martina's reaction to the surprise he had waiting for her at their modest rental cottage. In deep debt with the bills they faced after losing Lenny and Denny, they had moved out of their first house into a tiny one with only one real bedroom, just big enough for their double bed and a single dresser. They shared a cramped bathroom with a metal shower stall, old-fashioned white ceramic fixtures, and hexagonal white tiles on the floor. But next to the bedroom there was a large alcove that was to serve as Donny's room, and Derek had spent days transforming the nondescript space into a nursery, a miniature bedroom for a little boy. *His* little boy. He pasted luminescent stars to the ceiling, painted the walls deep blue with lighter blue trim, and placed a canvas shower curtain on a rod over the entrance to the alcove to serve as a makeshift door and muffle the house noise when Donny was sleeping. Derek was particularly happy he had found a curtain emblazoned with the logos of his favorite professional football and baseball teams

The crib had been Derek's own as a baby, and Albert's before him. He had salvaged it from the garage sale his family held after his mother was moved into a nursing home. He repainted it, fixed a few broken crib rails, put new casters on the legs, and covered the headboard and footboard with decals of sports teams like the ones on the curtain. Derek's big surprise for Martina was a hand-made mobile he had crafted on a jig saw at work. Ten small wooden sports figures hung in pairs from curved rods: a batter and pitcher, a quarterback about to toss a pass downfield, a tight end reaching for a pass, a soccer figure completing a banana kick, Dale Earnhardt's brightly decorated *Number 3* race car, Michael Jordan slamming home a dunk, another basketball player crouching at the foul line, and the unmistakable silhouettes of Arnold Palmer putting and Jack Nicklaus smashing a drive. It was a masterpiece, a work of love, and he hoped Donny would treasure it for his own children, just as he had saved his old crib for his son.

His son. He was bringing his son home.

Derek had hidden the mobile until today, the day his son was coming home. Now it was time. He held it out at arm's length in front of his wife. Martina had been delighted to see the small nursery take shape as Derek painted the alcove, hung the doorway curtain, and carried the refurbished crib in from his work area in the carport, but the mobile was so unexpected it overwhelmed her.

"Honey, this is…this is amazing. It's beautiful."

Martina was spellbound by the perfect details on the tiny figures, their shapes, the hand-painted uniforms they wore front and back, the expressions on their miniature faces. She examined each one, holding them gently with her fingertips, admiring the precision through tears that suddenly clouded her eyes.

"You did this all by yourself?"

Derek laughed as he said, "You think your husband can only hammer nails in planks?"

"I just have never seen anything like this before, it's incredible. It's so…it's so delicate, such fine work. How long did it take?"

"Not that long, actually, not once I got started. It took me a while to find just the right pictures in *Sports Illustrated* for models. The woodwork went real quick. The painting took some time, but I got really wrapped up in doing it. You like it, huh? You think Donny will like it?"

"Donny and I both love it, Honey, it's just beautiful."

***

Sarah Belden and Jimmy Yoder were also about to make major transitions in their professional lives. Sarah was finishing her pediatric residency and going into private practice. She felt good about the forthcoming change. The other pediatricians in private practice in the local pediatric community were glad she was staying in the area, and soon she would be on a first-name basis with them. The teaching faculty who had been her mentors were about to become colleagues. They would treat each other as equals, she would no longer feel she had to be deferential and always call them *Doctor*.

Sarah settled into a cozy leather seat in a corner booth of Ahmad's Café, surrounded by graduate students determined to ingest enough caffeine to offset their lack of actual sleep. She had arranged to meet with Giuliana Silvestre there for a farewell chat—and to ask for a specific piece of advice. When Silvestre arrived, Sarah took the bold step of greeting her by her first name.

"Hi Giuliana, how are you? Can I buy you a cup of coffee?"

The casual interaction felt good. Sarah was pleased she was at ease in the presence of the talented physician she held in such awe.

"Yes, of course. This place has an excellent Italian Roast, dark and strong. Not quite espresso, but it is good. Thank you, Sarah."

Sarah began speaking just as Giuliana took her first sip of coffee.

"I asked to meet with you to thank you for all the help you've given me over the years, and also to pick your brain one last time."

"You are most welcome, but there is no need to thank me, Sarah. You have been a delight to work with, one of our best residents ever. I'm not sure there is anything left in my brain for you to pick, but what is it you would like to know?"

"Thanks for those kind words, Giuliana. I'm going to see Donny Johnson tomorrow in your high-risk follow-up clinic at the University. Martina Johnson is likely to be the one who will bring him in. Do you have a transition plan for them?"

"Jimmy Yoder will be taking Donny on as a patient. Jimmy is will be doing a neonatology fellowship with us, so he will be able to care for this child for the next few years."

"Wow, that's unexpected news. Great to hear, but not what I every expected. Why would Jimmy go into neonatology? I always thought he would go back to his community and be a rural doctor among his people. In any case, that's great, you couldn't have done better than Jimmy. He may be the smartest resident we've had around here."

"You are not so dumb yourself, Dr. Belden, but yes, Jimmy Yoder is outstanding."

Sarah and Giuliana both knew that Jimmy Yoder had grown up in the isolation of the Mennonite community in Woodburn, Oregon, an enclave even further in time than in space from the urban life of Portland thirty-five miles away up the Willamette Valley. He was soft spoken and intense, compulsive and thoroughly dedicated. And very smart. But not worldly, not at all.

"We discussed his choice at some length before I accepted him into the neonatology fellowship. I wanted to be sure he was making the correct decision, exactly because of what you just mentioned, his dedication to his community. I believe there are a few conflicts he has been sorting through, but he has been quite clear in making his choice. Yes, he very much wants to serve his people, and he will not abandon them. But he has come to realize that his calling goes beyond the routine practice of general pediatrics, that he is stimulated by more complex problems than one faces in the office everyday."

The senior physician quickly realized she had indirectly slighted Sarah's chosen professional role.

"Forgive me, Sarah, I did not mean to belittle what the general pediatrician does."

"No need to apologize, Giuliana," Sarah said with a friendly smile. "I have thought about the seemingly mundane of a general pediatrician quite a bit. I came to realize that I actually love the fact that most of my time will be spent talking to mothers about normal growth and development and dealing with minor illnesses. Even," she laughed, "repeating the standard lecture about the different colors of stool that babies pass. It can be a bit like serving as a surrogate grandmother, watching hundreds, maybe thousands of children grow up. But there's a real challenge in the face of all the routine work: one needs to remain alert so as not to miss spotting the few children with serious illnesses, the high fever that is meningitis, not just the flu. But if you don't love that life, if you don't get personal satisfaction out of dealing with ordinary aspects of childhood, you can pretty well go sour and feel that you have wasted your medical training. So, yes, sure, I understand fully."

"We will see. Perhaps Jimmy Yoder will open a mid-level intensive care nursery in the hospital near his community. Of course it is a difficult thing to be the only well-trained physician to staff a nursery. But Jimmy Yoder must decide what Jimmy Yoder will do."

"Indeed," said Sarah.

Setting down her coffee cup and looking directly at Sarah, Silvestre made it clear that she had enough chit-chat and it was time for them to get to the point.

"What is it you wished to pick my brain about? I have the sense that you have something serious to discuss. Please, feel free to speak openly, Sarah."

"Thanks, Giuliana. I wanted to get your thoughts on what to say to Mrs. Johnson about Donny when I see her tomorrow—and to Mr. Johnson, if he shows up. I know the literature pretty well and I had a great experience working in the intensive care nurseries and your follow-up clinic, but I've spent so much time with the Johnson family, I'm not sure I have the best perspective. Maybe I'm not being objective about his condition. Since you have seen so many babies like him, I was hoping you could help me set the right tone. He's doing well right now after so many problems, but I know the future is not secure. What do I say to the parents?"

"It is always hard to find the right words. He was extremely small, and many such babies do have serious long-term problems. But many are essentially normal, at least once they make it out of infancy. It is not always easy to predict which ones will go in which direction. Of course, some are obviously afflicted even as infants. The ones with evident brain damage, those we can identify early on. But many of these infants surprise us. The ones we think are likely to be normal can end up with cerebral palsy or severe neurodevelopmental delay, and that can take years to diagnose.

Others worry us greatly at the start, and they actually grow up more or less entirely normal."

"What do you think about Donny Johnson?"

"I have seen him with you a number of times in our clinic, and I agree he is one of the tough cases. He looks like he is thriving, yet he seems somewhat flaccid, not physically strong. But it is much too early to be confident one way or the other. Whether his muscle tone will improve or not, whether it will prove to be a sign of severe handicaps from cerebral palsy or just a passing developmental phenomenon, I am afraid we cannot be sure at this point. It can be several years before any definite diagnosis of cerebral palsy could be made, or he might well be completely normal by then. Moreover, even if he turns out to have physical limitations he may have normal intelligence. Or, he may suffer from mental retardation. His mental acuity is even more difficult to predict until he is old enough to begin real testing and to see how well he learns."

"So…given all the uncertainties, what do I tell the family? I know that this meeting will have a lasting impression on them, since I will not be seeing him again. I do so want to be clear, as helpful as possible, but I don't want to mislead them. Either way."

"You have just the right concerns, Sarah. Perhaps the best message for them is that his organic, physical capacities are not fixed in place—they need to grow and develop over time. How his parents interact with him will be crucial. They must avoid creating—how do you say it—a *self-fulfilling prophecy*, no?"

Sarah nodded.

"If they believe he is a hopeless case and they do not make every effort to stimulate him mentally and to challenge him physically, he will be unable to reach his full potential, whatever that is. So it is quite important that they not think of him as fragile, or already broken for that matter. They must see him as a developing child who will benefit from all the nurturing they can provide. That is essential. If they give him his best chance and problems nevertheless ensue, so be it. But if they see their efforts as being a waste of time and they do not do their best by him, he will not have the opportunity to progress fully."

"So, how do I get that across without misleading them? Without setting their hopes too high, or too low? I have been thinking about that and I can't come up with just the right words. It's so difficult, isn't it?"

"Yes, of course, quite difficult. I have found that the most appropriate way to approach this is to stress to them that they should not expect him to be doing the things that other babies of the same chronological age can achieve. As we told his parents in the hospital, he was born some four months early. So it is not fair to compare him with other six-month old infants; developmentally, he's more like a two-month. The full-term babies were conceived long before he was. They had the full nine months to grow and develop inside their mothers. They should consider his age from the moment of conception, not from the time of birth. They should not expect him to compete successfully with babies born when he was. After a few years, that will equal out—or, unfortunately, his real difficulties will surface. That is the approach I take with parents of such premature infants."

"Thank you, that is very helpful. It is also reassuring that Jimmy Yoder will be caring for him. Jimmy will know how to assess Donny's development, and he will be able to identify whether he is lagging behind where he should be."

"Indeed. Dr. Yoder will be seeing many such babies in the high-risk follow-up clinic, and he will know what standard he should use to gauge Donny's development. And, as you say, Sarah, Dr. Yoder will have a more objective perspective, perhaps, than you might."

"Yes, Dr. Silvestre." In the dependent position of seeking advice from her mentor, Sarah had unconsciously reverted to a more formal tone.

Catching herself, she continued, "That has been bothering me, Giuliana. I have been wrapped up with this family for so many years that I worry I would not be able to see clearly what was going on if things were to take a turn for the worse with Donny. I would not want to be the one to deliver bad news to them ever again, so I might not see what I should see. When I think about what could go wrong with Donny, I am sometimes troubled about my decision to resuscitate such a tiny infant. At first I felt so good about saving him, but now I am afraid that my judgment is clouded. That is one reason I did not invite the Johnsons to bring Donny to my new office."

"You are wise beyond your years. Dr. Yoder will be very good for the family, and will be able to deal with anything that comes along. You can be honest with Mrs. Johnson without misleading her, and you can certainly reassure her that they are in good hands. In any case, our high-risk follow-up clinic is the best place for them to be seen for the next few years. We will give them access to many other services that are quite difficult for pediatricians in office-based practices such as yours to arrange: physical therapy, sub-specialty consultants, social services. So overall this is the right thing to do, you should not feel bad about leaving Donny Johnson with us."

"Thank you Giuliana." Sarah was back on even footing with her. "This was the most valuable cup of coffee I have ever had."

"Just one more thing, Sarah. What you said about being troubled by your decision to resuscitate Donny Johnson. You must never doubt that decision. We do not create life, but we have the great privilege to sustain lives that might otherwise end too early. You did what you were there to do in the delivery room, and you did it superbly. Everything went as it should have, you made no mistakes, no errors, and you saved a human life under circumstances more stressful than most people could imagine. Bravo! Well done, Dr. Belden, I say. Now it is up to us to continue to help this child achieve the most out of his life. But never again doubt your actions. You were a doctor doing what you were trained to do, what you are dedicated to do, and you should forever be pleased that you did it so expertly. I am most proud to have had you as a trainee, to see you gain such skill and expertise, and now to have you as a colleague. And, I would hope, as a friend."

"Of course, Giuliana, of course you and I will be friends always. Thank you so much. I will always remember what you said, and I will never again second-guess my decision to resuscitate Donny. At least I'll try. Thanks again."

"You are most welcome. And now, Ciao!"

"Ciao, Giuliana."

Chapter 11: Catching Up

"Donny looks great, Mrs. Johnson. He's gained almost a pound in the last two weeks. His lungs are clear, his color is good. He's coming along."

"Thanks, Dr. Belden, we're very happy. We wouldn't have Donny if it weren't for you and Dr. Silvestre. We'll always be grateful to you. You worked so hard for him, and for the....the..."

Martina Johnson's words trailed off, but Sarah knew that she was thinking about the other three boys, the ones Sarah had not been able to save. But she did not want to open more wounds than necessary, so she shifted the conversation quickly.

"I'm going to miss seeing you and Donny. He's come such a long way, it's a joy to watch him grow and develop."

Martina Johnson was beaming, her Nordic beauty restored by motherhood. Her smile amplified the sheen of her bright blond hair, once again brushed smooth, flowing gracefully over her shoulders. Her cheeks had a more robust pink glow than Sarah had ever seen before. Even her simple cotton print dress looked elegant on the striking once-again-young woman. Sarah treasured the return of her impression of Martina as a Russian *Madonna* illuminated by her baby.

"We'll miss you, also, Dr. Belden. Maybe when Derek's work picks up we'll come over to your office."

"That would be great, Mrs. Johnson."

"So, Donny's doing fine?"

Being asked point-blank whether Donny was doing fine drove home the uncomfortable reality of Sarah's relationship with Martina Johnson. Sarah was, above all, a doctor who had to mix caution with good news, and the happy mother was her patient. The baby the woman was holding was not quite normal despite his exceptional progress from being nearly stillborn. Sarah struggled to strike the right tone, to bring Martina into reality without destroying her euphoria. She had seen this coming, perhaps she shouldn't have let herself get so distracted by Martina. Maybe she overdid it by saying he looked great. Martina looked so happy now, how could she be the bad guy and let her down?

"He's coming along, yes, Mrs. Johnson," she nodded, maintaining a degree of separation by calling her 'Mrs.' "But of course," she added, "he's got a long way to go."

Martina raised her head toward Sarah Belden. Her face changed slightly, almost imperceptibly, but enough to confirm to Sarah that Martina also was well aware that they were doctor and patient, not just two women cooing over a baby.

"What…what do you mean, Dr. Belden?"

Sarah Belden gave Martina a reassuring smile and touched her arm. She had to pull herself out of the hole she had dug and fallen into. After all, there was nothing definitely wrong with Donny, she needn't burst Martina's bubble. Either he was going to be OK or he wasn't, she couldn't be sure yet. She had to let Martina have her moment, her hope. Most important, she had to refrain from by saying anything that, would lead Donny's parents to think of him as broken. She should not be the one to jeopardize Donny's full development by generating the self-fulfilling prophecy with her words that Giuliana Silvestre had warned her about.

"He is doing fine, Mrs. Johnson," she said, sounding fully confident. "Remember, even though we say he's six months old, he was so premature that it's as if he was just born about two months ago. He needs time to compensate for the fifteen or sixteen weeks he missed of developing inside you. And, he's already been through quite a bit, I don't have to remind you of that. So, yes, he's got a long way to go, but he's doing fine."

Sarah wasn't exactly lying, wasn't deceiving the young mother, she was simply stretching the truth. She *had* to do this, she assured herself, it was for Donny's benefit.

"We—you—need to give him time. It can take a few years before he is up to where kids his same birth age are. We can't expect him to make up for missing three or four very important months overnight."

Martina relaxed. Sarah could see the maternal glow that had never fully extinguished blossom again as her warm smile appeared.

"Yes, you and Dr. Silvestre have been very good about reminding us that he's not really as old as other babies his age—that sounds so funny to say! We won't rush things. Derek and I love him so much. We're happy he's with us and he's getting stronger all the time."

"That's right, and he needs all the help and support you can give him. You can tell his little arms and legs are just a bit weak, but that can improve rapidly over the next few months. We can't expect him to be on the same schedule as full-term babies, but these little ones have an amazing capacity to catch up."

"What about his head?"

Sarah's heart skipped a beat. She had hoped to avoid questions about whether Donny might have suffered any brain damage. But there it was. She fumbled for an answer.

"Well...there's no way to be sure yet. He could certainly have normal intelligence, but we can't tell for sure at this stage."

Martina smiled and choked back a laugh.

"I meant his *head*, not his brain, Dr. Belden. Look at his head—will that get better? Will he ever look normal?"

Sarah broke into an embarrassed smile as she understood that Martina was asking about the elongated, oblong shape of Donny's skull that made him look as though someone had squeezed his head in the jaws of a vise. Sarah had misinterpreted Martina's question because she was responding to a concern of her own about his brain rather than picking up on the more down-to-earth meaning of the mother's question.

Mortified, Sarah said, "I'm so sorry, Mrs. Johnson. I'm so used to seeing premature babies I don't even notice their heads anymore. The shape of his head is completely normal for such a small baby. A baby's head has to be squishy enough to change shape while passing through the birth canal, and in premature babies it stays that way even after they are outside the womb for several months. Their little skulls are so malleable, so flexible, they stay flat just from lying on the pads in their incubators. The shape of his head is no problem at all, just one more example of how much catching up a premature baby has to do. Once Donny starts sitting with his head up, it will take on a normal shape. By the time he is two years old his head will look just the way you would expect."

Satisfied, Martina shifted back into a palsy woman-to-woman mode.

"Do you know what his father did? He made the most incredible mobile to hang over Donny's crib."

Sarah readily accepted the return to more casual conversation, relieved that Martina had not pursued a discussion about Donny's brain.

"Mr. Johnson made a mobile for Donny? That's wonderful."

"It's fantastic. It has all these little cut-out figures of real people, sports heroes. You can even see their faces."

"I didn't know he did things like that."

"Me neither. I mean, he's a carpenter, he's very good with his hands, but he hadn't done anything like this before, it completely surprised me. His own wife, and I didn't know."

Sarah knew the time had come to end the appointment, indeed to pull out of their relationship. It had been nearly three years since that awful night when Martina's first baby turned out stillborn and grotesquely malformed. Then those long nights and days trying to save the twins, only to lose them both. But most of all she knew that those first experiences with Martina and Derek had influenced her decision the night Donny was born. Ever since that moment she had been plagued with a lingering sense of doubt, hoping against hope that she had made the right decision when she resuscitated him. Had she put too much of herself into trying to give this woman and her husband the son they so longed to have? But why was she having second thoughts? Once she helped Donny take that first breath, she had used up her options. The die had been cast, now all she could do would be to wait to see how Donny would turn out.

"It's been great seeing you and Donny, Mrs. Johnson. Maybe we'll keep in touch somehow. Keep up the good work, you have a precious little guy there."

"Thank you so much for everything. I'm sure we'll see each other again, Dr. Belden."

***

"Hi, Honey, what did the doctor say? How's Donny doing?"

Derek had come to the University with his wife and son, but had waited outside in his van. He had had enough of doctors and hospitals, and besides, Martina wouldn't really speak up and say everything that was on her mind if he had come along with her to see the doctor. She was better off dealing with Dr. Belden woman-to-woman, he thought. And hanging out in the parking lot he could sneak a few cigarettes without Martina noticing—he had promised to

81

give up smoking when Donny came home, just like the doctors had insisted, and he did quit, at least he quit around the house. But on the job, and those long drives to some of the worksites, that was the hard part. So he kept his stash of cigarettes in the van, and took advantage of time away from Martina to satisfy the urge he couldn't completely suppress. He would quit someday, he really meant it. Already he was down to less than a pack a day, he was getting there.

"Any problems?"

"He's doing great, of course. What else could she say?"

Martina was holding Donny wrapped in one of the baby blankets the nursing staff had given them, bright blue with circus animals dancing in all directions. Derek's face flushed from the warmth of her smile, his cheeks lighting up as they had when he first cast eyes on her in Olsen High.

"I don't know, just hard to believe he's OK after all that stuff he went through. He's still pretty small, huh?"

"Actually, that's what Dr. Belden kept reminding me about—he's not small, he's young. All the other babies who were born in early November are really three or four months older than he is—if you count from when they were, you know, conceived, anyway. So he's got to catch up."

"What about his head? Did she say anything about why his head is as flat as a flounder?"

"That's pretty funny—I asked her about his head, and she thought I meant his brain! Anyway, his head's still pretty soft, so it will be flat until he holds his head up on his own, then it will grow into a normal shape. You won't have to get special football helmets for him, Honey."

The image of tossing a football with his son triggered a surge of emotion that was different than anything he had allowed himself to think during Donny's long hospitalization. He felt—what was it? *Anticipation, expectation, hope, a future, a son to play with?* The future had never seemed tangible with the other babies, or with Donny until now. Mostly he'd had to deal with Martina's pregnancies, and the first three boys never left the hospital alive so their prospects were crushed before they had fully taken shape in his imagination. But now, here was his son, in his wife's arms, in their van. He could envision a future when the baby would be a little boy, then a bigger boy, then his buddy. He could teach him how to throw a spiral with a football, a slider with a baseball, just like he had learned from his own dad. If Donny wanted to play hockey or soccer or learn to ski, well, Derek would do his best to help his son even though those hadn't been his sports. The sense of anticipation made Derek choke up and turn away from Martina to catch his breath, to make sure his voice wouldn't crack when he spoke. He coughed once, twice, then felt confident enough to respond, "Nope, no special helmets for our boy."

***

Much to her surprise, Martina took quickly to Dr. Jimmy Yoder when she saw the warmth in his eyes. Dr. Jimmy lived to serve, he exuded caring and concern, he never seemed hurried, he listened carefully to every detail. Yes, he was different than Sarah Belden. He was far more reserved, and Martina could not feel the special woman-to-woman connection, of course. But he was so good with Donny, playful even, that Martina was comfortable with him. He hardly seemed to be examining Donny in any formal way, it was more like he was playing games with the baby and gathering information bit by bit as they played together.

Martina noticed that Dr. Jimmy didn't examine Donny in a ritualized sequence from top to bottom, he was able to put together a complete physical exam piecemeal, taking whatever opportunity the child gave him at any moment. He did not try to hold the boy down to press an ice-cold stethoscope against his bare skin, instead he kept the head of the instrument tucked in his armpit to warm and conceal it, then swung the shiny silver-and-black object dangling from its black rubber tubing like a metronome, touching it lightly to Donny's chest as part of their game. He felt Donny's belly between light pokes and tickles, he tested his reflexes with other delicate moves. He gauged the bony closure of Donny's soft spot, his anterior fontanelle, while gently patting his head.

Martina was impressed: Donny actually loved coming to see Dr. Yoder. He giggled in his funny way when the young doctor walked into the examining room, he never cried around him. Derek did not come into the clinic often, but the few times he did, he also liked the young doctor. Jimmy looked frail but he had a man's grip in his handshake, and the hands themselves told Derek this was someone who knew what physical labor was.

The Johnsons did not suspect that behind his youthful appearance and lighthearted demeanor, Jimmy Yoder was noting subtle signs that the baby who had survived so much was in for a great deal more yet to come. Certain primitive reflexes that babies are born with were persisting long after they should have disappeared. Donny seemed to prefer his right hand to an unusual extent, which confirmed Jimmy Yoder's assessment that his left side was not as strong as the right. Even taking the baby's severe prematurity into account, the child wasn't on schedule for rolling over or sitting up by himself. In fact, he was lagging far behind. By the Johnson's third visit, Jimmy Yoder was already calculating the probability that Donny Johnson had cerebral palsy, possibly with severely disabling loss of control of his arms and legs. The odds were growing stronger day by day. Jimmy Yoder knew that sometime in the next few months he would most likely have to break the news to the Johnsons that Donny needed further evaluation: testing, consultations, more visits to the clinic to see different specialists. The signs were growing stronger, and if they did not change soon, it would be clear even to the family that something was wrong.

Jimmy Yoder decided to wait and let the scenarios play out a bit longer. There was no need to rush. Either Donny's course would improve and he would blossom into a healthy child, or his disabilities would become obvious. Time would tell.

Chapter 12: Perfect Mix

Antonio O'Malley was in a very good mood. He had just finished putting together the biggest trade deal of his budding career at the Export-Import Bank of the United States. Because of his skillful efforts, the bank would now guarantee two hundred million dollars in letters of credit for a newly-independent eastern European country to purchase solar technology from a small company in Utah. Antonio was pleased with his accomplishment, the first big-time evidence that he would be successful at this job that he had worked so hard to prepare for. Born to immigrant parents, a father from Ireland and mother from Spain, he had inherited a marvelous mix of genes and culture. Both bloodlines had blessed him with blacker-than-black hair, tall slender stature, angular features, irresistible charm, free and independent spirit, quick intelligence, and boundless resourcefulness. With his M.B.A. from Georgetown in international trade, Antonio was coming into his own, and today's success made him feel he was finally a player on the international stage. He was at the top of his game.

Now, how to celebrate his triumph?

Closing the deal had not come easily. Antonio had persevered through months of negotiations, traveling back and forth between Utah and eastern Europe, places so culturally and geographically distinct from each other and from his own experience that it had been like commuting to alien planets. He had put in countless hours analyzing the financial stability of a relatively new and unproven foreign government and the capability of a small manufacturing company in the U.S.A. to expand its capacity and conduct international business deals. Helping these strange bedfellows work together had turned out to be entertaining as well as challenging: one side was a group of straitlaced teetotalers who partied with ice cream sundaes, the other a collection of raucous fellows fond of tumbler-sized glasses of neat vodka. But when it came to doing business they made a perfect match—the abstemious Utah entrepreneurs manufactured a product the earthier foreign team wanted to buy. The American loan guarantees that Antonio arranged had transformed the Utah manufacturer's tenuous export-related accounts receivable into financially-sound assets.

It was his success, his big accomplishment. The world's economy was one notch stronger tonight. He deserved to celebrate!

But how? His colleagues at the Ex-Im Bank had congratulated him, but they weren't the type to socialize and tie one on over what was, in the grand scheme of global finance, only a medium-sized deal. His highly accomplished mother and father, strange bedfellows themselves, would appreciate the complexity of the deal he had arranged, but spending a routine evening at the old homestead with his parents would hardly satisfy his urge to party. His mother, Mariana Húsares de O'Malley, had a doctorate in economics. An accomplished teacher and scholar on international economics, she prepared her son to understand the complex networks and balances that made a global economy possible—and vulnerable. His father, Sean O'Malley, was a philosopher with an active interest in the real world, and particularly in geopolitics. He complemented Mariana's technical world view with a deeper human perspective. Both parents had such confidence that great things would flow routinely from their son's work that they would view Antonio's first breakthrough as no more than was to be expected. Their enthusiasm, however genuine, would be muted, taking the edge off of his elation.

He decided he would treat himself to a fine dinner, even though it really sucked that he would be eating alone.

For Antonio O'Malley there was only one place to celebrate: *Ricardo O'Leary's,* his perfect restaurant. The Mexican-Irish cuisine allowed him to indulge either of his lineages, or both, depending on his mood. He had gone there the first time intrigued at hearing of a restaurant with a bi-cultural name like his own, and now he was a regular patron of *Ricardo O'Leary's.*

The only downside of walking into a restaurant where he was well known would be having to acknowledge to Ricardo O'Leary, the owner and maitre d', that yes, once again he would be dining solo. He would cover his embarrassment with a smile and an offhanded, "Just one tonight, Ricardo—unless I get lucky, that is."

Antonio's playful musing turned out to be prescient.

Sarah Belden had not dated much in college. She would still kick herself for having turned down an invitation from the one guy she really wanted to go out with, begging off with what now seemed a pathetically lame response: "Sorry, I have a Neurobiology final tomorrow, maybe you can call me next week?" But the call never came and not long afterward she spotted the rebuffed young man in a restaurant having a great time with another woman in her class. Medical school was another long social drought. Some of her female classmates managed to date once in a while, and a few even went out on weeknights and somehow still managed to graduate. But they were the ones who could clock in and clock out with random men, leave their brief encounters behind once they were over and return to studying at four in the morning after a date. She particularly remembered one friend who insisted, "Sex is just sport-fucking, it clears my mind, relieves all that tension so I can study better. You should try it, Sarah." But that was just not Sarah. She took relationships too seriously. The few she had managed to explore lingered forever in her mind. She rationalized her lack of a social life by insisting she would be too distracted to handle medical school if she got involved with someone. Then, how could she find time to date during her Internship and Residency when she was on duty in the hospital every other night? Plus, she chronically took her work home in her head, thinking about all those sick kids, all that responsibility, even when she was supposedly off duty. Hardly a good mind-set for romance. Now she was free, a doctor off on her own, she could enjoy herself at last. But she was still alone.

Then magic happened.

As Sarah went to board the elevator in her condo building a tall man she had not seen before stepped to one side and extended his arm to keep the door open for her. She smiled and said, "Thanks," then was struck by what she read on the nametag on the soft black leather satchel hanging from his shoulder. Without thinking she blurted out, "*Antonio O'Malley*? What's that?"

As her rash question reverberated around the enclosed space, she looked directly at her accidental companion and was instantly captivated by his strong features, his narrow, sharply chiseled face, his long, wavy, strikingly black hair. The blackest hair she had ever seen. When he returned her look she felt that he could see right through her eyes into her head and read her thoughts. She heard him answer her impulsive question in a pleasant, somewhat amused voice. "My name, of course, that's what *Antonio O'Malley* is. And what's your name, if I may ask?"

"Sarah Belden. But, I meant…what *kind* of name? *Antonio* doesn't seem to go with *O'Malley*, does it?"

He grinned, knowing full well what her question had meant. But he immediately wanted to extend their unexpected conversation for as long as he could, so he embarked on one of his fanciful stories about his origins.

"I was left in a basket in a church in a little village in Ireland, and the O'Malley family that took me home named me after Father Antonio, one of the Spanish missionary priests who found me," he said, affecting a faux-Irish brogue.

Sarah was so accustomed to being the concerned doctor, always taking people seriously, listening to their medical complaints at face value and pondering her response, that for a long moment she believed him. She couldn't wait to hear the rest of his fascinating history and said, "Oh my, go on, please. What a wonderful story." But he just started laughing without responding, laughing with the most alluring smile she had ever seen. At last she realized that the handsome man was teasing her. He was making a joke out of a question he had probably put up with all of his life, catching her unaware. At that very moment she fell in love with him right on the spot, somewhere between the 6th and 8th floors.

"OK, Mr. Melting Pot, OK, I get it. You're a hybrid."

"That's correct, one-half Spanish, one-half Irish. Half rice, half potato. Sometimes it's half tequila, half Irish whiskey. And you, Miss Belden? Or, is it Mrs. Belden?"

"It's Miss," she said, deliberately avoiding *"Doctor." "Miss"* would convey what she really wanted him to know: she was single, she was available. And, she realized, she was interested.

"Sarah, actually. Do you live in the building?" she asked, not daring to add the most important question: *"Are you going home to your wife and kids?"*

"Just moved in, one of those 'Junior one-bedrooms' on the 10th floor. More junior than one-bedroom, really a sleeping nook off the living-dining room and a tiny kitchenette, but that's plenty for me."

That was all she needed—he was letting her know he was single, he was available. *But, was he interested?*

"Then we're neighbors. I'm in an identical unit on the 11th floor. Maybe I'll come down to borrow a cup of sugar some time."

Sarah couldn't believe what she was saying. On the one hand she was being so forward her words sounded like they were coming from someone else. She had never had the courage to take a bold step like that with men. On the other hand she felt embarrassed that what she had managed so daringly to say was dreadfully trite, a cliché right off a soap opera. Not nearly what Lauren Bacall would have said at meeting Humphrey Bogart on an elevator. But her corny response worked.

"I haven't got any sugar, in fact I hardly cook at all. I can make strong coffee to get me started in the morning, but I drink it black with no sugar. And I go out to eat for almost all my meals." He paused briefly, then added, "Come to think of it, as soon as I drop my satchel off I was planning on catching dinner at *Ricardo O'Leary's* down the block. So, Miss Sarah Belden, would you like to join me? I would be delighted to introduce you to the joys of Spanish-Irish cooking. Well, actually, Mexican-Irish, but close enough."

The elevator stopped at the 10th floor, the door opened, he stood in the doorway waiting for her answer. Soon the door started to close, then bounced back after bumping against his shoe. After a few more seconds the elevator's aggravating buzzer began screeching at them and the door began to shut with more force.

Sarah had to decide quickly. Was this for real? Was she seriously about to go out for dinner with a guy she had met less than a minute ago?

"Sure," she replied, surprised not at her affirmative answer but at the enthusiasm she felt, and heard in her own voice. "See you in the lobby in fifteen minutes." Then, inexplicably, she yelled through the closed doors as the elevator started to rise, "Belden is mostly Irish."

***

Ricardo O'Leary's was crowded but a few quick words from Antonio to Ricardo got them a two-top along the wall next to the jam-packed bar. The walls were covered with the colors of both nations' flags, broad green and white stripes alternating with Irish orange and Mexican red. Waiters wearing crisp long-sleeved white shirts with black bow ties maneuvered deftly through the vibrant crowd, carrying as many as three large platters on each arm. Sarah loved the place immediately. It was the most exciting ambience she had experienced in years.

Telling Sarah not to bother looking at the menu, Antonio ordered dinner for both of them in fluent Spanish, speaking too rapidly for her to understand with the fledgling language skills she had acquired in high school.

When he finished ordering the food she asked, "So…what are we having?"

He feigned surprise. "Boiled white potatoes, spicy pigs' feet stew, and sweet Sangria, of course."

Again Sarah took him seriously for one brief moment, then laughed at herself for her repeated naïveté as she saw his mischievous smile broaden. "I hope you like seafood," he chuckled.

After downing the biggest, saltiest Margarita she had ever tasted, Sarah watched with delight as Antonio scooped large spoonfuls of paella onto their plates with a flourish. They ate gobs of rice, sausage and shellfish, along with thick pieces of Irish soda bread. They savored a fine *Miguel Torres Gran Coronas Reserva Black Label* wine, and somehow found room to share a sweet flan and a moist, fragrant chocolate potato cake, a dessert Sarah had no idea existed.

Sarah was charmed. More than charmed, she was intrigued, fascinated, infatuated. She had indeed fallen in love on the elevator and now felt as though they had known each other forever. After dinner at *Ricardo O'Leary's* she found herself suggesting they go to a nearby bar for nightcaps. Nearly four hours after they had met they were strolling along hand in hand, back to their apartment building. Neither wanted the evening to end.

Once back on the fateful elevator Sarah astonished them both by grabbing his hand as he went to push the buttons for the 10th and 11th floors. She kissed him lightly on the cheek and whispered, "I think we only need the 11th floor tonight, *hmm*?"

Her words echoed just what was running through Antonio's mind, but he had been reluctant to be the one to volunteer such a brash suggestion.

"Ah, yes," he replied, turning toward Sarah, still holding her hand but now wrapping his other arm around her, kissing her passionately.

Sarah returned his passion, stroking his neck, pressing her body against his until the elevator beeped and opened at the 11th floor. It was far too early to let the night end.

Chapter 13: Unraveling

Martina Johnson hardly recognized the face looking back at her in the mirror of the medicine cabinet in their tiny bathroom. For some time she had been avoiding her own image, glancing at her reflection only when it was inescapable while brushing her teeth or washing her hands. Now she was fixated on the ghastly sight of the person she was becoming. What was happening to her? Where was her beauty, her youth? How had this happened so quickly? *"My hair, oh my God, my hair!"* she cried aloud. Once the glamorous highlight of her exotic beauty, the exquisite capstone to a figure of elegance and strength, her blond tresses now looked like a witch's mane. The hair at the very top of her head lay flat, crushed against her scalp. A morass of split and uneven strands dangled listlessly at random lengths, some over her ears, some to her neck, others nearly to her waist. She tried to run a comb through the tangles but winced as the teeth got caught in a jungle of interwoven snarls. She saw the pained expression on her own face as the comb twisted the knots, then shifted her gaze to the furrows at the corners of her eyes, the bags under her eyes, the puffiness at the base of her nose, the cracked skin at the angles of her mouth.

Life with the two men she loved so very much had not turned out to be what Martina had anticipated, had longed for. Life with Derek was hardly life at all. Ever the well-meaning husband and father, he had labored diligently to earn enough money to keep his damaged family together, but the long hours at his several jobs and the stresses of their financial troubles had dropped a curtain between them that grew more impenetrable every day. And then, Donny. She could still cuddle with her son, play with the child, make him laugh. But now he was six years old and they had come to accept that the boy was not right, had not developed as they had hoped. He was responsive and seemed bright enough sometimes, but his efforts to communicate produced only inarticulate sounds. Martina could usually figure out what the boy wanted, but the noises he uttered were not language.

And, he couldn't walk. Years earlier, at the age most kids become toddlers who take endless spills but eventually learn to balance themselves and walk upright, he had moved around by dragging himself across the floor on his side like a wounded crab, pulling himself forward with his arms, then slithering ahead with his legs. His arms and legs were stiff, so Martina spent hours flexing them passively to keep them as limber as possible. He held his head off to one side with his mouth partially open. His eyes swirled in irregular patterns so that she was never sure where he was looking. Even now he could not attend to any of the normal everyday skills basic to a young child's life: she was still feeding, dressing and bathing him. He wore oversized diapers because she could not deal with lifting him on and off the toilet often enough by herself.

Mother and son shared precious few pleasurable moments. One activity they both enjoyed was watching television together. Donny seemed mesmerized by certain TV shows. He made happy sounds when she laughed and soft, high-pitched squeals when she cried. And when she had the strength to read to him, he would nuzzle up close to her and seemed to take pleasure in seeing the brightly-colored pictures in the large children's books that Derek brought home from time to time.

Martina had always wanted to be a mother and loved Donny with all her heart, but hers was not the motherhood she had craved. She stared at the aging young woman in her reflection watched tears stream down her weary face. How much longer could she keep this up? She was perpetually tired yet she could not stop caring for her son. She had nothing else, nothing but Donny. She was spending her life compensating for the limitations of his. She and Derek were hardly husband and wife any more. A wave of self-reproach washed over her. She could hardly blame Derek—how could any man possibly love someone who looked like the creature she had become? But she could never leave Donny long enough to go to the beauty parlor, and they couldn't afford such a luxury anyway. And not only had she stayed away from the beauty parlor for years herself, she had started cutting Derek's hair to save the cost of a barbershop. She grabbed at her hair with both hands and pulled hard, twisting the handfuls of matted blond hair until her scalp ached. At last she dropped her head and leaned against the sink, sobbing uncontrollably.

***

Nearly midnight, and Derek Johnson was on his way home from work at the end of another very long day. He was always at work these days, coming home between his two jobs barely long enough to clean himself up before heading out to the second one, then returning to the house later only to collapse for a few hours in bed before leaving for his morning work. He shook his head and blinked his eyes to fight off the intense urge to fall asleep at the wheel as he struggled to maneuver his van through the mist in the hills above the city. Dense fog would appear out of nowhere, seemingly always at the worst spots, where the road dipped, or on a sharp curve. Trapped between the cliff face on one side and the invisible steep slope on the other he had no place to pull over and rest.

"Where's the damn edge?" he said out loud to no one, unable to see the sheer drop-off in the fog. He kept yelling out loud, cursing randomly, perhaps hoping that the sound of his own voice would help keep him awake. The old van had no fog lights. He tried using the windshield wipers but they made the visibility even worse, smearing bugs into the heavy dew, coating the glass with a speckled paste of crushed insects.

Derek shuddered, despondent. His hopes had sunk to the most basic level: he could think no further than just getting home alive.

For his day job, Derek was usually on the road before dawn to arrive at the worksite at 7AM or even earlier. He was part of a crew building a spectacular 22,000 square-foot house sprawling on what had been an old farm nearly thirty miles out of town. A gifted carpenter, Derek knew which beams and boards to use, which ones to reject. His measurements were always accurate. When a line was supposed to be straight, it was straight. He could turn wood into any shape, bend handrails around soft corners, craft custom rosettes to decorate window or door frames. And the job was a good situation with a stable company and benefits, including health insurance. His boss appreciated his talents and the other regulars were usually fun to work with and carried their load. He even got to know a few of the day laborers who reappeared from time to time, and enjoyed seeing and joking with them in broken *Spanglish*.

At first, he loved his job and had even looked forward to the early-morning drives to the different construction sites. The work had been great fun back when he had been able to hang out with the guys for a few beers on Friday afternoons while looking forward to a relaxing weekend with Martina.

But that was before Donny was born. Work was not fun any more. Even with health insurance from the construction company, the money was not enough to carry their crushing debt, and he was too worn out to enjoy much of anything. His day didn't end when all the other workers finished. He couldn't just go home for the evening and relax with his wife and tell her stories about the construction crew. All he could do was drive to the house, spend a few minutes doing whatever chores Martina put aside for him, get out of his sweaty outfit, take a shower, change into the cleanest blue jeans he could find and head off to the store where he supplemented his pay from the construction work.

What kind of life was this? What the hell was he doing?

Derek worked construction five days a week plus as many weekend hours as he could get for the precious overtime pay. His second job was re-stocking large appliances and other heavy items at a big discount warehouse store. He would go to the store four evenings each week, and sometimes on Sundays if sales had been above expectations. Now he was heading back home and he was tired, very tired.

As his van rounded a curve the headlights of an oncoming truck startled him wide awake, lighting up his view so he suddenly saw that the wheels of his van were only inches from the cliff-side edge of the roadway. Trembling now, he fought with the steering wheel to regain control and managed to swerve back onto the pavement just before the van would have tumbled down the side of the hill all the way to the river. After the truck passed by he slapped himself in the face, knowing he had come close to disaster. Too close. The chronic exhaustion was taking its toll.

Awake now from the adrenaline surge of his brush with death, he allowed himself a moment of reflection.

Martina was home with Donny. She was tired, too. What the hell had they gotten themselves into? They had no sleep, no time together, no money. Forget sex, that was impossible. Martina had carried four baby boys, but three graves and Donny was all they had to show for it. Three dead and one... He couldn't bring himself to say, *"one worse than dead,"* but deep down that ugly thought threatened to creep into his consciousness at moments like this. What kind of life did Donny have? What kind of life did any of them have? Every day, every night, dealing with Donny. Lifting him, watching Martina care for him, feed him, try so hard to teach him to speak. Visions of tossing a football with his son, of even walking him to school, had all faded bitterly into a distant past. How long could this go on?

When he came to a relatively straight stretch of road Derek opened his window, pulled a cigarette from the pack in his shirt pocket, lit it, and drew deeply on the smoke. The instant nicotine high stimulated and relaxed him. The cigarettes might be killing him little by little, he thought, but for now they were his only pleasure.

The cigarette and the close call with the cliff edge had cleared his head enough to drive the rest of the way home. He said a silent prayer of thanks for his successful journey as he finally pulled into the driveway of their bungalow. He was home now, but he didn't go into the house right away. He stood in their driveway, leaning against his van, smoking a cigarette. And thinking.

Derek had never been mean or harsh with Martina, he loved her and Donny to his very core, but he was no longer the easygoing young man he had been in high school. He was worried, tense all the time. He remembered being so happy when he got the construction job. The health insurance seemed like a miracle that would solve their financial problems. The company's plan had what seemed an astronomically high half-million-dollar lifetime limit. Who would ever have imagined that the bills could be more than that? He and Martina thought they were finally safe, finally in a position where they wouldn't have to worry about medical bills. But as it turned out, the hospital bills alone were much more than a half-million dollars, then there were all those doctor bills, lab tests, wheelchairs, all those other things. And all the old bills they couldn't pay off. They were in serious financial trouble and he could see no way out. He had kept their precarious situation to himself but now he decided to reveal the gravity of their financial problems to Martina. She had to know. He had to speak with her, he just had to. It wouldn't be easy. Nothing was easy with Martina any more, but this would be as bad as it gets. She wouldn't want to hear what he had to say, but he had to tell her. He couldn't keep it in any longer, it was killing him.

Derek took one long, last drag on the cigarette, dropped the butt on the driveway and ground it to shreds with his work boot, venting his tension on the tiny stub of paper and tobacco shards.

He let himself in the side door from the carport as he always did, walked through the kitchen, and stopped still when he saw his wife staring into the mirror in their bathroom. He could see her reflection but she didn't seem to see his.

Derek said softly, "Hi, Honey." The words triggered only a tiny movement of her expressionless face in the mirror. She established eye contact with him through the reflection only briefly then looked away. He walked closer, touched her shoulders, kissed her lightly on the back of her head, and whispered, "Martina, Honey, I hate to unload this on you, I know you don't need something else to worry about, but we have big money problems."

He was expecting her to turn and look at him, but she continued to stare in the mirror and didn't say a word. He hesitated. Maybe this wasn't a good time. *Hell, there was no good time.* He took a weary breath and continued, "We're in debt up to our ears. There are bills from everywhere, all sorts of things. Memorial General is still billing us for all three pregnancies. We got bills from the University for Lenny's open-heart surgery, bills from many of the doctors, and more bills from the labs for all kinds of tests and things. We have killer bills for Donny's months in the NICU and special care unit after our insurance ran out. Now the bills are mounting for Donny's physical therapy and for his braces and wheelchair and other special equipment."

Martina turned a deaf ear to her husband. She could not listen to a cacophony of troubles on top of all the problems she had at home just getting through each day. Besides, there was nothing new about their money problems, why was Derek bothering her about them now? She had tried to help with their finances in her own way by dealing with the endless paperwork and tedium of applying for whatever aid they might get from public programs. At first their applications had been rejected. Married couples and their kids, she learned, couldn't qualify for public assistance no matter how poor they were. So they had years and years of bills with no help from the government. At last her efforts paid off a bit when Donny officially qualified as being seriously disabled so Medicaid and disability kicked in. But disability brought in meager cash payments and Medicaid didn't do anything about their old medical bills. And there was no end to the crushing frustration of dealing with the vagaries of the public programs she'd had to endure. Every so often Donny would get dropped off the disability and Medicaid rolls, sometimes by mistake, sometimes when the state wanted to save money and changed the rules, and sometimes when Derek had a good few months of work and their income went up enough to put them over the limits for the public programs. Then, when their income dropped again and they were eligible to re-enroll, she would traipse all over town with Donny to spend endless hours waiting in lines at agencies, filling out the same application forms repeatedly, dealing with clerks who were overwhelmed themselves and not much help, even the ones who seemed to mean well.

So Martina didn't want to listen to Derek because she thought she already knew how bad things were. She had long since stopped counting but she knew they had hundreds of thousands of dollars in medical bills, debts amounting to more money than Derek would likely earn in his entire lifetime, more than they had ever even thought of spending on a home or anything else.

So why did Derek have to keep reminding her?

And what more did he expect her to do? She was already spending every waking hour taking care of Donny. At last she turned toward him and asked, "What are you saying? Do you want me to get a job, or what?"

Derek backed up a few steps, a few steps back from his wife and a few steps back from the message he was delivering. He didn't know what he was asking of her.

"No, Sweetheart, no, of course not. I know that's not realistic. Anyway, you couldn't earn enough to dent these bills either. Someone's got to care for Donny, and you're doing a good job. A great job. I know it's hard on you, it's very hard. I guess I'm not asking you to do anything. I don't know what I'm saying, I just wanted to let you know. I'll deal with it as best I can."

He was still soft with her, not loving in the old way, but caring, understanding. Weaker men might have taken out their frustration and anger on her or on Donny, but Derek just kept it in. He cursed himself for his stupidity in unloading on his wife. He had already told her plenty about how bad things were, she was already overwhelmed. What was he thinking? Martina couldn't help. It was all up to him.

Chapter 14: Breaking Point

Unwilling to burden Martina further, Derek agonized on his own over what to do, where to turn. His little family had suffered unthinkable tragedies with the boys four times over. Martina's days and nights were consumed caring for their son, the rest of her life shot to hell. He had a good job and worked a second one several nights each week but they were drowning in a sea of debt and he was exhausted all the time.

And now, on top of the personal crosses they bore, they were facing a real crisis. He was not even sure exactly how much they owed the hospitals and doctors, but whatever it added up to, it was about to destroy them. The collection agencies came after him constantly. They pestered him at home, at work, they wouldn't leave him alone. He went to a credit counselor and did everything she told him to do. Calling from pay phones during breaks at work, he spent countless precious hours trying to set up partial-payment schedules for the bills, but nothing seemed to be enough to satisfy the creditors. Some of the health care providers he tried to negotiate with wouldn't cooperate at all, and the ones who had done so were always complaining that he was falling behind, he was violating their agreement.

Now they were at the breaking point: he couldn't pay their rent and they were facing eviction. What would they do if they were thrown out on the street? He shuddered at the thought that if they became homeless the authorities might take Donny away from them, put him in a foster home. Or some kind of institution. That would kill Martina, she couldn't take it. He couldn't let that happen, he just couldn't.

Derek was past the end of his rope, falling hard with nothing to grasp on to. He needed help but where could he turn? Then he thought about his brother, Albert. He would be humiliated asking him for money but what else could he do? Albert didn't have much himself, but Derek was desperate and knew his brother would lend a hand if he could.

Albert was a compact version of Derek—his face, his hands, the way he walked, all the features were similar but compressed into a shorter, stockier body. The brothers agreed to meet in the 24/7 Roadside Diner they had gone to since they were kids. The two Johnson men settled into one of the booths below a wood-paneled wall covered with deer heads and other taxidermied hunting trophies. A furry tail end of a deer mounted above the entrance to the men's toilet mooned the patrons. The brothers ordered black coffee. Derek wanted to add a piece of the banana cream pie he loved, but he barely had the money for two cups of coffee and he was determined to pay the tab.

Derek told his brother just enough to make him realize how bad things were, then added the desperate punch line: "Bro, we are on the verge of being evicted. Donny, Martina and me…we'll be out on the street." He choked on the words.

Albert's eyes opened wide with shock. He shook his head and said, "Derek, I'm so, so sorry. What a friggin' nightmare. That's terrible, we can't let that happen. We won't."

Derek coughed and found his voice again. "I can't make it anymore and I don't have the heart to tell Martina. I don't know what else to do, and I…I hate so much to ask, Albert, but can you possibly lend me a thousand dollars or so, just enough so we can at least pay the rent for a couple of months and keep our place for now? You know I'm good for it, I'll find a way to pay you back."

"Sure, sure, I'll do what I can."

"Thanks, Bro, I knew I could count on you. And it's only a loan, I'll make it up to you."

"I'm not worried about that. But maybe… Look, Derek, I've got to tell you something. We've also had some hard times. Remember four years ago, when Marcie lost her job? She ended up out of work for six months. We were broke, dead broke. You know what we did? We filed for bankruptcy, that's what. We went to a lawyer and filed for bankruptcy, we had no choice."

"Oh, Albert, I'm sorry, I didn't know. Don't worry about the money, forget it, we'll get by. I'll manage."

"Nah, it's OK, I'm not begging off. We're doing a little better now, I can spare you a few dollars. But I'm telling you our story because maybe you need to think about this bankruptcy thing yourself."

All Derek knew about bankruptcy was that it was some kind of stigma to be avoided, some legal way to avoid paying what you owed. The word was riddled with the sound of failure. But, maybe '*bankrupt*' was exactly what they were. The truth was, he couldn't pay his bills. And his wife and child would soon be thrown out of their home.

"OK," he said softly, "what do I do?"

Albert gave him the address and phone number of the lawyer and said, "He's not a bad guy, you'll like him right off. Straight-shooter, no mumbo-jumbo. Just make an appointment to see him, and I'll cover his bill for you. If it doesn't work out, get back to me and we'll see what else we can do to help."

"Albert…thanks, thanks so much. I hate to put this on you, you've got plenty to deal with yourself, but I'm really stuck, I'm…"

"It's OK, Derek." With a smile, Albert said, "You're a big boy, I don't worry about you, but I can't have my sister-in-law and nephew out on the street, can I? You know, if it comes down to it you guys can move in with us. We haven't got a big place but we've always got room for you."

The brothers shook hands warmly, then Derek impulsively hugged Albert, doing his best to keep from breaking into tears.

"Thanks, Albert, thanks again."

***

Derek was as uncomfortable as he could ever remember being as he drove to his meeting with the bankruptcy lawyer. He felt even further out of his element as he parked his dilapidated van next to the fancy cars in the parking lot behind the lawyer's office building. When he entered he wasn't sure where to go—he was in a spacious reception area with a high cathedral ceiling that arched over a huge stone fireplace. A ring of offices encircled the big room but there was no receptionist or information desk. As he looked around and tried to get his bearings, a man came out of one of the doors and greeted him.

"Mr. Johnson, it is, right? I understand your brother Albert referred you. I'm Curtis Crescenzi," said the man, extending his hand toward Derek.

Derek returned the greeting and shook the lawyer's hand. Crescenzi was an amiable man of indeterminate age with an easy smile, but Derek was surprised by his appearance. Empty jowls framed his sagging round face, hinting at some monumental weight loss his skin had not yet caught up with. The sleeves of his ill-fitting suit coat extended well over his wrists, the cuffs of his pants bunched up on his shoes. Derek couldn't help wondering whether the bankruptcy lawyer didn't have money enough to buy himself a new suit since he was always dealing with clients who had gone broke and might not be able to pay him. Well, whatever the man's reason was for being dressed like that, he had done well by Albert, that's what mattered.

Crescenzi led Derek into his office, a comfortable but not pretentious wood-paneled room with a large, cluttered desk and a small conference table. "Please, Mr. Johnson, have a seat," he said, pointing to a chair at the table. "Would you like some coffee? Water? I'm afraid I only have Diet Coke if you'd prefer a soda."

"I'm good, thanks. Sorry, but I'm in kind of a hurry, I took time off work and need to get back on the job as soon as I can."

"I totally understand, of course. Now, looks like you have something to show me?"

Derek handed the lawyer the stack of papers he had gathered in secret so Martina wouldn't know he was up to something. After some forty minutes scrutinizing the papers and listening carefully to Derek's story, Crescenzi looked at him with sympathetic eyes and said, "Mr. Johnson, I regret to tell you that you are indeed in a position to file for bankruptcy. You do not have nearly enough funds or other assets to pay your debts, and I am sure you realize you wouldn't be able to pay them off if you live to be two hundred years old at the rate you're going. If you do decide to file for bankruptcy I will help you, that's my job. And I will handle your case as inexpensively as possible, and prepare you to deal with the legal consequences of declaring bankruptcy. But, Mr. Johnson, in the interests of full disclosure I feel I should inform you that there may be an alternative."

"An alternative?" Derek said eagerly, immediately filled with an unexpected surge of hope. Maybe he could avoid the shame of going bankrupt, of admitting that he had failed to live up to his responsibility to care for his family?

"Even though this may not be in my own best interest, I must advise you that before you go down the path of bankruptcy you might consider filing a medical malpractice case to cover your bills and get the money you need to take care of Donny. I am not a malpractice lawyer and I have no idea whether you would have a good case, but after hearing about your son's problems I think it might be worth exploring the possibility. If you would like to learn more about your options, I can refer you to the best medical malpractice lawyer in this state, Fred Vagram. His firm is called Vagram & Marin, and I've known Fred for most of my career."

"Another lawyer? How could I afford to do that? I had to borrow money from my brother to come in to talk with you, and we could never pay a big law firm for something like a real lawsuit."

"Yes, your brother. Mr. Albert Johnson, good fellow, your brother. I am pleased to hear that he is back on his feet sufficiently to help you, and that he was willing to recommend our services. But, Mr. Johnson, that's the good part—a malpractice case won't cost you anything. The consultation to see if you have a good case is free and if do you file a lawsuit they won't charge you a legal fee unless you win the case. If Fred Vagram and his lawyers don't think you can win a malpractice case, so be it. If that happens, come back and see me and we will take care of you. We will work something out, and go through the procedures of declaring bankruptcy. But I would recommend that you speak with them first."

"My wife isn't going to like this. She won't want to sue Donny's doctors."

"You told me that she doesn't know that you are considering bankruptcy because you are on the verge of being evicted. Perhaps she will feel different about a malpractice lawsuit if she understands exactly why you have consulted with me about your financial picture."

Derek had a terrible vision of Martina sitting on the street with their disabled child.

"OK, you're right, I'll discuss it with my wife. Thank you, Mr. Crescenzi."

***

"*No!*" Martina screamed, "No, no, no! We can't do that, we can't. How could you ask me to do that?"

She collapsed onto their bed, sobbing uncontrollably, pounding her fists on the mattress.

Martina's reaction to the thought of suing Donny's doctors was even more impassioned than Derek had expected. He knew she had nothing but good feelings toward all the doctors who had taken care of her and her four baby boys, but he had not anticipated such extreme emotion. He waited silently. Finally, she stopped sobbing and looked up at him.

"Those doctors saved Donny's life, Derek. It was a miracle. Donny is a blessing, he is a gift from God that the doctors brought to me, to us. I know we have problems, Donny has problems, but who doesn't? No, I can't turn against those doctors, against Dr. Sarah Belden. She's so wonderful, so dedicated. She worked so hard for Donny, just like she did for Lenny and Denny. She suffered with us, I know she did. Please, Derek, please don't ask me to do that."

Derek was straining to be patient. He steeled himself for the worst message of all, that they were facing eviction from their little home, the only home the three of them had ever known together.

"Yes, Honey, I agree. Totally. Dr. Belden, Dr. Yoder, Dr. Silvestre, lots of the doctors have been good to us and Donny. And of course I am grateful for having Donny, I love him with all my heart, you know that. But the hospital, the labs, the other doctors, they're killing us. We are broke, way beyond broke. Honey, here's how bad it is: we may get evicted. Evicted, out on the street, no roof over our heads, no home for you, for me, for Donny. I am already working as hard as I can, and we can't keep up with the bills. I can't go on, Sweetheart. We have to do something. Let's just talk with the lawyers, see what they say. We don't have to decide anything yet, nothing final, just a conversation. It won't cost anything, nothing at all. Just one time. Please. I…I."

The words caught in his throat. It was painful enough admitting failure to himself, let alone to his wife.

Martina began sobbing again. She was lost, this was too much for her. She had never seen Derek plead like this, never heard his voice break with emotion, never imagined they might be out on the street. She had hardly noticed that Derek was wearing thin. All of her energy had gone into taking care of Donny. She was too stunned to speak for a few torturous moments. At last she stammered, "E…*evicted*? We might be evicted from this house, from our home? Donny out on the street?" Another long pause, then she nodded and said softly, "OK, we can talk with them."

Chapter 15: Counsel For The Plaintiffs

Driving to work in the pre-dawn haze a few days after his meeting with the bankruptcy lawyer, Derek's eyes were drawn to a brilliantly-lit billboard that emerged through the mist. The advertisement was dominated by an gigantic photo of a man's face with a huge, toothy smile. *FRED VAGRAM, ATTORNEY* was printed in enormous letters above the face. A sudden flash of recognition went through Derek: this was the malpractice lawyer Curtis Crescenzi had recommended. He pulled his van to the side of the road to read the rest of the sign:

Are You One of the Many Victims of Medical Malpractice?
Get All The Money You Are Entitled To!
FRED VAGRAM is Your Lawyer
No Legal Fee Unless FRED Wins Your Case
Vagram & Marin—The Most Successful
Personal Injury Law Firm in America
Call FRED Today: 1-555-GET-EVEN

Staring at the photo, Derek realized he had seen that face many times—not only on billboards by the side of every major road but also on countless television ads, on the back cover of the phone book, on buses and taxis, seemingly everywhere in the town. As he pulled back into traffic, Derek was impressed by the lawyer's prominence. If he was taking his problems to such a big-shot lawyer, he must be doing the right thing. And it wouldn't cost him anything. He would call Fred Vagram as soon as he could get to a phone.

***

Fred Vagram's associate, Dr. Sanjay Fijam, Esquire, was in a quandary. Sitting at his desk in one of the expensively furnished offices in a lavish suite that Vagram had personally designed to impress potential clients, Sanjay Fijam stared at the thick file in front of him. Vagram had ordered Fijam to do a preliminary assessment of the medical record on the case that the young Johnson man had brought to the law firm on the recommendation of Curtis Crescenzi. Fijam was to determine whether there was a strong enough malpractice case for Vagram & Marin to bother with. He had gone through the six-inch thick copy of Donny Johnson's medical records over and over for nearly three days, and he still wasn't sure whether the firm should take the case. At first blush, the child's plight seemed to have all the features of a very strong malpractice lawsuit: a tragic, sympathetic plaintiff who would need many millions of dollars in damages to pay for a lifetime of medical expenses and surgical procedures, special education, physical therapy, customized braces, wheelchairs, personal care services. Even more money to compensate for pain and suffering the child would have to endure for as long as he lived, and the pain and suffering his parents went through every day. More money for lost wages, since this child would never be able to get a job and lead a normal life.

And most important to his boss, Fred Vagram, if they prevailed in the lawsuit the law firm would end up with one-third or more of the money.

Fijam knew that a heartbreaking case like this would win over any jury—if they could get to trial. Jurors would melt out of sympathy when the family wheeled the child into the courtroom. They would feel such pity for this poor little boy and his long-suffering parents they would award them a big bundle of money out of pure compassion even if their legal case wasn't all that strong. Lots of juries would think that it was better to take money from some rich doctors and big hospitals than to let the family bear an excruciating financial burden on top of a horrendous personal tragedy. Besides, everyone knew the money really came from insurance companies anyway, and no one loved insurance companies.

Representing a helpless, crippled little boy and his tortured parents in a lawsuit would give the law firm the chance to ease the family's burdens. Even the threat of going to trial against the notorious Fred Vagram might pressure the other side to settle the case quickly.

Donny Johnson was almost the perfect plaintiff.

Almost.

The dilemma for Sanjay Fijam was that to have a viable chance of getting the case in front of a jury they would have to convince a judge that they met the legal requirements to let their case go forward. But having been trained not only as a lawyer but also as a physician, he could not swear that there was a serious problem with the medical care that this child had received. Everything that was done for Donny Johnson seemed to comply with standard medical practice.

As always, Fijam had done his homework. He had carefully refreshed his knowledge of pediatrics by studying sections of *Nelson's Textbook on Pediatrics* from the 11th edition in 1979 through the 14th edition from 1992, had read through numerous neonatology texts and several other reference books to check on what standard medical practice in caring for premature babies was from the late-1980s through the early 1990s, had searched diligently through scientific journals for any breakthroughs in treatment. Studying Donny Johnson's medical records, Fijam had spotted a few things here and there he might find fault with: a low oxygen reading that took a bit longer to correct than it should have, a point at which the pH of the boy's blood was marginally too far into the acid range for a few hours. But it would be impossible to show that this child's problems resulted directly from a handful of minor slip-ups. After all his research he could find no lapse from standard medical or nursing care that he could in good faith claim was the cause of Donny Johnson's many difficulties. The child presented a tragic situation indeed, but Sanjay Fijam concluded that there was no way to prove medical negligence. That meant no chance of ever getting Donny Johnson in front of a jury, let alone winning a lawsuit. No negligence, no malpractice, no multi-million dollar recovery. Case dismissed.

Sanjay Fijam was trapped between the imperatives of his two professions. As a physician, Sanjay Fijam knew that this child had gotten devoted and skilled medical care and tireless, expert nursing care, and that his physical and mental problems were probably unavoidable. And Fijam was sensitive to the harm he could wreak to the psyche and even the careers of physicians if he accused them of malpractice when they had really done the best job they or anyone could have done. But Sanjay Fijam was Donny Johnson's lawyer, not his doctor. His job as a lawyer was to find a way to help his client, not to worry about collateral damage to innocent doctors.

And it wasn't just legal and medical considerations that gnawed at Sanjay Fijam: the family had been tormented mercilessly by the business side of health care. Fijam was repulsed by the stack of unimaginable bills, threatening letters, dire warnings from bill collectors, that was as thick as the child's medical records. If he could figure out a way to move the case forward, Fijam would take some deep satisfaction in the rough justice of draining a few dollars from the bloated medical enterprise to alleviate the unfortunate lives of Donny and his devoted parents.

Sanjay Fijam had not intended to become a lawyer when he immigrated to the United States. Quite the opposite—he had cherished hopes of practicing medicine in his adopted country. But his dream had been crushed by legal obstacles, bureaucracy, and outright prejudice that would forever deny him a medical license. So he had found himself driving a taxi for a meager living. He had come to accept that driving a cab was to be his dire fate—until a Hindu Goddess rescued him late one October night. The four-handed Goddess Lakshmi, who is said to bless with prosperity those she finds awake on the full-moon night of Kojagari Poornima, bestowed her blessing on Fijam while he was cruising for passengers under a stunning harvest moon. He had been flagged down by a man who got into his cab and stunned Fijam with a stentorious voice that reverberated around the confines of the cab like shock waves from field artillery blasts. The man with the booming voice turned out to be Fred Vagram, who engaged Fijam in conversation and asked why an obviously well-educated man like him was driving a taxi. When Fijam told him that he was a physician but had been rebuffed in his efforts to practice medicine in this country, Vagram surprised him by offering him a job. He explained that he was a lawyer who was looking for someone with medical training to do investigations of potential malpractice cases.

The pain in Fijam's ears from Vagram's bellowing voice melted away at the prospect of a professional position. Vagram's offer would liberate him from the disgrace of working behind the steering wheel of a taxi. As soon as he got home he told his wife about the miracle that had just happened under the Kojagari Poornima moon and the couple immediately offered prayers of thanks to Lakshmi.

After only a few months on the new job, Fijam realized he actually enjoyed the work, so he enrolled in law school at night, secretly taking one course that first semester. Ultimately, he graduated at the top of his class, passed the bar exam, and became a Junior Associate lawyer at Vagram & Marin. As a lowly Associate,

Fijam was well aware that he was being exploited ruthlessly and had little likelihood of becoming a partner in the firm, but he harbored no resentment. After all, Fred Vagram had saved him from daily humiliation in the taxi and given him a new, relatively prosperous life. And he had no real options, since suing doctors as a plaintiff's attorney was the final kiss of death for his longstanding dream of practicing medicine in the U.S. So be it, he thought. He was putting his medical training to good use, even if he was no longer a real doctor.

He reviewed Donny Johnson's file one more time before reaching his difficult conclusion: the firm should not take the case. As sympathetic as he was to the plight of this dreadfully handicapped child, he was sure the legal case just wasn't there. The case would be dismissed before it ever got to a jury. He folded up the case file in front of him and added an additional folder on top with his analysis, a one-page summary that read:

"*Medical analysis*: My medical opinion is that, although there have been significant advances in the care of severely premature infants since the time of this child's birth, nearly everything that was done to and for this child met the standard of care at the time it was delivered.

Legal analysis: Since there was no breach of the standard of care that can be shown to have caused this child's problems, there was no medical negligence.

Conclusion: I believe it is too risky for the firm to take this case, since a favorable outcome is not supported in the medical or legal analysis."

Fijam handed the neat stack to Fred Vagram's receptionist, a young man named Tommy.

"This is for my meeting Thursday at 10 with Mr. Vagram."

Tommy looked up at Sanjay with his ambiguously flirtatious smile that never failed to be slightly disconcerting and said in his lilting voice, "Just let me check." He opened Vagram's appointment calendar and said, "Ah, yes, there it is, you bet. I'll see you then, *Doctor* Fijam."

Sanjay could feel Tommy's eyes on his back as he left the outer office and headed down the hallway.

***

Fred Vagram conducted business from the penthouse suite of a modern 12-story office building with a spectacular vista of the city's

108

skyline. The rest of the attorneys in the firm had offices one level down, occupying an entire floor that connected with Vagram's penthouse via an elaborate interior circular stairway. When Tommy ushered Sanjay up the staircase and into Fred Vagram's expansive office, the senior partner looked up from the file folder with Fijam's analysis of the Johnson case and greeted him with his customary, "Hey, Doc." Vagram's welcome was a backhanded compliment—it acknowledged Fijam's medical background but could not conceal a tinge of the antagonism Vagram harbored toward any physician. "So you don't think we've got a case here, huh?" he said, speaking as loud as if Sanjay were disappearing down the staircase out of earshot and he wanted to call him back.

Fred Vagram's deep voice was always several decibels louder than necessary. Everyone except people who were stone deaf found the voice annoying, so grating it was often excruciating for them to be in his presence. But Vagram didn't seem to notice, and at this point in his life no one in his circle dared to complain. At first people would presume he was compensating for being hard of hearing, but they soon learned that was a dangerous assumption. Vagram's hearing was excellent. He was able to pick up careless chatter down a hallway or across a large room, and had no compunction about using information he had overheard against those who thought he must be deaf.

As successful as Fred Vagram had been, part of him still felt unfulfilled. There was one goal he had set that remained for him to accomplish: winning million-dollar judgments against *every* hospital in town. Vagram had announced that objective early in his career, and had gone on to win so many big malpractice cases that the legal community had long since assumed that he had hit his target. The rumor of his having achieved universal success in suing hospitals was so often repeated that it became legendary in legal circles. But Fred Vagram knew there was one hospital left: Memorial General. He had never won a million-dollar judgment against Memorial General because it had been a public hospital and the law provided government agencies with limited immunity against lawsuits. All his big victories had been against private hospitals. But now things had changed: like a lot of public hospitals that wanted to cash in on Medicare, Medicaid and private insurance, Memorial General had become a public-private corporation. The special protections against a big lawsuit it had long enjoyed might no longer be a barrier. Fred

Vagram relished the thought that this case might give him that long-awaited opportunity to complete his collection, to achieve a perfect score, to get a million dollars or more out of every hospital in town, no matter what.

Sanjay Fijam started to explain—actually, he felt more like he had to defend—his opinion.

"Mr. Vagram," he began, almost apologetically, "I do not believe that the medical care in this case failed to meet the standard of care, and thus we cannot establish negligence."

Even after a decade of working his way up in the firm, Sanjay did not feel that he had the prerogative to address the firm's *Name Partner* by his first name.

"You know what, Doc?" Vagram boomed. "I think I have a pretty good idea of what it takes to win a case of medical negligence. But what else might we have going for us here? What else did you learn when you won that Torts Prize in law school, huh?"

Sanjay recognized yet another backhanded compliment, but his skin had hardened to Vagram's derisive jabs.

"Most juries would be extremely sympathetic to the child and his family once they saw how severely handicapped he was and heard how much the family has suffered."

"Yeah, but you didn't learn that in law school, you learned that right here in this law firm. What else?"

"What else, Mr. Vagram?" he replied softly, raising his eyes in thought as he repeated the words to stall for time. Sanjay was trying to figure out what was running through the crafty mind of his boss. He had spent three days thinking about this case, and his report contained every thought that had come to him, but he could sense now that he had missed something. Vagram had a legal trick up his sleeve that Sanjay had not anticipated. "*What else? What else?*" he asked himself.

"OK, Doc, you say that the medical care was up to par—at least the medical care that was generally accepted *at the time this kid was born*. How about a few years later? How about now?"

"Yes, I have also looked into current practice, and you are certainly correct. Treatments for babies this small with his problems have improved dramatically since then. Now there are artificial substances that are sprayed into the baby's lungs to help them stay open, they mimic the natural 'surfactant' such young babies are not yet producing enough of. There are new imaging machines that let us see hemorrhages into their brains, and new techniques for avoiding some of the consequences. There are new surgical operations and even some non-surgical methods of dealing with the heart problems such babies often experience. But none of that was available back then in most hospitals, it was all just being developed at major research centers. This baby got treated well with the medical care that was generally available, and that is the legal requirement. So, Mr. Vagram, I am not sure how these subsequent advances in care are relevant for this particular case?"

"Were any of those fancy new things available in this town when this baby was born? How about University Hospital? Were they doing those things then?"

Fijam hesitated. He sensed that Vagram was leading him into a trap. "Yes, there were several research protocols underway at University Hospital at that time. The University was part of a network of research centers across the country that were conducting studies that ultimately led to a number of the breakthrough treatments we now have. But this baby was at Memorial General Hospital, not University Hospital."

"What if they should never have tried to treat him at Memorial? What if they should have transferred him immediately? Did the doctors who took care of him at Memorial know about the new treatments that were available at the University?"

A thoroughly competent, albeit not highly creative, lawyer, Sanjay Fijam immediately realized where Fred Vagram was going. The cagey lawyer's point struck him like a sharp punch squarely between the eyes. Or worse, like a one-two punch to his guts and his nuts. Once again Vagram had demonstrated his skill at crafting ingenious legal theories when there was a very large amount of money at stake. He also knew Vagram would not be asking these questions if he did not already know the answers, so Fijam was relieved that he, too, now saw the legal implications of Vagram's questions.

"Again, you are quite right, Mr. Vagram. Dr. Giuliana Silvestre was the attending physician at Memorial General on this case, and she was also on the staff at the University. In fact, she was the Principal Investigator for many of the research studies I referred to that led to the breakthroughs that are now generally accepted. And, Sir, if Memorial General should never have tried to treat this baby at all, if caring for this baby was beyond its capabilities and the

111

doctors knew that there were alternatives, then perhaps we are not even considering a case of simple Medical Negligence. We may well be able to show Gross Negligence, a flagrant disregard for this baby's interests. In that case the consequences would be quite different."

"And if it's Gross Negligence, Doc, just what are those consequences?" continued Fred Vagram, getting excited and turning the seemingly limitless volume switch on his voice up another few clicks.

Sanjay had seen this coming as well.

"We could be looking at punitive damages as well as compensatory damages."

"You know, Doc, I knew you were a good doctor, that's why I hired you. And now you're a good lawyer."

Sanjay nodded in appreciation, but he had learned that this was Fred Vagram's style: compliments cost him nothing. Vagram had only hired him because his medical background came at a bargain price and helped the blustery lawyer get rich.

"One caveat, however, Mr. Vagram, if you please. It may be difficult to establish causation. I am not sure that we can show that the failure to transfer him to the University caused his handicaps. The scientific studies, the medical literature, suggest that the majority of cases of cerebral palsy are of unknown cause. The rate of cerebral palsy is higher in premature infants, but the reasons are not fully understood. The cause is most likely some intrauterine trauma that could not be avoided."

"Ah, Doc, you may have all the science stuff right, but you're forgetting the most important thing. When we get in a courtroom, statistics don't make a damn bit of difference to a jury. To them, it's what they believe about this kid, just this one kid that's sitting in his wheelchair right in front of them. You're not saying that the medical care he received—and the more advanced care he missed out on—*could not* have caused the problems, are you?"

"Certainly not, Mr. Vagram. Medical care could be implicated, of course. In any particular case that would be a possibility, however unlikely."

"So that gives us enough for the judge to let this get to a jury, and if a jury ever sees this kid, they aren't going to be worrying about statistics, believe me. And when we convince them that he wasn't even treated at the right place, in addition to the compensation they'll give this kid to cover his medical bills and other treatments and all the pain and suffering he and his family have endured, they'll want to punish Memorial General and these doctors for grossly disregarding their duty to this child. Punitive damages, Doc. Punitive means punishment, big punishment. We ask for millions of dollars, however much it would take to teach them a lesson. Three times as much as compensatory damages, maybe ten times as much, however much it takes. Still think we should take a pass on this case, Doc?"

Sanjay Fijam said nothing, simply nodding his assent.

"Then OK, that's it for today. Let's get going on this."

As he collected his file and withdrew from Vagram's office, Fijam had to admit that Fred Vagram was right. Vagram had come up with something that he had missed. Again. As he walked back down the circular staircase to his own office his ears were still throbbing from Vagram's voice.

Fijam returned to his desk to ponder the new strategy, but Fred Vagram was done for the day. Vagram was enjoying his small triumph over a doctor and savoring the prospect of nailing Memorial General for millions of dollars. He had earned a bit of a celebration, dinner at an expensive restaurant with his long-time assistant, Sally Lindores. Before he and Sally could leave the office together, however, Vagram had to make a phone call, the one call he never asked Sally to place for him: a call to tell his wife that he would be out late entertaining an important client who showed up at the last minute. Delivered in his softest voice, the one reserved for such moments, the statement was partly true: he would indeed be out late entertaining, only not with a client, and certainly not with someone who had shown up unexpectedly. He would be with his assistant. His very personal assistant.

Chapter 16: The Case

Martina Johnson sat folded inside herself, her legs crossed at the knee, her right foot twisted around her left calf, her chin tucked tightly against her chest, her arms wrapped around her torso as though she were trying to endure a winter wind with no coat. Already deeply troubled by what she and Derek were doing and disconcerted at the sight of the plush offices of the Vagram law firm, she was rattled to the breaking point by the strange lawyer's overpowering voice. She looked up and pleaded softly, "Mr. Vagram, please, isn't there any way we could do this without suing Dr. Belden? She's such a dedicated doctor. She worked so hard to save Donny, this will just kill her. Please, can't we just leave her out of this?"

"Mrs. Johnson, to get what Donny needs we must make decisions that are necessary under our legal system. Sometimes those decisions may not feel right to you."

Fred Vagram was trying to sound sympathetic, but his words came out with such bombastic force that they lost whatever consoling tone he may have intended.

"Dr. Belden could well be a fine doctor, a wonderful person, but that isn't what this lawsuit is all about. This is about using the law to provide enough money for you to take care of Donny and pay off your bills. If we leave Dr. Belden out, the hospital and the other doctors will just confuse things by blaming her. They will say that we left out the key doctor and we cannot hold them accountable without her."

Martina nodded halfheartedly, intending to signal that she understood his point, not that she agreed with the course of action. A thought was forming in her head. She opened her mouth to speak, but Vagram just continued talking. His voice overwhelmed her. She could not think, let alone argue with this man.

114

Fred Vagram was gifted at dealing with hesitant clients.

"Let me tell you one other thing: I know that people hate the idea of being sued and hauled into court, but doctors are used to it. For them it's just a nuisance that happens all the time in their line of work."

Speaking with such force that neither Martina nor Derek could do anything but hear him out, Vagram was reciting a falsehood he had reiterated hundreds of times in the early stages of lawsuits. He found that wavering clients who were anxious about offending their revered physicians often wanted to believe his reassuring misrepresentations.

"Not that doctors are happy or complacent about getting sued, of course not. Doctors generally despise lawyers. They complain bitterly about the malpractice system. But they know better than to take it personally. Because it really isn't personal, it's part of their business. They don't even stand to lose money since nothing will come out of their own pockets. They pay big premiums to have malpractice insurance, and they know their insurance company will foot the bill. And since the insurance company stands to lose, they'll also pay for excellent lawyers to defend them. So the doctors don't lose money. And they don't have to worry about being forced to stop practicing medicine no matter how bad their mistakes are since they never lose their licenses. In any case, how the doctors feel doesn't make any difference. We have to name all the doctors in this lawsuit or we would shoot ourselves in the foot. I can't do that. I can't let you bring a defective lawsuit that will fail before it gets started. We owe it to Donny to give it our best shot. So you understand, we must include Dr. Belden."

He was making a statement, not asking their permission to sue Sarah Belden. Derek nodded in agreement, but Martina didn't move. She sat frozen, silent, not agreeing or disagreeing, not even trying to speak, still trying to retreat into a cocoon that could protect her from the alien surroundings.

Vagram paused only briefly, then continued.

"I want to explain to you what will be happening. After Mr. Johnson's first visit with us, we got copies of all the medical records from Donny's birth, from all those months in Memorial General." Gesturing toward the small, olive-skinned man sitting quietly off to one side, Vagram continued, "My colleague, Dr. Sanjay Fijam—he's both a lawyer and a doctor, strange as that may sound—spent several

115

days looking through your son's records. He has also studied a number of medical books and spoken with experts. We have reached a very serious conclusion: Donny should *never* have been treated at Memorial General. They kept him from getting proper medical care."

More liberties, more half-truths, since it was Vagram, not Fijam, who had teased out that conclusion.

"No, no, that's not right, that's not what happened," cried Martina, breaking through her protective shell. She jumped up from her chair and stepped toward Fred Vagram, waving her arms back and forth in disagreement. "No! How can you say that? I had all my babies at Memorial General. The doctors there were wonderful. That can't be right. Not take care of Donny there? I *wanted* to go to Memorial General, I didn't want to go anywhere else."

She had started to defend the hospital and the doctors without thinking, then just as suddenly a pang of guilt washed over her like a torrent of icy water, sending a cold chill through her body. She felt faint and went pale as the blood drained from her head. Her knees buckled under her and she collapsed back into her chair.

"Oh, oh my God," she gasped. "Are you saying I shouldn't have gone there? I went to the wrong hospital? Was this my fault? What was I supposed to do? I…I didn't know what else to do. I…"

Martina's panic-stricken voice trailed off as the weight of the implication that she might have caused Donny's problems descended on her. She raised her eyes toward Derek, but her husband had no answer to her pleading, just a helpless look on his face, as though he didn't quite understand what Vagram was getting at either.

"Not at all, Mrs. Johnson, you went to the right hospital." For the first time, Vagram lowered his volume. "It wasn't your fault, that's not what we're saying, not at all. *After* Donny was born, he should have been transferred to the University. Donny was so small he needed even more specialized care than he received at Memorial General. They had never had a baby his size there before. They were not able to give him everything he needed."

Derek found his voice. "I don't understand, Mr. Vagram. Donny was in an intensive care unit with other little babies. He was on a breathing machine, and they kept him in an incubator. How could they have moved him across town, even if he would have been better off at the University?"

"That is not so difficult, actually," interjected Sanjay Fijam in soft tones, his calm medical air a relief to the Johnsons after the booming Vagram voice. He was well practiced now in forming his words carefully, delivering them slowly, keeping the pitch of his voice flat to minimize the sing-song cadence of the English spoken in his native India. "You see, Mr. and Mrs. Johnson, small babies, sick babies, get born in different hospitals all over the state, some far away in quite rural areas. It turns out there is a very sophisticated system to transport babies to the University. Sometimes they are carried by ambulance, sometimes by helicopter. Highly trained nurses go along, and sometimes the neonatologist as well. The baby stays in an incubator and gets help breathing the whole time. It's like a mobile Intensive Care Unit. And that system was in place when Donny was born, in fact it had been working quite well for almost ten years by then. There was no reason he could not have been transferred a few short miles across town."

As if on cue, Martina and Derek both slumped back in their chairs. They had anticipated that the lawyers might tell them that maybe, just maybe, something had gone wrong at Memorial General that had caused Donny's problems or made them worse. But not this. It had never crossed their minds that Donny should have been sent to another hospital, should have been taken care of somewhere else.

Derek wiped at the drops of sweat streaming down his brow and felt a tinge of—of what? Anger? Confusion? Heartbreak?

Still unsure just what he was feeling, Derek said, "Are you telling us that Donny might…might have been normal if he had been sent to the other hospital? We—Donny—we're going through all of this for no good reason? Is that what you're saying?"

Fred Vagram had no problem stretching another point to drive it home, however heartless the impact on the distraught couple. Decades of maneuvering through the emotional maelstroms his potential clients were experiencing had taught him how to close the deal, how to get their assent, their signatures on a retainer agreement. He had to overcome their reluctance to go up against the doctors and the hospital. Besides, he told himself, he was drawing legal conclusions, not medical ones. He wasn't the one who was responsible for judging the science, he was responsible for knowing what the legal consequences of the doctors' actions might be. And mostly he was the one who knew how a jury might react to his story. He was doing it all for the benefit of the Johnson family.

117

"Yes," he said, even more emphatically. "That's what we are saying. That's what I am telling you now, and that's what we will prove in this lawsuit."

Martina gasped.

"Oh my God, my God. All Donny's suffering, all his problems. Not necessary? How? How could that be?"

"My colleague, Dr. Fijam, can explain in more detail later on. But the simple explanation is this: the doctors and nurses at Memorial General tried hard, I'll give them that credit, but the deck was stacked against them. They didn't have the latest equipment, the newest medicines. They just weren't able to provide the most up-to-date medical care. They did the best they could with what they had. So I understand why you think kindly of them." Then, unwilling to soften the blow further, he exaggerated Sanjay Fijam's initial report of some minor errors in Donny's care, adding, "We actually think there were some serious mistakes made at that hospital as well, and we will include those in our lawsuit. But the bigger picture is that the University had different ways to treat Donny, better ways. Some of those treatments were still being tested, some were pretty well proven to work. And just about everything that was available there when Donny was born has now come into use everywhere—even at Memorial General. But back then, Memorial General was behind the times, *and they knew it.*"

Derek fumbled for words. "So…they…they didn't…What does all of that mean?"

"This is very important, a crucial legal point, actually. Let me explain. They knew things weren't up to date at Memorial General because the very same doctors who were taking care of him there would have been in charge of his case at the University. Dr. Giuliana Silvestre knew all about the more sophisticated care at the University because that's where she worked most of the time. And she was doing a lot of the important research that now has paid off. Dr. Belden had spent months at the University Hospital, she knew what they could do there. Lots of babies like Donny turn out entirely normal when they get more modern care. So the heart of our lawsuit is that Donny was never given a fair chance. He had no opportunity to get the kind of medical care that would have made a difference. For whatever reason, the doctors and the hospital kept him from being treated properly. That's just not right, they should not be allowed to get away with what they did to Donny, and we will not let them."

"I just...I just don't know," Martina stammered, unable to form a complete response.

Derek clenched his teeth to suppress the rage welling up inside him at the thought that Donny might have been normal if he had been moved to the other hospital. But then he realized that it didn't help to think about whether things might have turned out any different. They couldn't change the past. Donny was who he was, and he needed a lot of attention. Expensive attention. And he and Martina couldn't give their son what he needed if they didn't get help. Derek knew what he had to do: he had to make Martina understand how desperate they were.

"Honey, we're stuck. It's either this, or we have to go back to the other lawyer and file bankruptcy. And even if we did, we still wouldn't have enough money to care properly for Donny, not ever. This is our...this is Donny's only real chance, Honey. Please."

Like a used car salesman acting out the charade of having extracted a once-in-a-lifetime price concession from his sales manager, Fred Vagram was ready with his final argument, the huckster pitch that would close the deal.

"And, Mr. and Mrs. Johnson, our law firm will take care of your creditors and the bill collection agencies right now, we'll get them to back off. You won't be evicted. You won't have to declare bankruptcy. It's our money that will be on the line to protect you while the case goes forward, you don't have to risk anything. This is a no-lose situation for you, with a very good chance that all of your financial troubles will be behind you forever."

A little more than one hour later, Derek and Martina had signed the retainer agreement and were in Derek's van, heading home to relieve their babysitter. Derek had modified his aging van for transporting Donny. He built a portable wooden ramp to slide the wheelchair through the side door, and set a low frame on the floor to hold the chair more or less in place. When his co-workers chided him about the jerry-rigged contraption made of plywood and two-by-fours instead of steel he retorted defensively, "I'm a carpenter, not a welder." But in truth he was deeply embarrassed that he could not even afford materials for a proper homemade transport, let alone a real van conversion. Derek was troubled not just because the whole thing looked embarrassingly homemade, but more important, he knew that the restraining frame was not up to any standards, certainly not like real brackets. He tried to reassure himself that it was OK because it worked fairly well and he was a careful driver. But he knew better. The frame was barely adequate since it simply formed a low wall around the chair's large wheels to keep the chair from rolling around in the van. The old leather straps he belted onto the wheels of the chair did not provide any real security for a sudden stop. And god forbid what would happen if his van were to roll over. It hurt him deeply that this was the best he could do for his son, that there was no way he could afford to buy a specially-equipped van, a proper one with a power ramp and a hydraulic lift and heavy-duty steel braces to hold the chair. The lawsuit was their only hope.

As they drove home, Derek strained to reassure his wife.

"We're doing the right thing, Sweetheart, we have to try to help Donny. We can't afford to take care of him properly. It's killing us and we're not doing right by him."

Derek knew Martina would never fully agree. She didn't know what it was like to feel responsible for paying the bills, she had no idea what Derek was going through trying to make a decent life in the face of their desperate financial situation. Martina didn't take the calls from the bill collectors, she didn't hear the threats that they would be evicted. But he was deeply sympathetic with her, not angry. Martina had her own cross to bear. She had to endure the constant strain of staying home and nursing Donny. Fair enough, he told himself, he was infinitely grateful to Martina for caring for their damaged boy, he had no idea what he could possibly have done without her. They were in this together, but what they were in was so, so painful.

Derek waited for Martina to respond, but once again she was curled up tight, this time in her usual spot on the passenger side of the van's wide cab. Her legs were tucked up under her on the seat, her head slumped against the passenger-side door, her arms crossed tightly over her chest. Her unattached seat belt flopped uselessly across the seat of the van, its buckle dangling onto the floor, the shoulder-harness end still hanging in place on the sidewall. Her recklessness irritated him. Why wouldn't Martina use the goddamn seat belt? What was the matter with her, anyway? Did she want to end up in a wheelchair like Donny?

He rebuked himself instantly for his angry thought. His frustration with his wife over their recurring seat belt disagreement was not the most important issue to worry about at the moment. He tried again to console her.

"It's OK, Sweetheart, it'll be OK."

Still Martina said nothing. Not expecting her to respond, Derek continued. "Dr. Belden was good to you, good to all of us, yes. She tried so hard, she was so nice. But we need to watch out for Donny. We need to watch out for our son."

The last words choked in his throat. Our son. He's our son, our only son. He's all we've got.

Martina's only response was to curl up even tighter, tucking her face into her skirt between her knees, sobbing loudly. She never said a word, hardly moved at all until they pulled into the driveway of their home when she suddenly opened the door and jumped out before Derek had brought the van to a complete stop.

"Don't do that, Martina, don't open the door while the van is moving," Derek yelled for what seemed the ten-thousandth time, but as usual it had no effect on his wife. She was running across the grass to get back to Donny and was in the house before Derek had parked the van and shut down the engine. Derek came in through the side door of the tiny bungalow and saw Martina hugging Donny, tears running down her face. Donny was giggling contentedly in his mother's arms.

Derek greeted Charlie Brand, their neighbor's twenty-year old son who lived at home and couldn't find regular work, so he watched Donny once in a while for the few dollars the Johnsons could pay him. "Hi Charlie, how was Donny?"

"Not bad, he slept for a while, then we mostly watched television. He likes just about anything I put on."

"Thanks for sitting with him."

"Oh, it was OK, I didn't have to do much."

"Well, that's good, considering you'll never get rich on this job," Derek said as he handed Charlie everything he had in his wallet: seven dollars.

"Thanks, Mr. Johnson. What's the matter with Mrs. Johnson?" Charlie was looking at Martina, who was still holding Donny and crying.

"She's fine, she doesn't get away from Donny much, I guess. So she gets worried. Do you want a ride anywhere?" Derek was almost hoping that Charlie would ask to be driven downtown, anywhere.

"Nah, thanks, I'm just going home, I'll walk."

"Well, thanks again."

"Sure. See you."

Charlie walked closer to Martina and Donny.

"Good-bye Mrs. Johnson. So long Donny."

Martina didn't turn around or respond. Donny moved his right hand to wave at Charlie, but couldn't quite get it free from his mother's embrace. The child made a few friendly sounds, inarticulate noises that everyone understood was his way of saying farewell.

Derek stepped outside with Charlie and lit a cigarette as the young man walked away. He took a deep drag, filling his throat and lungs with warm smoke as he lowered himself onto the front step of the porch. Time enough to go into the house, into the world of problems that loomed inside. He needed to be outside, to be alone for a few minutes. He leaned against the base of one of the porch's support posts. Derek had fixed up those posts lovingly when they first moved in, had repaired and painted them bright red and was so proud of how they lit up the front of the house. Now he cringed as his eyes focused on the lower end of the post—the paint was chipping and peeling, exposed raw wood was showing through the heavily worn finish.

"This is rough," Derek sighed aloud to himself. "I thought I'd have this place sparkling by now and we'd own it, it'd be ours." No one was listening but somehow he had to let out the thoughts that were careening through his head, bouncing painfully off the bones of his skull, stinging his brain. He took another deep drag on the cigarette and exhaled slowly. "We're in it pretty deep. Those lawyers had better be right, or we're going to be even worse off. She's on the edge and I'm getting close. Those lawyers had better be right."

Chapter 17: At Your Service

Despite his university education and multi-lingual fluency, the one skill that had sustained Chih-Wheh Chon when he emigrated from Beijing to the United States was his ability to maneuver a bicycle through the teeming streets of a crowded city, however sloppy and miserable the weather. For several long years he had survived as a bicycle messenger, delivering packages for a pittance. But now he had risen up, he had found a new job. Yes, he was still a delivery man but this was different, very different. Now his countless trips around the city paid well, at least $100 each, half for him, half for the company. Now he traveled mostly by bus or cab, riding his bicycle only when he wanted the exercise or the bike was the easiest way to get where he needed to go. Now he was making personal deliveries, packages he had to give directly to the people they were addressed to. The new job did have one unsavory part: just about every person he delivered one of these packages to reacted as if they wanted to kill him, or kill themselves, or kill someone else. But he was compensated well enough to put up with a few tirades now and then.

***

As she finished her routine check-up of the bruising toddler with those long blond curls mothers love and fathers can't wait to have the barber cut off, Dr. Sarah Belden smiled at Freddie Anthony's mother and said, "What a good-looking boy, you've got, Mrs. Anthony. He's big, strong, and way ahead of all his landmarks for his age. When you get home you should childproof all the cabinets and drawers with anything that might be toxic: drugs, cleaning solutions, whatever is hazardous. It's pretty much his full-time job to get into anything he can for the next few years and he'll be very good at exploring everything in your house. But he doesn't

123

know what's dangerous and what isn't yet. He needs to learn, so don't let up or he'll learn the hard way. Boys really will be boys, you'll discover just how true that is. We'll see him again in six months, then, Mrs. Anthony."

Dr. Sarah Belden savored the sight of the picture-perfect child in his overalls and lumberjack shirt and reflected on how much she loved being a pediatrician in private practice. She truly enjoyed watching normal children like Freddie grow and develop while helping their parents learn about and deal with the different stages of childhood. She never tired of giving the same short educational speeches five or ten or twenty times every day. For the youngest ones the problems were pretty much the same as they had been for generations. *"She never seems to eat anything, will she starve?" "Is it normal for his stool to be green like that?" "What's that purple spot on his back?" "She just won't sleep at night, she cries all the time, what can we do?"* Then there were questions that had arisen in more recent times. *"Do immunizations really cause autism?" "Why does she get so many colds since she started day care?"*

The questions were more complex and the answers more elusive when her patients were adolescents experimenting with deadly temptations: cars, alcohol, sex, drugs, steroids. Then her role wasn't so agreeable, but she was motivated to help them and their families understand what was going on and how to cope.

Whatever the child's age, the many routine visits were her stock in trade. No matter how often she heard the same questions she never tired of giving the answers. But a deeper sense of accomplishment came from her ability to stay alert in the tsunami of everyday complaints and not be dulled into missing the few kids who had real problems, serious illnesses. She felt like she was really using her advanced medical training when she identified a young child who *actually* didn't eat anything, or had truly abnormal bowel movements, or had skin rashes that were signs of grave diseases, or whose frequent colds were asthma or the result of immune deficiencies. Or when she recognized the older ones whose adolescent rages or social withdrawal were actually warning signs of suicidal or homicidal tendencies or other serious mental illness.

Private practice wasn't the only big change in her life. She and Antonio had a toddler of their own, Ricardo Belden O'Malley. In her private life as a wife and mother she was known as Sarah Belden

O'Malley. In the office she was still Dr. Sarah Belden, but she felt like a different doctor now that she was a mother.

Having experienced the pain and pleasure of pregnancy and now frequently surprised by the many twists and turns of her own child's growth and development, Sarah wondered how she had dared to practice pediatrics before she had a kid of her own. At the time she had been so self-confident preaching her textbook-learning to women who were mothers many times over, but now that seemed as absurd as a celibate priest giving sex counseling to couples that had lived together for years. Not that she was really saying anything all that different than what she had always told parents, just that she was far more insightful into what her words meant to them about the landmarks they were noting and the problems they were having with their kids.

Sarah was sitting at the desk in her office writing notes on Freddie Anthony's chart when her intercom began buzzing.

"Dr. Belden, there's a man here to see you," the nurse said.

"A man? Does he have a child with him? Is he the parent of one of our patients?"

"No, I asked him that. He said he needs to see you personally. He said he can wait until you're free and he won't need more than a few seconds. He's just sitting here in the waiting room."

"What does he want to see me for? If he's a detail rep from a drug company tell him I don't grant personal interviews during office hours, ever."

"No, he doesn't look like a drug rep. He's…he's clean and all, but he's not dressed like a drug rep. And he's not carrying a big sample case, just a small portfolio under his arm." Then, lowering her voice into the phone, she added, *"He's Chinese."*

***

One down, six more to go and Chih-Wheh Chon could call it a day, a profitable, seven-hundred dollar day. Dr. Sarah Belden had been so easy to get to. One receptionist, very pleasant and eager to please, and a short wait of only a few minutes before Dr. Belden came out to greet him personally. The young doctor had such a lovely smile and greeted him in such a friendly way that Chih-Wheh was glad she didn't quite seem to understand what had just happened before he was out the door. He wondered if the others could possibly be this easy. He was sure there would be barriers to keep him from getting to the CEO at Memorial General, but at least he could give

125

the package to any representative of the hospital, he did not need to get to Everett Kappel himself. Next would be Giuliana Silvestre, then cardiologist Lesley Kahn and cardiac surgeon Morton Scheld, back across town to Dr. Jane Zimmerman, and finally Obstetrician and Gynecologist Dr. Fred Trilling.

Chih-Wheh Chon was very good at his occupation. He knew how to be polite, what not to say to scare people off, and how to extract himself if the situation became dangerous. His Hong Kong British accent gave the words *"You've been served"* a hint of deferential treatment, as though he were a tuxedoed waiter who had just put a snifter of brandy in front of a member of an exclusive club. Yes, being a process server might not make him wealthy but it was better than slogging through the rain on a bicycle.

Chapter 18: Counsel for the Defense

Jerry Janckovich looked up from his desk as Sarah Belden shuffled through the doorway into his office, her head down, shoulders stooped. The enormous man stood to greet her like a giant uncoiling from a crouch, his huge body ascending in stages until it straightened and towered over his chair.

"Welcome, Dr. Belden," he said, his soft and fluid voice a warm *basso profundo*. Coming around his dark mahogany desk he extended a mammoth hand to Sarah, which she took automatically, without reacting to its oversized scale. But Janckovich immediately felt the cold dampness of the much smaller hand she placed in his. Her hand did not shake, but he sensed that she was on the verge of trembling.

Jerry Janckovich was accustomed to dealing with situations like this. He had seen the entire range of emotions in physicians the first time they were sued for malpractice. Some were like Dr. Sarah Belden, filled with anxiety and fear of the unknown, trying desperately to come to grips with the shock. Others were despondent, full of self-doubt and guilt, too stunned even to try to deal with the situation. But most were so angry, so outraged, felt so violated that all they could do was rant and curse for the first few hours. How many times had he heard one of the doctors say with insincere apology, "No offense, Mr. Janckovich, but lawyers are the scum of the earth. Whoever said we should first kill all the lawyers had it right."

Sarah Belden was awed by the gargantuan size of the man who was to be her lawyer, an enormous bald man nearly six and a half feet tall who had to weigh 300 pounds or more. His dark black suit was precisely fitted to a huge, athletic frame. He came across to Sarah as no teddy bear, too muscular and too bald to seem warm and fuzzy, yet somehow his presence felt reassuring. Twice her weight and nearly a foot taller than she was, he would scare the bejesus out of any adversary. It was like having the biggest kid on the block on your side in a schoolyard rumble.

Janckovich gestured for her to sit in a chair facing him, then dropped his bulky frame into the seat behind his desk and said, "Dr. Belden, I understand that this is difficult for you. Perhaps the best way to start would be for me to tell you a bit about this firm and what we will do for you. OK?"

She nodded.

"Good. Our law firm, *Sorano, Janckovich, English & Weil,* has a rather unique focus that stems from the experience of the firm's founder, Seymour Weill. We do only one type of law: we defend doctors and hospitals. Period. I'm sure you can appreciate that this is not a world in which the lawyers can have it both ways, suing doctors in one case and defending them in the next. Doctors would have difficulty working with lawyers as their defense counsel if they knew those same lawyers also sued doctors. We have chosen to pick sides and stick with our choice. I played defense on the football field, and I play defense here.

"Seymour Weill built this law firm around defending doctors and hospitals because of what happened to his father, who had been a tireless General Practitioner. Old Doctor Weill devoted his life to his patients and didn't have an uncaring bone in his body. Tragically, Seymour Weill saw his father's medical career—and his life, he was sure—destroyed by a baseless malpractice suit. So he devoted his law firm to the medical side of malpractice lawsuits. That's what we're here for, that's all we do."

Janckovich paused, giving Sarah an opportunity to respond. She felt that she should say something, anything, but her head was swimming, she was out of her element. No words came. Mercifully, the big man did not push her. He simply picked up speaking after a few seconds.

"Dr. Belden, I am sure that being sued by one of your patients has come as a great shock to you. I want to reassure you that we have a great deal of experience defending physicians just like you. And we are very successful—over ninety-five percent of our cases are settled without ever going to court, and well over two-thirds of the time the doctor is fully vindicated. *Fully* vindicated. Right now, that may not mean much to you, but it will as we go along. Right now, you probably need time to take this all in, to adjust to what is happening. I believe it will help if we give you a clear idea about what is going to take place. But before we get to that, I would like to stop for a moment and have you tell me your story about taking care of Donny Johnson."

Sarah was taken aback by the request, too stunned to respond. She didn't have a story to tell, she had a life that was being torn apart. She couldn't begin to think about what had happened with Donny Johnson, all she could think was, *What is happening to me?* Donny Johnson, Martina and Derek Johnson, the three dead Johnson babies, they were all jumbled together with all the other families she had known, all the babies and kids and teenagers she had taken care of. This was not a story, this was real life. Her life. The work she loved might be over, her career could end right here in this office, she could lose her medical practice. What would all of this do to her husband, to her precious child?

Seeing that the last traces of color had now drained out of Sarah's face, Janckovich stood up again, walked over to her, and put his massive hand gently on her shoulder.

"Please, take your time, don't feel like you have to say anything until you're ready. Maybe you'd like some water."

He opened a bottle of spring water, poured it into a glass on the table near her chair, and placed a box of tissues next to the glass, as if to offer them as napkins but really to have them close at hand for her to wipe away tears. Jerry Janckovich had been through this before.

Sarah took a sip from the glass of water. Glancing at the box of tissues she immediately understood their purpose. The implication that she might burst into tears filled her with resolve to be strong, not to give in. She could do this. She would keep her head just as she would during a medical emergency. She was not going to break down, she was not going to cry. Not now, not here, not in front of this man. But she wasn't ready to start speaking yet, either. She took another sip of water and said nothing.

Jerry Janckovich intervened, again taking a cue from her silence.

"Let me give you a little background on the legal situation. I'll go over this in general terms now, but we'll have plenty of time to discuss it all in more detail later on. First of all, you should know that you are not alone, you are not being singled out. Everyone involved in caring for the Johnson child is being sued: all the doctors, the hospital, everyone the other side can think of. And then they added in a bunch of *'Persons unknown'* in case they missed someone. That's very common for a couple of reasons. It can be difficult in a complicated case to know what, if anything, went wrong, and whom to blame, so the plaintiffs—the people who are bringing the lawsuit—sue everybody, whether they were at fault or not. They don't want the doctors and hospitals named in the lawsuit confusing things by pointing fingers at the ones who weren't sued. Also, that way they have more sources of money to go after—we call that looking for *'deep pockets.'* Each of you—all the defendants—will have your own lawyers. In your case, the hospital has long had a special arrangement with our firm to provide legal defense services. Dr. Giuliana Silvestre's malpractice insurance company has hired us as well, so our firm will defend both of you but each of you will have your own principal attorney in this firm. Is this clear so far?"

Sarah nodded, thankful to be listening rather than speaking, but then his words started to reverberate in her mind. *Sued. Went wrong. Blame. Money.* Her *story*, whatever it was, was starting to take shape, a ghastly tale that filled her with dread. She stayed silent and took a long, deep breath to ward off the anxiety threatening to explode in her chest.

Janckovich continued.

"Since there are so many different defendants, we have to be careful about how we proceed. The other side will try to pit us against each other, will try to get us to accuse each other. If it comes to that, fine—my job is to defend you. In the last analysis we can't worry about the other defendants."

Sarah thought about Giuliana Silvestre. Whatever would she do if she found herself pitted against her mentor, her friend, the physician she so admired? She wanted to tell Janckovich she would never take sides against Giuliana, but she still had not found her voice.

"Now," said Janckovich, "I'm going to give you my first piece of legal advice, plain and simple: you should always tell the truth. To me and the other lawyers in this firm, you tell *all* of the truth, whatever you remember. Don't hold anything back. Everything you tell us will remain inside these walls. You can say whatever you want to say here, and no one can force us to repeat it outside. That's called the attorney-client privilege.

"Your first encounter with the other side will almost certainly be when they take your deposition. That's when they will ask you a lot of questions in a formal setting, probably in our conference room or somewhere similar. You will be under oath even though you won't be in a courtroom and there will be no judge present. So you should also tell the truth when you are speaking with the other side in your deposition. But there's a very important difference between telling me the truth and telling them the truth: you need not tell them more of the truth than necessary. I cannot emphasize this too much—tell the truth, yes, but don't volunteer anything you haven't been asked. How much is necessary? *Whatever it takes to answer a question honestly, but only enough to answer the question.* If they ask what color something was, you say, 'Blue,' if it was blue. You don't say something like, 'Blue, and that made me realize I should pick up the green one instead.' Me, I'm your lawyer, you tell me about the green one and why you think it might be important. But when they ask you questions under oath, you answer truthfully but you only answer what is asked. Don't add anything. Nothing. Don't worry, we'll go over this many times. We will have the opportunity to prepare you for any depositions. Is this clear so far?"

Sarah nodded, then at last spoke, saying, "It was a very long time ago. Years ago. I was still single, I…"

She started to say something else, but the words caught in her throat, so she sipped some more water and sat silent, listening intently.

"Yes, it has been a long time," Janckovich agreed. "That's the second point I wanted to go over. In most cases, a medical malpractice lawsuit would not be allowed to proceed after so many years. In this state, the statute of limitations has been cut way down—the medical association and the hospitals lobbied the legislature to shorten the statute of limitations to only two years. So people who want to sue for medical malpractice have only two years to do so, and most cases would be tossed out at this point. But when the lawsuit is brought on behalf of a child, the time limit doesn't run out until the child turns eighteen years old in this state. We have the longest period for such lawsuits in the country. Here, the time period for filing a lawsuit is pretty much unlimited until the child is grown up. So we can't get this suit dismissed just because what happened was so long ago. I have to tell you, that can make it hard to defend. What we have on our side are your memories from many years ago, whatever old medical records still exist, and the witnesses we can find. What they have is a child with very serious disabilities, heart-wrenching problems that would be obvious to every juror at a trial. You need to understand the situation, but we've done this before, many times, so we know how to help you."

Sarah finally found the words she had stumbled over a moment earlier. "It was a very long time ago. I was still in my residency. I was there when the first Johnson baby was born dead, and later on I took care of their twins that died. I knew how much they wanted a baby. I did everything I could to save Donny."

Again, she felt more words, the words of *her story*, building up, but this was all that she could squeeze out at the moment.

The experienced defense lawyer made a mental note about the fact that Sarah Belden had been involved in caring for three other Johnson babies, reflecting how that could cut two entirely different ways. On the one hand, a jury might be sympathetic to her, feeling bad for what must have been a devastating experience for a young doctor to go through. But on the other hand, the wily lawyers for the plaintiff might twist that around, making Sarah Belden appear to have been so blinded by her involvement with the loss of three other babies that it clouded her judgment in taking care of Donny. Or, even worse, they might imply that she had somehow been responsible for the earlier tragedies. Janckovich filed the thought away for another day.

"Let's talk a bit about the fact that you were still in your residency then," said Janckovich. "You were an employee of Memorial General, right?"

"Yes. I think so, yes. Sure. We wore Memorial General nametags and carried hospital ID cards. That's where our paychecks came from."

"But you also held a license to practice medicine?"

"Oh, yes, I guess so, at least by the time Donny was born. After our first year of residency we were eligible to get a medical license. Once we were licensed we could be the physicians in charge in the hospital when we were on call. And if we had spare time—what a joke—being licensed also meant that we could moonlight at other hospitals on our own or fill in for doctors in their practices for a little extra money."

"OK, that could have some legal importance. Let me explain. When somebody is sued for things that happened on their job, the law usually holds their employer responsible. Let's say the UPS guy is negligent and drops a box on your foot, you collect from UPS, not from the delivery guy. *Respondeat superior,* that's what the law calls it, in Latin of course. A lot of doctors aren't anyone's employees, however, they're in their own medical practice, maybe a partnership. So this rule often doesn't apply in medical malpractice cases. But you were an employee of the hospital while you were still a resident, so it should apply here. The malpractice insurance company which covered the hospital should be responsible for paying for your defense. That means they will be paying our bills. They should also be liable for any judgments against you if it were ever to come to that, but there are a few complications on that front that I'll explain in a minute. For now, you should know the general picture of where things stand. Are you with me so far?"

Sarah nodded, not sure whether she really understood, but she got the point: having been a resident at Memorial General might be important.

"So, you were an employee of the hospital," the big, gentle man continued. "But Memorial General is a special type of hospital, a sort of quasi-public hospital. Now, that has certain implications, the complications I mentioned a minute ago. You see, Dr. Belden, in this country there are limitations on suing the government, and public hospitals count as part of the government. The government is protected against lawsuits by a legal doctrine known as *sovereign immunity,* a rule we borrowed from the English who thought that people shouldn't be able to sue the king. But we've carved some holes in that immunity, and we allow lawsuits against the government under certain circumstances, and up to certain limits. In our state the absolute limit is very low—no one can collect more than $175,000 from the state under most circumstances. Still with me?"

"I think so."

"OK. Now here's one of the complications we will have to confront: Memorial General is no longer a traditional public hospital, so this protection might or might not apply. No one knows for sure because their new status just hasn't been tested in court yet. I know this is a lot to digest but it all comes down to this: if the other side can't get enough money from the hospital they will want to hold the doctors responsible and make them pay. Clear enough?"

"It's pretty confusing, actually."

"That's for sure. But that's what I'm here for, you don't have to worry about all of these details."

"Thanks. Is that all? My head is swimming with all these legal twists."

"Understood. But hang in there, because there's another bit of complexity I need to tell you. As you know, this lawsuit accuses the doctors and hospital of being negligent, but the allegations go further. Negligence is what is involved in a typical malpractice case. We use the term '*simple negligence*' even though there's nothing simple about it. For simple negligence, it's clear that your former employer, Memorial General Hospital, would bear the legal costs. But this particular case adds something unusual to the mix: the other side also alleges '*gross negligence.*' Now, gross negligence is different. It hardly ever applies because it's rare and difficult to prove. But, if they can prove gross negligence, the other side can look to the hospital for more money than the limits I mentioned. Unfortunately, having gross negligence as part of this lawsuit clouds the picture for you as well. You were an employee, but the law says that employers may not be held liable if their employees behaved so badly that what they did rises to gross negligence. And since you were a licensed doctor, not just an employee, the worst-case scenario is that you might end up being held liable. Back to the UPS driver dropping a box on someone while working. If he's just careless, UPS foots the bill. But if he's drunk or it's after hours, he could be on his own.

"This is a whole pile of stuff, I know, Dr. Belden. How are we doing?"

Sarah nodded as if she understood, but she didn't understand, not one bit. Janckovich's words were like repeated slaps on the face, one after another, each slap more hurtful than the previous one. This was too much, she didn't deserve to be attacked like this. Surprising herself, she blurted out, "*Negligent?* They're saying I was negligent? *Worse* than negligent? I was so incompetent I was guilty of gross negligence? I gave part of my life to this child and that was gross negligence? I suffered with Martina Johnson over three dead babies and saved her fourth, and that was gross negligence? What is going on here?"

Before Janckovich could respond, the dam burst and Sarah Belden's story started flowing out of her. Random bits and pieces at first, then a torrent of memories and feelings, whatever flew through her mind when she remembered her deep concern for that family and their tiny baby. She recounted agonizing over her decision to resuscitate Donny, the stress of getting his heart beating, his lungs breathing, the long hours in the neonatal intensive care unit, the conferences with the family, with the surgeons, with Giuliana Silvestre. Protecting Donny's eyes, his lungs, his brain, his heart. Giving up her nights and weekends when she wasn't on call to visit with Martina. Feeling so fulfilled when she saw the baby being fed by his mother at last. Standing in the doorway of Memorial General in tears as the family finally took him home.

She had no idea how long she went on like this. Jerry Janckovich never interrupted her, never seemed impatient, just sat at his desk looking as though every word fascinated him more than the previous one.

When her effusion had finally run its course, she sat back in her chair, drained. She was exhausted, more tired than she could ever remember being as a resident. She had no idea if her rant had made sense, but at least it was out there, no longer just whirling inside her.

Janckovich pursed his lips, nodded his head very slowly, and said, soothingly, "I think that's more than enough for today, Dr. Belden. You go home and try to rest. You probably feel as though you've been smacked in the head with a two-by-four, and in a real sense, you have. I know this isn't much comfort now, but in my experience coming to grips with the situation at the start is just about the hardest part. It will never be easy, but once the shock is over and you become familiar with what's going on you'll find that you can deal with this unpleasantness. And always remember that we're here to help you. We'll start collecting all the records, start planning what our strategy will be, maybe have a few conversations with the lawyers defending the other doctors. You go home to your family now, and tomorrow go back to work. You're a mother and a doctor, and this is a bad moment that will pass."

Sarah looked at her watch, and realized she must have been talking for over two-and-a-half hours. She wanted to put all this behind her, go home to her husband and her little boy.

She said softly, "I'm so sorry I went on like that, I had no idea how long I was talking. Thank you so much for being patient, Mr. Janckovich."

When they shook hands this time, Sarah looked down at the giant hand that engulfed hers and wondered how she had not noticed its size earlier. She decided she would go to the front desk and ask to use the office phone so she could call Antonio to come and get her. She just couldn't face hailing a cab and riding home alone. She stepped out into the waiting room and saw one of the most beautiful sights she had ever seen: her handsome husband was sitting there in the waiting room, holding her precious Ricardo. Antonio didn't say a word, he just took her into his arms. Her husband and son wrapped their arms around her and kissed her, and she realized she had never loved him, never loved her family, so much as she did right then.

Chapter 19: Empathy

The exquisitely dressed woman rose gracefully from her desk and walked toward Giuliana Silvestre with strikingly perfect posture. "Hello, Dr. Silvestre," she said, extending her hand. "I am Stephanie Sorano, and I'm going to help you with this lawsuit. Please come in and have a seat."

Silvestre immediately felt a bond with Sorano. She came across as precisely the kind of woman Silvestre was comfortable dealing with: highly accomplished, no nonsense, all business. Both were consummate professionals who had no problem dealing with the fact that they were also exceptionally attractive women. Neither was particularly tall, but each had an undeniable presence, an aura of authority. They both wore fashionable dark wool suits, a minimal amount of expensive jewelry, and soft leather shoes with high, wide heels that were stylish yet comfortable. Silvestre noted that the main difference in their attire was their choice of blouses—she sported a colorful silk one with large pointy collars that spread over her jacket, while Sorano wore an off-white blouse that billowed up at her neckline. Musing that they could have been sisters separated at birth, she wondered if Sorano had any Italian blood in her heritage.

Stephanie Sorano got right down to business.

"Just by way of background, I want you to know that in addition to being a lawyer I am also a physician, or at least I was a physician once. If you wouldn't mind bearing with me for a few minutes I'd like to tell you my history right up front so you will see that I really do understand what you are going through."

"Yes, Dr. Sorano, I was aware that you were qualified as both a physician and a lawyer. I am most interested in hearing your history. But please, call me Giuliana."

"Thank you Giuliana, and of course, call me Stephanie. I'm not a doctor here, and besides, we're going to be spending a lot of time together. So I'd prefer to be on a first-name basis."

"I would be most comfortable with that, Stephanie."

"OK, Giuliana. I'll try to keep this short so we can get on with your case. As you can imagine, I loved being a doctor, it was what I had always wanted to do. I was a surgeon with a very successful practice. I went to work full of energy every day, no matter how hard it had been the night before. I loved performing the most challenging operations, and I was getting lots of referrals of difficult cases. I didn't even mind taking shifts in the ER where I would see mainly people who had minor illnesses and didn't really need emergency care, because I realized that people who go to an ER are having a problem and they need help, they aren't there for fun.

"Now, here's the point of imposing on you to listen to my history: I know what it is like to be falsely accused. After several years of trying to protect patients from a truly incompetent doctor, I filed charges against him with the hospital. I went through all the proper procedures. It turned out that he was untouchable because he was their biggest money-maker. So the hospital leadership turned things upside-down and went after me instead. They dredged up some unhappy patients and got some sleazy personal-injury lawyers to sue me for malpractice. They brought a professional review action against me and pressured me to resign from the hospital. It was all bogus; those people all got excellent care, their complications were completely unavoidable. But I was trapped. I was abandoned by everyone, shunned by doctors who had been my friends, my colleagues. Guilty by innuendo. I was so bitter I probably overreacted, but I ended up quitting medicine entirely. So here I am, a lawyer.

"Having learned the hard way that the malpractice system was completely out of control I decided to do something about it. I have no tolerance for plaintiffs' attorneys no matter how sympathetic their cases might be. They are bloodsuckers going for money and don't care whose life they destroy. Well, they have to go through me to get to you, and it won't be easy, I assure you."

"Thank you, Stephanie. I greatly regret that you had such a difficult experience, but as you said, it is indeed reassuring to me to know that you do understand my situation."

"Thanks, Giuliana—what a beautiful name, by the way. I apologize for taking the time to tell you my life story, but I thought it would help you to get to know me and have confidence in me. Most of my clients are doctors. By and large they are hard working, highly motivated people. For the most part they do well financially, yes. But by the time I see them they are struggling uphill against dysfunctional legal and hospital administrative systems that make physicians their scapegoats. And don't get me started about the hassles they have to go through dealing with health insurance companies or the corporations that are gobbling up medical practices and hospitals and destroying them. Of course, I see some lousy doctors, no doubt about it. But I defend them, too, because a malpractice suit isn't going to make them better doctors. OK, that's enough about me—you can see that I have strong feelings about all of this. Let's talk about this lawsuit."

"Yes, certainly. I will tell you everything I can. But, please, do not apologize for telling me about yourself. I feel much better knowing that you are so dedicated, so knowledgeable, that you have such empathy. All of this is very strange to me. I have no understanding of the legal system in this country, and I am quite reassured to be in the hands of someone who knows what this is all about and also knows what being a doctor really is."

"Empathy is right. I spent many long hours sitting on your side of this desk. Now, tell me about the case of Donny Johnson."

Giuliana Silvestre started with the call to leave St. Anne Moray and rush over to Memorial General, then spoke about how small the baby was, how skilled the Senior Resident, Sarah Belden, had been. She described the first few hours, into the first full day. Then, when she was about to mention her fateful conversation with Everett Kappel, she stopped short, not sure what to say, uncertain how much to tell Stephanie Sorano.

"I need to ask you something before I go on, Stephanie, if you will. If there is something that is important but might be, how do you say it, incriminating for me in some way, should I tell you?"

"Absolutely. Thank you for asking, this is very, very important. No matter what you know, you must tell me. I cannot defend you properly if there might be surprises, if there might be something the other side could use against us that I don't have any way to prepare us for. What you tell me is between us, it is a privileged communication. That means I cannot be forced to release it unless you tell me to do so. It's like the seal of the confessional, even stronger than the protections of the doctor-patient relationship that you are familiar with. Nothing you say here can be used against you. What is it that you were thinking about?"

"Fine, thank you. I certainly want to tell you the full story. I understand that an important part of the lawsuit has to do with whether we should have transferred Donny Johnson to the University, correct?"

"Yes, exactly. That is why they are alleging gross negligence. What can you tell me about why he was not transferred?"

"Stephanie, I'm sorry to say but the truth is that I never thought we should treat the baby at Memorial General. I wanted to transfer him to the University as soon as we were able to do so safely. We did not have the resources—the experienced nurses, the medical specialists, the equipment—at Memorial General. And no baby that small had ever been treated there. The right thing to do was to transfer him."

Stephanie Sorano sat up and leaned forward, her already-intense gaze magnified even further. "Tell me, would anything have been done differently if he had been transferred? Who would have taken care of him at the University?"

"Good, that is an excellent point. It is likely that at the University he would have gotten some innovative treatments that we were testing then, treatments that are widely accepted now but back then were more or less in the experimental stages. And there would have been more highly trained personnel caring for him all around the clock. However, I would still have been his attending physician."

"And would he have been better off in the long run? Would he be more likely to have recovered fully? In short, would he be, shall we say, a normal child?"

"No, I do not think so. I firmly believe that his disabilities were not caused by any complications that were not treated properly. These unfortunate outcomes are most often due to intrauterine insults, as you probably know, not medical care after birth. So, in retrospect, thinking about what we actually did for him, I am confident it did not make any difference whether he was transferred or not. But it was not right to keep him at Memorial General, and it was not what I thought we should do at the time."

"So, why didn't you transfer him?"

"That is the worrisome part, the reason I asked about whether to tell you about something that might be incriminating. I was prepared to order the transfer, but the hospital administrator, Mr. Everett Kappel, kept me from carrying out my order."

"Take your time, please. Tell me exactly what transpired."

"Of course. The baby's birth had attracted a lot of attention. The newspapers, the television reporters, all had stories about the tiny baby and how he was being saved at Memorial General."

"Yes, I remember that. Even at the time, I was surprised that a baby of such extremely low birthweight was being treated at that hospital. Go on, I'm sorry for interrupting you."

"I knew that this attention, this publicity, was important, so I decided to tell the administrator that it was going to end because I was transferring Baby J—that's what we called Donny then. He was very upset, and told me not to do it."

"What, exactly, did he say?"

Giuliana Silvestre gathered her thoughts. So many years had gone by. She had forgotten all about that unfortunate encounter with the little man who hid behind the mustache that concealed the scar on his upper lip.

"I will try to remember. I came into his office and told him what I thought was best for the baby. He resisted, said we could do a fine job at Memorial General. I said no, the baby needed to go to the University. He kept insisting. I was just about to walk out and defy him—after all, I was the physician in charge, he could not tell me how to practice medicine."

"Did he actually order you to keep the baby in the hospital? Is that what he did? This would be very important to know, please think carefully."

Giuliana Silvestre paused for nearly a minute, then bit her lip and shook her head slightly as the details of her encounter with Everett Kappel began to resurface. She shook her head slowly and said with resignation, "No, in truth I do not think so, not in so many words. I cannot say that Mr. Kappel actually ordered me not to transfer the baby. He told me that the hospital needed the baby, it needed some positive exposure with the public. The hospital was especially dependent on the revenue it earned through the neonatal intensive care unit. The negative publicity that would follow if Memorial General had to admit it was sending sick babies to other hospitals would be bad for the hospital. He said the hospital might fail, the county commissioners might even close it and then all the poor people would have nowhere to go. It was all quite dramatic, a truly horrible prospect. This was a consequence I had never imagined. I was startled, I did not know what to say. I just felt that I could not take the responsibility for a disaster such as he predicted. In retrospect, now I suppose he was scaring me, he was making up an extreme scenario that was probably never going to happen, but I did not have any way of knowing then."

"So, who finally decided to keep the baby at Memorial General?"

"I did."

Chapter 20: More Than Two Sides

Every morning and evening Everett Kappel walked—prowled, many said, though not to his face—around the Memorial General campus, feigning interest in the inhabitants of his realm: nurses, maintenance workers, doctors, admission clerks, orderlies. But the aloof little executive's awkward attempts to play a man of the people fooled no one. The hospital employees smiled and greeted him on his rounds with apparent respect, but behind his back they mocked his transparent efforts to simulate rapport with them. They realized all too well that the visits were intended only to remind his minions that he was in charge, that he was always looking over their shoulders like a lord of the manor circulating among the peasants on horseback. And when real business was transacted, it was always in Mr. Kappel's office, nowhere else, that was one of Kappel's rules.

Frank Faison, General Counsel of Memorial General, was no minor subordinate yet even he was subject to Kappel's rigid protocol, an irritation that nagged at him as he walked down the elaborate hallway into the CEO's office. In a modest gesture of deference to his senior lawyer, Kappel stood up from his oversized desk and joined Faison at his imposing conference table, a rectangular glass slab on wrought iron that dominated more than half of the CEO's expansive office. Even with just the two of them, Kappel presided from his usual chair at the head of the table, the one with the highest back and padded seat and arm rests. Faison piled his file folders on top of the table and sat in the second chair on Kappel's left side, leaving a comfortable buffer between him and his superior.

"Mr. Kappel," began Faison, observing another rule of decorum in dealings with Kappel: no one called him "Everett" in the hospital, no mater how senior they were. Neither was anyone known to socialize with him in a setting where his first name might have

143

seemed appropriate. The lawyer had heard it repeatedly from the little man: *"Propriety, a proper respect, must be maintained at all times."*

"As you know, we have been sued by the family of one Donny Johnson, a young man who was born here a number of years ago. I believe you will remember him—he was quite a small baby, and the hospital received a great deal of positive publicity when he survived."

Kappel nodded in silent assent. *That* was not an episode he would ever forget. His expressionless face gave Faison no hint of the pleasure he was savoring from the memory of his triumph over Giuliana Silvestre and how he had parlayed the publicity from keeping the tiny baby in his hospital into funding from the County for a new medical-surgical building.

Faison continued, determined that Kappel understand their legal predicament fully.

"We have, of course, been sued before. But this time the situation is different. It's a bit more complicated, legally. Because we had been a public institution we have not had many dealings with the plaintiff's attorney, Fred Vagram. He is the bane of all the private hospitals in town but he showed little inclination to sue us because we were generally protected from big lawsuits by the *sovereign immunity* doctrine in this state. Vagram was not interested in going after peanuts, which is all our legal status offered for the likes of him. But, as you know, we are no longer simply a public hospital, so our legal liability might be much greater."

Again Kappel nodded silently, savoring another personal triumph: converting the old money-losing charity hospital into a successful business enterprise.

"The legal effects of our change in status have not yet been tested. In short, we may or may not still have some legal protections against simple malpractice as a quasi-public institution. We just don't know yet. However that may play out, Vagram has devised a way to try to hit us hard: he is charging us with gross negligence. Of course, he is also alleging ordinary medical malpractice, he cannot leave that out. But his real strategy here is to allege that this baby should not have been treated in our hospital, that we should have transferred him to the University. So even if we still have some protection against lawsuits we are not necessarily immune from a very big award if he can prove his case for gross negligence. We could be liable for millions. Should that happen, the County would have to find a great deal of money somewhere."

Kappel nodded silently a third time, but now his thoughts were on the consequences for him personally. If the hospital once again became a major financial drain on the County, that would be the end for him. The County Commissioners would run for cover, he would be fired in an instant.

"Please tell me everything you can remember about the decision to keep Donny Johnson here, Mr. Kappel. I need to understand how strong or how precarious our position is."

Kappel replayed his long-ago meeting with Giuliana Silvestre in his mind, as he had done a hundred times since first hearing about the lawsuit. He had decided to circle the wagons, remain detached, minimize his role in the affair. He delivered the lie to Faison with cold calm. "I know almost nothing about that."

"Did you ever speak with the doctors about this baby?"

"Of course, many times. You are aware that I do not seclude myself in this office. I am constantly on-site, I know every employee and every square foot of this hospital," replied Kappel, putting on his man-of-the-people façade. "Fred Trilling, the obstetrician, Giuliana Silvestre, the neonatologist, I may even have exchanged a few words with the pediatric residents, whoever they were. I probably spent more time on the wards than usual then. Reporters were swarming over our grounds in the first few days after the Johnson baby was born and I needed to know what to tell them since I was the spokesman for the hospital."

"Did anyone ever discuss transferring the Johnson baby to the University?"

"I had one meeting with Silvestre where that might have come up. She told me the baby was doing well, the nurses and housestaff were working very hard to keep him going. At one point she mentioned that he could develop some complications that might require him to be transferred."

"How did you respond?"

"Mr. Faison," Kappel spun his reconstructed version of history, "I said exactly what I always tell our doctors. I said that medical decisions are entirely up to them. I would never presume to tell them how to practice medicine. I never heard another word from her about wanting to transfer that baby."

"Anything else that you recall, Mr. Kappel? Any other discussions with the doctors, with any other staff? Anything at all?"

"As I said, I was in constant communication with many of my staff about this baby. It was important for me to know what was happening, whether our hospital was living up to expectations. I do not recall any other conversations with Dr. Silvestre. To the best of my recollection she came to this office only once."

Faison's long experience in dealing with Kappel told him that the man was not being forthcoming. The sly little man sounded as if he were reading from a script one line at a time, not replying spontaneously to Faison's questions. He was sure Kappel was leaving out some critical part of his narration.

"What about other employees? Did anyone else discuss transferring the baby with you?"

The hardened lawyer stared hard at Kappel with his most intimidating look. But he doubted that he could ever squeeze the truth out of him.

"My senior employees report to me regularly as well, of course. It is quite likely that some of them brought me information from time to time about the progress of the baby, since he was here in the hospital for many months. Certainly I paid close attention to his course with us. At first, it was a financial blessing for Memorial General—after all, most of our patients are uninsured or on Medicaid and the Johnsons' health insurance from the father's job paid us much better than we were used to receiving. So the revenue from their insurance quite naturally caught my attention, and I was grateful for that. Eventually, however, their health insurance ran out and we started to have bills that weren't collected. So I reviewed their case many times. But I always left the medical decisions up to the doctors. That's their job. I was doing my job, and they were doing theirs."

Faison realized he would get no useful information from Kappel. Whatever Kappel had done, whatever he knew, Faison could see that all the little man would ever reveal would be his canned version of reality. Faison would have to find out what happened piece by piece from whatever sources he could dig up before he could decide whether he could successfully defend the hospital or have to throw in the towel.

Faison decided he should keep his suspicions to himself. He said simply, "Thank you, Mr. Kappel. I will do my best to defend

Memorial General. We are up against the toughest lawyers anywhere, but we will do everything in our power to protect the hospital."

"I have every confidence in you, Mr. Faison."

Chapter 21: *Anniversary Celebration*

Sarah and Antonio had planned to celebrate their anniversary with a special dinner at *Ricardo O'Leary's*, then drinks and dancing at the *Top of the Tower*, the most romantic nightspot in town. Anticipating that the forthcoming deposition would be her personal Inquisition complete with torture rack and thumbscrews, Sarah had resolved that she and her husband would enjoy one wonderful celebration before the ordeal was to start, a brief time-out to sustain her through the ensuing nightmare.

But the much-anticipated date night with Antonio was not to be. Their baby sitter appeared in her office that Friday afternoon with a high fever and deep cough, in no shape to baby-sit later that evening. Sarah was distressed and couldn't believe her bad luck but she had no choice other than sending the teenager home to bed and start working on a new plan.

Getting a replacement sitter at such short notice proved futile—the handful of teenagers she would trust with Ricardo were already taken by other families. So she decided on another plan: she would cook dinner at home for Antonio. She would cook something romantic. But what was romantic enough? *Cioppino* would be romantic, but she didn't have time to assemble all the different types of seafood and she didn't dare try to compete with one of Ricardo O'Leary's specialties. Irish cuisine was off-limits for the same reason. At last she thought of *Coq au vin*. She would do Coq au vin, she had all the spices, all she needed to do would be to pick up some chicken breasts and vegetables, and a bottle of cheap red wine to use in the sauce and let the pot simmer while they sipped champagne. After Ricardo went to bed of course.

"Perfect," she said out loud, to no one but herself as she headed out to the grocery store.

Sarah was walking past the soup-and-pasta shelves toward the meat department in *Rimme's Market* when she noticed a vaguely familiar figure at the end of the aisle, a thin woman wearing only a frayed cotton print dress and old leather sandals. As she pushed her shopping cart closer, their eyes met. Sarah's heart jumped and skipped a beat as she realized she was looking at Martina Johnson. But this was a shop-worn, rapidly aging facsimile of the beautiful blond woman Sarah had known as Martina Johnson.

"Dr. Belden," the woman said softly, her voice cracking, her face looking just as astounded as Sarah felt. "Dr. Belden. I'm so...so... Dr. Belden, I'm sorry, so sorry. I didn't...I never..."

The last words trailed away as the woman's eyes filled with tears. Her head dropped until her chin came to rest on her slender chest, her shoulders slumped in total dejection. Sarah could hear her sobbing but no more words were forthcoming.

Sarah was so taken aback she could not respond. Now her heart was pounding in her chest and she felt a sudden vacuum in the pit of her stomach, as though a trap door had opened somewhere, dropping the contents of her chest into her belly. The shock drained her and she began to feel faint, wobbly on her feet. Grasping her shopping cart to steady herself, Sarah started to speak, but all she could get out was a faint, "Mrs. Johnson..."

The woman raised her head slightly and stood there motionless, tears streaming down her face. She made no further effort to speak. Sarah Belden and Martina Johnson were locked in each other's bewildered stare for a few seconds, then Sarah walked past her, unable even to remember where she was heading, why she was in a grocery store. She didn't feel anger or sorrow or anything else, just confusion, disorientation. She needed to get away.

Sarah let her body lead her without conscious direction, let it take her wherever she had been intending to go. Soon she found herself in front of a vast array of chicken breasts. Yes, chicken, that was it, chicken breasts for *coq au vin*. But the sea of fleshy pale animal parts sent a spurt of bile into Sarah's mouth. Fearing she might vomit into the refrigerated display case, or faint and fall in head-first, she grabbed onto the edge of the case, closed her eyes for a moment, took a deep breath and strained to regain her composure.

Anniversary dinner. Antonio. Champagne and fine wine. Her memory came back bit by bit, but as it did she knew she could not go home and cook the dinner, could no longer put together the evening

149

she had planned. Wandering aimlessly away from the fresh meat counter, Sarah found herself in the familiar prepared-food section. Dinner could be salvaged. She selected a simmering chicken concoction that vaguely resembled *Coq au vin*, then asked for some risotto with pine nuts, a small container of broccoli and cauliflower with no sauce, a large container of Caesar salad, and three large pieces of six-layer chocolate cake.

As Sarah entered their apartment Antonio handed her an elegant arrangement of long-stemmed pink and red roses.

"Thanks, Honey," she said listlessly, laying the flowers on the kitchen counter, making no effort to put them in a vase with water.

Antonio read his wife's perfunctory response correctly. Something serious had happened to her, something very serious. Had she lost a patient? What could have gone wrong? Kissing her more tenderly than romantically, he poured two glasses of champagne, then said, "I'll take care of the boy, and you rest a bit. Then we'll celebrate, sweetheart."

After feeding Ricardo some chicken tenders and peas, Antonio put their son to bed, then went to the kitchen to reheat the food Sarah had brought home. As they waited to begin dinner he slowly coaxed a version of the encounter with Martina Johnson out of his wife. They ate in spurts, with the champagne and a bottle of wine soothing over the day's horror, then sat on the living room couch. Antonio hugged his wife, not seeking romance, just providing the warmth, the tenderness he knew she needed. When they went to bed she tried to sleep, but the scene in the grocery store wouldn't leave her all night.

Chapter 22: The Other Pockets

"We should have no problem getting you dismissed from this case, Dr. Trilling," said Woodrow L. Tharpe, attorney-at-law. Tharpe was not particularly fond of doctors, since he had seen and defended too many inexcusable cases of malpractice. But he knew the law and some medicine quite well, and he particularly understood the strategy that a plaintiff's attorney like Fred Vagram was likely to adopt.

"I believe it is clear that you met every standard that an Obstetrician is supposed to meet with respect to the delivery of Donny Johnson. Once that baby was born, any problems he had were the responsibility of either Mother Nature or the pediatricians or other doctors. The one point that we need to be strong on is whether you had any real chance, any medical opportunity, to keep the baby from being born so prematurely, or in any other way to have protected him from the consequences of being born too soon. We need to know if the prenatal care the mother received during the pregnancy, or the care she got when she went into labor, could have been different in some way. In short, could she could have received some other treatment that might have led to a more favorable outcome?"

Tall, slender, relaxed, Fred Trilling exuded confidence. Trilling was prospering in private practice. A pair of five-hundred dollar "*Italian kangaroo*" cowboy boots, actually made in Texas, stuck out below his precisely-creased chinos. He wore a burgundy-colored long-sleeved polo shirt, open at the collar, below a casual denim jacket. The temples on the stylish black frames of his slightly tinted eyeglasses disappeared under the long dark hair that covered his ears and hung down to his neckline.

"Nah, not a chance. I never saw that woman, Martina Johnson, until the ambulance brought her in. By then her labor was well advanced, the baby was almost out. You know, that's what kills babies or really screws them up, when a medical student or some cop or cab driver tries to keep a baby in that needs to pop. Once the labor is that far along, the placenta is going to separate from the uterus pretty soon, and that baby has got to get out and breathe on its own or it will suffocate in the birth canal. No way he could have been stopped. No competent doctor would ever say otherwise."

Short and stocky, with closely trimmed salt-and-pepper hair and small wire-rimmed eyeglasses, wearing a slightly frumpy but respectable pin-striped suit that coordinated well with his white linen shirt and dark tie, Woodrow Tharpe couldn't have looked any more the opposite of Fred Trilling. But he liked the way the doctor came across. Straightforward, honest, self-assured.

"Excellent. You would be a good witness, if it ever comes to that, but I do not think it will," Tharpe said, all the while eyeing the designer cowboy boots and thinking privately that if Trilling ever were to be in front of a jury he would need to avoid appearing overly cavalier. He continued, "Fine. How about earlier in the pregnancy. Were there any warning signs that Mrs. Johnson might go into labor early on?"

"None that I know of, but that's based on looking over her medical records since she had seen other doctors for her prenatal care, not me. It appears she was very cautious—you may or may not know, she had lost three babies already and didn't want to take any chances with this one. What's that saying, '*Be careful what you wish for, you might get it*'?"

"That's a hard lesson for all of us, isn't it? So there were no suggestions, nothing to warn of possible complications ahead of time?"

Woodrow Tharpe knew how to keep a witness on point, how to dredge out exactly what he was seeking.

"Nothing. I glanced at her medical records when she showed up in labor, then after the baby was born I reviewed them in more detail. She had started her prenatal care right on time, early in her first trimester, and had not missed an appointment. She was being seen in our high-risk Ob-Gyn clinic because of the earlier pregnancy outcomes: one malformed stillbirth, twins who died early on. So she was seeing our best obstetricians, the perinatologists, our maternal-fetal medicine specialists. Everything was routine. No hints of any problems, all tests normal, she didn't skip any appointments. There were no warnings at all. That, unfortunately, is all too common. More than half the time there's no advance notice of something going wrong until labor starts."

"What about once she got to Memorial General? Was there any delay in taking care of her? "

"Same situation. I was on-call at General when the two-way radio notice from the ambulance came in, so I met them myself in the ER. I spoke to her and did a very quick exam—her water had broken hours earlier, she was obviously having real contractions very close together. I knew immediately we had no time to waste so I wheeled her up to the delivery suite myself, no delay whatsoever."

"Good, very good. I'm sure the records will confirm the sequence of events. Now, even if you could not have delayed the delivery, were there, perhaps, any medications or any other treatments you could have given this mother to help prevent the baby's later problems from occurring?"

"No treatments like that were available back then, no. Not even now, there's still nothing that could have helped him. There just wasn't anything I could have done, not then, not today. That muffin was on its way out of the oven long before it was fully baked, but it was out of our control."

Tharpe could stomach the Italian kangaroo boots for now, but the muffin analogy provoked an immediate caution. "I take the point, and appreciate your medical opinion. Just a word of advice, however, if you will permit me. If we are ever in a more formal situation, in a deposition or before a jury, you would do well to avoid any lighthearted references to the baby, however picturesque. Even well-intentioned statements might come across as blithe. You might be mistakenly seen as disrespectful, and we don't need any distractions from the medical facts."

"Gotcha. You bet, counselor. Nothing but medical jargon for the lawyers. No more muffins and ovens. I won't embarrass you."

"That's most reassuring, but it never crossed my mind that you could embarrass us. At this point, the most important thing is for you to be sure I know everything, anything at all that could be harmful or helpful."

"Sure. So what happens next? Most of my colleagues have been sued at least once, that's all they talk about, but this is my first time. This is all new to me. Looks like I'm in good hands with you, and that's great because I haven't got a clue what to expect."

"Our next step is to put some distance between us and the other defendants. Not everyone on this side of the lawsuit belongs there, and we do not all have the same interests here. I was convinced even before I saw you that there was no reason for you to stay on as a defendant, and now I'm quite hopeful that we should be able to get you dismissed from this case."

"So…if I'm dismissed from this lawsuit, how does that help me?"

"The benefits are several. First of all, that ends it for you. That is the most important consequence from the point of view of most of the physicians I deal with. You will not have to put up with us lawyers any further—no more time away from your practice, no tedious depositions, no trial preparation or testimony, no listening to us giving you advice all the time."

"No offense, Counselor, but that would be terrific. I'm a busy guy, and this is one gigantic pain in the you-know-where."

"Understood, and no offense taken. I've heard the same sentiment expressed far less delicately, shall we say, by other members of your profession. Second, even though you played a relatively limited role in Donny Johnson's course, being dismissed from the case protects you from some consequences you might not be aware of. For example, if you were to remain as a defendant and our side were to lose the case, there is the small but real chance that you could end up with the entire liability for any verdict, despite your modest role. In this state we follow the traditional rule of *joint and several liability*. That means that any defendant who is found to be liable, even if there are ten different defendants in the same position, any single one of them can get stuck for the whole amount of the judgment, no matter how large it is. Then you would have to sue the other defendants on your own to get a fair contribution from each of them—you and your insurance company, that is."

"What? Are you saying I could get stuck for the whole thing if we lost? Even if there are lots of others who lose the case? Ouch! What kind of bullshit is that?"

"That is the way the law in this state can work, unfortunately. And the other side will do everything it can to keep you and your colleagues in the lawsuit because the more defendants with deep pockets, the more likely the full judgment can be collected. But that is precisely why we prefer to have the case against you dismissed."

"OK, let's go for it, tell me what you think. Can you get me dismissed quickly?"

Without breaking a smile, Tharpe permitted himself a touch of humor.

"I believe so, but you should realize I get paid by the hour, so the longer it takes, the better off I am. But I will do my best to have you dismissed as expeditiously as possible."

Given Tharpe's serious demeanor to that point, Fred Trilling didn't take the unexpected remark as a joke at first. Then he saw a small grin pulling back Woodrow Tharpe's chubby cheeks. The guy had a lighter side after all.

"OK, counselor, take your time, I wouldn't want you to starve on my behalf."

"Not a problem, Dr. Trilling."

***

"*Scoundrels. Bloodsuckers. Miserable sons of bitches. Filthy rotten bastards,*" Dr. Morton Scheld muttered audibly as he entered the elevator of a downtown office building. "*Goddamn them all, goddamn them to Hell. They should be skinned alive and left to die.*"

Scheld was oblivious to the older couple already in the elevator who shrank away to the far corner to get as far as possible from him as he unleashed the rapid storm of obscenities. They were convinced that a raging madman had just trapped them in the cramped space and held tight to each other and to the brass elevator handrail. Fortunately, while they were still wondering how they could escape from the ranting lunatic he blew out of the elevator two flights later and the door closed safely behind him.

Scheld flew down the hallway, so distracted by his fury that he passed right by the office he was heading for, then had to double-back when he came to the blind end of the corridor. The misstep triggered a further outburst of obscenities that would have done a drunken sailor with *Tourette's Syndrome* proud. Finally, he saw the door with the name he was looking for, *Fairley and Fairley, LLC, Attorneys and Counselors at Law*, pushed it open and strode in, seemingly ready to dare anyone to impede his course.

The first person Scheld encountered was his partner, Lesley Kahn, the pediatric cardiologist. He had consulted on Baby Johnson at Kahn's request, and had seen the baby only once. He had never thought about that case again until that Chinese guy sweet-talked his way in past his office staff to serve him with papers. Seeing Kahn,

155

Scheld abruptly reverted to his customary state of military composure, still intense but now socially acceptable, no longer likely to terrify old couples on elevators. This capacity to restore his self-control instantaneously in the wake of a storm of excitement had served him well as a surgeon.

Kahn was standing in front of an open door, beyond which were the offices for the *Fairley & Fairley* lawyers. She was speaking with another woman, a well-appointed blonde whom Scheld assumed was the receptionist. He restrained his surprise when Kahn turned to him and said, "Morton, I would like you meet our lawyer, Bernardine Pekings. Ms. Pekings, this is Dr. Morton Scheld, the eminent cardiac surgeon."

Picking up on Kahn's gratuitous compliment, Bernadine Pekings said, "Yes, of course, I am well aware of Dr. Scheld's reputation, and it's a great honor to meet you, Sir."

Mollified by the praise, Scheld suppressed his primal misogynistic reaction to finding that he must deal with yet another woman, particularly a young one who evidently felt the need to be overly deferential. He extended his hand with practiced courtesy, saying, "Except for the circumstances, I'm pleased to meet you, Ms. Pekings." It had taken him more than a decade before he had finally admitted to himself, however grudgingly, that the young women physicians he had trained had actually proved to be exceptionally competent surgeons. Perhaps, he told himself, this one might be a good enough lawyer. Only time would tell.

"Please, follow me."

Bernardine Pekings led Doctors Kahn and Scheld down a well-lit corridor into her office, a comfortable room with a broad U-shaped work center at one end and a brightly polished oval table surrounded by four high-backed leather chairs at the other. The files and books that filled the shelves along two of the walls were lined up perfectly. Nothing sat on the desktop itself but a telephone and a computer monitor, a keyboard neatly stowed below the angled work surface that connected the desk and hutch.

Scheld was pleased with the orderly appearance of her office, but what impressed him most was the quick glance he had taken at the identically-framed diplomas and certificates mounted behind her desk. He immediately recognized his own alma mater's anachronistic Latin, *Universitatis Yalensis* in large print below the gold seal emblazoned with *Lux et Veritas* on her law school diploma.

Yale. Maybe she knows what she's doing after all, he permitted himself to think, but said only, "What the hell is going on here? What business do these bastards have suing me, suing us?"

Kahn chimed in immediately in her blunt, cold manner. "Ms. Pekings, what I believe Dr. Scheld is expressing is that this state of affairs has got to be ended quickly. We have no time for frivolous lawsuits. I had to reschedule a cardiac catheterization on a four-year old child to come here today. Our time is precious. Children's lives are at stake."

Bernardine Pekings had done her homework well. She understood that Donny Johnson's current problems did not stem from anything these two cardiac specialists might have done. Knowing that her clients should in no way be held responsible, she struggled to dredge up a modicum of sympathy for these two extremely disagreeable people. With a look of commiseration that appeared more sincere than she actually felt, she said, "Tell me about your contact with the Johnsons and Donny Johnson."

Scheld, ever the senior partner, answered first.

"I had operated on one of this couple's twins, but that was from an earlier pregnancy, it has nothing to do with this case. Dr. Kahn asked me to consult on this one, but there was no surgery contemplated, so I never saw him again, just that one time."

He stopped, sat back, and passed the conversation torch over to his partner.

Lesley Kahn said, "Donny Johnson had a very mild case of persistent fetal circulation that resolved spontaneously. Neither his PDA nor his *patent foramen ovale* lasted long enough to require further treatment."

A physiology honor student in college, Bernardine Pekings fully understood Kahn's medical jargon about the way blood flows through the fetus. But she needed to get these doctors to speak in plain English if they were ever to testify in front of a judge or jury.

Abandoning her professional persona enough to hint at playing the dumb blonde, she looked at the cardiologist and said, "I realize that you are highly specialized doctors who deal with these problems every day, but please try to explain the baby's condition in more common terms so that a lay jury might be able to understand the situation."

Lesley Kahn was taken aback, but caught her breath and contemplated what the lawyer had said. When she started again she spoke with obvious condescension, as if Bernardine Pekings were indeed a dumb blonde. "OK. I'm sure that in junior high school you saw those pretty pictures with red blood in the arteries and blue blood in the veins. The left side of the heart pumps the red blood to deliver oxygen around the body, and when the oxygen gets used up, the veins return the blue blood to the right side of the heart. Then the blue blood is pumped to the lungs where it gets fresh oxygen and turns into the pretty red blood, and the whole cycle continues."

Bernardine Pekings smiled, nodding with satisfaction as though Kahn had just explained some mystery that had stupefied her blonde's brain for years.

"Yes. Good, Dr. Kahn. Please continue."

"When the baby is in the womb—the uterus—all the oxygen the baby needs is coming from the mother through the placenta. So the lungs remain collapsed, like a couple of flat, empty balloons. They don't do any work until the baby is born and takes its first breath. You know, when the doctor holds the baby upside-down and gives it a pat on the butt to start the baby screaming—and breathing. That first breath fills the lungs with air and they open up. Before then, when the baby is still inside the uterus, the fetal lungs stay flattened, squished-up tight. The baby's heart can hardly pump blood through them because when they're squeezed so tight they provide too much resistance. It's like trying to run water through a hose that has a lot of crimps in it. So far, so good?"

"Yes, that's very clear. Please, continue."

"OK. While the baby is still inside the womb the red and blue blood actually mix with each other in a couple of places, both within the heart and in some of the big blood vessels. One place where they mix is a little hole in the wall between the right and left side of the heart called the *foramen ovale*, which I mentioned a minute ago. That hole in the heart should close once the baby is born but if it stays open it can become a problem and would need surgery to close it. The other place where the red and blue blood mix is a little tube outside the heart that connects the aorta and the pulmonary artery. Again, in normal babies this little tube, called the *ductus arteriosus*, shuts down and closes soon after birth, but in these very small babies it can stay open for a while. If it stays open too long, that's what I referred to earlier as 'PDA,' for *patent ductus arteriosus* and it needs to be closed. In Donny Johnson's case, neither the hole in the heart nor the *ductus arteriosus* ever needed surgery, so Dr. Scheld only saw the baby that one time, just to check to see if surgery might be necessary."

Bernardine Pekings was impressed and pleased by Kahn's evident ability to communicate reasonably well when forced to. Kahn would not be a perfect witness, a bit pedantic, still too reliant on jargon, but she could be taught to speak simply enough to get through to the average juror.

"So Dr. Scheld had only that one contact. How about you, Dr. Kahn? What further involvement did you have?"

"I checked on the baby a number of times over the coming months to see if he might need surgery, which he didn't. I also was called in to consult when the baby had some mild congestive heart failure, maybe from getting too much IV fluid. But this baby never showed any signs of serious heart problems, so my consultations were all rather routine. I don't think I saw him after about six weeks or so, he was doing so well."

"Very good. I think both of you should be in the clear without too much trouble. We will prepare the motions to have you dismissed from the lawsuit as soon as possible. We '*never say never*' in the law, the same as in medicine, but I would anticipate that you should face no liability in this case. You may need to testify, however, as witnesses. You are likely to have to produce documents as well, anything bearing on the Johnson case. I'm sure you are already well aware of this, but you should not alter or destroy any records or notes, no matter what they say, now that the lawsuit has been filed."

"It's been several years since this baby was born. What if some of our records have already been discarded?"

"Good question. If something has already been trashed as a matter of routine in your office, that's perfectly acceptable legally. Unfortunately it could still work to your disadvantage, because when something is missing the other side can allege that it said just about anything that serves their purpose and you don't have the document to prove them wrong. Another important point: don't talk about this case outside of this office. Our conversations are privileged, but whatever you discuss with someone who is not your lawyer is not privileged. Do you have any questions?"

Bernardine Pekings had delivered her advice in such a confident and concise manner that Morton Scheld had to admit she impressed him.

Scheld replied, "No. Thank you." Somewhere deep inside of him a nascent thought that women might actually be able to handle certain professions struggled to emerge but failed, remaining inchoate, never actually surfacing into his consciousness.

Lesley Kahn simply nodded, and followed her partner out of the office. She would never have tolerated Scheld's Paleolithic attitudes toward women if he hadn't been such a gifted surgeon. Smart, competent professional women like Pekings were her norm. She allowed herself to believe that perhaps, having met Pekings, Morton Scheld might have taken yet another baby step toward realizing that intellect was not determined by the presence of a Y chromosome. Walking behind him she was pleased that Morton Scheld could not see the look of smug satisfaction on her face.

Chapter 23: Face-to-Face

As she sat through the sessions with Jerry Janckovich and Stephanie Sorano prepping her for the upcoming deposition, Sarah Belden felt like an understudy being rushed into the lead role. Was this really happening to her? Wasn't there some other person all of this was meant for? Feeling utterly out of place in the briefing room with the two lawyers, she had to force herself to listen attentively as they walked the fine line of coaching her without ever putting words in her mouth. They avoided explicitly suggesting what her answers should be, and often reminded Sarah that they were *not* telling her what to say. She should always use her own words and tell the truth. In that way, if asked—as she probably would be—Sarah could always answer truthfully, *"No, my lawyers did not tell me what to say."*

In one of the first sessions Janckovich said, "Dr. Belden, I need to warn you that the rules for depositions are different than in court. We don't have nearly as much control over the situation in a deposition as we would in court. There is no judge to intervene. We cannot stop the other side's lawyers from asking questions unless they are extremely inappropriate. Most of the time we can only file objections for the record, and try later to get the questions and answers excluded on various legal grounds. But during the actual deposition we can do little to control what you are asked, unless the situation gets so out of hand that we simply call an end to it and instruct you to cease answering questions entirely. If that happens, which isn't very often, we'll go fight it out before the judge to determine the ground rules for a further deposition."

"That's pretty scary, Mr. Janckovich. You mean they can ask me just about anything?"

"If it has any relevance to the case, yes, almost anything. But don't worry, we'll be right there with you. And, Dr. Belden, you're

161

doing fine, we don't think you have anything to be concerned about. You're smart, you're a good student, you've probably been through much worse oral exams in your time."

Janckovich's words were hardly reassuring, since they served to remind Sarah of the two days of oral exams she had suffered through to become board-certified in pediatrics. And, as it turned out, despite the hours of preparation, this time Sarah was not at all ready for the ordeal that ensued.

The first shock came when she walked into the big conference room in the offices of Sorano, Janckovich, English & Weill and realized that the deposition would be a far bigger production than she had imagined. She was to be Dr. Sarah Belden onstage under bright lights, performing before a much larger audience than the one or two lawyers and stenographer she had expected. In addition to Jerry Janckovich, close to a dozen people were crowded into the room, anonymous men and women dressed in dark business suits, all sitting bolt upright around the table, staring at her like vultures eyeing their prey. There was a stenographer like the one she had pictured from courtroom scenes on television, an older woman with wire glasses who looked like an off-duty librarian, with her fingers poised over the keyboard of a small boxy instrument on a tripod stand. But it was clear to her that the stenographer was merely an adjunct, an anachronistic backup to more modern systems that would capture her every word and gesture. Wires and cables criss-crossed the room, connecting stacks of audio and video equipment. A studio-sized television camera would record not just what she said but also her facial expressions, body language, and tone of voice for all to see and hear. A technician wandered around the room testing the sound and picture and organizing boxes of videotapes.

A speakerphone resembling a large black starfish loomed in the center of the table, alerting her that there would be people listening that she couldn't even see. For reasons she couldn't understand, the thought of strangers off in unknown places hearing her every word was even more unnerving than facing the crowd in the room. She already felt uncomfortable that she couldn't tell friend from foe among the ones she could see and now she had to worry about some invisible listeners.

Sarah didn't have long to obsess over the remote participants on the phone line before she received the second shock of the deposition. As soon as she took her seat a man at the head of the big table stood, looked directly at her, and bellowed, "Dr. Belden, I am Fred Vagram. My law firm represents the Johnson family. I will be conducting the proceedings today."

The words were so loud they sent Sarah's head reeling backward.

In the closed room the earsplitting sound of the man's voice nearly undid Sarah Belden's last grasp on self-control. Jerry Janckovich had repeatedly warned Sarah not to be startled by the strident way that Fred Vagram spoke, but nothing could have prepared her for actually hearing his piercing, stabbing voice in person. The noise blasted directly into her head, unnerving her. She looked around and realized she had no possibility of escape.

Still speaking in his thunderous voice the man gestured toward a slight, brown-skinned man in a perfectly-fitting but nondescript dark suit next to him, saying, "With me is my colleague, Dr. Sanjay Fijam, who is also a lawyer. I will be the only person asking you questions today but I may consult with Dr. Fijam from time to time. Have you been made aware of the procedure?"

Straining to keep from over-reacting to the noise level, Sarah nodded silently in response to Vagram's question. She paid an immediate price for relying on body language: Vagram unleashed a shrill rebuke, his imposing presence magnified by the volume of his voice.

"Dr. Belden," Vagram boomed, "despite the video you must speak out loud, since all of your responses will be recorded and transcribed for the record."

Sarah turned toward Jerry Janckovich. Well attuned to Fred Vagram's techniques for unsettling witnesses, her enormous ally was already responding to Vagram. "Dr. Belden knows what she needs to do, Fred. Just ask your questions and she will answer them." Janckovich spoke in a firm, though not hostile tone, his impressive *basso profundo* carrying the clear message that their side was not going to be intimidated.

"I have no doubt she has been well prepared, Jerry," replied Vagram, clearly insinuating that she had been coached carefully on what to say and what not to say. Intimating that he could squeeze the truth out of her no matter how well she had been rehearsed he added, "and we eagerly await her responses to our questions." Turning back to Sarah he said, "OK, Dr. Belden, are you ready to begin?"

Janckovich looked at Sarah. "Dr. Belden?"

"Sure. Wait, can I please have a glass of water?"

Janckovich pointed to the glass of water and an unopened bottle sitting right in front of her on the table. Sarah had not noticed either one. Embarrassed, she gulped down a mouthful of water. This was definitely not a good start. What was wrong with her if she couldn't even see that there was water right in front of her?

"Fine, thanks," she said, recovering. "You can start."

A young man flipped several switches on different pieces of equipment, positioned a pair of heavily padded headphones over his ears, and spoke directly into the big camera. He recited the name of the lawsuit, the date, time and location of the deposition, his name, the name of his company, the fact that he was certified as a legal videographer, and that about every two hours he would need to interrupt the proceedings to change the videotape. He turned the camera so that it pointed at Sarah Belden and stated the identity of the witness. Then he panned the room and recorded all of the attendees as each said their name and identified their affiliation. He repeated the drill for two lawyers on the phone who had been stranded at O'Hare Airport.

Sarah had wondered who all the people in the room were, but their brief self-descriptions were all a blur to her. She was in a fog, feeling as though she was watching the proceedings rather than being the central attraction. She came back into the moment when she was asked to swear that she would tell the truth, the whole truth, and nothing but the truth, so help her God. Sarah said, "I do," and the deposition began.

Fred Vagram rose at his place and roared, "Please state your full name, date of birth, and address, Dr. Belden."

Despite the startling intensity of Vagram's voice, Sarah was momentarily distracted by a sudden cry of anguish from the technician monitoring the sound level of the proceedings. Looking in the poor fellow's direction, she caught a glimpse of the needle on some sort of meter vibrating wildly in the red zone on the instrument's dial as Vagram's booming voice coursed directly into the man's head through his bulky earphones.

Sarah had been repeating her own name, date of birth, and address over and over to herself during the past few seconds, just to be sure she got them right. Now, like airing the contents of a tape that had been playing silently in her head, she heard her voice saying,

"Sarah Jane Belden O'Malley. I am known professionally as Dr. Sarah Belden. I was born August 1, 1963. I live at 300 West Park Lane, Apartment 6B."

As she spoke, the unsettling image of her encounter with Martina Johnson in the grocery store coursed through her brain, sending her mind floating away. Once again she was wandering aimlessly down the aisles, then staring at the repulsive mounds of chicken flesh. But just as quickly as her consciousness had been commandeered by the memory, a booming voice cut through her, startling her back into the moment. Fred Vagram was apparently repeating a question she had missed during the flashback.

"Dr. Belden, I asked you to describe your medical training and credentials. You are a pediatrician, correct?"

The force of Vagram's voice got Sarah back into gear. First her mind returned, then her own voice, until at last she was in full control of herself, of her part of this interrogation, her role in this unfamiliar drama. Yes, she was indeed a pediatrician. She recounted her medical school years and her progression through the post-graduate pediatric training. Then she was answering more and more questions, all bellowed at her with uncomfortable volume. Yes, she knew Martina Johnson, Derek Johnson, Donny Johnson. Yes, she was on duty the morning of Sunday, November 10, 1988. Yes, she was involved in the delivery-room care of Donny Johnson that morning. Yes, she had performed the immediate resuscitation of the baby, giving him his first breath some 45 seconds after he was born, some 25 seconds after she began the successful endotracheal intubation, all as recorded by the nurse's note in his chart.

"Dr. Belden, what was your rank, your status at the time Donny Johnson was born?"

"I was the Senior Resident in Pediatrics, the highest-ranking pediatric staff doctor on site in the hospital."

"Were you a neonatologist?"

"Objection," said Jerry Janckovich, "she answered the question about her status."

Janckovich spoke as much to establish a pattern as to intervene on this particular question. He would object many times during the deposition, not jumping up dramatically as actors did on television shows, although he was capable of spectacular histrionics when necessary in a real courtroom. This was a deposition where he could not easily cut off a question, so he was speaking for the record, for a possible hearing before a judge someday. But mainly he was reminding Vagram that Sarah Jane Belden was not alone in this room, she had her defender, a big one at that, and nothing truly out of line would be tolerated.

"No, as I said, I was a pediatric resident."

"Was there a neonatologist in the delivery room with you?"

"No."

Sarah was tempted to say more, to describe how she had called for the neonatologist and been told that Giuliana Silvestre was on her way, but she knew better. Janckovich's oft-repeated guidance echoed in her memory, *"Answer the question that is asked, only that, nothing more. Don't give them information they haven't asked for."*

"Why was there no neonatologist there?" asked Vagram. Sarah knew full well where he was going.

"We had no advance warning that a high-risk delivery was going to take place, so there was no time to call the neonatologist beforehand," Sarah said, trying to put the best light on the absence of a fully-qualified specialist.

"Where were you when you were called to the delivery?"

"In the housestaff on-call room."

"And where was the neonatologist?"

"My understanding is that she was at St. Anne Moray hospital."

"So she was not physically present in Memorial General Hospital when Donny Johnson was born?"

"Objection, answered" said Jerry Janckovich.

"No, she was not. Or maybe I should say, yes, she was not. She was not present."

"Was there another neonatologist in Memorial General at that time?"

"Objection, answered."

"Not that I am aware of."

"Why not?"

"I am not the person who determined where the neonatologists were stationed, so I cannot tell you why."

She had responded to similar questions many times in her preparatory sessions with Jerry Janckovich, so she knew that she could limit her answer to matters that she had first-hand knowledge of. At least she could try.

Vagram was unfazed. He knew how to recast a question to force an answer.

"In your personal experience, were there ever neonatologists immediately available at Memorial General?"

"Yes."

"Yes? Under what circumstances, Dr. Belden?" Vagram asked, appearing slightly puzzled by her reply. After all, his case was centered around the absence of appropriate staffing and resources at Memorial General to take care of Donny Johnson.

"When we knew that a high-risk delivery was going to take place, we would call ahead and have a neonatologist present."

"Ah," said Vagram, showing that he realized her explanation presented no unexpected problem. In fact, he thought it provided him with an opening to pursue precisely the course he wanted to follow. "You would call ahead. Where would you call, Dr. Belden?"

"We would call the paging number for the neonatologist on call."

"So the neonatologists were only present at Memorial General Hospital when they knew a high-risk baby was about to be born?"

"Yes, in my experience, unless they were there for some other reason."

"Such as?"

"If we had another sick baby in the intensive care nursery, the neonatologist might happen to be in the hospital when an unexpected high-risk birth was taking place."

"So that would only occur by happenstance, correct?"

"Yes."

"When did the neonatologist arrive in the case of Donny Johnson?"

"Shortly after we took him to the neonatal intensive care unit."

"So you were responsible for all the medical care in the delivery room?"

"For the baby. Yes."

"And how long before the baby was in the neonatal intensive care unit and the neonatologist was on the scene?"

"I'm not sure, but I believe it was about fifteen to twenty minutes."

"Who was that neonatologist?"

"Dr. Giuliana Silvestre."

"Who was responsible for the baby's care from that point on?"

"I stayed on the nursery and neonatal intensive care unit rotation for the rest of the month, then another Senior Resident took over."

"So you were in charge?"

"Ultimately, Dr. Silvestre was in charge. She was the Attending Physician for the entire hospitalization."

Sarah wondered briefly whether she might have just unintentionally compromised Giuliana Silvestre somehow, but she had no time to worry about any such consequences. She had to answer the questions as asked. Truthfully.

"So from that point forward, Dr. Silvestre was at Memorial General, full-time, twenty-four hours per day?"

"Objection," said Jerry Janckovich.

"No, she made regular rounds, but she was not in the hospital full-time."

"Doesn't a baby like Donny Johnson require full-time medical attention?"

"Yes, and he got it, twenty-four hours a day, from the Senior Residents in the hospital."

"But not from a neonatologist?"

"No."

"How about the neonatologists-in-training, the Neonatology Fellows, I believe they are called? Were they there twenty-four hours a day?"

"No."

"Why not?"

"The neonatology fellows are based at the University, they do not come to Memorial General."

Sarah stopped, upset with herself for answering a question that she could have deflected on the grounds that it was not her place to know *why*.

"How about neonatal nurse specialists? Were they there twenty-four hours per day?"

"There were nurses in the neonatal intensive care unit at all times, as far as I know."

"But were they specially-trained as neonatal nurse specialists?"

"Objection."

"I am not in a position to be aware of their training background."

Better, she told herself, that was a better answer.

"So no neonatologist, no neonatology fellows, no neonatal nurse specialist, is that correct?"

"Objection. Already stated."

"As far as I know, yes."

"Dr. Belden, you stated that you attended medical school at the University. Did you spend any time in the Neonatal Intensive Care Unit there?"

"Yes. Four weeks in my third year, and another four weeks in my senior year."

"And since then?"

"The pediatric residents at Memorial General have two months of elective time every year. I spent one of those elective periods, four weeks, as a second-year resident at the University in the neonatal intensive care unit."

"So you are familiar with the way that the intensive care unit operates at the University?"

"From a medical student's or second-year resident's perspective, yes."

"In your experience, were there neonatology fellows in the intensive care unit twenty-four hours per day?"

"Physically present at all times in the unit itself? No, not that I recall."

"Readily available, then, in the hospital with easy access to the neonatal intensive care unit?"

"Yes."

"Neonatal nurse specialists?"

"Yes."

"Attending neonatologists?"

"Not twenty-four hours every day, no."

"How frequently?"

"Objection."

"Based on my experience, a lot of the time."

"What is 'a lot'?"

"Pretty much whenever there was a very sick or very small baby."

"Was that more the rule or the exception?"

"More the rule, I suppose."

"And how about other specialists with particular expertise in taking care of extremely tiny or sick newborn babies? Cardiologists? Cardiac surgeons? Neurologists? Neurosurgeons?"

"They were not in the hospital twenty-four hours per day every day, no, not to my knowledge."

"How about advanced trainees, Fellows, in each of those fields?"

"Yes."

"Yes, what?"

"Yes, I believe the University has fellowships in all of those subspecialties and they were in the hospital twenty-four hours a day as far as I remember."

Vagram's questioning continued like this for another three hours. Specialty by specialty, he asked about every physician who had been called to examine Donny Johnson. He made her describe every piece of equipment, every advanced technology that could possibly be used to diagnose or treat problems in small babies, all the medical breakthroughs that Sanjay Fijam's research had identified.

"*When did MRIs become available at Memorial General?*"

"I do not know."

"*Were you using surfactant replacement therapy to keep premature babies' lungs inflated?*"

"I believe surfactant replacement was unknown at the time."

"*What type of Oxygen sensors were in use, and were they able to servo-control the oxygen content automatically?*"

"I do not recall the brand of sensors, but I do not believe they controlled the oxygen flow directly."

On and on it went. Over and over, Vagram emphasized the distinction between care that such a baby might have gotten at the University and the care he actually received at Memorial General.

During the lunch break, Sarah followed Jerry Janckovich into a private room just down the corridor from the Great Hall of The Inquisition.

"That voice," said Sarah, "I've never heard anything like that in my life. It's deafening. It's so loud, it's actually hard to concentrate on what he's saying, especially in a closed room like that. My head aches. My ears are ringing."

Just then Stephanie Sorano came in, casually it seemed. Sarah was glad to see her, another face, a friendly, female face.

170

"How's she doing, Jerry?" asked Stephanie.

"She's great, just great. Calm, responsive but not overly chatty, no problems at all. She's rather taken with Fred's voice, though," he chuckled.

Sarah wondered if his praise of her performance was his honest assessment or if it were meant to bolster her morale, but she didn't care. She was grateful for the positive words either way.

"I figured as much. With your experience and her brains, I knew she'd do fine. Don't let that guy's voice bother you, Dr. Belden. He's always been like that and no one knows how to get him to tone down."

"I just can't imagine being around him all day. It positively hurts just to hear him talk."

"Yes, I know what it's like, I've had to sit through many depositions with him," Sorano responded sympathetically. "I've even seen judges threaten him with contempt because of his volume, but they never have actually done so."

Then Sorano returned to the subject.

"Where are they going with their questions?"

"Exactly where we expected," replied Janckovich. "They want to lay a foundation for their gross negligence charge. They are essentially arguing that Memorial General was some kind of primitive backwater that hardly deserved to be licensed as a hospital, let alone allowed to take care of sick babies. That argument can only go so far—after all, no one could deny that this baby would not have lived at all if he hadn't gotten the advanced medical care he received at Memorial General. He'd be in the ground with his siblings."

He stopped, annoyed with himself for having made reference to the other Johnson babies in front of Sarah Belden. He was relieved when she broke a small smile and said, "That's OK, I remember the others all the time anyway, you can't make it any worse. Excuse me, just a minute, please."

Sarah's smile covered the shudder that raced through her body from Janckovich's words, not the mention of the lost Johnson babies but saying that *this baby would not have lived at all if he hadn't gotten the advanced medical care he received at Memorial General.* Too true, Sarah sighed, all too true. Donny would not have lived at all if she had let him be.

Sarah needed a moment to herself. She went into the private rest room down the hall, the one reserved exclusively for deposition witnesses to spare them any potentially embarrassing confrontations with lawyers from the other side when they were in a vulnerable moment attending to biological needs. She headed straight to the sink and doused her face with cold water for the better part of a minute. Grateful that the law firm stocked its rest rooms with soft, thick linen hand towels, she padded her face dry, brushed her hair, and did her best to refresh her basic make-up, which was limited to a light touch of nearly transparent lipstick and just a hint of color on her cheeks, no eye shadow or mascara.

Once Sarah had finished with the sink she took a long stop in the stall, as much for the peace and quiet as to relieve herself. When she returned to the private meeting room Jerry Janckovich and Stephanie Sorano were just finishing thick roast beef sandwiches on croissants. Turkey shards on Janckovich's plate told her the roast beef had not been the big man's only sandwich. She stared at the array of food on the credenza off to one side, not sure if she were famished or too tense to eat, but finally took what looked like turkey breast and Swiss, also on a croissant, with butter. The bread was excellent, so good it made her want to finish the sandwich and nibble at a second one. Estimating that there was still enough food left for another eight or ten people, she hoped that the food would not be wasted, that office staff would get to share the bounty. After all, she realized, it would all be charged to her insurance company. She was cheered a bit by the thought that something good might come out of this nightmare after all: she was, in effect, about to take the office staff to lunch.

When the deposition resumed, Fred Vagram opened with what seemed like the same line of questioning, but soon started down a somewhat different path.

"Dr. Belden, you realize you are still under oath?" he bellowed.

Sarah had her bearings now. She looked directly at Fred Vagram with a new sense of confidence and said, "Sure. Yes."

"Before Baby Johnson, had you ever taken care of a baby in the 600-gram range?"

"Yes."

"At Memorial General?"

"No."

"Where?"

"During my rotations at the University."

"How about at Memorial General?"

"Objection. Answered."

Jerry Janckovich knew where this was heading and wanted to reestablish his presence.

"As I said, not at Memorial General."

"Were any babies in the 600-gram range born at Memorial General while you were there?"

"We had some small babies, well under 1,000 grams, but I don't remember how small."

"And were they treated at Memorial General?"

"I took care of two or three in the delivery room, and initially in the neonatal intensive care unit."

"Initially?" roared Vagram. "What do you mean, 'initially'?"

Sarah scolded herself for adding an unnecessary word, but didn't lose her composure. "I don't remember how long I was on their cases, not very long."

"The hospital records show that in the last 15 years, no baby less than 1,000 grams was treated at Memorial General for more than two days until Donny Johnson. All the others died or were transferred to the University."

Vagram paused, too long for Jerry Janckovich.

"Objection. Dr. Belden is not here to testify to the entire history of the hospital. What's the question that addresses her own experience and knowledge?"

"Just catching my breath, counselor." Then, to Sarah, "Is that consistent with your experience at Memorial General?"

"Yes."

One word this time, no embellishment.

"Did you think that the Johnson baby should be transferred to the University?"

"Objection."

Sarah was perfectly willing to respond.

"I do not remember thinking that we should transfer that baby, no."

"Did you ever discuss transferring him? With Dr. Giuliana Silvestre? With any other doctors? With anyone?"

"I do not recall any discussions along that line."

"Let me show you some excerpts from the nursing notes in Donny Johnson's chart. I'm going to ask you to look them over and see if they refresh your memory."

Vagram handed Sarah a small stack of papers and passed another set to Janckovich. The papers looked like photocopies of pages from a hospital chart. Each sheet was divided into two wide columns. The left-hand side, where the nurses recorded vital signs and other measurements, occupied about one-third of each page, and the larger right-hand side held handwritten notes by the doctors or other clinicians. The perfect script in the left-hand column unmistakably identified those as nursing notes—no doctor she knew, herself included, ever wrote that clearly once they had advanced in school beyond about the 6th grade.

"Document and copies yet to be authenticated," intoned Jerry Janckovich for the record. "I would remind Counsel that Dr. Belden is not required to comment on documents that she has not had time to review."

"Take as long as you need, Dr. Belden," said Fred Vagram.

Sarah and Janckovich read through their copies in silence.

"Thursday, November 14, 10:21 AM. Combined staff conference to discuss Baby Johnson. Dr. Giuliana Silvestre, Dr. Sarah Belden, Dr. Jane Zimmerman, Patti Jennings (day nurse), Melinda Brady (overnight nurse), present. Cindy Portugal, pediatric units administrator joined after few minutes. Discussed plans for baby. Patti asked whether baby was to be transferred to University. Silvestre asked why. Patti said nurses worried, baby's care very demanding, requires full-time attention of the only nurses with more than few months in NICU. Pressure getting to them. Also X-ray techs not getting clear pictures, retaking over and over, lab techs complaining needed larger blood samples, respiratory techs saying they were spending half their shifts on one baby. Silvestre said baby doing well, will stay at Mem. Gen. Everyone to keep up good work, not ready to consider transfer. Further questions for 5-10 minutes, similar responses, no transfer. Portugal thanked everyone, said that what the doctors decided was consistent with the Hospital Administration's views. Meeting ended 10:50AM."

"Do you recall this meeting, Dr. Belden?"

"It seems familiar, but I don't remember this one in particular. We had a lot of meetings about this baby and all the others."

"Do you recall discussing the possibility of transferring the baby?"

"Objection, answered."

"To the best of your knowledge, do you have any reason to doubt that these notes reflect a meeting that you attended?"

"As I said, it seems familiar, so I would assume it happened. I just don't remember the particular meeting."

"Did you ever recommend that the baby be transferred?"

"Objection. Answered."

"I believe, Counselor, that my previous question was whether Dr. Belden *thought* the baby should be transferred, not whether she *recommended* he be transferred. Would you like the transcript to be read back to Dr. Belden?"

Janckovich regretted interrupting Vagram, not just because he immediately realized his objection was not quite accurate, but mainly because it gave Vagram an excuse to turn his already-piercing volume up a click or two for emphasis.

"No. Proceed," said Janckovich.

"Not that I recall, no. I don't think so," Sarah responded.

"Did you feel that the baby was getting optimal care at Memorial General?"

"We were doing the best we could for the baby. He was getting very good care."

"But did you think he would have been better off at the University?"

"It wasn't for me to decide. I was a Resident at Memorial General, my job was to take care of my patients."

Vagram looked at Sarah Belden for a long moment, then surprised everyone by saying, "Five minute break, OK?"

"We should be the ones to ask for breaks," said Janckovich. "But sure, Counselor, we'll accommodate you."

"Videotape stopped," said the videographer, adding the exact time, "at 1:32 PM."

Vagram did not get up from the table as Sarah and Janckovich walked into the corridor. He started thumbing through stacks of paper with the assistance of his silent colleague.

"What's that about?" Sarah asked.

"No reason to speculate, we'll find out soon enough. He probably forgot where he was going next, and needed to look at something. Not a problem, you're doing great. Do you want to go back into the small conference room?"

"Not really. Can we just walk around for a few minutes?"

"You bet. The building is like a large rectangular donut—all the corridors just go in one big loop around a central courtyard. Let's get some exercise."

175

"Thanks."

After they had circled the entire floor, they stopped at the deposition room. Janckovich tapped on the glass wall and made eye contact with Fred Vagram, who held up his index finger, asking for a bit more time. When Janckovich nodded his assent, Sarah felt relieved. She would take all the time out of the deposition room she could get. They made one more lap of the building before Vagram gave them the thumbs-up sign that he was ready.

When the entire group was reassembled around the large table the videographer asked, "Are you ready to proceed?"

Vagram and Janckovich both said yes, as did Sarah, and the videographer said, "Videotape resumed at 1:55 PM."

"Dr. Belden," Vagram began. His volume had diminished slightly, which Sarah unexpectedly found unnerving. What was he up to? Why had his overwhelming presence shifted? Why was he appearing to be less aggressive?

"Dr. Belden, when you attended to Donny Johnson in the delivery room, what condition were you in?"

"Excuse me? What do you mean?"

"Were you tired? Had you been working long hours? Were you at your best?"

"Objection."

"I was fine. We always worked hard, but I was fine."

Stop, she reminded herself. She should not try to explain any more. She should just answer the question.

"How much sleep had you gotten?"

"Not much."

"How much is that, Dr. Belden?"

"Ten or fifteen minutes."

"And you had been working all the previous day, all that evening, and into the night and early morning before you got to bed, is that correct?"

"Yes."

"You had a number of serious problems to deal with that day and evening, right?"

"We were always faced with serious problems."

"Did you take any breaks, any time off? Any naps? Did you have any rest at all between 6AM Saturday morning when your shift started and 3:15 AM Sunday when you were paged to the delivery room?"

"No."

"So you were tired, went to bed, and got called to the delivery room after ten or fifteen minutes, is that correct?"

Vagram's volume knob was clicking back up, question by question.

"Yes."

"Dr. Belden, were you in any shape to attend to that baby under those circumstances?"

"Objection."

"Everything went well, so I must have been in good shape."

Sarah briefly thought she had gotten the better of him, but soon realized he was not so easily defeated.

"Ah, yes, everything went well, you say. Everything you were able to do for that baby in that delivery room in that hospital went well. And if things had not gone well—what then?"

"Objection. Calls for speculation."

"You already told us there was no neonatologist, no neonatology fellow, no one more experienced than you available at that time, isn't that correct?"

"Yes."

"So Donny Johnson was fortunate—in the delivery room. But from that moment on, he was still in a place with a limited capacity to care for him, right?"

"He was still at Memorial General Hospital."

"With limited resources, isn't that correct?"

"Every hospital has limits to its resources."

"In this case, the precise resources needed to provide state-of-the-art care for a baby this size were present at the University and not at Memorial General?"

"I am a general Pediatrician, I'm not an expert in state-of-the-art neonatal care."

"So your answer is…?"

"I don't know the answer."

"Let me rephrase my question."

Now Vagram's volume was in the red zone, any louder it would have been screaming, hollering, intolerable.

"Were the resources to care for such a small baby far greater at the University than at Memorial General?"

"I suppose so. Sure. Yes."

"Thank you Dr. Belden." Then to Sarah's amazement, he said, "That's all for today. Counselor, do you have any remarks for the record?"

Jerry Janckovich shook his expansive head and said "No."

The Videographer calculated the expired time at exactly six hours, and announced that the tape was ending. As he shut down his equipment the room exploded with the voices of the dozen or so talkative professionals suddenly liberated from their uncomfortable roles as silent yet attentive spectators. Multiple conversations broke out as they released their pent-up energy and chatted among themselves.

Sarah stood up and felt her knees start to buckle. She grabbed the back of her chair to steady herself and blinked several times as Martina Johnson's utterly hapless face in the grocery store aisle once again flashed before her eyes. What was to become of her?

Chapter 24: New Game Plan

Stephanie Sorano sat across from Jerry Janckovich at the table in one of the firm's small meeting rooms, her elbows on the table top, her hands wrapped around her heavily stained coffee mug, covering the inscription: *Go Ahead, Make My Day—Sue Me*. As usual she was dressed well in an expensive two-piece tweed pants suit with one of her billowing blouses. But her fashionable clothes couldn't conceal the toll that stress and long hours were taking. Frazzled strands of hair hung listlessly over her ears, dark puffiness under her eyes betrayed her lack of sleep. She looked at her colleague and said, "We're not positioned exactly the same, Jerry. Your client, Dr. Belden, may end up in the clear, but my Dr. Silvestre is in some heavy doo-doo."

"Uh-huh, my thoughts precisely. There's no evidence that the medical care Dr. Belden delivered failed to meet the standard at that time, none at all. Or that she withheld anything from the baby that he would have received at other comparable hospitals. So I agree, on the charge of medical malpractice, they can't prove the key element against her, that she breached the standard of care in a way that caused harm to Donny Johnson. And whoever was responsible for keeping him at Memorial General, it wasn't her. So, yes, I think we have a good chance to get Belden out of this case. Once everything is in place, we'll file a motion to dismiss her from the suit on the grounds that the other side has not made a *prima facie* case that she was negligent or that she made the decision to keep the baby at Memorial General. If that doesn't work we'll settle her out for a minimal sum. I don't want to be too optimistic just yet, but that seems to be a likely scenario."

"Yes, exactly. She was an employee in a subordinate role. She didn't do anything wrong, and she had no power to order the baby to be transferred, even if they can make the case that he would have been better off at the University. Not her pay grade, not her duty."

"Yup. After that deposition, she was most likely transformed from a defendant into a witness. For her sake, let's hope so. She's not what that screaming idiot Vagram wants anyway. He wants big bucks from Memorial General and from Dr. Silvestre and her lucrative neonatology group for gross negligence, punitive damages. That's what that *'state-of-the-art'* questioning was all about."

"But to get to gross negligence, Vagram needs to show that Silvestre and the hospital had a duty to the baby to get him care at a level much higher than what they were able to provide at Memorial General. Think he's getting there?"

"Not sure. It's not like there are a lot of similar cases to draw on. Hard to know how difficult your Italian lady's situation is."

"She's hardly Italian any more, Jerry—she's been a citizen here for many years."

"Yeah, yeah, you know what I mean. OK, I won't refer to her as Italian."

"You're hopeless. Unfortunately, her prospects are even worse than you know."

"How's that?"

"She told me she thought the baby needed to be transferred to the University."

"What? Why didn't you tell me this sooner?"

"Haven't had a chance, helping you prepare for Dr. Belden's deposition. And, I wanted to hear Belden testify first."

"OK. So, why didn't Silvestre send the baby over to the University?"

"Hospital administration threatened her, scared her into keeping the baby at Memorial General. She says that miserable little twerp Kappel thought the publicity was good for them, and he also wanted the money from the Johnson's insurance company as long as it lasted."

"What exactly did he do? Did he overrule her to keep the baby at Memorial General?"

"That's a problem. A *big* problem for Silvestre. He covered his ass, paid lip service to not interfering with the practice of medicine, spouted platitudes about how medical decisions were up to the doctors. But then he told her she could be responsible for closing Memorial General if she transferred the baby. He said that all the poor people in town would suffer, they would have nowhere to go to get care if Memorial closed."

"She bought that crap from Kappel?"

"He was good at selling it, no doubt. On the face of it, he left it up to her, he didn't force her to keep the baby there. But in her mind, he put her in a position where she had no choice whatsoever."

"She was intimidated? That lady was intimidated?"

"I wouldn't say intimidated, but she was seriously disconcerted. He knocked her off track and she didn't insist on going ahead with the transfer."

"You're right, she's in a bad situation. Very worst case, the hospital gets off free and she's guilty of gross negligence. That would be a killer for her and her partners. If that happens they'll be out on the street like those idiot surgeons in the *Frontage Hospital* case years ago who let their one-eyed partner keep cutting on people, covering up his casualties. They never saw the *gross negligence* charge coming, they had no idea they would be personally liable for so much money. They went bust and most of them never practiced medicine again. Riches to rags in one lawsuit. Hopefully, Silvestre has a better case than those guys did. After all, unlike Kappel, Silvestre had absolutely nothing to gain by keeping the baby at Memorial General, by not transferring him to the University. If jurors ever get this case and hear her and Kappel testify in person I think they are likely to believe her story that he overwhelmed her with pressure. Then the hospital most likely would share the liability with the neonatologists."

"Whether the hospital shares the liability or not she would take a big hit either way, maybe even a fatal one financially. And who knows what it might do to her professionally, or personally. Any other thoughts?"

Janckovich hesitated momentarily, wondering how much Stephanie Sorano's own tortured experience as a physician had shaped her feelings about what could await Giuliana Silvestre. Putting the thought out of his mind as not helpful to his assessment of the problem he said, "Not much. As for getting her off completely, we've got only two options that I see: undermine their gross negligence charge entirely, or stick it all on the hospital. Either way it's not going to be easy. Most of what she told you goes against her at least as much as it implicates the hospital. No matter what Kappel said to her, if she didn't exercise her best independent *medical* judgment, she wasn't meeting her duty to Donny Johnson."

"Uh-huh. That's the rub. At least on paper the buck stops with the doctor, even if the doctors are being pushed around by some corporation that ends up with most of the money."

"Exactly. Doctors nowadays are getting stuck with malpractice suits by patients when it was the managed care plan that wouldn't approve the right medical care, not anything the doctors did wrong. At least in theory the docs are still supposed to make sure their patients get what they need. But this is different because Silvestre could have ordered the transfer. She admitted she had that authority, it was under her control, even if she were intimidated by Kappel."

"So it was," Stephanie Sorano sighed, "so it was."

She hesitated, a dejected look sweeping across her face, something Janckovich had never seen from his strong-willed colleague. Again he wondered whether some connection between this case and the collapse of her own medical career was affecting her judgment. Then, to his relief, she brightened up and began speaking like the brilliant colleague he knew she was.

"You know, Jerry, we can defend her decisions on *medical* grounds. Babies that size mostly die, but they saved Donny Johnson at Memorial General. That's the central point here. Were other therapies, other specialists, other nurses, available at the University? Maybe so. *But transferring him wouldn't have made any difference*—that's what we need to prove. I think the evidence is strong. When babies like this survive, the evidence shows that it is quite common for them to have handicaps. I'll bet we can demonstrate that many of the preemies this size who survived at the University ended up more or less like Donny Johnson."

He was reassured. Sorano had not been distracted by reflections on her own previous life, had never lost her train of thought. She had only been contemplating their legal situation, analyzing her client's case, crafting a new strategy. He was the one who had been lapsing into thinking about her past, not her.

"Can we prove that?"

"We'll have to try."

"Anything else on our side?"

"Yes, that's actually the strongest part," Stephanie Sorano said, her voice rising with emotion. "Most of the early literature on the handicaps and other major problems experienced by tiny preemies who survived involved studies of such kids when they were

182

still pretty young. Very few studies followed those kids up until they were school-age, let alone for years and years afterward. The press really picked up on the early reports about how bad the physical and mental problems were for extreme preemies who survived. You know, all those stories about how modern medicine was spawning a generation of children who were seriously disabled by saving smaller and smaller infants. Those scare stories were so widely publicized it became generally accepted that extremely small infants would be permanently damaged if they managed to live long enough. But now we have some long-term research showing that many of these tiny babies are more resilient than we had thought. Much more resilient. A lot of them catch up, and even the ones with serious physical handicaps often are able to cope quite well when they get older."

"Damn, it's great having a doctor around," said Janckovich. "I can't tell you how many times I've tried to read the medical literature but I just can't do it, not like you. You not only understand that stuff, you get excited reading it."

"Well, yeah, sometimes I still do, I guess. The part that I think is important is that a fair number of those handicapped kids have actually done well in life, becoming independent enough to shatter the stereotype that they would need to be cared for every moment of their life. Many have had success in high school and college, and have found jobs and are living independently. The biggest dividing line is whether those severely premature babies lived or died. If they make it out of the hospital and beyond the first year or two of life, a surprisingly high proportion of them look fairly good in terms of what they can accomplish. Even the ones who suffer from some pretty serious physical handicaps and other limitations can do quite well. We've learned that disabled doesn't mean retarded. Their brains can be just fine even if the rest of their bodies have limitations."

Janckovich mulled over his partner's words. Something she had said was circling in his mind, searching for its connection to a distant memory. Then his eyes lit up and he came alive, blurting out, "Stephanie, that's brilliant, you just said something absolutely brilliant! You reminded me of Jeremy Wolke! We can use Jeremy Wolke!"

Stephanie had never seen him get so excited in all the years they worked together.

"Wolke is perfect," Janckovich continued. "Why didn't I think of him already? What an idiot I am!"

"Who is this Jeremy Wolke you're so ecstatic about?"

"He's a doctor of some kind, not an MD medical doctor, but a medical scientist. PhD, I think. Very smart, highly accomplished. Famous, even. He's the perfect expert witness."

"Why does he fit in this case?"

"Wait 'till you see him."

Chapter 25: Internecine Warfare

As always, Everett Kappel perched on his oversized chair at one end of the massive glass-top table in his office as if he were presiding from a throne. But this time he was not in charge. This was Frank Faison's meeting.

"Mr. Kappel, Ms. Portugal," Faison began, "I asked to meet with you to bring you up to date on the Johnson case, and to ask a few questions."

Faison sat to one side, as always leaving an empty place between him and Kappel. On the other side of the table Cindy Portugal separated herself even farther from her boss, so far that Faison had to twist his head when he shifted his gaze between her and Kappel. But since he also avoided sitting right next to the little tyrant he knew better than to ask her to move closer to Kappel.

Faison glanced at Portugal, then turned in Kappel's direction.

"There is some tentatively good news and some not-so-good news. The better part is that counsel defending Drs. Belden and Silvestre are preparing to make the case that this child is not so seriously harmed as he appears. They will argue that although Donny Johnson has major physical limitations, the scientific evidence shows that he may well be able to look forward to a fairly independent and even productive life. If they can establish that point it would greatly benefit our side of the case by undermining the plaintiff's arguments that Memorial General destroyed the child's potential for a worthwhile life. And if they prove that he has a decent chance to make it on his own, that would reduce the estimate of any damages in terms of financial support and future medical care costs. Most important of all, such a showing undercuts the argument that we—Memorial General Hospital—deserve to be *punished* for keeping him here. If he was not severely harmed by remaining in this hospital, then we should be able to argue that deciding not to transfer him was not gross negligence on our part. That's a very positive development for us. No gross negligence, no punitive damages, much less bad press."

"Fine. Good. What about the bad news?" Kappel said brusquely, his lips pursed into a snarl as he posed the question.

Faison responded in his normal speaking voice, showing no reaction to the hostile glare.

"As we anticipated, the pediatricians are preparing a 'Divide and Conquer' strategy that would put distance between them and the hospital. In short, they would blame any decision to keep him here on the hospital administration. The plaintiffs are actually giving them a hook to hang this on by making a point over one of the meetings they found in the nurse's notes, a meeting Ms. Portugal apparently attended."

He turned toward Cindy Portugal as he mentioned her name, but kept a dispassionate look on his face to avoid making any accusatory glances at her. He knew that Kappel would sell out his loyal assistant in an instant if given the opportunity, and Faison was determined to prevent Kappel from seizing the opportunity to make a scapegoat out of her. So, before Kappel could speak, Faison rotated back toward the head of the table, fixed his eyes on Kappel and said dispassionately, "Dr. Silvestre will testify that you brought undue pressure on her to keep the baby here, Mr. Kappel. The Portugal meeting is simply being used to bolster that argument."

Faison's attempt at a preemptive strike had little apparent effect on the impervious Kappel, who said, "Ms. Portugal attended such meetings as part of her responsibility as the pediatric unit administrator. I have every confidence in her and she often acts on her own, as I have delegated authority to her to run those units. Whatever she did, I am sure she believed it was in the best interests of the patients, as well as the hospital."

Cindy Portugal gasped, nearly choking at the blatant lie. Kappel had ordered her to attend that meeting to spy on the doctors and nurses and report back their every word to him. She had been little more than a scribe, with no authority whatsoever to make decisions.

Portugal struggled to contain the torrent of expletives and insults that cascaded through her head, all the while stiffening her resolve not to take a fall for this duplicitous man. She took a deep breath and, hoping her voice would not crack, she stared at Kappel and said icily, "I do not believe I did or said anything to suggest a particular course of action. I was there at your request, Mr. Kappel, as an *observer*. It was Dr. Silvestre who told the combined staff that Donny Johnson would remain at Memorial General. I simply stated that such a decision was consistent with the hospital administration's views." Turning toward Faison she continued, "My statement about the administration's views was based on my discussions with Mr. Kappel both before and after the staff meeting. Mr. Kappel will recall that I had argued in favor of transferring the baby to the University, but he was of a different opinion."

As gratified as he was to see Portugal's look of fierce determination in standing up to Kappel, Faison immediately realized that an internecine struggle could only hurt his real client, the hospital. If the other side got wind of the tensions between Kappel and his staff they could provoke them to attack each other and rip their defense to shreds. And Faison knew full well that Portugal was hardly the only hospital employee who couldn't stomach Kappel. A jury that saw how much he alienated his own staff would soon believe that the man hiding behind the mustache was indeed capable of sacrificing a baby's well being for his own interests.

Faison had anticipated some disagreement between Portugal and Kappel, but was caught off guard by the ease with which their enmity could be exposed. If they fought openly they would be sitting ducks for the other side and bring the hospital down with them. For the first time he began to consider that they might need to settle the case, however difficult it would be to come up with enough funds for a settlement that would satisfy Fred Vagram.

This would be rough. He needed time, this meeting wasn't helping.

Gathering up his papers abruptly Faison said, "Thank you both. I apologize for cutting this off so quickly, but a few considerations have crossed my mind that I need to explore."

Before Kappel could speak, Faison was out the door. Cindy Portugal quickly pushed back her chair, glared one last time at Kappel, and followed close behind Faison, unwilling to spend even a short moment alone in the room with Everett Kappel.

Chapter 26: Aligning Interests

Jerry Janckovich was just finishing a session in the gym at the health club when he looked up to see Frank Faison approaching him, a large green-and-white towel wrapped around his waist. "Hi Frank. Haven't seen you around here much."

"Yes," said Faison pleasantly. "I really need to get more exercise. I'm not the athlete you were...eh, sorry, *are.*" He moved closer, lowered his voice, and said softly, "Look, Jerry, I need to have a little chat with you. Off the record, nothing formal. Outside of your billing hours, if you get my drift."

Janckovich looked questioningly at Faison, wondering what this invitation was about. Although they weren't close friends they had a personal bond from the shared experience of having to deal with the problems that the doctors and administrators created for themselves and their institutions. Try as they might, a hospital's lawyers could only do so much to protect the hospital against itself. They could introduce measures that would lower the risks for patients but if those controls ever interfered with the institution's bottom line or threatened the medical rainmakers who brought in the big revenue, they would be squelched immediately. More than once Janckovich and Faison had commiserated, telling each other they should get over trying to change things and just accept that was how hospitals operated. And be thankful, since the intransigence of the hospital's leadership to change was why lawyers like them had jobs.

Janckovich nodded in acceptance. "Sure. If you're telling me we're not going to be talking about anything related to a particular case or client, my meter won't be ticking. Bit dicey for me to talk about a case without informing my client, as you know."

"Just a hypothetical discussion, nothing official. No need to have any record that we ever got together."

The serious look on Faison's face told Janckovich that something was up, but also that the locker room wasn't the place to find out what it was. Faison continued, "You know where *Jimmy's Diner* is? How about 7AM day after tomorrow?"

"Hypotheticals are for law school exams and I don't generally eat breakfast, but I like *Jimmy's*. See you there."

Two days later, Jerry Janckovich looked around *Jimmy's Diner* and was satisfied that he had picked a good spot for their meeting: none of the half-dozen truck drivers or the assorted downtrodden men pouring tablespoons of sugar and several ounces of cream into their coffee mugs looked like the kinds of folks who would have any interest in their discussion even if they did overhear their conversation. He did acknowledge that it was always possible that someone in that crowd would recognize him from his football days, but decided the risk was low. Most of the customers appeared unlikely to remember an aging former lineman.

Having surveyed the other patrons, Jerry Janckovich looked across the table at his breakfast companion and wondered what he was about to hear. Janckovich wasn't hungry. He had gotten up at his habitual 5AM and begun his day with his customary three large mugs of *Peet's Italian Roast* coffee. Most of the time he did not eat any food for breakfast, starting his real eating with an early lunch. But this morning at *Jimmy's* he ordered scrambled eggs, sausage and hash browns, and Texas toast, rationalizing his self-indulgence by telling himself he had to do something while Faison ate.

"Thanks for meeting me, Jerry," Faison said pleasantly after they had placed their orders.

"No problem, Frank. It's good to see you, even if you're forcing me to eat stuff that ought to trigger a red alert to my cardiologist. What's up?"

Faison wasted no more time on pleasantries.

"We're paddling upstream without a paddle, and our hands are getting more and more fouled every day. I'm referring to that hypothetical case, of course."

Faison avoided saying any names out loud—even in an out-of-the-way place like *Jimmy's*, someone might know the Johnson family or recognize Donny Johnson's name from the newspapers or television. Even more important, speaking in the abstract was indispensable if they were to sustain the pretense that they were not discussing the Johnson lawsuit.

"My hospital and your doctors are more or less on the same side, at least for now. So I'll be candid: the underlying charges are bogus, I'm convinced. Everything that was done medically came out better than anyone had a right to expect, and the other side hasn't identified specific acts that were not up to standard. But even so, we are not in a great position. Neither of us. Their boy is not someone we want a jury of twelve parents and grandparents to see in a courtroom."

"What you're saying sounds pretty real, Frank, not hypothetical. But we can speak in generalities. I agree that there are often reasons not to let some plaintiffs get in front of a jury, but we don't think we'll ever be in that position. Our people should be in the clear. There's no real case for liability, we expect to get that taken care of. And the fact that the kid is alive is what really counts—a fact that we believe we can drive home, even if it ends up in front of a jury."

"I don't disagree, not at all. But there's another facet to all of this: the interaction between my hospital administrator and your lady neonatologist is toxic. Having our sides fight back and forth over who made what decision will not serve either of us well. We're both likely to be dragged down by that kind of struggle. And if we go, your lady and her partners could get the worst of it—taking big bucks from a more-or-less public hospital is a lot more difficult for the citizens on a jury than sticking it to a doctor's malpractice insurance company. Jurors are sophisticated enough to understand that a lot of that hospital's dollars would come out of their own tax money one way or another. And, as you are well aware, there is the technical legal point about who's in control: hospitals don't discharge or transfer patients, doctors do."

The two lawyers looked at each other knowingly, tacitly acknowledging that they had veered off their agreed-upon course. They were speaking too loud and in too much detail to be chatting about a hypothetical situation. They needed to lower their voices and keep the discussion between themselves.

"You know as well as I do that these days the idea that the doctors are really in control is little more than fantasy in the real world. The docs are often third in line in real decision-making power, behind the managed care companies and the hospital administration."

"Point taken, but that's not the law, as *you* well know. And that's not what would be before this particular jury. They would only hear that a particular doctor made a decision not to transfer this baby—and then your client and mine will point fingers at each other over why that happened. Fighting like that will only make things worse."

Janckovich nodded, fully grasping his counterpart's argument. "Yes, I've been mulling that very point over myself. So what would you suggest we consider to avoid such a situation?"

"We should figure out a way to settle this so that we're never in that position."

"Nice idea in theory. But *Mr. Boom-box Voice* is gunning for big stakes here. How do we satisfy him?"

"That's why I'm buying you breakfast. I thought a little grease circulating through your bloodstream might stimulate that uncanny legal mind of yours."

The short-order cook pushed through the swinging door at the end of the counter, emerging from the kitchen with two large platters of food.

"Hey, Jimmy, are you all alone back there today?" said Frank Faison. He didn't come to the diner regularly, but he was there often enough to be on a first-name basis with the proprietor.

"You ever try to keep steady help in a diner?" responded the owner. "One thing I've learned, you own the place, you own the work. No gol-dang job description for me," he said as he put the egg-and-sausage dish in front of Jerry Janckovich and a huge waffle topped off with a large scoop of butter on Faison's side of the table. "I was here late last night, now I'll probably have to cook and serve through lunch. I'm working like one of those interns you've got in your hospital, Frank. Any more coffee, gentlemen? OJ?"

"We're good, thanks, Jimmy."

They both let the remark about interns and hospitals pass and ate in silence for a few minutes. "I always forget how much I love fried eggs and sausage," Janckovich said quietly, his guilt receding in the pure pleasure of eating forbidden food.

Janckovich watched Faison spread butter neatly across his waffle, then pour what looked like half the pitcher of syrup on top of the butter. Faison carved the mess into square-inch portions along the waffle grid lines and loaded three big pieces onto his fork at one time. He crammed the load of food into his mouth in one swift bite, making Janckovich wonder if Jimmy knew how to perform a *Heimlich* maneuver.

"Actually, this meeting is timely. I might have an approach…" Janckovich began, but he couldn't complete the sentence—he was choking on a piece of sausage half the size of his enormous thumb that cut off his air entirely. A wave of panic swept over him—he was the one who needed a *Heimlich* now. Janckovich looked at his breakfast companion with eyes that were beginning to bulge, but Faison had his head down as he shoveled more huge waffle squares into his mouth. He would never notice Janckovich's ensuing death from a fatal lump of sausage until the big man collapsed on the table.

Jerry Janckovich's mind was racing to a strange place as he was choking. Rather than trying to get Faison's attention to summon help he felt relieved that his desperate plight was invisible to his companion. *I can't let Frank see me like this. I do not want to die in Jimmy's Diner, what a fucking stupid way to die…* Just as he thought he was about to fall dead face-first into his breakfast, he felt the sausage move slightly in his throat. He told himself to keep from inhaling, that would be fatal. Gathering all his strength for one last attempt to force air out of his chest he opened his mouth like an opera singer about to fill a concert hall with a ponderous note, stiffened his throat, and forcefully contracted every fiber of muscle in his well-developed chest. The move suddenly expelled a burst of air that propelled the oversized bite of sausage up and out of his windpipe, flying from his mouth. With his athlete's reflexes, he caught the chunk of meat with his enormous hand just before it would have lofted across the table onto Faison's plate—or right into his face. He put the soggy lump back on his plate, carved it into four pieces, and returned one chunk into his mouth, this time chewing and swallowing thoroughly.

Vowing to be more careful with the rest of his food, he lectured himself on his carelessness. He felt overwhelmed, not with the shock he would have expected after coming close to dying, but with chagrin at the banality of what his final thoughts on this Earth might have been. His life had been about to end and all he cared about was the ignominy of dying in a diner from a jumbo lump of grease and pork? He had been embarrassed over where he was dying instead of seeing his life pass before his eyes or having profound thoughts for the ages? He felt extremely stupid.

A humiliating death quietly averted, Janckovich was all the more determined to find a way to get past the personalities and narrow interests and get this case over with. They needed to do something to help Donny Johnson and his family while not breaking the bank for their clients.

Faison looked up from his orderly assault on the waffle to resume the conversation that had nearly been terminated for a reason he would never know. "You were saying you had an approach, Jerry?"

"It's all in the money," Janckovich replied, clearing his throat on the first few words but still not sounding quite like himself. "Boom-box voice got wealthy by knowing when to sign on to the best deal—the key is getting him into that position."

Chastened a bit by the sausage incident, he put a modest portion of hash browns into his mouth and started chewing methodically.

"It sounds like we're on the same page, we've been thinking along the same lines. But how do we get there?"

The hash browns safely negotiated through his mouth and on their way to his stomach, Janckovich took a sip of water and described the strategy he was formulating.

"OK, I see three critical steps." His deep voice had returned, the vocal chords having suffered no apparent damage from the chunk of sausage that had been wedged atop them minutes earlier. "First, it's necessary to offset the potential appeal of a highly sympathetic plaintiff. If that's done right, the other side has to realize they're in danger of losing on the most lucrative count, punitive damages. Second, actually at the same time, we pull the rug out from under the lesser charges of simple negligence. We make a convincing case that the other side might get nothing. That elevates the chances of getting home free, and we need to push that point. But that's too risky to count on. So, number three, we also need to put some real assets on our side of the table to make it more attractive for them to settle. When we get close to a number they like, they'll start to think about getting out."

"Have you got all this worked out yet, Jerry?"

"We're balancing on a tightrope, Frank. We're working on a strategy to offset the appeal of a sympathetic plaintiff. But there's a lot at stake. If we don't succeed, there will be far-reaching consequences."

"No doubt about that. OK, enough said. I suggest that we should stop our conversation at this point."

"Agreed. I can't go too much further without chatting with my colleagues, not to mention my clients."

"I have the same considerations on my side. And I have some ideas on how to get a certain person to see the light as well."

"Thanks for breakfast. It'll take a month in the gym for either of us to work off Jimmy's fine cooking."

"Yeah, I shouldn't come here as often as I do. And this breakfast is a cash deal. Personal expense, no reimbursement records. What's the next step? Ball's in your court, right?"

"Yes, I'll be in touch. So long, Frank." Janckovich slid out of the booth, uncoiling his large frame into its full upright position, and extending his oversized hand to Frank Faison.

"See you in the steam room, Jerry," said Faison. As Janckovich's enormous hand engulfed his own, Faison mused, *Jeez, is that a hand or a ham hock?* But he kept the thought to himself, simply smiling broadly at his towering counterpart.

Jerry Janckovich smiled back at his companion, grateful that the meeting had not ended with paramedics pronouncing him a tragic casualty of Jimmy's sausage. Who knew what other dangers lay ahead?

Chapter 27: Witness for the Defense

As an expert witness in the right kind of lawsuit, Jeremy Wolke was the stuff that lawyers dream of—reverie for one side, nightmares for the other. When you went against Jeremy Wolke, you had to consider all of your options, including getting out of the lawsuit as quickly and painlessly as possible. He was part Stephen Hawking, part Robert De Niro. Having earned highest honors in the Stanford Human Biology program as an undergraduate, Wolke had long anticipated attending medical school despite universal cautions from family, friends, counselors, and numerous physicians not to attempt that route because of his physical limitations. Determined to prove yet again his ability to overcome challenges no matter how extreme, he was doggedly insistent on pursuing no career other than his chosen one. But then something changed him forever.

Jeremy Wolke may have been confined to a wheelchair because his stiff, withered legs could not support his body, but he had powerful hands and arms. He trained as hard as he studied, winning gold medals in his category of the 400 and 800 meter wheelchair races in the U.S. Paralympics Championships. With his extraordinary scholarship and athletic success, Wolke went off to Oxford as a Rhodes Scholar, the first ever who used success in the Paralympics to meet the criterion in Cecil Rhodes' will that Scholars should demonstrate *"energy to use one's talents to the full, as exemplified by fondness for and success in sports."*

Wolke's undergraduate courses at Stanford had given him the impression that medicine was a highly scientific field, that diagnosis and treatment were based on the best evidence possible, that physicians were dedicated to applying scientific principles to their work at all times. His experiences at Oxford shattered his naiveté.

In England Wolke discovered that the National Health Service was a world leader in applying real science to studying the effectiveness of medical care. The turning point for him came one day while accompanying medical students on their rounds in Guy's Hospital in London with their tutor, Sir Charles Handleman. Wolke was inspired by the way Sir Charles introduced the physicians-in-training to critical thinking.

"Tell me," Sir Charles would ask a medical students, "just what do you propose to do for this patient?" He would listen patiently to the usual answer that the student would order numerous laboratory tests and X-rays and then prescribe various pharmaceuticals depending on the diagnosis. Then he would follow up with, "Now, tell me, just what evidence is there that what you are proposing to do will actually benefit this patient?"

Wolke was often stunned by the inadequate answers the medical students came up with. They would struggle to respond to his probing query, having never anticipated that their mentor might cause them to question the efficacy of medical care.

"This is what Mr. Scarleton told us was the routine practice in cases such as this, Sir Charles."

"I have been on this ward for two months, Sir Charles, and this is what we always do."

"This is what we did for a patient last year, Sir Charles, and that patient did quite nicely."

Only infrequently did Sir Charles' insistence on solid evidence provoke the scholarly response he was seeking, a reply such as, *"There was a large review article in The Lancet that included numerous controlled clinical trials that established the value of this treatment, Sir Charles."*

During their private tutorials Sir Charles, in his eloquent but never pompous tone, would say, "Mr. Wolke, I regret to tell you that much of medical care is simply what doctors do because that's what other doctors before them have always done. It is indeed little more than 'medical folklore.' Doctors do what they have been taught to do, whether it has a solid scientific basis or not. And entirely without regard for how much it might cost. For all of its limitations, our National Health Service has led the way in studying the effectiveness of medical care, following the vision of our own Dr. Archie Cochrane. Archie had a simple mantra: *'Either we know something works, Gentlemen, or we don't know whether it works.'* In his genteel style he would insist that we base our treatments on evidence, and where

196

there was none, we must use the scientific method to collect evidence. Thankfully, many here listened."

"Why—here,—why—in—the—UK?" asked Wolke, still coping with the unsettling news that medicine might not be entirely scientific.

Words came fluently from Jeremy Wolke, with great precision, but slowly, drawn out to several times their usual length, with atypical inflection points. His speaking ability was constrained by defective neurological controls over his voicebox, resulting in the drawn-out, somewhat distorted speech pattern characteristic of some persons with cerebral palsy. It was almost painful to wait patiently for his words as his exceptional brain struggled to transform thoughts into sounds.

"In the National Health Service we have limited budgets for health care, quite different from your situation in the States. That restriction has forced us to impose discipline on ourselves. We must assess the value of treatments and technologies to help decide what to pay for or to invest in. Archie Cochrane's initiative promised both to save money and improve care, and that was quite appealing. Indeed, we have found that such studies offer economic benefits to the NHS as well as better medical care. Now his approach is taking hold here, and we foresee that it will lead to a worldwide movement to vastly expand the scientific evidence base for the practice of medicine. We are quite proud of this in our own way."

Jeremy Wolke had found his calling. He would not become a physician, but he would not abandon his medical dream; he would follow in Archie Cochrane's footsteps.

Shortly before leaving England, Wolke went to see Sir Charles in his office. He was surprised to find that Sir Charles was quartered in a strikingly small, overcrowded mess of a place that hardly seemed appropriate for someone who had been knighted by the Queen. Evidently, Wolke thought, a knighthood was more impressive to Americans than to the English.

"Sir—Charles,—I—am—here—to—thank—you—for— helping—me—find—my—way. When—I—return—to—the— U.S.,—I—intend—to—pursue—a—Ph.D.—in—clinical— epidemiology—at—the—Johns—Hopkins—University—School— of—Hygiene—and—Public—Health. I—wish—to—devote— myself—to—the—study—of—the—effectiveness—of—medical— care. I—will—also—be—doing—advanced—work—in—

biostatistics—and—health—policy. Afterward,—I—hope—to—spend—two—years—in—a—postdoctoral—fellowship—at—the—National—Institute—of—Child—Health—and—Human—Development. For—leading—me—in—this—direction,—you—have—my—profound—gratitude."

Sir Charles smiled approvingly and said, "That is indeed a wise decision. You are a brilliant scholar and you have much to contribute. I had feared that all too much of your time and energy would have been expended needlessly in overcoming the prejudice and the physical barriers you regrettably but surely would have encountered in studying and practicing medicine. Not that I had any doubt you would have triumphed, but this is a far better use of your talents and a more efficient way to spend your finite time on this Earth. As important as caring for patients one at a time is, you have the potential to advance the science of the field, which will benefit countless people. You have my blessing, as well as my admiration. I know you will be an immense success, and I will follow your career with great delight."

Fulfilling every one of Sir Charles' expectations, Jeremy Wolke had become the leading expert in the world on the growth and development of children with a variety of disorders, including his own affliction, cerebral palsy. Wolke was among the first to dispute the widespread but unfounded belief that all babies who were very small at birth or suffered from serious complications in the newborn period would inevitably be dependent on their families and society for their entire lives. Adhering to Cochrane's maxim, *"Either we know, or we don't know,"* Wolke had designed and carried out long-term studies that followed severely premature infants well into their teens and afterward. His research had shown that the stereotype of physically disabled people being wholly dependent was as undeserved for many others as it had been for him. Sir Charles had watched his rise from afar, taking pleasure from the role he had played in helping Jeremy Wolke become an internationally acclaimed scientist.

***

Fred Vagram had heard all about Jeremy Wolke and decided to enlist him as an expert witness for the plaintiff's side in Donny Johnson's case. Vagram's strategy was a preemptive strike: whether Wolke would be helpful to them or not, signing him up would keep the famous scientist from assisting the other side. Vagram assigned

Dr. Sanjay Fijam to the task of recruiting Wolke, in the hope that Fijam's medical background would help bring Wolke on board.

Vagram's gamble backfired.

"Thank—you—for—your—interest—in—me,—Dr.—Fijam," Wolke said, "but—from—what—you—have—told—me—about—this—case,—I—must—decline—your—kind—offer. I—regret—to—tell—you—that—the—science—is—simply—not—on—your—side—of—this—lawsuit,—however—needy—Donny—Johnson—and—his—family—might—be. Indeed,—fortunately—for—him—the—evidence—is—actually—very—much—on—his—side—as—far—as—his—future—is—concerned. The—odds—are—favorable—that—he—can—expect—to—have—a—much—brighter—and—more—productive—life—than—you—would—care—to—have—me—testify—to."

Wolke was highly selective in accepting requests to serve as an expert in legal cases, not wanting to take the time from his own studies. So he would only agree when he thought a particular lawsuit stood for some important principle. Donny Johnson's case was tempting, but not on the child's side. Bursting stereotypes was Jeremy Wolke's passion, particularly ones that were based on myths or tradition rather than good science, so when he subsequently received a request from Dr. Stephanie Sorano to serve as an expert for the defense, he did not hesitate to accept. He would use this case as a forum to educate the public—and the law—about the rich potential that many children such as Donny Johnson had, far beyond the role into which they had long been typecast.

***

"Hey Doc, they got Wolke!" boomed Vagram when he received the expert witness list from *Sorano, Janckovich, English & Weill*. "This could put us in deep kimchee."

"Kimchee?" said Sanjay Fijam, confused. He enjoyed the pungent taste of the fermented Korean cabbage staple, so he was at a loss to understand the negative connotation of Vagram's expression.

Vagram read the puzzled expression on Fijam's face and added, "You might like eating that stuff, but I can't get within five feet of it, and I sure wouldn't want to be swimming in it like we could be now. Wolke testifying for the other side could kill us. He'll make the jury think that Donny Johnson will grow up to win a Nobel Prize. I knew we had to get Wolke on our side, Doc. Now we've got to get rid of him."

"Get rid of him? How?" Sanjay Fijam was momentarily terrified by the thought that his gruff senior partner was actually contemplating physical violence against the disabled scientist. "But Mr. Vagram, they are entitled to use any expert witness they want to, and you know how qualified Dr. Wolke is."

"Yeah, of course, that's why I sent you to get him in the first place. We've got to find a way to get him disqualified as an expert. We can't do it on his raw credentials—the guy has a résumé that would knock the socks off any judge, let alone your average Joe or Jane sitting on a jury. Besides, if we tried to discredit him the other side would reveal that we had sought to get him as an expert, and that would make us look duplicitous arguing that he wasn't qualified. OK, Doc, what are our options?"

Cautious as always in responding on the fly, Fijam hesitated, then replied, "I am not sure that we have any good options, Mr. Vagram." As Fijam spoke he recoiled inside himself at hearing the sing-song pattern return to his voice, betraying his nervousness. Then, quickly realizing that Vagram was in no mood to grant him a long period of contemplation, he took a deep breath and was instantly relieved to find a solid thought forming in his brain. As the idea crystallized, Fijam continued, his voice steady now. "We might agree that he is highly qualified in many ways, a distinguished scientist indeed, but argue that his particular expertise had not been applied properly in this specific case. We might press that argument based on the rules in this state regarding expert testimony. As you know well, Mr. Vagram, we have adopted a version of the federal courts' *Daubert* test. It is not sufficient to show that someone has expertise in a given field. For their testimony to be admissible they must also demonstrate that it is based on solid scientific methods and procedures applied properly to the case at hand. We might get his testimony excluded, even if we could not undermine his status to qualify as an expert."

Vagram was silent for a long moment, a much longer silence than any Fijam could remember. Was he about to blast back with some penetrating criticism?

When the words came from Vagram this time they were like music to Sanjay Fijam's ears.

"Not bad, Doc, not bad."

Fijam allowed himself a moment of satisfaction, thinking how good it felt to come up with a response under pressure and get praise from Vagram. How very good.

But Vagram's next words quickly broke the spell.

"OK, Doc, how would you go about that approach?"

The fluctuating pitch returned to Fijam's voice.

"Again, I am not quite sure. I would like some time to consider the alternatives," he said, retreating once again from the discomfort that plagued him when trying to think on the spot in front of Vagram.

Vagram had no more patience with the hesitant Sanjay Fijam. He wasn't in a mood to postpone the discussion. The volume of his voice rose perceptibly.

"C'mon, Doc, give me some help here, let's get this started."

"Well, Mr. Vagram," Fijam forced himself to think as he spoke, "for one thing, Wolke is not a medical doctor. Perhaps we can try to show that it would require medical credentials to assess the clinical condition of Donny Johnson and that Wolke is not qualified to perform such an assessment."

"Not bad, not bad for starters," Vagram thundered enthusiastically.

Fijam continued, "We would have another distinguished scientist review his expert report and apply the *Daubert* guidelines. We would then move to have his report excluded on the grounds that he had not applied scientific principles appropriately in preparing his analysis."

"Doc, I may have to take the prod to you to move you into the corral, but once you're there, you buck with the best of the broncos."

Fijam had no idea what Vagram's comment meant, but it was evidently a compliment of some sort, so he smiled back and said deferentially, "I will continue to pursue our options, Mr. Vagram."

"OK, Doc. We'll give that a try. But here's something to mull over: what do we do if your approach doesn't work and we can't discredit his testimony? Let's say Wolke is just as tough to deal with as we expect, that he comes across as a witness who could turn any jury against our own disabled kid. If that happens, we need Plan B."

"Do you have anything in mind, Mr. Vagram?"

"Yeah, but you aren't going to like this, Doc. I'm thinking that if our backs are up against the wall we might counter Wolke by getting other cripples into the courtroom. You know, ones who are really hopeless, who can't speak or feed themselves or do anything without assistance. If we can parade a little crowd of them around the courtroom the jury will melt. They'll believe that Donny Johnson is going to end up in a sorry state like them, he'll never be like Wolke. How's that for a Plan B, Doc?"

Dr. Sanjay Fijam, the physician inside the lawyer, was speechless. The man who had built his now-forsaken medical career around caring for the ill, the helpless, the disabled, felt a knot forming in his gut. What was he doing in the employ of a man who spoke about such unfortunate children as cripples to be paraded around in public just to win a lawsuit? He stared at the creature he now took orders from and said nothing.

Chapter 28: Science and Theater

As soon as Wolke entered the deposition room, Fred Vagram stifled a curse. He watched spellbound as Wolke politely shrugged off any help lifting his slender frame out of his wheelchair and onto one of the ordinary chairs around the conference table. The transfer process itself was attention-gathering, time-consuming, and—worst of all from its likely impact on a jury, Vagram knew—downright riveting. As though in slow motion, Wolke pressed his powerful athletic arms on the side rails of his wheelchair, lifted his contorted body up and out of the chair, then stood, slightly hunched over on his arm-crutches. With one sweep of a crutch he pushed his wheelchair away and slid one heavily braced leg at a time toward the table. He turned the witness chair just enough to give him room to step in front of it, and slowly lowered himself onto the seat. Finally, he scooted the chair forward to its proper position in very small increments. The entire process created an almost-irresistible urge in the onlookers to jump up and help him, but none dared to do so, sensing that offering unsought assistance would have violated some unwritten code of respect.

Vagram agonized over Wolke's mesmerizing entrance. Scenes like this were precisely why he had wanted the handicapped scientist on Donny Johnson's side, or at least neutralized. A jury would be eating out of the palm of his hand before he said a single word. The only chance they had was to get his testimony disqualified.

The videographer began the session as usual, explaining the process and asking everyone in the room to identify themselves. Wolke spoke in his broken cadence, each word coming so slowly that the listener would wrongly assume that he was about to falter, unable to find or to form the next word, that he would fail to complete the thought. But syllable by syllable the words came, perfectly aligned in a rhythm that listeners adapted to the longer it went on.

"My—name—is—Jeremy—Wolke. I—have—a—doctor—of—Philosophy—degree—from—the—Johns—Hopkins—University—and—honorary—doctorates—from—six—universities,—including—Stanford,—the—University—of—Chicago,—and—Oxford,—from—which—I—also—have—a—Masters—degree."

Wolke had an unexpectedly playful side that he revealed under social circumstances, startling people who were straining to pretend they didn't notice his disabilities by making self-deprecating, politically incorrect jokes to put them at ease. "*G—g—g—good—th—th—th—thing—I—d—d—don't—st—st—st—stutter—as—w—well,*" was one of his favorite lines to tease people with, or "*Would—you—please—adjust—my—playback—button—to—the—normal—speed?*" or "*I'm—not—stupid, I—just—have—a—Western—drawl.*" But in formal settings such as testifying in court or at a deposition, he maintained his professional demeanor throughout. He was well practiced in how to capitalize on his speech patterns to enhance the drama of his presentation.

When Fred Vagram started to question Jeremy Wolke, the renowned scientist initially misjudged the explanation for the lawyer's strident voice, thinking Vagram was condescending to him by speaking so loud, as though his physical disabilities meant he was incapable of normal conversation. Perhaps Vagram was like many hapless souls who raise their voices to people who don't understand their language, as though higher volume can overcome lack of fluency. Wolke was tempted to resort to one of his stock sarcasms, "*I'm—just—slow-moving,—not—slow-witted,*" but he made no retort. Later, when he realized that Vagram always spoke that way no matter who the listener was, he was grateful he had not begun his testimony with such a major *faux pas*.

"Dr. Wolke," Vagram boomed, "in your expert report, you go to great lengths to describe what a person with Donny Johnson's handicaps might achieve in life. Did you examine Donny Johnson?"

"No,—I—did—not."

Wolke initially was parsimonious in his responses, both because he was well versed in sticking to the point in depositions, and also because of the strain on both himself and his listeners when he spoke at length. He was masterful at using his speech patterns to filibuster or extort sympathy when either served his purposes, but not now, not at the beginning of the interrogation. He would see where this braying questioner was going first.

"Why not, Dr. Wolke?"

"That—is—not—my—role."

"Not your role? Are you not able to diagnose conditions such as those that Donny Johnson suffers from? Aren't you a doctor, Dr. Wolke?"

"I—am—not—a—medical—doctor."

Vagram took the bait, momentarily thinking he was on his way to discrediting Wolke's testimony.

"So all of your conclusions about Donny Johnson's conditions are based on someone else's diagnoses, someone else's medical training? You are not able to tell us just what conditions Donny Johnson has, is that correct?"

Wolke sat with his shoulders twisted, the left one several inches above the right, his head tipped back slightly, the fingers of both hands spread open and moving in awkward patterns, as though they were pantomiming in front of a bright light to cast shadow-figures on a wall. His dependent appearance was misleading. The brilliant man inside the distorted body fully understood where Vagram was headed and knew how to get his questioner off course, how to take control of the situation.

"The—description—of—this—young—man's—medical—condition—that—I—have—analyzed—came—from—the—documents—that—you—filed—in—this—lawsuit,—Mr.—Vagram. Another—person—might—question—those—assertions, but—that—is—not—what—I—am—here—for.—Assuming—your—descriptions—are—correct,—my—expertise—is—knowing—what—someone—with—those—conditions—has—to—look—forward—to—in—life.—You—are—the—lawyer,—sir,—but—I—understand—my—role—is—to—explain—what—caused—Mr.—Johnson's—conditions—and—what—the—consequences,—the—damages,—are—likely—to—be,—not—to—diagnose—his—affliction."

Vagram was deflated, but at the same time greatly impressed. He had expected no less from the famous Dr. Wolke based on his reputation, but dealing with his intellect in person was another story. Wolke was indeed a worthy opponent. Vagram also appreciated the courtroom value of what he was seeing. Wolke had not wasted a single word, yet had taken nearly four minutes to deliver four sentences, four long minutes during which a jury would be hanging on his every word. Prolonged, hostile questioning would only increase their sympathy for this man as a witness and they would give his testimony even greater weight than it deserved. Vagram continued to press Wolke on his lack of medical training, but only dug himself in deeper.

"How can you purport to understand the anatomy, the physiology, the biochemistry of Donny Johnson's conditions if you have not studied those subjects, Dr. Wolke?"

"One—doesn't—need—to—be—a—physician—to—draw—proper—conclusions—from—scientific—facts. I—have—actually—studied—the—subjects—you—mentioned,—but—do—not—purport—to—be—qualified—as—an—expert—in—any—of—them.—What—I—do—have—is—scientific—knowledge—that—allows—me—to—draw—conclusions—from—evidence—about—those—conditions,—and—in—that—capacity—I—believe—I—am—recognized—as—an—expert."

After two and a half hours, Vagram accepted that Fijam strategy number one was doomed. Wolke had such strong credentials and so many scientific accomplishments that his expertise was beyond question. And, although not literally so, he was quick on his feet. His nimble mind quickly deflected any assault on the admissibility of his testimony in this case. Vagram no longer believed that there could be any line of attack that would neutralize Wolke as a witness. They needed a Plan B.

First, though, it was time for lunch. The deposition had not begun until just after 10AM, and it was now approaching 1PM. Vagram needed a break. He took his frustrations out on a thick Ruben sandwich waiting for him in the private room next to the large conference room. He bit into the Ruben impatiently, not caring that the corned beef had cooled off to room temperature or that the pumpernickel bread was so soggy with meat drippings and Russian dressing that he had to hold the sandwich wrapped in his napkin and maneuver the sloppy mess with both hands as he devoured it. The Ruben vanished far more quickly than two of Jeremy Wolke's sentences. Meanwhile, at the same table, Sanjay Fijam ate slowly, taking his time chewing his pita bread sandwich of boiled egg with sprinkled curry, cucumber, and yogurt.

Fijam wiped his face carefully and cleared his throat with a soft *'uhmnn'* before speaking.

"Dr. Wolke is a strong witness, Mr. Vagram. It does not appear that we will be able to turn him to our advantage." He braced himself for a room-filling retort.

Vagram, however, responded in relatively tones, only slightly above conversational levels.

"I think we've seen the writing on the wall, Doc. Let's see how this afternoon goes, but if it turns out as bad as this morning, we're going to have to reconsider our options. That guy's not only smart, he's a great actor—he knows how to use his disabilities as well as his abilities. This is as bad as I feared. Worse, even."

Fijam was stunned. He had heard Vagram make difficult decisions many times to cut his losses, always choosing what Vagram called the 'least worst alternative'. But those were all strategic retreats—this sounded like Vagram was mulling over terms of surrender. Fijam had never imagined that Vagram would capitulate quickly in this case, the case that was to have been the jewel in his legal career's crown, his capstone million-dollar victory. He had no response, he simply stared in silence at his senior colleague, as stunned as a soccer fan who just watched a legendary all-star miss a game-ending penalty shot.

The afternoon turned out to be even rougher for Fred Vagram. He tested Wolke on every requirement of the *Daubert* test for expert testimony, every aspect of the rule that was intended to keep "junk science" out of the courts by admitting into evidence only expert testimony proven according to the rules of science. Vagram painfully concluded that this strategy was demolished. Wolke established that everything he testified to was clearly based on methods and procedures that were widely accepted in the scientific community. His work had been published in the most prestigious scientific journals spanning many disciplines—medicine, public health, child development and psychology. And he had even been widely quoted in law review articles and previous court cases that cited his breakthrough work, a point that obviously impressed all the lawyers in the room. Any judge would go nuts over hearing Wolke testify.

Only Sanjay Fijam heard Vagram mutter, *"Law reviews, goddamn it,"* in a highly uncharacteristic *sotto voce*. His boss was visibly defeated as Wolke drew his testimony to a conclusion.

"Being—born—like—Donny—Johnson—is—no—longer—
just—a—curse,—no—longer—a—final—sentence—to—a—
lifetime—of—pain—and—dependence.—About—one-half—of—
the—babies—his—size—don't—live,—but—most—of—those—
who—do—survive—can—look—forward—to—quite—normal—
lives.—Donny—is—alive.—He—made—it—this—far—so—he—
is—likely—to—graduate—from—high—school,—maybe—
college,—and—support—himself.——If—he—has—trouble—
with—employment,—it—is—more—likely—to—be—due—to—
prejudice—against—people—who—talk—funny—or—can't—
walk,—than—to—his—own—limitations."

When Wolke got to that last sentence, Vagram knew his case
was cooked. The brilliant, albeit disabled, scientist would keep
reminding a jury about his own accomplishments, the incredible
success he had achieved despite serious physical disabilities. Even
though Wolke would never be allowed to testify directly about
himself, he didn't need to say a word about his own life. His very
presence would be more than enough to strike a chord with any jury,
to remind them that this slow-talking, physically disabled witness was
a world-class scientist who had been a Rhodes Scholar. And they
could easily draw the conclusion that Donny Johnson might turn out
to be as successful as Wolke, or at least that his future wasn't
unequivocally bleak. Worst of all as far as Vagram was concerned,
despite Wolke's tortured speech he was a masterful communicator,
he could explain complex subjects in words that anyone could follow.
And follow they would, entranced by his gripping performance.
Vagram's case was cooked, cooked more thoroughly than the Ruben
that was making his belly more and more uncomfortable as the
deposition went on.

Case cooked, but Fred Vagram wasn't quite ready to quit.
Not yet.

When the deposition ended, Vagram and Fijam walked to the
street to hail a couple of taxicabs. Vagram turned to his junior
colleague and asked, "Doc, did you come up with anything?"

Sanjay Fijam had anticipated this moment and was
prepared—prepared to duck the question for a few hours. Generally
he would not have tested Vagram's patience by pleading for a delay,
but he saw that the senior lawyer was too worn out from the day with
Jeremy Wolke to object.

"Yes, Mr. Vagram. I will go over some ideas with you first thing in the morning."

As Fijam stepped into a taxi a deflated Vagram simply responded, "OK, see you tomorrow, Doc."

Sanjay Fijam made no reply. He was enjoying his secret personal triumph: getting into the back seat of a cab. Being a paying passenger in a taxi was one of his small joys in life. He couldn't wait to see what the nationality of the driver would be.

Chapter 29: Home Life

Steering his old van straight into the carport outside their little house, Derek slumped against the steering wheel as the van rolled to a stop. He shut his eyes and blew out a long, slow breath, relieved to be home. As he got out of the van he saw that lights were on in the house. After midnight, but Martina must be awake. He squashed the remains of a cigarette on the concrete with his shoe and let himself into the house through the side door into the kitchen.

"Hi Honey," Derek said, as he bent to kiss Martina, who was sitting at the Formica-top kitchen table.

Late as it was, Martina held a half-full mug of coffee, and looked as though she hadn't slept in a week. Her once-elegant blond hair was protruding from her head at wild angles, little bunches of it sticking nearly straight up, other clumps matted down. Her forehead was ribbed as though she had been resting her head on an old-fashioned washboard. She glanced up at her husband with a blank expression and turned a sallow cheek to receive his kiss. She made no effort to kiss him back or greet him in any other way.

Derek was exhausted, desperate to get to bed, to go to sleep. But it was not to be bedtime yet, his rest would once again have to be put off. He could not walk away from Martina when she was like this.

"Where's Donny? Asleep? What's up—anything I need to do?"

"Phone messages," Martina muttered.

"What? What messages?"

"Bills. They're calling again."

Flat, no emotion, just lukewarm words devoid of feeling.

Derek was growing tense, he could feel the center of his chest tighten. "What bills? Who's calling?" he barked, then recoiled at the severity in his own voice. He must calm down, take it easy. This was not her fault. Martina just answered the phone, she was not the problem.

"Sorry, Honey, I'm not mad at you, I just can't believe they're bothering us again. The lawyers said they would get them to hold off. All the big bills are on payment schedules, we're doing all we can."

"I don't spend any money," Martina said. "I only spend what I have to."

He felt a sharp pang of guilt as he realized Martina thought he was criticizing her. Yet her words came mechanically, just hollow words, a pale reaction to what she had taken as an accusation. No anger, no sign of irritation, nothing but the words.

"Yes, Honey, I know, you're very good about it. I'm so sorry you have to be the one who deals with this stuff. Sunday, on Sunday I'll have time to go over things, I won't be working at the store on Sunday. Don't worry, I know it's rough, but we'll get to the end of this."

Derek was trying to reassure her, but he sensed her emotional pallor wasn't just about the bills and phone calls. It was everything, it was her life. Looking at Martina he felt a surge of love, but love tinged with shame, with guilt. He was filled with remorse over leaving her alone all day to care for Donny, over coming home barely long enough to eat and sleep. He knew that she agonized over suing Dr. Belden, tormented to the extreme that she wouldn't even return to the supermarket ever since her encounter there with Dr. Belden. No wonder she was like this, so blank, so desperate. It was too much, he had asked too much of her. He could see the life draining out of her.

"It'll be OK, Honey, I'll take care of it."

Derek made the promise to ease his wife's pain, but he had no idea how he would take care of the bills. They had no money in the bank, they barely made it from paycheck to paycheck, they bought nothing except what Donny needed, their food, and gas for the truck. He sighed, reproaching himself over spending money to buy cigarettes, too much money, he knew. But he needed the cigarettes, he couldn't give them up.

"The lawyer, too. The lawyer's office called. Said we need to talk."

"When?"

"Today, called today," she replied, misinterpreting the question.

"Sorry, Honey, I meant, when does he want to talk?"

211

"I don't know. I didn't know when we could, when you could get off work."

"Get off work! How can I get off work again? I've missed so many days on the site, if they didn't need me so bad I'd have been fired long ago." Derek strained to control his anxiety, his consuming frustration, knowing how vulnerable his wife would be to any hint of criticism. "I'll have to check. Did he mean soon? How soon?"

"Didn't say. You'd call, I said you would call."

Derek again struggled to keep his voice soft, to stop his burgeoning anger from being directed at his wife.

"Did they say anything else? About why they want to talk?"

Deep inside he felt a glimmer of hope, hope that maybe, just maybe, the call from the lawyer meant their case might be getting somewhere, they might have something to look forward to, some relief from their financial pressures, their suffocating life. He told himself not to think about it, just to find a time and go talk to the lawyers. It could be another great big nothing, nothing at all. Or worse, it could be bad news. He mustn't get his hopes up. He knew that he and Martina and Donny were most likely going to have to live like this for years and years.

"Just, *We have to talk.*' Nothing else that I remember."

"OK, Honey, I'll call tomorrow. Honey…I'm tired, I'm so tired. I need to go to bed."

Derek was still stunned from nearly driving the van off the road that night. He was left near the point of collapse after the burst of adrenalin from his confrontation with death had subsided, so drained he wondered whether he would be able to drag himself out of bed again in less than five hours or whether his body would just give out. He couldn't stand much more of this endless series of struggles.

Then he looked down at Martina and remembered he wasn't the only one who was tired. She stared at him, her own extreme fatigue palpable on her face, in her hollow eyes, in her drooping body.

He walked across the kitchen, kissed her softly, again on the cheek she offered him, and stepped through the doorway into the small living room that led to the rest of the little house. A tiny house, but it had unusually wide doorways and was all on one level, so the entire place was open to Donny's wheelchair. Derek pushed aside the thick curtain that served as an improvised door to the alcove, stepped the few feet over to his son's bedside, and bent over to deliver another kiss on another cheek. A soft kiss, a father's loving kiss. His eyes filled with tears as he felt the dry skin of his son's face on his lips. He whispered, "Good night, Donny, I love you. I wish I could help you, son. I'm doing everything I know how to do. I love you." Derek moved away when he saw the boy stir slightly. He didn't want to wake him. If Donny awoke now there would be hell to pay from Martina. And no one would get any sleep. He couldn't face another night like that. His tears turned to sobs, his heart filled with anguish. He couldn't do anything to help his son. Or his wife. Or himself.

Chapter 30: Plan B

The order from the court was short and to the point. Motions *Granted* to exclude as defendants cardiologist Lesley Kahn, cardiac surgeon Morton Scheld, pediatrician Jane Zimmerman, and obstetrician/gynecologist Fred Trilling, for failure to allege sufficient facts against them to establish a charge of Medical Negligence. Motions to dismiss the case against pediatrician Sarah Belden, a.k.a. Sarah Belden O'Malley, neonatologist Giuliana Silvestre, and Memorial General Hospital, *Denied* as to Medical Negligence and *Denied* as to Gross Negligence. The court set a trial date in three months and ordered the remaining parties to pursue settlement negotiations in good faith.

Told that she had a telephone call from Bernardine Pekings, Lesley Kahn picked up the phone with no thought that it might connote bad news. Winning, as always for her, was simply the only outcome. She listened to the lawyer, then said, "Thank you. I will tell Morton," hung up the phone without asking a single question or expressing any relief, and went back to reviewing the echocardiogram that had absorbed her interest. Hours later she saw Morton Scheld in the hallway of the cardiac catheterization lab suite and said nonchalantly, "Lawyer called, we're out. Case closed, as far as we're concerned."

Scheld looked at his partner, pursed his lips, and nodded his head slightly, not ruffling the perfectly-coiffed grey hair that capped off his distinguished look. "About time," he replied with not a trace of the initial outrage he had felt when he first heard of the lawsuit. Just simple acceptance that a minor distraction from the truly important work of his life was over.

Sarah Belden got a very different phone call. After reciting the judge's ruling, Stephanie Sorano said, "We need to discuss where things stand at this point."

Sarah felt a noose tightening around her neck. What had begun as a jumble of legalisms, noise and confusion was now coming clear: decisions would be made soon that could destroy her life.

***

Sanjay Fijam looked across the table at Fred Vagram, expecting the usual thunderous command to proceed. But Vagram merely looked at him and said, in a voice not soft by normal standards but moderate for Fred Vagram, "OK, Doc, what's your Plan B?"

"Thank you, Mr. Vagram. I believe that we cannot hope to exclude the scientific evidence that Dr. Wolke would provide in his testimony. But I have been considering the suggestion you made for this Plan B. As you said, we may indeed be able to counter the emotional impact of his appearance in front of a jury."

"OK. You mean you came up with a way for us to parade a bunch of helpless cripples into that courtroom?" The sarcasm was evident despite his voice having regained its customary volume.

Struggling to control his disgust with Vagram's callous, almost obscene way of referring to seriously disabled children, Fijam said, "Not quite, Mr. Vagram. We must proceed in a way that would not seem disrespectful to Dr. Wolke, to Donny Johnson, or to anyone else with Cerebral Palsy. With all due respect, we should do so without, as you say, parading them around the courtroom."

"So are you going to tell me just how we can go about doing that?"

"Yes, I believe I have an idea. Our purpose will be to exploit the stereotypes about disabled people that jurors already have, but to do so with without giving offense. That is, people on the jury will be predisposed to believe that disabled persons are totally dependent on caregivers and will remain so throughout their lives. We are concerned that seeing the brilliant and successful Dr. Wolke would weaken the jurors' existing prejudices, and thereby undermine our argument that Donny Johnson has been rendered nearly helpless. We could mitigate that effect without bringing the children themselves into the courtroom. All we need is for the jury hear stories about other disabled individuals, similarly afflicted people who can accomplish nothing such as Dr. Wolke has achieved. Hopeless

215

individuals who require ongoing care. Vivid descriptions of the difficult situations many disabled persons and their families face. That will be sufficient to reinforce the stereotypes the jurors will bring with them into the courtroom. That will give them reason to see Dr. Wolke as a rare exception to their pre-existing ideas about disabled persons."

"Yes, Doc, that's the idea, but just how would you get a judge to let such testimony into the courtroom, and how would you impress the jury without bringing in the kids themselves?"

A glimmer of admiration began to form in Fred Vagram as he reflected on the changes he was seeing in Sanjay Fijam. Fijam was getting the killer instinct he needed for this work. He even thought that the doctor-lawyer had grown a pair of balls—*now, if only he could learn to get to the point quickly*.

"Dr. Wolke will testify that the outlook for people with Cerebral Palsy has greatly improved. He will say that severely disabled individuals are now able to be less dependent, that they may well be able to support themselves, live independently, and get along on their own. We will introduce testimony to counter his evidence. In short, we would present other expert witnesses who would be speaking to the points Dr. Wolke will make, and thus their testimony will be accepted by the court. They would portray the difficulties that many disabled persons and their families still have to deal with. Our witnesses would not seek to refute Dr. Wolke's evidence entirely. That would likely be futile, since he is, indeed, the world's leading scientist on this subject. Instead of countering his testimony with other research, we would have them describe individual cases about families that have suffered great hardship. Anecdotes, however tragic they might be, would not be sufficient to convince a scientist, of course. But they would have an impact on the lay members of a jury that will reaffirm their prior prejudices."

"Anecdotes, hmm? You know, I think you got something there, Doc. Anecdotes are always more powerful than data with average folk. Talk to me, Doc—just where would you get these witnesses? Would you walk up to parents with kids in wheelchairs and ask them to testify about their problems?"

"Not at all, Mr. Vagram," Sanjay Fijam said, brimming with confidence although not knowing just how seriously he should take the question. "I have spoken with the leadership of the major associations that represent disabled people. They have a high regard

216

for Dr. Wolke, a great deal of respect for him and all he has accomplished. But they are concerned that the publicity surrounding this case could damage their cause in the long run if it were to create the widespread impression that people with disabilities need no special attention or support. They do not want to reinforce the old stereotypes, to be sure, but they also do not want the public to believe we can now ignore the special needs of the people they represent. They would much prefer that we achieve a confidential settlement instead of going to trial since they would not like to be accused of discrediting Dr. Wolke in public. But they would provide support for our position even to the point of having some of their members testify in court if that were to prove necessary. I believe that we can walk a fine enough line to make the point that the jurors cannot be sure that Donny Johnson will live an independent, productive life, whatever the scientific evidence may show. And, of course, that is all we would need to accomplish since we have only to establish the point for our client, not for everyone with Cerebral Palsy."

His voice restored to its full force, Fred Vagram said, "Damn! Damn nice work, Sanjay."

Sanjay Fijam was beaming. Fred Vagram had praised him and called him by his given name.

Chapter 31: Widening Cracks

On the other side of the lawsuit Frank Faison had also worked out a strategy to end the Johnson case: he would scare Everett Kappel into agreeing to settle by laying out the legal consequences he was facing. He called another meeting, this time just with Kappel.

"Mr. Kappel, there is another aspect of this case that I must advise you on, one that poses a potentially serious problem for you. When I say for *you*, I do mean for you personally, not just the hospital."

Frank Faison had decided to paint the worst-case scenario for Kappel to make him realize just how much was at stake. The lawyer felt that Kappel had gotten something of a free ride so far, but now he had to make sure the man understood his own personal exposure. Faison did not allow himself to savor the moment overtly, that would have been unseemly, unprofessional. But he did look forward to bringing the elevated little man down several notches.

Everett Kappel sensed a change in Faison's demeanor. Faison had never been fawning or docile in his presence, yet Kappel had always felt that his General Counsel knew which one of them was in charge. Today something seemed very different. Faison had established a distance between them that Kappel had not known previously. It seemed to Kappel as though he was talking with *someone else's lawyer*, rather than his own.

Faison's next words confirmed Kappel's concern.

"We need to consider the possibility that you will require your own counsel in this case. I may no longer be in a position to advise you."

"What are you talking about? You work for *me!*"

The little man was doing his best to control his outrage, but he was near the point of losing control. He had never anticipated such a development.

"I report to you, Sir, but as Memorial General's lawyer my duty is to the hospital, to the corporation, to the Board of Trustees. Thus far, there has been no conflict between that role and defending your interests, since you are the senior officer and you represent the hospital. But now I must advise you that the Johnson case raises the prospect, however unlikely, of a partition between yourself and the hospital, in which case I would have to defend the interests of the hospital. And in that case you would be well served to have your own legal counsel."

Kappel did not respond. He glowered at Faison, who noticed that Kappel's upper lip was protruding further than usual under pressure from the tip of his tongue.

Faison's voice was cool and direct, not threatening but not in the least reassuring.

"Mr. Kappel, this institution stands behind you for all acts within the scope of your duties as an officer of the hospital. That extends to any charges of negligence in the performance of your duties. You have an indemnity clause to that effect in your contract, so the hospital would have to pay any damages in a work-related judgment against you as well as your legal costs of defending yourself. We have never had reason to discuss the limits of that protection before today. This case charges the hospital with gross negligence, and, again, there would normally be no division between your interests and those of Memorial General, insofar as you were at all times acting within the scope of your responsibilities."

Faison looked intently at Kappel to emphasize the next point, the potentially devastating message he had come to deliver.

"But now that the allegation has emerged that you ordered the baby to stay here—an unproved allegation for sure, but nevertheless an allegation—we must recognize that the situation could change. The hospital is not obligated to defend you, or pay any claims against you, if you did something quite wrong *intentionally*. It would not be within the scope of your duties to, say, walk up to a patient and slap them in the face because you felt like doing so, or deliberately run over a nurse in the parking lot. At some point, actions can be shown to be outside the scope of your employment— and at that point, you are, to put it bluntly, on your own. In fact, the hospital would be *obligated* to distance itself from you if you were to harm someone intentionally."

Kappel could hardly speak. What was he hearing? How was this possible? The hospital was his life and he was the hospital's life, the man who created it, sustained it. Without him there would be nothing there, just the shell of the old buildings. Whatever he had said to Giuliana Silvestre was only for the sake of the hospital. He strained to keep his mouth shut, to regain control, to wait until he had something coherent to say.

Faison knew he had positioned Kappel precisely where he had hoped to get him. He watched a single drop of sweat appear at Kappel's hairline, roll down his forehead and along the right side of his nose, then pause momentarily above his nostril before disappearing into his mustache. A second drop of sweat followed, then another, then a continuous stream. Faison surprised himself at feeling a deeper satisfaction in deflating Kappel than he had anticipated. Years of repressed resentment cascaded out of him in a as he savored having the advantage over the overbearing hospital executive. A most unlawyerly thought passed through his mind: *I've got you now, you miserable little shit.*

Having pushed the knife into Kappel's gut, Faison now twisted it unremorsefully.

"The hospital cannot be in the position of appearing to support acts by its employees that are intended to harm people. That would be an intolerable position. This is an institution that is responsible to the people of this county as well as to its patients."

Kappel finally found a few words.

"What are you suggesting?" he stammered.

Faison remained poised, the consummate legal professional now that he had the better of Kappel. He needed to keep from acting out of pure antagonism to exact some long-deferred retribution, however satisfying it would feel to teach Kappel a painful lesson. Faison could not let this be about vengeance, it was about doing his best for his client—his real client, Memorial General Hospital. He could kick Kappel in the teeth some other time if it came to that, but not now. It was enough for now just to maneuver Kappel into a position where he would go along with Faison's sense of what would be best for the hospital.

"We need to put this entire incident behind us. There is no need for us to admit anything, but we must find a way to get out of this case. It will not be easy—the protection from big damages in lawsuits that this hospital had long enjoyed under *Sovereign Immunity* means that we have no ready source of funds in reserve for large damage payments."

He paused to let this sink in. He had softened Kappel up with the threat of personal liability, now he would make the point he had been building up to all along: Kappel needed to agree to settle the lawsuit.

"Fred Vagram will not give in for peanuts. If we are to settle this case we must find more money. A lot more."

"Where? How?"

"One way would be for you to use your powerful contacts on the County Commission and the Board of the hospital, people with influence. You would need to call in your chits with them."

"We can't go to them for millions of dollars. They won't appropriate funds like that, and even if they did…"

Kappel realized that going to the Commission for a huge sum would be signing his own death warrant. If those powerful people were forced to come up with a great deal of money, he would be out on the street in five minutes.

Faison knew exactly what Kappel was thinking: the man's self-interest was overriding any unease over the effect on the hospital or on the people who depended on it for medical care or for their jobs. He felt like swearing at the little man, letting the disgust that was bubbling up inside him erupt in a vindictive tirade, but he responded with lawyerly moderation.

"The Commission and Board would have no choice but to find the funds for a settlement if they were under a court order in a final judgment. But we might be able to avoid going down that path. I have a thought about how we might not need to present it to them that way. I would like to meet formally with the other defense counsel, Jerry Janckovich, to discuss a possible joint settlement proposal."

Faison added the *'formally'* out of an excess of lawyerly caution. Kappel had no way of knowing that Faison had already held the off-the-record breakfast chat with Janckovich at Jimmy's Diner, but if that meeting ever came to light he might face a charge of having jeopardized his client's interests without authorization. He wanted Kappel to ratify the earlier meeting, however indirectly.

"Here's what I have in mind for a joint offer. The bulk of the money will come from Janckovich's clients, or their insurance companies. The hospital will put mainly in-kind benefits on the table. That is, we release the family from their existing debts to us for Donny Johnson's unpaid medical bills and, in addition, we offer to provide all the medical care and support services this child will ever need at our expense. Doctors, hospital care, social services, physical and occupational therapy, we've got just about everything he needs. We can make the same offer for his parents."

"Do you believe that will work? Would they accept such an offer?"

"The Johnsons might accept, but one serious obstacle will be getting Vagram to agree to in-kind damages being a major part of the settlement. He wants as much cash as possible up front for his big contingent fee. We might have to find some funds to throw in. Then, of course, there is the real possibility that the family will want to have nothing to do with this hospital any more. If worse comes to worst, we get agreement on the concept that we're responsible for their medical benefits and support services, but the Johnsons refuse to come to this hospital. Then we have to pay for them to get medical care elsewhere instead of actually providing it here. That would be much more expensive for us, of course, but if that proves to be necessary we can reduce our expenditures by agreeing to pay the costs over time as they use the services. That way there would be no need for us to pay a huge lump sum up front."

Kappel began to regain his self-control, although he hadn't stopped sweating entirely.

"What chance does this have? Why would Vagram go for it?"

"I won't know until I discuss it officially with Janckovich and we take something to Vagram. We need to make every effort to avoid the high-side risk for us, which is enormous. Especially for you personally, as I have explained." Faison hoped that he would gain Kappel's assent by emphasizing the individual jeopardy he might face if the hospital were to distance itself from its President and CEO. "Should you and the hospital have a parting of the ways there would be much at stake. I feel we need to pursue any option that is more favorable to the hospital—more favorable to all concerned, including you, of course."

"But Vagram would not have gotten into this if he didn't think he had a powerful case and was going to take us for millions of dollars."

"That is certainly true, but I believe that, as threatening as their case is for us, Vagram has to realize that it might well fail. Accusing the hospital and doctors of ordinary negligence for causing Donny Johnson's disabilities is one thing, but they are pushing a unique position by claiming gross negligence. Vagram knows it is hard to prove such a charge. The child is alive, against the medical odds, and courts are not amenable to 'wrongful life' lawsuits. Life is still precious under the law, and we would do all we could to characterize their argument as penalizing the gift of life. Vagram is counting on a jury taking one look at Donny Johnson and his impoverished family and ignoring the letter of the law, and he's good at that. The best. But Dr. Jeremy Wolke presents the opposite message, and Vagram has got to realize that makes his case vulnerable. He knows the jury would be so impressed with Wolke they might look past their stereotypes about Donny's future. Nevertheless, we won't know whether he would be open to an offer like this until we try. I'm looking to you for authorization to take this approach forward in settlement negotiations.

"Do what you think best."

"Thank you, Mr. Kappel. I have prepared a short document to that effect for you to sign. It provides me with full authorization to meet with Mr. Janckovich on behalf of the hospital for the purpose of exploring a joint settlement offer."

"Sign? Why do I need to sign any document?"

Faison could not say what he was thinking: he could not trust Kappel to admit he had agreed to this plan if it went awry. Nor was he about to mention that the wording of his authorization would cover his previous meeting with Janckovich at Jimmy's Diner. He said simply, "A necessary formality to document that we have followed proper procedures in carrying out our responsibilities to the hospital."

"OK, I'll sign. But you will need to alert me well ahead of time if you foresee any separation between the hospital's interests and...and anyone's else's."

"I assure you, Mr. Kappel, you will be the first to know."

Chapter 32: Middle Ground

The lawsuit had begun as an out-of-body experience for Sarah Belden, as though it were happening to someone else. She felt like an outsider, a spectator captivated by a disturbing drama that swirled around her but wasn't at the core of her life. But as the potentially grave consequences of the legal proceedings grew on her, the lawsuit began tearing at her, straining her emotional bonds with her husband and son and distracting her when she was caring for patients. As she and Giuliana Silvestre sat together waiting for a meeting with Jerry Janckovich and Stephanie Sorano, Sarah envied Silvestre's steady, calm demeanor and wished she could be more like her. Giuliana's composure never wavered. She displayed the same confidence with the lawyers that she did with sick babies in the nursery. Sarah just grew more and more anxious, consumed with dread at what might lie ahead.

The two lawyers entered the law firm's conference room and greeted the two physicians casually with nods and smiles. Janckovich's deep voice was calm, reassuring.

"Dr. Silvestre, Dr. Belden, welcome. In a few moments we will bring in Mr. Frank Faison, General Counsel for Memorial General Hospital. You will recall that Dr. Sorano and I asked your permission to speak with him to explore our common interests. He is here to discuss the outlines of a potential settlement offer, after we explain a few things. Dr. Sorano will summarize the situation."

"Thanks, Jerry. Dr. Silvestre, Dr. Belden, this shouldn't take too long. As you know, the Court has thrown out the case against the other physicians, so the two of you and the hospital are the only defendants remaining in the case. The case against the other doctors failed because what was alleged against them would not have met the most basic requirements of negligence even if it had been proved at trial. So they are out."

"*And I'm done for?*" blurted Sarah, then felt her face flush with embarrassment at the desperation in her voice.

"Not at all. This ruling does not mean that the Court has decided against you. Far from it. It just means that if a jury were to believe the facts that the other side has alleged, that would be enough under the law to hold you responsible. But they have proved nothing yet. We will have our opportunity to counter their allegations with our own arguments and evidence, and we believe our case is very strong. There is nothing substantial in the record to support the charge of ordinary medical negligence, of malpractice. We are convinced we can prove that the medical care that Donny Johnson received was up to the standard required for babies like him in nurseries such as the one at Memorial General."

"Perhaps then you could explain why we are still being charged with negligence, and with gross negligence," Giuliana Silvestre asked, her voice inquisitive but without rancor.

"Of course. The plaintiff's case has two things going for it. First, as I mentioned a moment ago, the Court simply accepted on its face their argument that the care Donny received *could be* shown to have been below the standard of care, and that the inadequate medical care caused his problems. In short, the court has given them the opportunity to make their case. We will have the opportunity to rebut their arguments with our defense, our own experts, none of which the court has taken into account at this point. So far, so good?"

Sarah and Giuliana nodded.

"Second, the Court accepted their argument that they might be able to show that the baby should have been transferred to a hospital where he could have gotten even better care, and that keeping him at Memorial General was Gross Negligence. Again, that's their one-sided argument. We believe we can answer this, but there is one possible weak point in our defense to that allegation: Dr. Silvestre and Mr. Kappel engaged in a potentially troublesome conversation about whether Donny should be transferred to the University."

This was news to Sarah Belden. Her eyes widened with surprise as she looked inquiringly at her colleague. Giuliana Silvestre nodded at her with a hint of resignation and said, "Yes, Sarah, it is so.

I wanted to transfer the baby to the University and I told Mr. Kappel what I thought. He said there would be harsh consequences for many people if the public thought Memorial General could not handle the case, consequences that I never imagined happening."

Silvestre turned back toward Sorano and said, "So, are you saying that my discussion with Mr. Kappel is fatal to our case?"

"No, but it is something we must deal with. Hearing that the transfer was discussed at a high level but rejected might allow a sympathetic jury to find against us on that count. That is one of the reasons we are here today to meet with Mr. Faison, the hospital's lawyer. As strong as our counter arguments are, we must recognize that we have a real problem if this case ever goes to trial in front of a jury. What I am referring to involves considerations that have little to do with the law or even the true facts, and a lot to do with human nature. The plaintiff's lawyers would have something important on their side if they get Donny Johnson into a courtroom in front of a jury: their client is, indeed, extremely sympathetic to behold. Juries might take one look at someone with his problems and have a tough time not wanting to do something to help the unfortunate little boy."

Giuliana Silvestre nodded, saying, "I believe I know what you are saying. That is the way I feel when I see Tiny Tim in *A Christmas Carol*. I always cry at his plight."

"Good analogy, Dr. Silvestre, that's exactly how the jurors are likely to react when they see Donny Johnson. If they are given any legal hook to hang a verdict on, some juries will do just about anything for plaintiffs like him.

"Any other questions at this point?"

Giuliana Silvestre and Sarah Belden O'Malley looked at each other. Once again Sarah envied the confidence emanating from the other woman's eyes, her poise, her evident grasp of what Stephanie Sorano had just said. Even in the face of being told that she may have made a terrible error in her conversation with Everett Kappel about transferring Donny to the university, Giuliana remained composed and proceeded to ask questions about the implications of what she had done. Sarah felt that she, too, understood the legal mumbo-jumbo, more or less, but she couldn't get her brain to focus on where this was all leading. Nothing came to her mind except to wonder how this had happened to her, what she had done to deserve being tormented like this. All she knew was that she had made a decision to resuscitate Donny Johnson, to rescue Martina and Derek's fourth baby boy, and she had done her job well. And for that she was being punished.

Giuliana Silvestre, who had the most to lose of the people present in the room, said calmly, "I understand. The law could be clear, but some good-hearted citizens might take it upon themselves to help the boy nonetheless. Yes, that is human nature. Please, if you will, I have a question on a different matter."

"Of course. Go ahead, Dr. Silvestre."

"Perhaps you will get to this question in a moment, but I would like to know if the two of us and the hospital are truly all in this together, or if we may become adversaries among ourselves."

She had directed the question to Stephanie Sorano, but Jerry Janckovich answered.

"That is indeed a perceptive question, Dr. Silvestre. We will be dealing with that issue in a few minutes with Mr. Faison. For now, the short answer is yes, such a partition is imaginable. But our goal is to keep that from happening. We want all of the parties at interest here to be fully aligned, and thereby put an end to the case. But that is not a sure thing, we will have to work at it."

"Thank you Mr. Janckovich."

Stephanie Sorano continued.

"There is, of course, a critical point on our side. We believe that what you did really comes down to this: you saved Donny Johnson's life."

Sorano's words were meant to reassure the two physicians, but they had the opposite effect on Sarah. Hearing once again how she had saved Donny Johnson only to relegate him to a life with serious disabilities cut through Sarah like a blowtorch, searing her mind yet again with the finality of her decision, her spur-of-the-moment, irreversible decision to resuscitate the tiny baby. What good was the life she had saved? Had she really accomplished anything worthwhile? Why couldn't she have left well enough alone and not inflicted so much pain on so many people? Sarah fought with herself to expunge such dreadful thoughts, to stifle the self-doubt and return to listening. She shook her head slightly in several short side-to-side jerks, movements not even big enough to be noticed by the others, but more than enough to make her feel as though her brain was smacking against the insides of her skull.

Stephanie Sorano continued. "The law places a very high value on life, and most jurors see life as a gift from God. It is quite difficult to use the law to punish someone for keeping someone alive, just as it should be. Yet that is really what their case amounts to, at least in one sense. If Donny Johnson had died or been stillborn we would not be here today."

The words made Sarah's head quiver again, faintly but uncontrollably. She was afraid she might scream if she heard one more time about the consequences of her life-saving resuscitation.

Sorano went on, oblivious to Sarah's inner turmoil.

"They are drawing a fine line here. They wish to make the case that you, collectively, are responsible not just for his life, which is a very good thing, but also for his disabilities. We believe we can counter that argument and show that you most likely did not cause his problems. We have a witness who is a consummate example of how much someone like Donny can accomplish in life: Dr. Jeremy Wolke. He will be testifying for us, for the defense."

"Excuse me," interrupted Giuliana Silvestre, "I am aware that Dr. Wolke is the most renowned scientist in the world in the field of childhood disability and human potential. His studies are the cornerstone of everything we know about the future we are giving to the babies we save. He is, indeed, a brilliant and highly accomplished scientist, and I am most gratified to hear that he is willing to help defend us. But, I am sorry to say, despite my highest regard for that gentleman, I have seen him at professional meetings, and he has great difficulty speaking. He often has other persons read his papers out loud, and then answers some questions himself. Once he even used a computer-generated voice to broadcast from the text he had entered into the program, but that did not go well. How could he testify in court?"

Again, it was Janckovich's deep, resonant voice that responded to a question directed at Sorano.

"What you say is quite true, Dr. Silvestre, but it turns out that Dr. Wolke is even more skilled at communicating than any of us appreciated. He will help us not only on the science but also with neutralizing the impact on the jurors of seeing Donny Johnson in person. His presentation in his deposition was masterful. He demonstrated that he is not only an unassailable and unflappable expert, but is also an exceptionally dramatic performer. Dr. Wolke speaks slowly and with agonizing difficulty, yes, but he uses his disability to great effect, drawing out his answers in a way that is nearly mesmerizing. Perhaps scientists at a professional meeting are less patient, but ordinary people will hang on his every word, their attention will not lag for an instant. A jury would be drawn into his aura; they would accept everything he said. Moreover, his very presence has a great effect on people even when he does not speak. He can simply sit there and the jury can see for itself that Donny Johnson is not necessarily condemned to a hopeless existence since it is possible for someone like him to become a world-famous scientist like the one in front of them at that very moment. He's a tremendous asset for our side."

Sorano picked up the thread.

"I completely agree with Jerry—I was also totally taken with the man. In addition, it is important to note that the other side tried to get Dr. Wolke as their expert first, and he refused. Most likely they would have had him write a report but never be called to testify in open court. They tried to neutralize him, so they must understand what he can do. And, his presence must be all the more threatening to them since he refused to work with their side but joined ours. That put them on notice that he likely feels quite strongly about the correctness of our position."

Sarah found her voice at last.

"This sounds like...like theater, like a stage play or a game, not like...not like a way to find the truth or decide what's really fair."

Having found her voice, Dr. Sarah Belden instantly regretted the words that she had uttered. She was coming across as such a simpleton. Of course it was theater, she already knew that courts weren't there to find truth, they were there to see who gets to win and who has to pay, she knew that. She tried to recover.

"Where I'm going is, will Dr. Wolke's participation help us get this over with? Soon? Will we still have to go to trial?"

Stephanie Sorano rescued her.

"Keeping us from going to trial is exactly what we are here to discuss, and how we intend to use Dr. Wolke to achieve that end. We think that the combination of expertise and presence he brings, plus the threat that if he were to appear in front of a jury he would counteract the impact of Donny Johnson's unfortunate appearance, will be enough to make them want to cooperate at the settlement table. We feel that we now have the prospect of reasonable terms for ending this."

Janckovich summarized the point simply, saying, "We believe we have a very strong position, and we will press for a practical, immediate outcome."

Silvestre saw that there must be another aspect to this, it all sounded too good to be true.

"So, if we are confident that Dr. Wolke is a weapon they cannot, they will not, take a chance on fighting, why should we settle at all? Why should we not take the case before a jury, or simply refuse to settle and force them to drop the case?"

Janckovich smiled at Silvestre, once again appreciating her discerning mind.

"In part, we have no choice. We must respect the judge's order to engage in good faith in pre-trial settlement negotiations. But, yes, that's the central question: how desperate would they be if we pushed them to the wall? And the problem is, we do not know, there are no sure bets in this…in this situation."

He had started to say *"in this game,"* the allusion that came naturally to his athlete's mind, but he thought better about using those words after Sarah Belden's outburst about their deliberations being theater.

"Do we think we would win if we take this to court? Yes. But we must always keep in mind that we could be wrong. The same jurors who would be impressed by Dr. Wolke might be overcome with emotion when they saw Donny Johnson. And, there would be other witnesses with nearly the same credentials, if not the same appeal, as Dr. Wolke. They might counteract his effect enough to let the jury worry more about Donny Johnson's future than they will immediately after Dr. Wolke is through testifying. And, of course, Fred Vagram might have something else up his sleeve. He is nobody's fool."

"I can appreciate your points, Mr. Janckovich. Are there any other possible weaknesses in our position?"

Giuliana Silvestre was focused, intense, assembling all the information she could so that she fully understood where things stood legally.

"Yes, there is one additional factor, the conversation I referred to earlier. We don't know what the effect might be of the testimony about you and Mr. Kappel having had a discussion that led to Donny Johnson not being transferred. Even if the two of you disagree about who was responsible for what was said or for the final decision to keep him at Memorial General, a jury could decide that the defense had done something wrong and covered it up. That is a gamble we should not take if it can be avoided. The stakes are too high."

He realized that he had reverted to a gaming analogy but didn't try to change his words. After all, he acknowledged silently, that's what a lawsuit really is, a game of sorts. A big game, but a game nonetheless in which one side will win, the other will lose, there's going to be a final score and then it's over, done. Time runs out, the world has a winner to celebrate and a loser to scorn. Period. Just like football.

Janckovich shared none of his thoughts with his colleague or their clients. Instead he looked around the room and said, "I believe it is now time to bring in Mr. Faison." He caught Sorano's eyes for a moment and saw her nod in agreement. The big man stood, went to the door, and passed through into the luxurious waiting area.

"Hi Frank, please join us now. Stephanie and I have brought the doctors up to speed."

Janckovich ushered the man into the conference room, saying, "Dr. Sarah Belden, Dr. Giuliana Silvestre, this is Mr. Frank Faison, the attorney for the hospital."

The two physicians stood up and shook hands with him, first Silvestre, then Sarah.

"Dr. Silvestre, Dr. Belden, good to meet you at last," said Frank Faison. "It always amazes me that I can work in the same place as someone for many years and never meet them."

Sarah and Giuliana nodded in agreement, a knowing half-smile on their faces.

"As you know, I am here on behalf of Memorial General Hospital to explore the possibility of putting together a united front. If we can work out a global offer that we all participate in, and get the other side to accept it, then the case will be over and we will never be pitted against each other. If we go to trial, it's all much more complicated. The hospital will have to assert its rights under the state law doctrine of *sovereign immunity*, which might provide the hospital—but no one else—with substantial protection against high damages. In that case, the bulk of a large award might well fall to you and your insurance company."

"Why, Sir, would you be willing to pay more in a settlement than you might face in a jury verdict?" asked Giuliana Silvestre.

"Because we don't know for sure what financial exposure the hospital might face if we go to trial—it could be less than in a settlement, but it might be far greater. We have to face the fact that once we are in a courtroom, all bets are off."

"I understand," said Silvestre. "Thank you."

"OK. Then, this is what we are thinking. I believe you are aware of the legal barrier to lawsuits that Memorial General has enjoyed, the principle of *sovereign immunity?*"

The two physicians nodded, and Stephanie Sorano said, "Yes, we have discussed that legal construct with them. Thanks."

"The problem is that we are in unknown territory with respect to the legal status of *sovereign immunity* now. The doctrine has not been tested since the hospital became a quasi-public corporation. Raising the issue in this case would mean that we would be faced with an exceptionally complicated situation that would likely involve years of appeals. Such a prolonged lawsuit would be costly and might end up producing a precedent we wouldn't want to live with. We cannot be sure the Court would uphold our traditional immunity and keep us in the situation in which we have very limited liability. Our concern is that it might go in the opposite direction and remove the protection entirely, or modify it in some unforeseen way. So we would prefer to end this now, to know precisely where we stand."

"And if we went to trial, this case would remain in the public's view for a long time, to the detriment of the hospital," added Stephanie Sorano.

Sorano was alluding to what she knew was the hospital's real motivation for considering a settlement: its very survival. But she could not know that there was another reason why the hospital might settle. Frank Faison could not share his strategy of making Kappel so terror-stricken at the prospect of ending up with personal liability and public disgrace that he was willing to cooperate in a more generous settlement than the hospital would otherwise accept.

Jerry Janckovich's deep voice prodded them forward to the matter at hand. "So, let's talk turkey."

"Sure," said Faison. "Let me outline the terms of the offer that we wish to propose. Memorial General will pay in cash only up to its traditional statutory limit to avoid admitting to any change in our *sovereign immunity* defense. We will also forgive all of the Johnsons' earlier debts and provide in-kind benefits going forward in the form of lifelong medical and support services at no charge. Should the family decide they do not want to receive care at Memorial General, we will arrange to pay for those services elsewhere. For your part, Dr. Silvestre and Dr. Belden, you will each be apportioned a certain amount of the liability. In your case, Dr. Silvestre, you would pay no more out of pocket than the deductible on your malpractice insurance. Dr. Belden, you would be covered as an employee of the hospital and thus have no financial obligation to bear. Our legal fees are already being paid by the malpractice insurer and the hospital."

"Is this something they will accept?" asked Sarah Belden. She was relieved to hear her own voice sounding calm and professional,.

"The other side will have to figure out how the settlement money would be divvied up to pay Vagram's contingent fee and costs. That might be the biggest stumbling block, but no one will know for sure until we put the offer on the table."

"What are you asking us to do?" said Sarah.

"You have the right to review any settlement, so we need your approval."

"And what are the consequences for us as physicians?" said Silvestre.

"Good question, and the answer is that there should be none if we reach a settlement. The terms will be sealed, they will be kept confidential, protected from disclosure even under Freedom of Information Act lawsuits. We will have to report the details to the State Medical Board and to the National Practitioner Data Bank, but in this state the public does not have access to the Medical Board's information, and the federal data bank also keeps its files confidential from the public. Most important, we will not admit any fault."

Sarah Belden understood the value of doing everything in secret, but she was taken with the bigger picture beyond the immediate impact on her own life.

"Isn't that a bit disingenuous? We pay hundreds of thousands, maybe millions of dollars, presumably for doing something wrong, but we don't admit we were at fault. What about the truth?"

The lawyers simply nodded, raised their eyebrows, and shrugged slightly, but said nothing in response.

"It is satisfactory to me," said Giuliana Silvestre. "I wish to get on with my work."

"OK by me, sure," added Sarah, following Silvestre's lead.

"Thank you Dr. Silvestre, Dr. Belden. We will be in touch as soon as the other side responds."

***

"Hey, Doc, come into my office."

Whenever Vagram called him on the phone Sanjay Fijam would hold the receiver several inches from his ear to avoid the anticipated explosion of sound, but this time it was not necessary. His senior partner sounded almost normal.

"Of course, Mr. Vagram, I will be there shortly."

Fijam mounted the interior staircase slowly, deliberately. He needed to give himself time to think. Something must have happened. But was it good news or bad news? Fijam got no immediate answer when he walked into Vagram's office and saw the blank expression on the man's face.

"Come in, Doc, come in. Sit down." Again, the moderated volume that Fijam inexplicably found disarming. "The other side has made a settlement offer."

"Did they receive our list of proposed witnesses? Is that the reason?"

"They got the list, yes, but this sounds like they've been thinking about settling for some time."

"Are the terms acceptable, Mr. Vagram?"

Vagram hesitated, tossing a pen back and forth between his hands.

"Maybe yes, maybe no. The offer will include enough cash to cover our expenses and provide some relief for the Johnsons. But much of it will be in-kind: debt forgiveness, free medical care. And the settlement would be structured, one lump sum up front, the rest stretched out over time."

Fijam could see that Vagram was thinking about something other than the Johnson family: for Fred Vagram this case had always been about completing the set, getting the last trophy in his million-dollar victory case. He had to be questioning whether the terms of this settlement offer would make for a worthy capstone to his longtime goal. If it took a team of actuaries and accountants to place a million-dollar value on the outcome, if the calculation were too complicated for a simple headline proclaiming his triumph, Vagram would have little satisfaction.

Fijam was surprised when Vagram added, in a thoughtful, almost soft voice, "These things are always complicated, Doc. Maybe

234

I'll get that last million, maybe not. Since it's a formal offer we have no choice but to present it to our clients and see how they react."

"And you, what is your reaction, if I may ask?"

Vagram sighed, catching Fijam off guard. He had never seen the blustery man troubled like this.

"I'm leaning toward acceptance, Doc. We have a strong case. Most juries would melt when they see our client. But Jeremy Wolke is a wild card. I think it's less than fifty-fifty if we go to trial and he gets into the witness box. This may well be the best we can do. Take a look at the details and let's talk again, Sanjay."

Sanjay Fijam once again was thrilled at hearing Fred Vagram call him *Sanjay* and seem genuinely to want his opinion.

"Yes, Mr. Vagram, I will. And, I do understand…"

Fijam could not bring himself to finish the thought, to say that he knew Vagram was balancing completing his personal quest against the interests of his clients.

Vagram looked directly at Fijam. "You know, Sanjay, that's the thing about taking cases on a contingent fee. You win some, you lose some."

Chapter 33: Settling Matters

Derek Johnson could not believe what he was hearing. He felt as though the floor had gone out from under his feet and he was in free fall. When Sanjay Fijam called and asked Derek and Martina to come to the office to discuss a settlement offer, they had allowed a glimmer of optimism to light up their gloom. But now—*this? This was the settlement?* Derek wasn't sure he understood all the details, but the bottom line was coming across bright and clear: he and Martina might end up with nearly nothing.

At first the numbers sounded promising: one hundred and seventy-five thousand dollars from the hospital and four hundred thousand dollars from the doctors. That was real money. But then Derek heard Vagram say that his legal fees, and their taxes, and paying off all the old bills, would eat up just about every penny. And if any money was left over, Medicaid might go after them to claw back whatever it could for the government.

No cash, no money in the bank. Not for them, anyway. They had endured so much pain for so long, they were both exhausted to the point that they could barely get through most days, and they had been hoping against hope that the settlement would bail them out. They weren't looking for a big windfall, just a little cushion. But now that hope was dead. There would be nothing to help them start over. What would they do?

Derek was groping for the words to explain what he was thinking. He looked at Martina. She was sobbing quietly, her face in her hands, a clear sign that she had also understood how little this settlement would mean for them. He couldn't contain his anger any longer.

"So, that's it? What the hell good is that? My wife is so guilty about suing the doctors she feels worse now than before we got into this lawsuit, and I'm working all day and night to make enough for us to survive. And we will still be taking care of Donny by ourselves. How could you give up like this? We've been through so much and you'll leave us with next to nothing to show for it?"

Fred Vagram was attempting to be conciliatory, to sound compassionate, but he was already looking forward to his next case.

"This is the way the system works, Mr. and Mrs. Johnson. We made the strongest case we could, and now we have to make the best decision open to us under the circumstances. If we were to pursue the lawsuit to trial we very well might lose, and you would get nothing. At least this settlement means that you won't have to worry about all those old bills anymore. And you'll all get free medical care at Memorial General Hospital."

Martina said, "I don't ...don't ... I don't like that place anymore. I can't go back there, ever, ever again. Please, no."

"You are not required to use Memorial General for medical care. The agreement allows you to decide and the hospital has to pay for Donny's care if you go somewhere else. The advantage for you of Memorial General is that it has so many services there: medical, social services, rehabilitation, special education programs. They would even come and pick Donny up in a handicapped van."

"Handicapped van," mumbled Derek, the words burning through him. He had his own *handicapped van*, and it was falling apart. He would never be able to get a better one, not with this deal. He'd be driving his jerry-rigged contraption until the wheels came off.

Martina stopped sobbing but seemed to have checked out of the meeting. She was staring blankly off into the distance, somewhere beyond her husband, beyond the walls of the conference room. Her mind was elsewhere, worrying about Donny. Charlie Brand had been too busy to babysit, having gotten a job bagging groceries, so Martina had been reduced to begging her sister, Ivana, to watch Donny for a few hours. Ivana and her husband, Hector, lived a long way from Martina and Derek, in an upscale subdivision in the very hills that Derek drove past each morning on his way to work at the construction site. Martina wanted to get out of the lawyer's office and get back to Donny. Her son wouldn't have any idea where he was— he had never been to Ivana's house before and he wouldn't know why his mother wasn't there with him. He would feel abandoned. And on top of it all, Ivana would explode if Donny were still there when Hector came home from work.

"Mr. Vagram, please, I have to ask you. How did it come to this?" Derek asked, still trying to grasp their situation. "Is that it, we're just done for? We have to take what they're offering and give up? You told us you could prove that it was their fault that Donny didn't end up right. What happened?"

"We had a lot going for us, yes, and we made a strong case. But it was an uphill struggle all the way. We were up against the law that has always protected public hospitals. We had to devise a unique approach and argue that Donny should have been transferred and that their failure to transfer him was so wrong that they deserved to be punished with punitive damages."

"But you knew all of that when you took the case, didn't you?"

Vagram nodded but said nothing for a long moment. Then he said, "Well, yes, that's right. We knew all along this wouldn't be easy but we thought we could deal with things. Unfortunately, something came up that caught us off guard. They lined up an expert who's a brilliant scientist—and he's also severely disabled. He would be a very tough witness for us to go up against. When the jury sees him they're likely to think that your son will be able to overcome his physical limitations and do just fine on his own."

"This is a damn awful mess," said Derek, trying to keep from screaming, or crying, or jumping across the table and pummeling the loudmouthed lawyer. "You gave us the impression you were sure you could win."

"We are winning. This is a good settlement. Granted, it's not everything we had hoped for. But we aren't losing—and we might have lost if we had gone to trial, especially now that they have this new expert."

Martina uttered a few words too softly for anyone to hear, drowned out by Vagram's voice.

"I'm sorry, Honey, what did you say?" Derek cut Vagram off to let his wife speak.

"Nothing. Never mind," Martina whispered.

Sanjay Fijam's soft voice broke in. "Please, Mrs. Johnson, please feel free to offer any thoughts you might have."

Fijam's understated reassurance struck a chord with Martina, giving her the strength to speak up, to let out her anger and her profound sadness and say the one thing that mattered to her amid all the talk about money and legal details. Struggling to keep her voice from breaking she said, "I just wanted to say that I never doubted that Donny got good care from Dr. Belden. I never wanted to do this to her, or to Dr. Silvestre. They are wonderful doctors and I hate the pain we are causing them, I always have."

Martina's tormented words filled Derek with guilt. He had pressured Martina to go along with the lawsuit. He had raised her hopes but in the end he had only brought her pain and heartbreak and done nothing to help her or Donny. He had failed as a husband and a father. The lawyers had no idea what he and Martina were going through. It was all Derek could do to avoid crying, sobbing out loud. He wanted this to end, it had to end, he couldn't take this any longer, and neither could she. He was on the verge of losing his self-control, not with anger so much as with heartache and remorse.

"What the hell future does our boy have? He'll be in a wheelchair all his life, maybe able to speak a little, watch TV all day. He can't be a carpenter, let alone go to college. He can't even toss a goddamn football with his father."

"In cases like this, both sides bring in their experts, and the jury has to decide which expert can best predict what the future will look like. Their new witness is the leading expert in the field—and he's in a wheelchair from Cerebral Palsy just like Donny. We're concerned that if he goes before a jury in his wheelchair he would neutralize a lot of the emotional response we were counting on. The jury would not feel as sympathetic toward Donny once they saw what someone with the same physical problems had been able to accomplish. At this point, we are fortunate the other side is willing to settle for real money."

Almost inaudibly Derek mumbled, "Real money for you, not for Donny, not for us."

Then he spoke up, his voice desperate.

"Now what do we do?"

"We'll take care of everything. You sign the settlement agreement, and we'll take it before the judge to be turned into a final judgment of the court. You'll be able to start getting Donny's free medical care right away, and we'll make sure you get your money as soon as possible."

Derek looked at Martina.

"Honey? What do you think?"

He saw right away that she had retreated again into her cocoon. She was gone from him. Maybe forever.

Martina answered so softly that he could barely hear her words.

"I just want to get Donny from Ivana's and go home."

Derek saw tears streaming across the creases that cut into his wife's once-beautiful face, a face now drained of all depth, a face with no color, no features. Just pain, dreadful pain. Her eyes were pointed in his direction, but they were focused somewhere else, she wasn't really looking at him.

"Please. I want to get Donny and go home."

Derek turned back to Fred Vagram. "Do we have any choice? What can we do?"

"You can do as you like, of course. It's up to you in the end, it's your lawsuit, Donny's lawsuit. But I've given you my best advice, and that's what I'm here for. I've been involved in many lawsuits, and one thing that I've learned is that when it's time to get out, it's time. I believe it is time for you to take this offer and be done with it. Donny will be better off, and so will you and Mrs. Johnson. But I cannot force you to accept this offer. If you tell me to turn them down and go to trial, I will do what you say. I must tell you that if we do go further, my best judgment is that you have less than a fifty-fifty chance of getting a better result. In other words, I believe that if we go to trial it is more likely that you will get less, maybe much less, than what you will get from this settlement. Or you might end up with nothing at all." Vagram did not mention that he would get no contingency fee if the case went to trial and they lost.

Derek wasn't highly educated, but he understood their legal situation perfectly: he and Martina and Donny were screwed. He got the message loud and clear. Vagram wanted to get his money and get it over with. A few months of work and Vagram gets a truckload of money, hundreds of thousands of dollars. Anger boiled up inside Derek. He couldn't help thinking that even if he and Martina actually told him to keep the case going, Vagram would never work on it with any real enthusiasm. Not when the lawyer thought he would be losing money every day.

Derek Johnson gave in. Gave up. He would resign himself to their hopeless situation, anything to let him and Martina get out of the office.

"OK, Mr. Vagram, we're done. Where do we sign?"

Vagram slid a stack of papers across the table. Derek picked up a pen and reached for the papers but just then a slender brown hand grasped his wrist gently but firmly and he heard a soft voice say, "Please, Mr. Johnson, do not sign that settlement agreement."

Dropping the pen on the table, Derek looked into the face of Sanjay Fijam. To that moment, the man had been so quiet, so deferential, he had melted into the background, muted by Vagram's voice and obscured by the senior lawyer's dominating presence.

Steeling up more courage than he had ever before found inside himself, more than he had even imagined he could possibly muster, Sanjay Fijam said, "Excuse me so much, Mr. and Mrs. Johnson. Mr. Vagram, please pardon me, Sir, but, with all due respect, I must speak my mind."

Fijam felt stark terror course through his body as he uttered the words, but he could not stop. He realized that he did not care what Fred Vagram did to him, he could not let this go forward with Vagram pocketing most of the cash and the Johnson family cursed with their burdens for the rest of their lives. He would not bring honor to Goddess Lakshmi if he remained silent. Unable to look directly at his senior partner and uncomfortable facing the Johnsons, he continued speaking with his head down. He did not dare look around for support, for permission to proceed with the interruption. His faint voice was the only sound in the room

"I apologize for intervening at this point but only now do I appreciate fully the limitations of this settlement from the family's perspective. I have long agreed with what Mr. Vagram has said about the difficulties with our position in this case. My review of the medical care failed to detect negligence that could be blamed for young Mr. Johnson's problems. We have argued that his transfer to the University would have made a substantial difference for him, but, in truth, it is not clear that he would have benefitted to such a great extent as we alleged. And yet, even as I saw the weakness of our case, I did not press my position because, ultimately, it is up to a jury to decide what occurred and what the cause of his difficulties was, and there was always the possibility that our side would prevail. But now I realize that I have been ignoring what may be the most telling consideration, so I must say that I do not feel that this is an appropriate settlement for the Johnson family."

Fijam paused briefly, an habitual act of ingrained deference ill-suited to a moment as precarious as this. A prolonged lull might tempt a dismissive interjection from Fred Vagram, even an order for Sanjay to be silent or to leave the room. But no sound whatsoever came from his senior partner. Fijam restarted his impromptu speech, the words flowing from his heart more than his brain in an uncontrollable cascade that was so out of character for him he could scarcely believe that they were coming through his own mouth.

"Sir, with all due respect, we must do better. Upon reflection, I realized that science and the legalities of causation are not the principal factors that we must address. There is something of much greater importance that we must redress: Mr. and Mrs. Johnson did nothing wrong and do not deserve to be abandoned. In fact, they did everything the way our society calls on them to do. All they had in mind was raising a family, and—you will excuse me for saying so, please, Mr. and Mrs. Johnson—in return they have suffered repeated tragedies, none of which was of their making. True enough, we must all deal with our own lot in life, but the tragedies that happened to them were not predictable. We have looked carefully into the scientific evidence and there is no explanation for their repeated tragedies other than bad luck. There is nothing the Johnsons could have done to avoid them. What has transpired could have befallen any of us, yet they bear all the costs. And that is not proper, not fair. The debts they have incurred are vastly greater than they should be. They were charged prices for medical care that were inflated beyond any rational level. Mr. Johnson has worked two jobs, yet even when he had the benefit of health insurance it covered only a fraction of the enormous expense. They have been pushed to the very edge of bankruptcy, harassed by bill collectors, strained beyond anyone's breaking point. And yet they persist, they try to pay exorbitant debts, to meet financial liabilities that they could not have bargained for and that will ruin them. They should not stand alone. In truth, they have received no real support from the rest of us, from society, as any family should that is struck with such random misfortune. That is the principle that I believe we must assert here. Perhaps it is not perfectly fair to allocate a portion of their burdens to a hospital and doctors who may have done little wrong, but it is no less fair than saddling the family forever with grossly unconscionable debts. It is our place to help them, Mr. Vagram. Indeed, it is our duty to do so."

At long last Fijam lifted his head, looked at the young couple and said, "Mr. and Mrs. Johnson, I believe you must have a net recovery that will allow you to deal with your son's situation in a much better fashion than what is currently in the offer before you. All of us, society at large, must help you. If this lawsuit is the only means that exists to spread the losses more broadly, then so be it. It is our obligation, our responsibility, in fact it is our great opportunity, to help you."

Fijam stopped. What had he done? In the silence of the room he thought he could hear his heart pounding, his stomach churning, every organ in his body screaming in pain. He saw his own career tumbling before his eyes, but he found the strength to look directly at Derek and Martina and say, "I cannot advise you to sign this settlement agreement."

Derek Johnson sat up in his chair and nodded his head slowly at Sanjay Fijam. Even Martina was moved by the soft-spoken lawyer's speech, touched deeply for the first time in the many months of dealing with the lawsuit. Six eyes now turned on Fred Vagram, three people awaiting a response from the famously strong-willed lawyer.

Fred Vagram hesitated for a long moment, a terrifying delay that Fijam struggled to endure. Vagram was silent because he was quite surprised at his own reaction to Fijam's plea. He was not stunned, not angry, not embarrassed—he felt none of the emotions everyone in the inner circle of his life, from his mother to his wife to anyone who had dealt with him in a courtroom, would have expected him to feel at being challenged by Fijam in this way. He was curiously proud of Sanjay Fijam, felt a rush of new respect for the man he had always regarded as an inadequate warrior. He looked at Fijam, delighted at the thought that the man had indeed grown a pair of balls.

"I'll be damned," Vagram blurted out to the great surprise of everyone in the room, *"the sonofabitch is right!"* Then he looked his colleague squarely in the eyes, smiled, and in the softest voice anyone had ever heard from him, said only, "You know what, Sanjay, you have a point." He turned toward the Johnsons and said, "Mr. and Mrs. Johnson, I beg your pardon. Let us go over this settlement again. I think we can find another approach."

Sanjay Fijam felt the most pressing need to urinate that he had ever experienced. Still polite even as his bladder was threatening to explode he said, "Thank you, Mr. Vagram, thank you so much. Perhaps the Johnsons would like to take a break for a few minutes."

***

As they pulled into Ivana's driveway, Derek was about to warn Martina not to open her door until the van came to a stop but

Martina jumped out the instant the van slowed down. Derek didn't yell at her or move, he simply watched her run to be reunited with Donny. Martina seemed to have found a new bolt of energy and knocked rapidly on Ivana's door. Derek watched as her sister let her in, then he got out of the van and lit a cigarette. He needed to relax, to let it all sink in. The cigarette gave him something to do, and the stimulation helped him think, for better or worse. He allowed himself a grain of hope that maybe things were about to turn around. Maybe this was about to end, things would be OK after all. That guy, Vagram, sounded so sure he could reach a better settlement. Well, they would see. After all, Vagram had always sounded sure, and so far they still had very little to show for it. In the meantime, Derek had to get his family home so he could get back to the store tonight. There was a big shipment coming in and he would pull down overtime.

Ivana's piercing command broke through his dazed thoughts. "Derek! You come help your wife."

His sister-in-law was standing in her doorway with her arms folded, looking impatiently at Derek. Derek felt the insults in Ivana's look, he knew she thought of him as an uneducated loser who had dragged her sister down into a deplorable life. He could sense her thoughts, her disdain for seeing him stopping to smoke a cigarette and rest while she and Martina dealt with Donny.

"You know she can't get Donny out by herself. Put out that cigarette and come help your wife."

Derek stared at his sister-in-law and saw a contorted rendering of the strength, elegance and loveliness that his wife had once shared with her. Ivana had been transformed into a caricature of a powerful Russian beauty. Her blond hair was rolled and plastered with hairspray into an unnatural sculpture of waves and curls that was no longer free to flow across her shoulders or blow in the wind. Her outfit was fashionable but as stiff as her hairdo: a tight blue wool pants suit, with loud multicolored designs appliquéd across the front of the coat. A Cossack's uniform. She still displayed the commanding stance, the defiantly uplifted chin, the self-confident presence that had long since been crushed out of Martina. Derek dropped his cigarette, squashed it on the ground, then, realizing his sister-in-law was scrutinizing his every move, bent over and picked up the butt and dropped it into his shirt pocket next to the box of fresh cigarettes.

"I'm coming, Ivana," he called obediently, and headed toward the front door.

Donny made happy noises of greeting toward his father, his arms and legs pounding up and down in excitement at the sight of Derek. The boy's welcoming gestures cut through Derek. As he bent over to kiss his son he felt tears trickling down his face. All his emotions, all his thoughts, all the hopelessness came together. Every feeling he had repressed all day came out at once, but he managed to whisper softly into the youngster's ear, "Hi there, Donny, how's my boy? Daddy's here, we're going home now, we're all going home together. We didn't leave you here, we're back."

Donny made more of his contented sounds, and Derek understood that his son was glad to see him. Derek grabbed the wheelchair by the handles and backed it gently down the four steps in the front of Ivana's house, then turned around and pushed it along the walkway toward the van. He slid the side door open, pulled out his makeshift ramp, and rolled Donny's chair up into the open area behind the front seat. When he snapped the crude wooden frame into place to stabilize the chair's wheels he realized it would not be up to the task much longer. One quick stop or light impact and Donny would go flying, the improvised chair restraint wouldn't hold him for an instant.

"I hope to hell we're going to be able to buy a new van soon," Derek told himself.

***

It did not take Fred Vagram long to craft his strategy for vastly enhancing the settlement. He did not reopen negotiations with the hospital, he did not even respond directly to the offer that was on the table, the offer he had verbally agreed to for his client. Instead, he sent a memo to Jerry Janckovich and Stephanie Sorano, and to Frank Faison, announcing that he had called a press conference for the following Thursday, two days hence. Vagram said that he intended to expose the horrors that the hospital had inflicted on Donny Johnson as well as their total disregard for the family's plight. The other side would have 48 hours to put a greatly improved settlement on the table, in which case the press conference would be a love fest among all the parties. But the public spectacle would go ahead either way. The media were already alerted and were planning to turn out in force, especially the television stations, to whom he had promised dramatic visuals of the family wheeling Donny Johnson onto the front steps of Memorial General Hospital for all the world to see. Vagram would stack replicas of the Johnson's medical bills on a table next to Donny, with large placards showing the extent of their sticker-price debts. He would have similar displays showing the merciless tactics of the bill collection agencies, highlighting quotes from their threatening messages to the Johnsons. If they were barred from assembling on the front steps of the hospital, Vagram would take the show to the sidewalk. And he would replace his law firm's peripatetic billboards and television ads with new ones highlighting the Johnson case, with large photos of Donny.

Fred Vagram made it clear that he was prepared to go to trial. He would try the case before the jury of the public.

Chapter 34: Donny's Legacy

Hospital staff, reporters, and an assortment of well-wishers and curiosity-seekers packed the enormous tent that had been set up on the hospital grounds for the press conference. Everett Kappel climbed up onto the podium that raised him above the bank of microphones so he appeared to be of normal height and looked out over the crowd. He was in his glory.

"We are here today to celebrate the Johnson family," he began. "Donny Johnson was the smallest baby ever to survive in this hospital, weighing just over one-and-a-quarter pounds at birth. He is a symbol of the wonders of modern medicine, a tribute to the dedication, perseverance, and skill of the physicians, nurses and all the staff here at Memorial General."

Kappel's words sounded vaguely familiar to the NICU staff gathered in one section of the audience. They shifted uncomfortably in their seats as he continued.

"His parents, Derek and Martina Johnson, demonstrated loving devotion to their son. The Johnsons had suffered the loss of three sons before Donny, and they were committed to providing him with every opportunity. Mr. Johnson worked two jobs and Mrs. Johnson devoted her life to her son."

Gesturing toward the front row Kappel raised his voice and said, "Please join with me in welcoming the Johnson Family to this celebration."

The audience erupted with applause and rose from their chairs to deliver a standing ovation that continued for several minutes. Martina and Derrick remained seated, embarrassed by all the attention. Donny sat quietly next to them in a wheelchair with the words, "Memorial General Hospital" stenciled on the side panels.

Kappel at last patted the air with both palms and said, "Please, take your seats so we can continue." When the crowd quieted and was seated, he said, "Today we are pleased to announce the many wonderful ways in which Memorial General Hospital will be helping to ensure a bright future for Donny and his family. First, a gift for young Donny." He smiled broadly and pointed to a large item covered with red wrapping paper sitting on one side of the stage. At Kappel's signal, an orderly lifted off the covering to reveal an elaborate motorized wheel chair. The crowd broke into another round of applause, until Kappel again signaled for them to stop. "When the ceremony is concluded," he said, "Donny will transfer to this state-of-the-art chair and ride in it to the brand-new, fully equipped van that is now parked in front of the hospital.

"This chair and the van are gifts made possible by the generosity of those who support this hospital. In addition, our supporters have made arrangements for substantial financial assistance for Donny and his family for many years to come. And, the hospital has agreed to provide all the medical care and supportive services Donny will ever need—at no cost."

Another prolonged round of applause, which Kappel let continue for a full minute. Basking in the adulation he said, "Coming to the aid of the Johnsons in this remarkable way is just one example of how Memorial General Hospital is devoted to its patients. We care for our patients when they are ill, and we also care for them in every aspect of their lives."

Anger seethed inside Sarah Belden. Kappel was shamelessly taking credit for actions that had been forced down his throat by a cunning lawyer. The man was a little monster who was exploiting Donny's disabilities to serve his own purposes. And, Kappel was largely responsible for creating the financial burdens the Johnsons had suffered under, and now he was accepting praise for alleviating them. *The man has no decency*, Sarah thought. *He should be ashamed of himself.*

Then Sarah's thoughts turned inward and her resentment toward Kappel was submerged in a wave of guilt. She agonized once again over the central role she had played in the Johnsons' misery, unable to curb the lingering feeling that all of this misfortune would never have fallen upon Derek and Martina if only she had let nature take its course in the delivery room.

Fighting off the negative thoughts, she reproached herself. She had done the right thing, the job she was there to do, and done it well. It was her duty to save his life and no one could foretell what the outcome would be. She had tried to reassure herself this way a thousand times, and heard the same words of comfort nearly as often from Giuliana Silvestre, yet she could not suppress a dreadful sense of failure, a profound remorse over the consequences of her actions.

Sitting next to Sarah, Giuliana Silvestre felt her younger colleague tense up. She sensed that Sarah was once again reeling under the weight of her doubts and guilt, and put an arm around her to console her. But even as she ached for Sarah she raged at Kappel. Kappel had deceived her into going against her own judgment and kept her from transferring Donny to the University Hospital. She had the urge to stand up and denounce him, rebuke him in front of the crowd. But she would never put on such a public display of anger, let alone do so at a tribute to the Johnson family. She remained composed, all the while boiling inside. Just as Sarah Belden would continue to be tormented with doubts over what she had done in the delivery room, a piece of Giuliana Silvestre would always regret having given in to this conniving little man.

Off in a far corner of the tent, Fred Vagram had a very different take on the self-serving spin Kappel was putting on what had transpired. To the hardened lawyer, Kappel was but a rather sorry example of the many arrogant hypocrites he had battled over the years. Vagram's principal concern was that this event had not turned out to be the press conference he had envisioned. Vagram had wanted a gathering that would highlight his grand achievement of having won a million-dollar settlement from every hospital in town. He began mulling over new strategies of how to use the Johnson case to generate publicity to bolster the reputation of his law firm. At that moment, his eyes came to rest on the shiny, new motorized wheelchair. Donny Johnson, he realized, would be spending much of his life in that chair. For the first time in his career, it dawned on him that he had actually done something good for someone. The chair, the money, the van—nothing would make Donny's problems go away, but what Vagram had done would help ameliorate them. An unfamiliar feeling came over him, an exquisite sense of gratification that he had accomplished something truly worthwhile for the Johnson family. He bowed his head and sighed as tears rolled down his cheeks.

While Sarah Belden, Giuliana Silvestre, and Fred Vagram were wrapped up in their own thoughts, Kappel was continuing to speak.

"Now I am pleased to announce just how we will be honoring Donny Johnson. We will expand and modernize the newborn nurseries, so that future babies like him will benefit from the best medical care possible. And we will memorialize his legacy by naming the new intensive care nursery the 'Donny Johnson Neonatal Intensive Care Unit.' Everyone who hears the name 'Donny Johnson' will forever think of the infants whose lives are saved in our neonatal intensive care unit. Donny will represent the thousands of babies who have been cared for here at Memorial General Hospital over the years with wonderful success, and the thousands more who will do so in the future."

Directing his gaze squarely into the television cameras, Kappel took on the earnest, pleading look of a professional fund solicitor skilled at cajoling people into opening their wallets for charitable causes. "To sustain this momentous tribute to this brave young family, we are embarking on a new fundraising drive that we are calling, 'The Campaign for Donny Johnson.' We are kicking off the campaign by setting aside a special fund of two hundred thousand dollars for this purpose, and we call upon the citizens of this community to honor this heroic little boy and his valiant family by giving generously to the Fund. Donny Johnson's life is a medical miracle, a miracle that will—with your support—be repeated many times over in the new nursery. I ask everyone here today and all of you watching on television to join in this life-giving tribute to a remarkable child and his family, and to help assure that his life, his triumph against the odds, will serve to benefit countless as-yet unborn babies. I ask you to contribute whatever you can to 'The Campaign for Donny Johnson.'"

The audience erupted in another long ovation, drowning out his final words. Kappel began bowing and waving his arms in wide arcs like a symphony conductor acknowledging enthusiastic applause at the end of a performance. The sensitive area of his repaired harelip tingled pleasantly under his mustache. This was his great moment, his triumph, his victory in the face of disaster.

Sarah Belden and Giuliana Silvestre applauded along with the rest of the crowd, but softly, out of respect for the Johnsons, not in tribute to the speaker on the podium. Silently, they cursed the vile self-serving man who was exploiting the Johnson family's tragedies and demeaning Donny's very life.

Just then Sarah was distracted by movement on the lawn outside the big tent and turned to look. What she saw instantly melted away her anger. With one hand on the joy stick of his new motorized chair, Donny was driving in circles around his father, who was stepping in and out in a game of tag. Martina was cheering them on and laughing as she watched her son and his father having the time of their lives.

For the first time in her long history with the Johnson family Sarah saw Martina and Derek unreservedly enjoying themselves. She felt a great weight lift off of her shoulders. She was certain now, no more doubts. No more guilt. She had made the right decision.

Acknowledgements

I deeply appreciate the assistance and encouragement generously provided by so many of my friends and colleagues, including three who have since passed away: editor Rachel Abram, literary agent and editor Tim Seldes, and astute former English teacher and avid reader Susan Vanselow. All were quite gracious and gentle in their insightful comments on my first attempts at producing a novel a number of years ago. Author Marc Smolonsky has been a tireless source of literary support. I am particularly grateful to my wife, Ta, for her careful proof-reading, creative suggestions and consistent encouragement. I extend my heartfelt apologies to anyone I have inadvertently failed to mention.

All shortcomings in this novel are my sole responsibility.

I also express my gratitude and affection for those of my fellow pediatricians and the neonatal intensive care nurses who continue to inspire me with their steadfast dedication to safeguarding the health of their patients even as the medical corporate enterprise engulfs them and corrupt elements seek to loot and distort healthcare in this country and despoil the medical profession.

Finally, I thank Ilya Haykinson for permission to use his photo on the cover.

Thank you all.

About the author

Peter Budetti trained as a physician (Columbia) and lawyer (Berkeley) but he has devoted most of his professional life to working on health care policy in Washington and in senior academic positions.

Having spent years as a university professor, he decided to write novels for the general public because he felt that he has stories worth telling but no desire to add to his numerous scholarly publications that languish in obscurity. His novels are inspired by real events, personal experiences, and his imagination.

To date, he has written four novels. *Resuscitated* draws on his earlier life as a pediatrician, as well as his legal background and experiences in Washington and academe. *Hemorrhage, Deadly Bargain,* and *Hacked to Death* form a trilogy of thrillers that features the exploits of a brilliant cybersleuth, Will Manningham. The trilogy grew out of his years combating fraud in healthcare.

He is now *Of Counsel* to Phillips and Cohen, LLP, the nation's most successful law firm representing whistleblowers. As a political appointee in President Obama's administration he was responsible for overseeing modernization of Medicare's outdated systems for detecting and preventing healthcare fraud; he thereby acquired the amusing moniker of *Healthcare Antifraud Czar.*

Previously he served for six years as Counsel, Subcommittee on Health and Environment, U.S. House of Representatives, under the Chairmanship of Congressman Henry A. Waxman; as a member of the health staff, Senate Finance Committee, under the Chairmanship of Senator Daniel Patrick Moynihan; and as a core legislative drafter for President Bill Clinton's Health Security Act.

In his academic life, he founded and directed health policy research centers and held tenured professorships at Northwestern University and The George Washington University, was a faculty member of the Institute for Health Policy Studies, University of California, San Francisco, and held an endowed chair as Professor in the College of Public Health, University of Oklahoma. He has published more than fifty scholarly articles and another forty-plus reports, book chapters, reviews, and editorials.

His undergraduate degree is from the University of Notre Dame. He is a board-certified pediatrician and member of the California Bar and District of Columbia Bar. He is married and has two grown children, seven grandchildren, and one Pekingese-mix rescue doggy. He and his wife live in Kansas City, Missouri, where they moved when they decided it was time to get away from Washington, D.C. They spend their free time at their lake house in Arkansas.